"I'm sorry, Jonah. I shouldn't have said all that."

He stood there, not knowing what to say. He hadn't expected Lovina's confession at all. Her words surprised him, especially since he loved Autumn, too. He hated to lose the baby when he'd grown so attached to her. Autumn could not stay with him and Lovina indefinitely—Jonah knew that. But it would break his heart once more when Bishop Yoder finally took the baby away.

"The bishop is trying to do what's best for Autumn," he said. "He won't give her to just anyone. She'll be loved by her new *familye*. Everything will work out fine."

Jonah didn't know why he bothered to reassure Lovina. Maybe he said the words out loud because he needed to hear them, too. But when she looked up at him, her eyes so wide and filled with doubt, he found himself suddenly longing to wrap his arms around her and kiss her tears away…

Leigh Bale is a *Publishers Weekly* bestselling author. She is the winner of the prestigious Golden Heart® Award and was a finalist for the Gayle Wilson Award of Excellence and the Booksellers' Best Award. The daughter of a retired US forest ranger, she holds a BA in history. Married in 1981 to the love of her life, Leigh and her professor husband have two children and two grandkids. You can reach her at leighbale.com.

Patricia Johns is a *Publishers Weekly* bestselling author who writes from Alberta, Canada. She has her Hon. BA in English literature and currently writes for Harlequin's Love Inspired and Heartwarming lines. She also writes Amish romance for Kensington Books. You can find her at patriciajohns.com.

LEIGH BALE

&

PATRICIA JOHNS

An Amish Christmas Baby

2 Uplifting Stories

The Midwife's Christmas Wish and
A Precious Christmas Gift

LOVE INSPIRED
INSPIRATIONAL ROMANCE

LOVE INSPIRED®

INSPIRATIONAL ROMANCE

Recycling programs for this product may not exist in your area.

ISBN-13: 978-1-335-45453-9

An Amish Christmas Baby

Copyright © 2023 by Harlequin Enterprises ULC

The Midwife's Christmas Wish
First published in 2021. This edition published in 2023.
Copyright © 2021 by Lora Lee Bale

A Precious Christmas Gift
First published in 2020. This edition published in 2023.
Copyright © 2020 by Patricia Johns

For questions and comments about the quality of this book, please contact us at CustomerService@Harlequin.com.

Harlequin Enterprises ULC
22 Adelaide St. West, 41st Floor
Toronto, Ontario M5H 4E3, Canada
www.LoveInspired.com

Printed in U.S.A.

CONTENTS

THE MIDWIFE'S CHRISTMAS WISH

Leigh Bale

Many thanks to Kim Woodard Osterholzer, who brings deeper meaning to safe and sacred home births. I appreciate your generosity, skill, insight and dedication to bringing God's children safely into the world. You, and other midwives like you, are amazing!

Why beholdest thou the mote that is in thy brother's eye, but considerest not the beam that is in thine own eye?... First cast out the beam out of thine own eye; and then shalt thou see clearly to cast out the mote out of thy brother's eye.

—*Matthew* 7:3, 7:5

Chapter One

A white haze of clouds filled the bleak afternoon sky. Misting rain sprinkled the black asphalt of the parking lot. The late October weather had been mild...up until today. Stepping out onto the front steps of the small cinder block hospital in Riverton, Colorado, Lovina Albrecht wished she'd worn her rubber boots instead of her plain black shoes. Just now, her feet felt cold and damp. A chilly breeze rushed past and she shivered, catching the tangy aroma of damp earth and sage. No doubt the storm would increase and she was eager to get home before it struck.

Hunching her shoulders beneath the overhanging portico, she watched as an *Englisch* woman opened an umbrella and scurried toward her from the sidewalk. Lovina stepped aside to give the stranger room to pass and smiled before shyly ducking her head as the lady went inside. Lifting her face, Lovina breathed in deep, grateful for the rain. In this area, the farmers lived in a constant state of drought. They'd take any moisture they could get and consider it a blessing for their crops.

The intensity of the storm strengthened. Maybe Lovina should go back inside. But no. She'd rather wait here where she could be alone to think. Tucking an errant strand of golden hair beneath her black traveling bonnet, she readjusted the weight of her heavy bag on her arm and exhaled a sigh of relief. She'd accomplished her mission today: safely delivering Norma Albrecht and her unborn baby to where they could receive proper medical care.

As an Amish woman, Lovina had worked hard to become a certified professional midwife. Thankfully, her *Ordnung* was progressive enough to see the benefit of having a CPM in their community. Since legal authorities across the nation were prosecuting Amish midwives for practicing without a license, Lovina felt especially grateful. Even still, she only took on low-risk clients and was extra vigilant of them and their baby's needs. If any mother exhibited symptoms of distress, Lovina immediately referred them and their unborn child to the hospital in town. Which left Lovina no choice but to bring Norma here where one of the two medical doctors could help her.

The automatic double doors to the front entrance whooshed open and Jonah Lapp joined her. He looked like every other Amish man in the area with gray broadfall pants, black suspenders and scuffed work boots. Tufts of sand-colored hair peeked out from beneath the brim of his black felt hat. And yet Lovina could never consider him plain. Not with his long forehead, high cheekbones, blunt chin and deep brown eyes that always seemed to smolder with quiet intelligence. From what she'd observed over the past four years since he'd moved here, Jonah was a good man and dedicated to his elderly grandfather and Amish faith. His clean-shaven face attested that he was unmarried but that didn't matter to Lovina. She wasn't interested in him or any man. Not with the many skeletons she had clustered in her closet.

As Jonah tugged at the collar of his blue chambray shirt, he glanced out at the dismal day and quickly shrugged into his warm winter coat. "Brr, it's cold. Darrin just arrived and is with Norma. I think we can go *heemet* now."

Yes, she wanted to go home, too. He spoke in *Deitsch*, the German dialect their Amish people used among themselves.

"*Ja*, I saw him a few minutes ago. He can help make decisions for Norma and the *boppli*'s care. I'll check on Norma tomorrow," she said.

Stepping out into the rain, Lovina held the handrail as she negotiated the slick steps. The temperature had dropped and the wind picked up, slashing against her lavender skirts and spitting a fine mist of grit into her face.

Jonah followed. He worked part-time for the hospital as a certified EMT. Because they believed higher learning led to *Hochmut*, the pride of men, the Amish only went to school through the eighth grade. Like Lovina, Jonah felt fortunate to have his EMT credential, too.

"You don't have any errands to run in town, do you?" Jonah asked.

"*Ne*, I'm ready to go."

"*Gut*. If we leave for *heemet* now, we should be able to beat the storm before it gets worse," Jonah said.

Lovina hoped so. She hated the thought of being caught on the county road with a horse and buggy while rain slashed against their windshield. She didn't mind the inclement weather but it could diminish their visibility, and it wasn't safe with *Englisch* cars zipping past them like rockets.

Lovina and her *familye* had originated from Lancaster County, Pennsylvania, and had moved to Colorado when she was fifteen. They got lots of snow in Pennsylvania, but Colorado was colder, with a much shorter growing season. The farmers here depended on the moisture to produce their crops.

"I was hoping to repair the fence in the south pasture but doubt I'll get to it today." Jonah glanced up, blinking as droplets of rain spiked his long eyelashes.

In addition to being an EMT, he also owned the small farm where Lovina lived. She'd rented his farmhouse almost three months earlier. Because they both were single and didn't want the appearance of impropriety, Jonah lived with his grandfather out back in the *dawdi haus*, a small four-room house they'd built for his grandpa's use. A *dawdi haus* was the Amish version of a retirement home. Bishop Yoder, the leader of their congregation, had made the arrangements. Jonah needed the extra income from Lovina's rent and she needed a quiet place to live and serve her expectant mothers. Since Lovina's mom had died several years earlier, it was a vast improvement over renting a room from various members of her *Gmay*, her Amish community. Now that Lovina occupied Jonah's entire house, she'd set up a nursery and bedroom just for her clients. Her midwife business had flourished and she felt like she had a real home for the first time in years. But that could end the moment Jonah decided to marry. Yet he didn't seem eager to wed. Not since his broken engagement with Fannie Fisher eight months earlier.

"Do you think the storm will be a hard one?" Lovina ducked her head as they headed down the sidewalk.

"I hope so. We need the moisture," he said.

Without her asking, Jonah took hold of her elbow in a solicitous gesture meant to steady her on the slippery path. His fingers felt warm and firm through the fabric of her winter shawl but Lovina couldn't help feeling uncomfortable with his touch. He was a handsome man. There was no getting around it. And though she longed to encourage him, he was a cloying reminder of what she could never have: a husband and *familye* of her own.

The intensity of the storm increased and they hurried across the parking lot. Jonah's horse and buggy were tethered on the far side where the town had set up a covered hitching post just for the Amish to use.

"Do you know who that is?" Jonah asked, jutting his chin toward a parked car.

Lovina looked up, her gaze taking in a silver vehicle through the haze of the storm. A young *Englisch* woman of perhaps eighteen years stood out in the drizzling rain, leaning against the car's front fender. She wore blue jeans, navy tennis shoes and a yellow slicker. Her shoulder-length blond hair was damp and hung around her shoulders in sodden strands. At first sight of them, she braced away from the car and stared openly.

"*Ne*, I don't know her," Lovina spoke in a quiet voice.

Jonah glanced toward the *Englisch* girl and shook his head. "Me either."

"*Ach*, she seems highly interested in us." Lovina forced herself not to stare back as she skirted a puddle of water.

She couldn't help feeling a tad uncomfortable with the girl's gawking. But many people gaped at the Amish. Their distinct clothes and horses and buggies were an oddity that many *Englisch* people couldn't disregard.

"Maybe she's never seen an Amish person before," Jonah said.

"*Ja*, you're probably right." And yet Lovina sensed the girl's curiosity was something more. Something she didn't understand.

"Just ignore her," Jonah said.

Lovina looked away, focusing instead on her feet. With the temperature dropping so fast, the rain might freeze on the road and make travel more treacherous. It was definitely time to go home. And at that moment, Jonah's presence comforted her. He was a skilled horseman and knew how to drive in this kind of weather. But out of her peripheral vision, Lovina saw the *Englisch* woman tracking them closely, never taking her gaze off them.

When they reached the buggy, Jonah opened the door for her. As she lifted a hand to pull herself up inside, a loud revving of an engine caught her attention and she glanced back at the silver car. The *Englisch* girl had hopped into the vehicle, put it into gear and sped out of the parking lot. In the process, her reckless driving caused her to nearly hit a parked truck. She swerved in time to avoid a collision, her brakes squealing as her tires spat gravel. Both Jonah and Lovina stared as she pulled onto the main road and raced away.

"What on earth got into her?" Lovina asked.

Jonah shrugged his wide shoulders and wiped his damp face with a calloused hand. "Beats me. She seems awfully young. Maybe she hasn't had her driver's license long. She sure doesn't act like she knows what she's doing."

Chuckling at the eccentricities of the *Englisch*, Lovina nodded and climbed into the buggy. She immediately saw a large wicker basket sitting on the back seat, covered with several receiving blankets. While Jonah hurried around to climb into the driver's seat, Lovina stared at the object, wondering how it got there.

"What's wrong?" Jonah asked, taking the leather lead lines into his practiced grip and releasing the driving brake.

She nodded toward the basket. "What is that?"

He swiveled around and looked over his shoulder, his eyebrows crinkled in a confused frown. "Where did that come from?"

Without answering, Lovina jumped out of the buggy and looked up and down the street. Ignoring the thick drops of rain striking her face, she sought some sign of the silver car, but the vehicle was long gone. And all at once, a horrible feeling blanketed her. The realization that the *Englisch* girl had been watching them for a specific reason permeated her dazed mind. She wished she'd thought to get the license plate number on the car but she'd had no reason to do so. Now, she feared she'd regret it.

Turning, she climbed back inside. Ignoring Jonah's look of confusion, she closed the door tightly, shutting out the brisk wind. The quiet thud of raindrops striking the overhang seemed to escalate her nerves.

"*Ach*, dear me," she murmured beneath her breath.

"What is it? What's going on?" he asked, his eyes, forehead and mouth quirked in an endearing frown.

Shaking her head, Lovina reached into the back seat and pulled the basket close so she could inspect the contents. Just as she feared. Nestled within the folds of the warm blankets, a very tiny baby lay sleeping peacefully.

Jonah gasped in horror. "Where did that come from?"

"That is a girl," Lovina whispered, noticing the miniature dress the baby wore. It was handmade, the stitches even and tidy. Not at all like the factory-sewn jumpers so many of the *Englischers* put on their babies.

"*Ach*, you poor *liebchen*," Lovina crooned as she rested her fingers against the babe's arm.

The infant moved briefly, sticking a diminutive hand out, but she didn't awaken. Her small rosebud lips made a little sucking motion. The tiny nose, cheeks, chin, faint outline of eyebrows and fringe of eyelashes were absolutely perfect. Wonderfully formed and beautiful. And no matter how many new babies Lovina helped to enter this world, she could never get over the feeling she was witnessing the perfect miracle of life every single time. But more than that, this moment reminded her of a day twelve years earlier when she'd held her own precious newborn babe within her arms. Lovina had been only fourteen years old at the time. The father of her babe had been barely fifteen. Way too young to support a wife and child. Lovina had given birth to a lovely little boy but he was born out of wedlock to parents who were too young to raise him. Lovina was willing to try. She'd loved and adored her baby at first sight…until he was cruelly taken away from her without her permission and given to a childless Amish couple to raise as their own.

"Oh, *ne*!" Lovina murmured beneath her breath.

Her heart gave a powerful squeeze. She'd heard of this happening to other midwives but this was her first. A baby abandoned into her care. For Lovina, it was personal. Because she'd had a child out of wedlock, she could hardly stand the thought that somewhere in this world, there was a young mother who felt desperate enough to leave her child in the hands of complete strangers.

"Do you think the *Englisch* girl is her *mudder*?" Jonah asked.

"*Ja*, I most certainly do," Lovina said, wondering when the baby had eaten last. She searched the buggy but found no bottles or diapers. And since new babies must eat every two or three hours, she was filled with urgency.

"Gucke!" Jonah picked up a folded piece of paper tucked within the folds of the blanket and handed it to Lovina.

His deferential treatment didn't pass her notice. He was always solicitous and respectful of her. Always helpful. Yet there was a giant wall between them and she figured it was because everyone in their *Gmay* knew she'd given birth out of wedlock. To top it off, her father had left their Amish faith. He'd divorced her mom and married an *Englisch* woman and Lovina hadn't seen him since. Things like that weren't kept secret for long, especially since she'd lived in this community for years.

Some people tried to hide from their past. That wasn't possible for the Amish. When they relocated to another state, the bishops of the new and old community corresponded, to ensure the new person was still in good standing with their faith. Otherwise, they would be shunned. And more than anything, Lovina wished no one knew about her past. That she could be a normal young woman who went out with nice young men, married and had a *familye* of her own. But her history made it impossible. Because she was damaged goods. No Amish man would want her now.

Jonah watched Lovina carefully as she read the note. A myriad of emotions flashed across her pretty face. Her high forehead creased in a frown, her slightly up-turned nose crinkled softly, and her full lips pursed in apprehension. Twining her finger around one of the black ribbons on her traveling bonnet, she gave a sad little gasp and her brilliant blue eyes widened before a flicker of dismay filled their depths.

"What does it say?" he asked.

She didn't answer for a moment, as if she was reading it a second time. Finally, she took a deep inhale and read out loud.

"'Dear Lovina Albrecht,

"'I've been told you are a midwife and are kind and generous. I can't be Amish anymore but I have no money to take care of my baby either. Her name is Autumn and she was born the second of this month. Her father is *Englisch* and wants nothing to do with us. I don't even know where he is. I want my *boppli* to be raised Amish by loving parents. That's why I'm giving her to you. Please don't try to find me. Take my daughter and care for her as your own. When she is old enough, tell her it's because I love her that I gave her up. One day, I hope she'll understand. Her life would be ruined if she stayed with me. *Gott* bless.'"

Lovina lowered the paper to her lap and pressed her fingertips against her mouth. Her expressive eyes glistened with tears and Jonah understood her consternation only too well. If anyone understood this situation, it was him. Having been raised by his grandparents, he'd lived the sadness and confusion of growing up never knowing his own mother. In fact, he had no idea who his father was. Little Autumn's mom had abandoned her, just like Jonah's mother had abandoned him shortly after he was born.

"What should we do?" Lovina lifted her pensive gaze to his.

Her eyes were filled with grief and a part of him hated to see her sad. Sighing, he knew exactly what his *Englisch* employers inside the hospital would want him to do. He should hand the baby over to the administrator. Right now. But in his heart, he knew that wasn't going to happen. Because he was Amish and so was this baby. And the Amish never, ever involved the *Englisch* in their lives unless it was absolutely, critically unavoidable.

"Her *mamm* was Amish, though it appears she has left her faith," Jonah said. "Her clothing looked *Englisch*. From her note, it's obvious she knows about you, so I'm guessing she must be from one of the Amish districts in our region."

"*Ja*, I think you're right. Little Autumn is definitely Amish," Lovina confirmed as she reached up and gently caressed the delicate stitching on the sleeping baby's lavender dress. The child wiggled and blinked her eyes open. She briefly made eye contact and remained calm. She wore a sober expression that seemed so wise and understanding, as if she understood her predicament but knew they would take care of her.

"*Ach*, she's so beautiful," Lovina whispered, leaning forward to gaze into the child's dark blue eyes.

"*Ja*, and she deserves better from her *mamm* than this," Jonah said.

Lovina jerked at the anger in his tone and he forced himself to calm down. Though he frequently assisted Lovina in childbirth throughout their *Gmay* and had seen his fair share of newborns, he thought Autumn was the prettiest baby of them all. Her button nose, cheeks and eyes were impeccably formed and his heart ached with sorrow to know she wasn't wanted by her own mom.

"How dare her *mudder* abandon her like this?" he muttered to himself.

Lovina lifted her head and stared at him with wide eyes. "We mustn't judge. We don't know what the circumstances are or what her *mamm* might be going through. She looked incredibly young. She may be destitute and have no way to provide for her child."

That might be true. But…

"What about her *familye*? Surely they would help her," he said.

Most Amish families were quite large, living near their grandparents, aunts, uncles, cousins and siblings. And if that failed, the members of their *Gmay* would always come to the rescue. Their Amish congregation consisted of more than regular church meetings and a shared faith in Christ. It was an entire community of support, no matter the need. The Amish stuck together and took care of their own.

Lovina gazed at the baby. "Maybe something else is amiss here. We won't know until we find the *mudder*."

He nodded, expecting nothing less than absolute compassion from Lovina. She was so good and kind. Always earnest and giving as she tended the expectant mothers in their *Gmay*. And she doted on their new babies. Like everyone else, he knew she'd given away her own child. Maybe she felt guilty for what she'd done and was trying to make amends. It didn't matter to him. The last thing he wanted was to get involved with another woman. Not after the way his ex-fiancée had fractured his heart when she'd dumped him to marry another man in their *Gmay*. He thought she'd loved him but she'd proven him wrong, just like his mother.

The intensity of the rain increased as he sat back and stared out the windshield. His mind raced in a melee of thoughts. Everyone in their community knew his mom ...ndoned him shortly after his birth. It wasn't a ...cret. But the Amish cherished all children, even illegitimate ones. Usually.

Although Jonah's grandparents raised him, he'd never felt like he belonged. Every woman he'd ever loved or cared about had abandoned him for one reason or other. First, his mom had ditched him for an *Englisch* life because she couldn't cope with being an unwed mother. Then his fiancée had dumped him when she learned his small farm was barely making ends meet. She feared the financial insecurity too much and married another man in their congregation whose *familye* owned one of the most prosperous farms in the area. Even Jonah's grandma had died when he was only thirteen. All these women had ducked out whenever things got rough. Other than his grandma, he'd been left feeling like he couldn't depend on any woman to stick it out with him.

Though the tenets of his faith taught that his primary goal should be to wed and raise a *familye* of his own, that would never happen. Not for him. Once upon a time, he'd wanted to marry. He dearly longed to belong to someone who cared about him. Someone he could shower his love upon in return. Now all he wanted was to sell his farm and move back east. As soon as he found the time, he'd speak with a real estate agent in town. A distant cousin in Ohio had offered him and his grandfather room and board in exchange for labor on his farm. Seeing his ex-fiancée so happy with her new husband at church and other gatherings had become too difficult for him to bear. It constantly rubbed salt in his wounded heart. He couldn't stay here anymore and watch her live a happy life with another man. He just couldn't!

Jonah glanced at Lovina, focusing on the matter at hand. Right now, they had to take care of this baby.

He inhaled a deep, settling breath and let it go. "According to the Safe Haven Law in Colorado, a *mudder* may deliver her uninjured *boppli* to a firefighter at a fire station or to a staff member at a hospital, with no questions asked. But the child can be no more than seventy-two hours old."

In unison, they turned and looked closely at Autumn, studying her wee little face. Jonah brushed the babe's hand with his index finger, checking her reflexes. She quickly tightened her grip around his thumb, which looked enormous in comparison to hers.

"According to the *mudder*'s note, this baby was born on October 2, which would make her twenty days old," he said. "Notice her face doesn't appear swollen and her eyes are quite clear and focused. She's definitely older than three days. I'm certain of it."

"*Ja*, I agree," Lovina said. "Maybe her *mamm* doesn't know about the Safe Haven Law."

Jonah agreed. The only reason he and Lovina knew about the law was because of their training as EMT and midwife.

The strong patter of rain caused Jonah to glance out the window. It was really coming down now.

"We should take her *heemet*," he said.

"*Ja*, I'd like to get her out of this damp air. But what will we do with her?" Lovina asked.

He peered through the dreary haze at the hospital. "We can't hand her over. This child isn't *Englisch*. And no matter what, the authorities will prosecute her *mudder* for abandonment and confiscate the *boppli*."

Lovina gasped, then made a sad noise in the back of her throat. Jonah knew the option of turning Autumn in upset her. It upset him, too. In his heart, he thought prosecution was the least the young mother deserved for abandoning her child but he knew the bishop of their *Gmay* would never agree. Autumn was Amish and they must take care of her, no matter what. It would be unacceptable for them to hand this innocent child over to the *Englisch* and their worldly ways. For Jonah, it was tantamount to throwing away one of *Gott*'s children when she was completely innocent and vulnerable. Jonah could never do that. Not ever!

Lovina shook her head. "If we turn Autumn in, social services will give her to an *Englisch familye* to raise. They'd never give her back to the Amish, especially if they find the *mudder* and prosecute her for abandonment."

Hearing his own fears verbalized caused Jonah's heart to clench. No matter what Autumn's mother had done, this baby deserved to be raised by her own people. She must remain Amish.

"We can't turn our backs on her," Lovina said.

"I agree," he said. "The *hoppli* might have grandparents who want her. We need to look into this matter further and see if we can find them."

"But if that were the case, wouldn't the *mudder* have left Autumn with her grandparents instead of bringing her to me?" Lovina asked.

Her quick intellect always impressed Jonah. She always seemed to think the same way he did. But the fact that she'd given away her own child, even if it was years earlier, stood like a giant wall between them. Why had she given up her baby? He wanted to ask but it was none of his business.

"That's true," he said, "but it's possible there's a greater problem here that we don't know about."

The concession was difficult for him. He'd always believed it was a mother's duty to put her child's welfare first. He couldn't condone abandoning a baby like this. Nor could he conceive of any scenario that would force a mother to do so. He didn't understand at all.

"Can't we consult with Bishop Yoder for his advice?" Lovina asked.

As usual, they were both on the same track. Jonah wasn't surprised. Frequently in their medical work together, they agreed on what to do.

"*Ja,* I think that would be best. We'll consult Bishop Yoder first," he said.

After all, everyone within the *Gmay* respected their bishop. He'd been elected to his position by the members of their congregation because he was devout, kind and generous and had a wisdom that seemed to surpass other men. He was also nonjudgmental and forgiving, doing everything in his power to lead and help the members of their congregation work, live and worship in joy and happiness. Rather than being domineering or dictatorial, he wanted their individual success. As a man of *Gott*, he truly seemed to want only what was right and good for others.

"We'll consult the bishop," Jonah confirmed.

With those final words, he slapped the lead lines against the horse's back and the buggy jerked forward.

As they pulled out of the parking lot, the rain intensified. Great, heavy drops of water pounded the windshield and saturated the hard, dry earth. Inwardly, Jonah smiled, knowing his farm was getting a good drenching.

He drove carefully, conscious of the horse's reactions to the rushing wind. The poor animal ducked his head and trotted forward, seeming eager to get home. No doubt the warm, dry barn and bale of hay beckoned to him. But Jonah didn't want to end up in a ditch. Not with Lovina and a newborn in the buggy. They should get the child indoors where she could be dry and warm as fast as possible, but he wouldn't travel at a breakneck pace, either.

Within fifteen minutes, Jonah saw his farm from a distance. Located just a mile outside of town, it was a lovely place with a fine house, a barn, corrals and fallow fields that had burgeoned with hay only weeks earlier. Now the harvest was over and Jonah could focus on his winter chores. The big drawback was that his place only had thirty acres of land. Jonah really needed thirty more to grow enough hay to be self-sufficient and provide feed for his horses and cattle. When he'd first bought the place, he'd thought it would be simple to buy more land. Hah! That was easier said than done. None of the surrounding farmers were interested in selling to him. Financially, it had become a hardship and he feared he might lose his farm. Then Bishop Yoder had asked if he'd be willing to study to become an EMT. Under the tutelage of Eli Stoltzfus, a member of their *Gmay* who was a certified paramedic, Jonah had gotten his certification and a part-time job at the hospital.

Then, several months earlier, the bishop had asked if Lovina could rent Jonah's farmhouse for her midwifery business. By that time, Jonah was certified and could occasionally assist with her work. Everyone, including the *Englisch* hospital administrators, thought it was an ideal situation. Because the *Englisch* doctors didn't understand their Amish ways, Jonah and Lovina were able to provide inroads to help their people receive better medical care. Everyone was happy, except Jonah. He didn't want to work with Lovina. He didn't want to spend any more time with her than necessary. And he felt guilty for feeling that way because he knew *Gott* wanted him to love everyone, even a woman who would abandon her baby. But the only reason he'd agreed to rent out his house to her was because he needed the extra income.

Between his farm work, the rent Lovina paid and his part-time EMT job, Jonah was finally making ends meet. Now would be an ideal time for him to marry. But with his fiancée breaking off their engagement last winter, he wasn't interested in any other woman. He had no reason to stay and try to make his farm prosper. It'd be better to sell it off and move on, which he planned to do just as soon as he could. Hopefully, it would only take a few months to sell. Then he could start fresh somewhere else where his ex-fiancée's betrayal wouldn't hurt so much.

Focusing on the road, his mind returned to the present. The bishop's farm was eight miles outside of town. Much too far to drive a new baby there in the middle of a rainstorm. Jonah didn't want to put Autumn at risk. He would drop the baby and Lovina off at his place, then go and fetch the bishop. It was the right thing to do. Because no matter what hurts he carried inside, he'd do anything in his power to protect this baby from harm.

Chapter Two

Lovina pushed the heavy barn door closed until she heard the latch click. Turning, she picked up a shiny metal bucket filled with frothy white goat's milk and made her way across the barnyard. She skirted mud puddles in the expansive driveway. The rain had stopped and the late-afternoon sun had begun its descent in the western sky. Jonah and the bishop should be returning any moment and she still hadn't fed the baby.

Focusing on the path in front of her, she struggled not to slosh any of the precious milk on the ground. Evie, the oldest of her black-and-white Nigerian dwarf goats, was normally docile and let Lovina milk her without trouble. But today, the goat had been obstinate and the process had taken longer than usual. And right now, Lovina was desperate to get back inside to feed Autumn. She'd left the baby sleeping peacefully in a wooden cradle in the nursery, but the child could awaken at any moment.

Gravel crunched beneath Lovina's feet as she scurried toward the house. A crisp, tangy scent of rain filled the air and she took a deep, calming breath.

Glancing up, she came to an abrupt halt. Darkness gathered around the white-frame, bi-level farmhouse. Two horses and buggies were parked beside the spacious garden plot. Lovina recognized one of them as Jonah's. The other one belonged to Bishop Yoder. Oh, dear! The two men were already inside. She must have been in the barn longer than she thought.

Hurrying on her way, she hoped Autumn hadn't woken up from her nap. It had been almost three hours since they'd found the baby in the hospital parking lot. She must be ravenous by now.

Flinging the screen door open, Lovina stepped inside the kitchen. With the cool temperature and rainstorm, the room felt chilly. After wiping her shoes on the large rag rug just inside the back door, she hurried to set the milk bucket on the kitchen counter, then reached for more wood to stoke the fire. She hesitated, noticing that someone had laid pieces of extra firewood in the bucket on the floor. Jonah, no doubt. Though he didn't seem to like her, he frequently brought her firewood whenever she met with an expectant mother. It was as if he knew she was occupied in caring for someone else and needed help. His consideration impressed her and, for one flashing moment, she wished they could be friends. But there always seemed to be an edge of irritation between them. As if they were purposefully trying not to like each other. And she knew *Gott* wouldn't approve of that. The Lord had taught that she should love everyone as herself. But no matter how hard she tried, Lovina still felt Jonah's censure.

The low sounds of men's voices filtered in from the living room, but she heard no cries from Autumn. Realizing the dinner hour had come and gone, she forced herself to remain calm as she stoked the fire, then quickly opened the gas-powered fridge. She lifted out a pot of chicken noodle soup she'd made early that morning and placed it on the propane-powered stove. With a quick twist of her wrist, she switched the burner on low. The soup would simmer while she prepared a bottle for the baby. Then she could offer the men something to eat. Her stomach rumbled with the thought of food and she realized neither she nor Jonah had eaten all day. But first things first.

Anxious to process the goat's milk, she went to see the men. Bishop Yoder sat on the plain brown couch. Jonah stood in front of the wide picture window, his legs slightly spread, his booted feet braced beneath him. It was a purely masculine stance but she forced herself not to dwell on that. Instead, she saw he was rocking gently back and forth, which was a bit odd. Again, she tried not to notice his lean hips, wide shoulders and muscular arms. She told herself his rugged good looks were worldly things she didn't care about.

"Hallo!" she called, startling both men.

The bishop immediately came to his feet in one quick movement as Jonah swiveled around to face her. He cradled little Autumn close against his chest and, all at once, Lovina understood why he'd been rocking.

"I didn't know you were here. You must have made *gut* time in the storm," she said, forcing a smile.

Standing beside Jonah, she gazed at Autumn's face, finding the baby wide-awake and sucking frantically on her tiny fist.

"We did. When we arrived, Autumn was lying in her cradle, screaming her head off. We didn't know where you were, so I changed her diaper, then picked her up," Jonah said.

Lovina stared. Jonah had changed Autumn's diaper? How surprising. After all, he'd never been married or raised a child of his own. But she tried not to bristle at the censure in his voice.

"*Ach*, I was out milking the goat so I have something to feed her. If you'll hold her a bit longer, I'll get the milk processed as quickly as I can," Lovina said.

He nodded, avoiding her eyes.

"Is there anything I can help with?" the bishop asked, his gray eyes creased in a genuine smile.

Since the bishop was a veteran husband and father of nine children, Lovina wasn't surprised by his kind offer.

"*Ne*, I can handle it. But *komm* into the kitchen and we can chat while I work." She turned toward the other room and headed that way, expecting them to follow. And they did.

The tantalizing aroma of her soup drew the two men over to the cook stove.

"Um, that smells *gut*," the bishop said, nodding at her bubbling soup.

She gave him a warm smile. "Are you hungry?"

"I am. Jonah arrived to get me just as we were sitting down to dinner."

Which meant Jonah must be ravenous, too. Her own stomach rumbled but Autumn's needs came first.

As if on cue, the baby gave an irritated squeak. It was a high, adorable sound that made Lovina smile. Once the little girl was a few months older, the noise would undoubtedly shoot right through them. But for now, the baby was so tiny and sweet that everything about her was cute.

"There, there, Itty-Bit. You'll have your bottle soon enough," Jonah soothed her.

Itty-Bit! Lovina hid a look of surprise. She would never have expected a solemn man like Jonah Lapp to use such a term of endearment for a tiny baby girl.

As he tucked the child into the crook of his arm, Autumn immediately quieted…for the time being. Knowing they didn't have much time before her impatient cries turned into an ear-splitting screech, Lovina hurried with her chore. Picking up a metal spoon, she prepared to process the milk.

"*Ach*, she's *allrecht* now you have her. You're *gut* with children, I see." Bishop Yoder beamed at Jonah.

Lovina dropped the spoon into the stainless steel sink. The baby jerked at the loud clatter and began to cry in earnest. Jonah bounced her harder.

As she retrieved a clean spoon, Lovina glanced at Jonah and saw a bit of panic in his eyes. Obviously he liked to hold babies…when they weren't crying.

"I'm glad you made it through the rainstorm okay.

Did it create much mud on the road leading to your farm?" Lovina turned toward the stove.

The bishop glanced out the window. The shadows of dusk were settling across the land. "*Ja*, it did. The storm seems to have let up for the time being but it could start raining again. I should get *heemet* soon."

"You're always welcome here, bishop." Lovina glanced at Jonah, hoping for his approval as she used a coffee filter to sieve the goat's milk into a shiny pan she'd set in the sink.

"Of course," Jonah said, his voice sounding a bit strained.

The bishop smiled and reached to rub Autumn's tiny arm. Though she'd stopped crying, the baby released several exasperated grunts.

"She sure seems to have taken to you. You're a natural at holding a *boppli*," the bishop told Jonah.

A flush of pink suffused Jonah's face and he looked embarrassed. Lovina felt the same way and, for the life of her, she didn't know why. She worked with babies almost every day of her life. So did Jonah. Being members of an Amish community that was constantly producing little ones provided lots of opportunities for both of them to hold and admire babies, not to mention their medical training. So why did this moment in time make her feel so uncomfortable?

Reaching for another pan, she prepared a double boiler to heat the milk. The back door opened and a rush of damp air that smelled of sagebrush filtered over them as Jonah's grandpa, Noah, came inside. Seeming to know the baby might be getting cold, Jonah tucked the warm blanket tighter around her little body, which won Lovina's approval.

"*Ach*, here you all are," Noah boomed in a cheery voice. "I saw Lovina come into the house after milking the goats." He glanced at her. "I brought you a bucket of chilled water from the well house. I figured you'd need it to process the milk."

"*Danke!*" Lovina smiled, thankful for his offering. Little Autumn's impatience was growing by the minute and she didn't want to leave right now to fetch the cold water.

"*Hallo, Dawdi,*" Jonah greeted his grandfather.

Dawdi Noah nodded at his grandson, then glanced at the bishop. "I put your horse in the barn with ours until you're ready to leave. To what do we owe this unexpected visit?"

The bishop smiled and jerked a thumb toward Autumn. "I came to see this little one."

"*Ach*, what a pretty *boppli*." *Dawdi* Noah gazed with adoration at Autumn, seeking to make eye contact with the little girl. The baby gazed at him for several moments with somber tolerance. Then she waved her little arms and let out an outraged squall.

"Is she hungry?" *Dawdi* Noah asked.

"*Ja*! We're trying to get her fed," Jonah exclaimed, glancing at Lovina.

Determined to remain unruffled, she proceeded with her work. After all, she was a midwife and knew better than to get upset and scurry around like a maniac. All that would do was confuse and upset the mothers and babies she cared for. Instead, she made each of her movements count as she quickly stirred the milk and reached for glass jars to store it in.

She wasn't surprised by *Dawdi* Noah's curiosity. If he saw someone come into the house that he knew, which was almost everyone who came to visit, he came inside the house to chat with them. Mothers and their babies were in and out of this house at all times on any given day. *Dawdi* always wanted to hug and admire every single one. With a full head of shocking white hair and a jovial face creased by age, the elderly man stooped slightly and walked with the aid of a cane. Otherwise, the mischievous twinkle in his eyes made him look much younger than his eighty-nine years.

"Whose *boppli* is she?" *Dawdi* asked.

"That's what we're about to discuss," the bishop replied.

Dawdi tilted his head in confusion. "What do you mean?"

"*Dawdi*, this is a unique situation. Please sit down and you'll soon learn what's going on," Jonah told him.

Giving a nod, *Dawdi* sat on one of the wooden chairs and remained quiet yet attentive. The baby's cries became heart-wrenching and Jonah shifted her in his arms once more but nothing he did eased her wails. She was out of patience.

"She needs something to eat. I still can't believe her *mudder* would abandon her like this," Jonah mumbled beneath his breath.

Dawdi's bushy eyebrows shot up at this but he kept silent, his intelligent eyes taking in every movement in the room.

Lovina frowned and responded a bit too forcefully. "As I said before, it's not for us to judge. The bottle is almost prepared. Give me just a few more moments."

When it was ready, Lovina placed the pan of hot milk into the bucket of chilled water *Dawdi* had brought in from the well house so it would cool down as fast as possible. That would help the milk retain its good flavor.

"Can I hold her?" *Dawdi* reached to take Autumn from Jonah and he handed the child over.

Dawdi's hands were shaky and he almost dropped the little bundle. Just like catching a new calf in his arms, Jonah made a quick save as Lovina gasped.

"Careful!" Jonah said.

Dawdi nodded as Jonah placed Autumn in his grandfather's arms. Jonah hesitated a moment, as if waiting to ensure all was well before he withdrew the support of his hands. Autumn was so small and helpless, completely dependent upon them for her every need. And that made Lovina feel fiercely protective of the child. She'd do almost anything to keep this little girl safe.

The bishop sat at the table with *Dawdi* Noah and watched Lovina move efficiently around the room. This was her home and she knew her business, keeping a close eye on everyone as she worked. Jonah merely leaned against the wall and folded his arms.

"Has Jonah explained everything to you?" Lovina finally asked with a quick peek at the bishop.

Though he'd removed his black felt hat, the bishop

still wore his coat and work boots. Otherwise, he was dressed just the same as Jonah and *Dawdi* Noah.

The bishop nodded. "*Ja*, he's told me how you found the *boppli* in your buggy in town and he let me read the note Autumn's *mudder* left her for you. I guess you weren't able to follow her."

Lovina laughed and lifted one hand in the air as she spoke in a teasing voice. "I'm afraid that would have been rather difficult."

The bishop chuckled. "Hmm, point taken. I know a horse and buggy could never catch a speeding car."

"Then you understand why we brought Autumn here instead of giving her to the hospital administrator," Lovina said. "We feared the *Englisch* would take her away for *gut*. Jonah thought it was for the best. So did I."

"I agree with your actions. From what Jonah has told me, Autumn's *mudder* would probably be prosecuted by the law for abandonment," the bishop said.

"That's correct." Lovina spoke as she worked. "If the *Englisch* took her, we might never get her back."

A dark frown deepened the furrows on the bishop's forehead. "That is unthinkable. Autumn is one of our *kinder*. She must be raised Amish. It's her birthright."

The bishop's words didn't surprise Lovina as she quickly prepared a five-ounce bottle, adding a mixture of powder especially for babies, which contained the proper ingredients to give Autumn enough calories, fat, protein and carbohydrates to keep her healthy.

As she reached for the tiny girl, Lovina almost tripped over Jonah's large feet. Without thinking, he shot out a hand to steady her. A feeling of shock and embarrassment prickled her skin where his strong fingers curled around her upper arm. She stared into his eyes, feeling transfixed for several moments. Then, she pulled away.

"I'm sorry," she murmured as he released her.

His startled expression told her he felt just as shocked as her.

"Um, if you don't need me anymore, I think I'll go outside and work on my chores," he said.

"That would be *allrecht*," the bishop said. "I'll speak with you again before I leave."

Jonah nodded and slipped out the back door. Watching him go, Lovina breathed a sigh of relief. She didn't know why she felt so jittery around him but she did. He'd made it clear what he thought about Autumn's mother and, because of her past, Lovina figured he must feel the same about her. And that realization set an ache in Lovina's heart that wouldn't go away.

In the barn, Jonah tossed grain to the chickens, then poured slop in the pig's trough. Normally, Lovina did the chores but she was occupied elsewhere.

It had grown dark, the sun hiding behind the western mountains. Not a single star gleamed in the night sky, and he figured they must be covered by rain clouds. The air felt damp and cold and he was eager to finish his chores and get something to eat. Right now, he was starving and thought about the delectable fragrance of Lovina's homemade chicken noodle soup. He dearly longed to eat a bowl or three but it was his habit to take his meals with *Dawdi* Noah in the *dawdi haus*.

Lovina was a good cook. Jonah couldn't deny it. He'd tasted her food at the church gatherings on numerous occasions. In fact, she was good at everything she did. When he'd been inside the farmhouse with the bishop, he couldn't help noticing how neat and tidy the rooms were now that she occupied the home. So different from the chaos that had reigned when he and *Dawdi* had lived there. By this time, Jonah had planned to be living there with Fannie, his ex-fiancée. Now he just wanted to leave town and go anywhere but here. And yet he sensed it was really his inner grief he longed to run away from.

His stomach rumbled again and he was eager to retire to the *dawdi haus* and whatever burnt dinner *Dawdi* planned to serve them tonight. Since it was so late, maybe they'd have a simple meal of store-bought bread, cold meat and cheese. And right now, that sounded like a feast.

He was just preparing to milk his two black-and-white Holsteins when *Dawdi* startled him out of his musings.

"Jonah, the bishop wants to see you again. Can you come up to the house?" the elderly man asked from the barn doors.

With a single nod, Jonah picked up the wood bucket and followed his grandfather. Wondering where the day had gone, Jonah walked through the dark farmyard toward the brightly lit house. His stomach churned with emptiness and he chafed at this delay. He didn't want to return to the house because he feared what the bishop might ask him to do.

Inside the farmhouse, he found Bishop Yoder sitting in the kitchen with Lovina. Steaming bowls of hot soup sat cooling on the table with a pile of warm biscuits and dishes of golden butter and honey. The baby was nowhere to be seen. Upon Jonah and *Dawdi*'s entry, Lovina stood and ladled two more bowls of soup for them. At first, Jonah just stared, his mouth salivating at the delicious aromas. Then he doffed his hat and sat down, too hungry to argue or refuse this kind offering.

When Lovina finally took a seat, the bishop smiled kindly. "I'm glad you're all here. Let us pray."

They each bowed their heads and prayed silently in their hearts. Jonah tried to focus on his Savior instead of the food sitting in front of him. Finally, the bishop released a low sigh and they each ate ravenously, the room silent except for the chink of spoons and knives against dishes.

After a few minutes, it occurred to Jonah that Lovina hadn't eaten today either. Yet she hadn't complained once. She'd merely ducked her head and done what she could for Autumn. And in that moment, Jonah couldn't help comparing her to Fannie. Though he'd been in love with his ex-fiancée, he realized she was naturally more high-strung…the complete opposite of Lovina. It was as if Fannie was uncertain of her own abilities and didn't know what to do. During their engagement, Jonah had thought she was young and fragile and needed a strong man to guide her. But now he wondered.

"It'll be *gut* for you to eat something hot before you take your journey *heemet*," Lovina said to the bishop.

"*Ja, danke* very much. It's delicious," the bishop replied, taking another bite.

As he reached for two warm biscuits, *Dawdi* smiled with delight. "*Ja, danke*, Lovina. This is *wundervoll*."

She nodded and blessed the old man with a smile so bright Jonah had to blink. And for one insane moment, Jonah wondered what it would be like for her to smile that way at him.

When both *Dawdi* and the bishop glanced at Jonah, he took a quick gulp of chilled milk from his glass.

"Don't you think the food is *gut*, Jonah?" *Dawdi* asked.

Jonah didn't meet his grandfather's gaze as he swallowed hard and nodded, feeling embarrassed by his rudeness. "*Ja*, it's very tasty."

. Lovina nodded but her smile didn't quite reach her eyes.

Avoiding her gaze, Jonah took another mouthful of soup, feeling grouchy because he didn't want to say thank you. In fact, he wished he was anywhere but here. But the food was absolutely yummy and he had no call to be discourteous. The Lord wouldn't approve.

"*Danke*, Lovina. It is very *gut*." He spoke without looking up, deciding it was right to speak the truth. He didn't want to like Lovina but the Lord would not endorse his ingratitude. Whether Jonah approved of this woman or not, she was one of *Gott*'s children and deserved his respect. He must not let his pride get the better of him. He should be humble and willing to help wherever he was needed.

"*Gaern gscheh*. You're welcome," she returned as she buttered a biscuit for herself.

"Where is the little one?" *Dawdi* asked.

"She went right to sleep after her bottle. Young *bopplin* sleep a lot, so I'm not concerned. She's only a few weeks old, after all. It's been a long, tiring day and she needs rest so she can grow strong," Lovina said.

"*Ach*, we have six Amish districts here in Colorado," the bishop said. "I'll send letters to each of their bishops to see if they know of any unwed *mudders* who might have run away. That way, we might be able to track down the *boppli*'s *mamm*."

Jonah chewed thoughtfully, then swallowed and set his spoon on the table. "That could take some time. If Autumn's *mudder* has run off, they might not know where she's gone."

"*Ja*," Bishop Yoder agreed. "But if she's Amish, then she's one of our own. She may not have been baptized as a member of our faith yet, so she cannot be shunned for what she's done. We don't want to lose her to the *Englisch* world, if we can prevent it. I'm hoping we can find her and bring her back."

"What would you like us to do in the meantime?" Lovina asked.

Jonah leaned forward, his ears pricked for the answer. He had a bad feeling about this. The situation had been foisted upon them and they must rise to the occasion, for Autumn's sake.

"If it's *allrecht* with you, I'd like Autumn to remain here in your care for the time being," the bishop said.

There was a long pause as this soaked into each of their minds.

"Of course. I can tend to all her needs. It's no trouble at all," Lovina agreed with enthusiasm.

"Not just you but Jonah, too," the bishop said, swiveling in his seat to look at Jonah. "Even at such a young age, a *kinder* needs two parents."

Jonah's mind scattered. What exactly was the bishop asking him to do?

Bishop Yoder dipped his head. "I'd like Jonah to assist Lovina in any way possible. We must put this *boppli*'s needs above our own. I don't want anything to happen to her while she's in our care. She deserves the best we can give her until we can locate her *familye*."

"Of course," Jonah agreed. But he still didn't understand. It only took one person to feed, bathe and diaper a baby. With chores and livestock to tend, Jonah wouldn't be much help with that.

"I want Jonah to protect Autumn and Lovina," the bishop continued. "We don't know what or who we're dealing with yet. It's possible Autumn's *vadder* could return and try to take the *boppli*. We don't know if the man is abusive or what his motives might be. And I don't want Lovina to get injured because she's in the way."

Aha! Jonah hadn't thought about this but he realized the bishop was right, though he couldn't say he was happy about it. He didn't mind helping tend to the baby, but being Lovina's protector was something else entirely. Of course, he didn't want Lovina to get hurt but helping her with Autumn would mean he had to spend even more time with her than he already did with her midwifery practice.

From Lovina's frown and pursed lips, Jonah figured she felt the same about him. And that's when he realized she didn't like him any more than he liked her. And for some crazy reason, that made him feel even worse.

"The bishops in the area might not know if a girl in their *Gmay* had a *hoppli* out of wedlock," Lovina said. "It would be quite easy to hide a pregnancy behind loose clothing."

"True, but we have to try," Bishop Yoder said. "It will take time to hear back through the mail. In the meantime, please take care of Autumn as if she were your own child."

Lovina nodded and looked away but not before Jonah saw tears glistening in her eyes. And that confused him even more. Other than the obvious reasons, why did she care what happened to this baby? Autumn wasn't her child. Lovina had given away her own babe years earlier, so why the show of emotion now?

"Will you have any problems if members of our *Gmay* ask questions? They can be rather nosy," the bishop said.

Lovina smiled at that. They all knew it was difficult to keep anything going on within the *Gmay* a secret for long. And that could work in their favor as they tried to find Autumn's mother.

"*Ne*, we'll simply speak the truth," Jonah said. "We'll

say Autumn's *mudder* has asked Lovina to look after the *boppli* for the time being. Since they all know Lovina is a midwife, I think they'll accept that without becoming too inquisitive."

"*Gut.* And you'll keep this quiet, too, won't you, Noah?" Bishop Yoder glanced at Jonah's grandfather.

Dawdi nodded, his expression one of integrity that none of them would ever question. He was old but he had lived a devout life and was wise and kind. His character was unimpeachable and they knew he could keep silent on something as important as this.

"Of course," *Dawdi* said. "It's vital that we protect this *boppli.* I won't say a word."

Satisfied by this, the bishop nodded. "And while I search for the *mudder,* I want Jonah to accompany Lovina whenever she leaves the farm with the *boppli.* We must ensure that both are safe at all times."

The man glanced at Jonah and completely missed Lovina's shocked expression. She tossed Jonah a withering look that could have melted wax. Jonah gazed at the bishop with suspicion. He'd heard the man periodically give assignments like this to other couples in their *Gmay,* hoping to get them together in marriage. Their Amish community was new and relatively small and the bishop was trying to help their *Gmay* grow, to ensure their success. In fact, the bishop had recently assigned Ben Yoder to accompany Caroline Schwartz after she'd been badly injured in a buggy accident. The two had not gotten along…at first. Now they were newlyweds. Was that what the bishop was doing now?

Trying to get Jonah and Lovina together? Because if so, it wouldn't work. Not for Jonah. All he wanted was a fresh start. But with the bishop's word on the matter, Jonah knew neither he nor Lovina could refuse. Jonah would obey, but that didn't mean he liked it.

"I'll look after them both to the best of my ability and do everything I can to protect them," Jonah promised.

It wouldn't be easy. Jonah had his part-time EMT job at the hospital and Lovina had to pay visits to her expectant moms throughout the week. They'd figure it out. Maybe they could stagger their schedules.

Slapping the palms of his hands against the tabletop, Bishop Yoder scraped back his chair and stood. "*Gut.* I'll leave it in your hands. Let's touch base again at church in a couple weeks. If you hear any news before then, just send me word."

Both Lovina and Jonah nodded as they accompanied Bishop Yoder to the back door.

"I'll walk out to the barn with you." Lifting his cane, *Dawdi* snatched up another biscuit, then stepped out into the frigid night air with the bishop.

Jonah watched the two men disappear from view, noticing how his grandfather limped heavily on his cane. He knew the two men would go to the barn and hitch up the bishop's horse and buggy.

He glanced at Lovina. The heat in the room had given her cheeks a pretty rose color. In the warm glow of the gas-powered light overhead, her profile looked beautiful. With an apron tied around her waist and a dish towel draped over her left shoulder, she seemed so domestic. For a fleeting moment, Jonah caught a vision of her as some Amish man's wife with a passel of kids, but he quickly blinked that away.

"Unless you want me for something else, I'll head back to the barn, too. I need to finish my chores before I turn in. I'll feed your goats while I'm out there," he said.

She met his gaze without flinching, her expression a tad severe. "*Ja, danke.* Autumn and I will be just fine here without you."

Ah, that hurt. It wasn't so much what she said but the harsh, final sound of her voice.

"*Gut nacht*, then." He placed his straw hat on his head, then ducked outside and followed the other men to the barn.

Within minutes, the bishop's buggy rattled down the graveled lane as he headed home and Jonah milked his cows by kerosene light. *Dawdi* soon joined him, offering to feed the three goats. They closed the double barn doors, preserving what warmth they could find in the expansive barn.

As he worked, Jonah gazed through the shadows and a feeling of anticipation warred with a cold, dark dread. He'd see Lovina again in the morning. She might need to pay a visit to some expectant mother or run errands in town. He would need to accompany her while keeping up with his work on the farm. How long this might go on, he couldn't say. And what if Bishop Yoder failed to locate Autumn's mother? What would happen to the baby then? How would Lovina cope if the child was taken away and turned in to the legal authorities? Jonah shouldn't care at all. But he did. And that's what confused him most of all.

Chapter Three

Lovina lifted Autumn out of the plastic tub she used to bathe small babies and wrapped the child in a soft, fluffy towel. Droplets of water dotted Lovina's hands as she laid the tiny girl on a soft pad set on the kitchen table to dry her off. The room was toasty warm as Autumn kicked her spindly legs and waved her arms, active and wide-awake.

Streams of sunlight blazed through the window in front of the sink. Outside in the barnyard, a rooster crowed and Lovina knew it was past time to gather eggs. It was barely six o'clock in the morning. Normally, Lovina was ready to hitch up her buggy and pay visits to her expectant mothers. But today, she was way behind schedule. No doubt the three feedings during the night had something to do with it. Lovina had slept late but she couldn't begrudge Autumn. The infant's cries were innocent pleas of hunger. And each time Lovina prepared a bottle and rocked the baby, she was reminded that some other woman had gotten up in the middle of the night to tend to her newborn son years earlier and she viewed this service as a labor of love.

Once she had the baby dressed, Lovina lifted her up and cradled her in her arms. She spoke quietly to the babe, kissing her cheeks, telling her how wonderful she was. With her tummy full, Autumn gave a wide yawn and made little contented sounds in the back of her throat. Her eyes soon began to droop.

"*Ach*, are you tired already? Such a sleepy girl," Lovina cooed.

The baby looked at her briefly, her mouth curving in a reflexive smile. Though Autumn was too young to be smiling for real, Lovina's heart melted.

"*Ach*, you little sweetums. My dear *liebchen*."

A knock on the back door distracted her and she looked up. Jonah stood there, waiting for admittance.

Carrying the baby, Lovina walked over and opened the door. He held two pails of milk and, from the froth on top, she could tell one was cow's milk and the other was from her goats.

"*Guder mariye*! *Komm* in." Lovina stood back so he could enter the room.

He barely glanced her way as he set the pails on the kitchen counter. He wasn't wearing his felt hat and, from the damp tendrils of hair curling against his nape, she could tell he'd recently washed. He smelled of hay, horses and spearmint toothpaste…a masculine scent she'd been raised with and had always liked. It meant he'd been in the barn, working with his livestock.

"Since you're tied up with the *boppli*, I went ahead

and fed and milked your goats. *Dawdi* is gathering the eggs for you now," he said.

How kind. For just a moment, a feeling of teamwork and *familye* washed over her. But then she reminded herself that this wasn't her *familye* and they never would be.

Jonah turned, his gaze sweeping the room. No doubt he saw the plastic tub she'd emptied and propped in the sink to drip dry and the bottle of baby lotion and thick towel she'd used on Autumn.

"*Danke*. That's very thoughtful of you," she said.

He looked at the baby and a half smile almost curved his full lips. Almost. His smile was so tentative she thought she must have imagined it. Regardless, she knew he liked the baby. A lot.

"Is she eating well?" he asked, lifting a finger to caress Autumn's tiny hand.

Lovina laughed. "Like a little piglet."

He nodded, his eyes sparkling with delight. But still, he didn't smile. "That's *gut*."

"Would you mind holding her a moment while I run upstairs?" Without permission, she placed Autumn in his arms.

A look of satisfaction curved his lips and Lovina knew he was pleased. As she turned toward the door, she wondered what it would take to get him to laugh.

Lifting Autumn to his shoulder, Jonah turned his face toward her little neck and inhaled deeply. "Mmm, she smells *gut*, just like a *boppli* should."

Lovina chuckled, pausing in the doorway. "Of course. She just had a bath and lotion. Most babies smell *gut*."

He cocked one eyebrow at her. "Unless they've spit up or, you know, messed their pants."

Lovina burst out laughing. She couldn't help it.

Jonah's cheeks flamed beet red, which made her laugh even harder. But he turned away, obviously embarrassed by what he'd said.

"Don't worry. If Autumn messes her pants, I'll let you change her," she said.

From his profile, she saw him frown and she realized she shouldn't tease him. He seemed so surly all the time and she wished he would let down his guard and give her a genuine smile.

Leaving the two of them, Lovina hurried to one of the bedrooms upstairs, retrieved extra diapers and blankets, and was back in a flash. As she entered the kitchen, she heard Jonah speaking baby gibberish. He sat in one of the wooden chairs and had laid Autumn on his long thighs, rocking his legs back and forth and holding her tiny hands as he gazed down and spoke to her. The sight was so endearing that Lovina's heart gave a little squeeze.

With the baby occupied, Lovina reached for two frying pans, then opened the fridge to retrieve milk and a bowl of eggs.

"Have you and *Dawdi* eaten yet?" she asked as she cracked eggs into one pan.

Jonah responded without looking up. "*Ne*, not yet."

"*Gut*! I'll have breakfast ready in a jiffy. You did some of my chores, now I can repay you by feeding you."

He glanced up, a look of refusal on his face, but

then he seemed to think better of it and glanced down. "*Danke*, I would appreciate that."

Lovina hid a satisfied smile. No doubt he was hungry and didn't want to pass on a good meal. But once more, that feeling of teamwork washed over her and she forced herself to shrug it off. She went about her work, processing the goat's milk as she had the night before, then prepared thick slices of homemade bread. She soon had oatmeal with raisins ready to round out their meal.

"Do you have a lot of work to do out in the fields today?" she asked as she worked.

He nodded. "*Ja*, there's a fence I need to repair before the cattle from the neighboring farm break through. We won't have rain today, so I thought I'd take advantage of the clear skies."

Holding a spatula aloft, she gazed at him. She hated to take him away from his work but there was something on her mind.

"I... I was wondering if I could buy two more goats," she finally said.

He looked up, lifting the baby to his shoulder. "You don't have enough already?"

She shook her head. He already knew she made goat cheese, which she sold to an *Englisch* grocery store in town every Friday. That left just enough milk to sell to some of the Amish mothers who wanted to supplement their baby's diets. Which meant there wasn't much left over for Autumn to eat.

"With the *boppli* requiring regular feedings, I fear I may run out of milk," she explained.

He nodded. "I see. We can't let that happen."

"*Ne*, of course not. I'm happy to pay you for the extra feed," she hurried on, fearing he might refuse her request.

He shrugged one powerful shoulder. "That won't be necessary. We can get you more goats if that's what you think we need. After all, it's for Autumn, and Bishop Yoder has asked us to care for her."

Yes, it was just an assignment from the bishop. That was all. Or was it? Somehow, teaming up with Jonah to care for this baby felt like so much more.

Lovina poured the fresh goat's milk into sterile jars and slid them into the fridge. She'd make cheese later this evening, once she had a few minutes for the chore. "I think it's best to buy two more goats but I have no idea how long Autumn will be here. If Bishop Yoder finds her *mudder* and she leaves in a few days, we could be stuck with two extra goats."

Glancing over her shoulder, she saw Jonah frown. Did the thought of extra goats bother him? Or did the baby leaving upset him as much as it did her? After all, Autumn's life was in flux and Lovina didn't want the child to return to a mother who didn't want her. Once Autumn left, Lovina knew she would worry about the little girl constantly. Memories of giving up her own child still clogged Lovina's chest, and she hated the thought of giving up another baby, even if Autumn didn't belong to her.

"I can drive you over to Mervin Schwartz's place this afternoon. He's got lots of extra goats. I'm sure he would sell us a couple of them. Would that be soon enough?" Jonah asked.

She nodded, feeling relieved by his offer. "*Ja*, that would be perfect."

Stepping over to the back door, she pushed the screen open and glanced around the expansive yard and outbuildings. It was warmer than the day before and the blue sky showed not a single cloud, which meant they would have no rain today.

"It's going to be a beautiful fall day. Where is *Dawdi*? He should *komm* inside and eat," she said.

"He was in the coop last I saw him. Over the next few days, we're going to clean it out and add new mulch and a propane light for winter," Jonah said.

"*Gut*! I can help, if we do it when Autumn goes down for her nap." Stepping out onto the back porch, she let the screen door clap closed behind her as she cupped a hand around her mouth.

"*Dawdi* Noah," she yelled twice.

When there was no sign of him, she reached for the bell mounted on the side of the house and pulled on the leather cord. She clanged it several times, to get *Dawdi*'s attention. It rang loud and clear, the sound reaching clear out to the farthest field. On a farm like this, the bell was used only to call the *familye* in for meals or to herald an emergency. This was the first time Lovina had used it and she felt a little shy as she tugged the cord one last time.

Within moments, *Dawdi* appeared at the barn door, looking surprised and a bit alarmed.

"*Hallo! Mariye-esse,*" she announced breakfast.

He grinned and limped heavily on his sturdy cane as he hurried toward the house with a basket of eggs.

Inside, Lovina took the eggs and served the men a delicious meal. They blessed the food, then explained to *Dawdi* their plan to buy more goats.

"That's *gut*. The *hoppli* will need plenty to eat," he said, biting into a piece of bread spread with butter and strawberry jam.

"We'll be going over to the Schwartzes' farm later this afternoon. Do you want to *komm* with?" Lovina asked, thinking the ride wouldn't seem quite so somber with *Dawdi* along. The elder man had a penchant for chatter, the complete opposite of Jonah. Plus it might be fun for *Dawdi* to get away from the farm for a short time.

Dawdi stared at her a moment, as if thinking this over. Then he shook his head. "*Ne*, I have chores I need to do."

Like what? Perhaps he planned to start on the chicken coop today. But he offered no explanation as he tucked into his eggs and oatmeal. Lovina was mildly surprised he didn't offer to tend to the baby while they were gone. But maybe that was best. He was rather frail and shaky and she feared he might drop the child. Instead, she'd prepare a diaper bag, bundle the baby up nice and warm, and take her along.

Jonah didn't say a word, just ate his meal in silence. Occasionally, he glanced at Autumn and his face would soften for a few moments. Then he'd look at Lovina and the stern scowl reappeared.

Once he'd finished eating, *Dawdi* sat back and released a satisfied sigh as he rested a hand over the slight bulge of his stomach. A sudden frown drew his eyebrows together and he scooted back his chair.

"*Ach*, I'll leave you two alone now," he said. "I'm not feeling well all of a sudden. I think I have indigestion. The food was so *gut*, I fear I overate."

Jonah's mouth dropped open and he showed a look of concern. "Are you *allrecht*?"

"*Ja*! *Ja*! I just need to lie down a while," the old man said.

Lovina hid a smile. *Dawdi* had eaten enough for two men. But she got the feeling that he was trying to get her and Jonah alone. Lovina didn't mind taking Autumn with her. The weather was warm enough and Jonah would be there if she needed a second pair of hands.

Hmm. Funny how she'd already come to rely on the two men's help. But she wasn't sure she wanted it. Spending a good portion of the afternoon alone with Jonah might not be fun. His brooding looks could really send a chill through her at times. Hence, it might be a long, uncomfortable afternoon. For both of them.

Lovina held the baby in one arm. Using her free hand, she spread strawberry preserves on a slice of bread and spooned oatmeal into her own bowl. By the time she finished eating, Autumn was sound asleep.

Gulping down the last of his chilled milk, Jonah nodded at the infant. "Shall I put her in her cradle for you?"

Surprised by the offer, Lovina shook her head. "*Ne*, I can do it."

She stood, trying to hide her flaming cheeks and wondering what was wrong with her. He was only trying to help. But she didn't want him roaming around the back bedrooms of her home, even if it was his house she was renting. It felt much too personal.

"I'll be heading out to the fields now. I'll see you later this afternoon and we'll go get your goats," Jonah said.

"While we're out, I also need to check on Norma and her new baby. Just a quick follow-up," she said.

He nodded and she hurried to the nursery. For some reason, she was suddenly desperate to get away from him.

When she heard the screen door close behind him, she breathed a sigh of relief. The bishop had asked the two of them to care for Autumn, but for some reason, this situation felt much too intimate for Lovina. With Jonah and his grandfather sitting in her kitchen, eating a meal she'd prepared, holding and marveling at the baby, it felt like they were a real *familye*. And they weren't. Not now, not ever. But it served Lovina right for inviting the men to share her meal. She'd tried to be friendly and helpful. After all, they'd milked her goats and gathered her eggs. But getting close to Jonah and his sweet grandfather was the last thing she wanted. Because their time together was temporary at best.

Jonah hurried out to the barn, where he gathered up his shovel and hammer and a bag of nails. Within minutes, he was headed out to the south pasture. As he stepped over furrows of damp, fertile soil, he gazed at the Wet Mountains where stands of aspen stood high up, shimmering in the sunshine. Thick stands of scrub oak trailed the fence line where his property bordered the fields of another *Englisch* farmer where the fields lay fallow. For two years now, no crops had grown there. Though Jonah had twice made an offer to buy the acreage, the elderly *Englisch* man who owned the land refused.

Shaking his head, Jonah pulled the brim of his felt hat lower to shade his eyes. Leaving good, fertile soil empty was such a waste. If Jonah owned the land, he'd fill it with hay or a little barley or oats.

Since he didn't have enough of his own land to plant, Jonah had to buy his barley and oats from another farmer. And though he knew it was wrong to covet what belonged to someone else, he admired the open fields surrounding his place. But then he thought better of it. Today or tomorrow, he'd speak to a real estate agent in town and hopefully sell his farm soon. At some point, he'd need to tell Lovina of his plans so she could find another place to live. He'd move back east where he could start anew. Maybe, in time, he'd even meet someone he could love. Someone who would love him in return. But right now, that seemed like a distant dream.

Adjusting the weight of the shovel in his hand, he thought about Lovina. She hadn't hesitated when the bishop asked her to care for Autumn. This morning, when she'd invited him and *Dawdi* to breakfast, he could see the fatigue in her eyes. No doubt, she'd been up throughout the night with the baby. And yet she hadn't grumbled about it. Not once. He couldn't help comparing her to Fannie, who'd exhibited great concern when he confided his farm wasn't making ends meet. Within a fortnight, she'd broken off their engagement. And though she hadn't said so, he knew she wanted more security than he could offer. His suspicions had been confirmed when she'd quickly become engaged to Alvin Fisher, whose father owned a lucrative farm.

Shaking his head, Jonah refocused his thoughts on his work. At the irrigation ditch, he studied the long rows where just weeks earlier he'd mowed his fall hay. He discovered several places where the rainwater had pooled and created a big sinkhole. He evened out the furrows and built up the side of the ditch so the winter moisture wouldn't cause more erosion.

As he worked, droplets of sweat formed on his brow in spite of the cool day. Standing up straight, he pushed back his hat and swiped his forehead with the sleeve of his shirt. He didn't know why he worked so hard on this place. Though he planned to sell the farm soon, he labored as if he planned to stay forever. It just wasn't in him to do anything half-heartedly. But there was nothing for him here now. He wasn't interested in any of the marriageable young women in his *Gmay*. And even if he was, he didn't know how he could open his heart again and let his guard down enough to fall in love with one of them. It hurt too much.

Once he was satisfied the irrigation ditch would run smoothly through the field, he walked to the south pasture. Several fence posts had fallen over, dragging the strands of barbed wire with them. A good farmer always kept his fences mended. Fences helped create good neighbors. But as he dug deeper post holes, he lost his sense of urgency. The *Englisch* farmer bordering his property had no cattle in his field this year and he wondered why. Again, Jonah thought it was such a waste. If he could buy the land, he'd put it to good use. But then he reminded himself he was leaving soon.

He reseated the posts before tamping them firmly into the damp soil. Then he restrung the barbed wire and tacked it into place. Within an hour, his work was finished. He looked up at the sky. The position of the sun and his rumbling stomach told him it was midday. Time to go in for lunch. And then he'd drive Lovina over to get her goats. He didn't mind so much except he never knew what to say to her during the journey.

Packing up his tools, he carried them back to the barn. As he walked, his gaze took in the status of his farm with the critical eye of a meticulous farmer. He scanned the fences for any more breakage. He noticed the outbuildings and his cattle grazing in the east pasture. His milk cows stood in the corral, chewing their cud and swishing their long tails. His two roan draft horses stood grazing beneath the stand of leafless poplar trees near the house. All his livestock appeared strong and healthy. And yet there was much work to do this winter if he was to prepare for spring planting. And since he didn't plan to be here then, he figured he'd do the work for the next farmer who bought this place.

Lovina's goats stayed close to the barn, eating everything in their path. That was good, to a certain extent. They kept the weeds mowed down but sometimes got into other trouble, such as breaking down the fence and wandering up onto the dangerous county road. The chickens pecked around in the yard while the pigs snorted and lounged in the cool dirt of their pen. Everything looked in good order. Though his farm was small, it was tidy and well-kept. The Realtor thought it would sell for a good price.

A flash of lavender caught Jonah's eye and he jerked his head in that direction. Lovina stood in the vegetable garden, her slender back bent as she gathered up tomato gates and stacked them neatly in the gardening shed. She raked compost into the furrows, then stood straight and arched her back before returning to her work. He'd thought about tending to the garden but never needed to do so. Lovina did her chores with an efficiency his farmer's mind could admire. And though he'd tried to grow tomatoes last year, he had to admit no one in the area grew plants as big or as nice as hers. With their cooler, shorter growing season, it was difficult at best. Maybe that was a topic he could address on their trip to buy the new goats. He could ask her to tell him the secret to growing good tomato plants in Colorado.

As he arrived at the barn, he saw Lovina lean her hoe and rake against the back door. She didn't seem to notice him as she went inside. No doubt Autumn was down for her morning nap. Jonah knew Lovina wouldn't leave the baby unattended for long.

Thinking how conscientious Lovina was about her duties, he washed up in the water barrel outside, letting the cold water invigorate him. Then he joined his grandfather in the *dawdi haus* for a lunch of ham sandwiches on store-bought bread. A part of him wished he was eating Lovina's food but it was best to keep his distance right now.

"Did you get the fence repaired?" *Dawdi* asked as he took a bite of his sandwich.

"Ja," Jonah grunted.

"Did you have any trouble?"

"Ne."

And that was the end of their conversation. Men seemed to say what needed to be said while women liked to chatter endlessly about anything and everything. As he washed a bite of bread down with a cool glass of milk, Jonah tried not to smile. Lovina loved to talk as much as any woman but her conversations were usually tied up with the farm and her clients... topics that interested him, too. And for some reason, he kind of liked listening to her talk, though he'd never admit it out loud.

Looking across the tiny table in the *dawdi haus*, he tried to focus on his grandfather.

"Are you feeling better this afternoon?" he asked.

The old man paused and blinked. "Of course. Why?"

"You weren't feeling well this morning. You said you didn't want to drive over to the Schwartz farm with Lovina and me."

"Ach, I'm feeling fine now but I think I need more rest. I'll stay home today," *Dawdi* said.

Jonah shook his head in confusion. And then a thought occurred to him. Was *Dawdi* purposely trying to get him and Lovina alone together? Had the bishop put *Dawdi* up to this? Because if that was the case, it wasn't going to work.

Soon, Jonah returned to the barn to hitch up the horse and buggy. No doubt Lovina would be ready to leave. She was punctual, organizing her day to accommodate her expectant mothers. And though he admired many of her qualities, Jonah dreaded the trip to the Schwartz farm. Because he'd have to spend several hours with Lovina. Alone. But that wasn't the biggest problem. Her lilting laughter sounded so sweet that he wanted to smile and talk with her. But he couldn't allow himself to be taken in by her beguiling ways. The price was too high. He was not interested in her or any woman. No, not ever again.

Chapter Four

By late morning, Lovina was ready to leave. Dressed warmly, she wrapped Autumn in an extra blanket. Because of her profession, Lovina had plenty of diapers and clothes on hand...for a newborn. But the little girl was growing fast and would soon need a larger size.

Carrying the baby against her shoulder, Lovina retrieved her diaper bag and went outside. The day was bright but the north breeze brought a distinct chill to the air. As she crossed the spacious driveway, Lovina shielded the baby's face from the cold wind.

Inside the barn, she found Jonah. He was just finishing up harnessing the horse to the buggy and hadn't noticed Lovina. She watched him work, noticing how his high forehead creased in concentration as he straightened the traces. A spray of dazzling sunlight pierced the shadows of the barn, landing squarely on his broad shoulders and head. She listened as he spoke softly to the horse, telling him what a fine animal he was. That touched her heart like nothing else could. She remembered the bishop saying once that you could tell the caliber of a man by how he treated his animals.

Jonah ran a hand over the horse's neck and shoulder, tugging gently on the collar to ensure it was firmly in position. It was a restful moment and she hated to disturb him. His profile looked lean and firm, his strong, capable hands threading the last leather strap through a buckle. Then he turned and saw her standing in the doorway with the baby. All at once, his expression changed. His lips tilted upward just a bit and she thought he almost smiled. Almost. But then the expression was gone, so fast she thought she must have imagined it.

"*Guder mariye*. Are you ready to go?" he asked, his words low and matter-of-fact.

Gone was the quiet, almost reverent voice he'd used to speak to the horse. Now he sounded a bit gruff and showed not a single hint of enthusiasm for their task ahead.

"I am. But I don't want to put you out. I can go alone. I think Autumn and I will be safe." She stepped over to the buggy, trying not to show her hurt feelings.

"*Ne*, I will drive you."

It wasn't so much his words but the way he said them. As if it were a command. And that made Lovina bristle. She was an independent woman who worked and paid her own way. She didn't like taking orders from anyone.

As Jonah opened the door, he took the diaper bag from her arm. Using both hands to cradle the baby, she forced herself not to flinch when Jonah clasped her elbow as she climbed inside.

"Danke." She spoke rather coolly, settling into the passenger seat. He handed her the diaper bag and she set it in the middle of the seat. It was a good barrier between them.

As he walked around the buggy and climbed into the driver's seat, she ignored him by fussing with the baby's knit cap. Maybe it had been a bad idea to ask for help on this errand but it would be difficult for her to tend Autumn, drive the buggy and deal with obstinate goats at the same time. And the bishop made it clear he wanted Jonah to accompany her on all her errands. Just now, Autumn was fast asleep and there wasn't much to do. Finally, Lovina sat still as Jonah took the leather leads into his hands, released the brake and urged the horse forward.

Soon they were moving down the dirt road at a fast trot. They didn't speak as they pulled onto the paved county road. The movement of the buggy increased the breeze that whispered past her window and she reached up to ensure it was closed all the way. Fields of drab brown and yellow opened up to Lovina's view, along with black-and-white cows grazing contentedly beside Cherry Creek as it meandered across Jonah's farm. Sedges and sticks of cattail lined the creek. Clusters of trees edged the roadside, their gold, red and brown leaves sparkling against a cerulean sky. It was beautiful here and she wished she could stay in her rented farmhouse forever. But all things came to an end and she knew she would have to leave one day, when Jonah took a wife.

Three miles outside of town, they rounded a bend

and Lovina caught sight of a lone Amish woman walking alongside the road. Carrying a wicker basket, she was dressed much like Lovina in a blue skirt, warm winter shawl and starched prayer *kapp*.

"Who is that?" Lovina asked, not recognizing the stranger. She glanced at Jonah and immediately noticed how his shoulders stiffened, his spine rigid and straight.

Lovina looked back at the woman and narrowed her eyes. It couldn't be, could it? Yes, it was!

"It's Fannie." Lovina spoke the obvious.

From the purse of displeasure on Jonah's lips, he'd already recognized his ex-fiancée. It wasn't surprising for the young woman to be here. After all, she lived with her new husband and his parents on their farm no more than a mile down the road.

As they drew closer, Lovina made a pretense of adjusting the baby in her arms. Jonah didn't decrease speed and she wondered if he would just blast right on past. Surely he wouldn't be so rude.

"You should ask if she needs a ride," Lovina said.

Out of her peripheral vision, she thought he rolled his eyes but when she glanced his way, he looked completely neutral. And yet there was a subtle tensing of his hands around the lead lines. It wasn't as if he was irritated but rather uneasy by this chance encounter. Even so, he slowed the horse as Fannie glanced over her shoulder and turned to face them.

Jonah pulled the buggy to a stop along the shoulder of the road.

Shielding the baby from the cool air, Lovina opened her window halfway. *"Hallo!"* she called with a wave.

"Guder mariye!" Fannie returned, her voice vibrating with excitement. Her gaze took them in and, once she recognized Jonah, she showed a nervous smile.

Jonah tugged respectfully on the brim of his hat but didn't look at her nor speak a word. And considering this was the girl who had shattered his heart, Lovina thought he was doing an admirable job of being polite. After all, the tenets of their faith dictated tolerance and love. Even if Fannie had broken off their engagement, the Lord expected Jonah to behave with a forgiving heart and realize that something better awaited him. But from the way he avoided Fannie's eyes, Lovina got the impression his faith wasn't coming easy for him today. And for some odd reason, that caused a surge of compassion to rise in her chest. She felt sorry for him. After all, she knew firsthand what it felt like to suffer a broken heart.

"Can we offer you a ride *heemet*?" Lovina asked the girl.

Fannie's eyes crinkled as she thought this over. Standing rigidly beside the buggy, she shook her head. *"Ne,* I better not. I only have a short way to go. I cut across the field and take a shortcut. It's faster than driving all the way around."

Lovina cringed. "You'll be careful of snakes as you go, won't you?"

Fannie's eyes rounded. "Snakes?"

Lovina shook her head, immediately regretting she'd mentioned it. "Probably not. I'm sure they're hibernating right now."

A strand of brown hair had come undone from Fannie's white prayer *kapp*. She tucked it back in place, looking at the field. "Do you really think so?"

"*Ja*, I'm sure of it. It's too cold for them now," Lovina said.

Fannie hesitated, as if she might change her mind and ask for a ride anyway. But one glance at Jonah and his stony profile nixed that. He didn't say a word as he stared straight ahead. He seemed so tense. Lovina wondered if he'd forgiven Fannie for ending their engagement. The thought that he might be harboring resentment toward the girl made Lovina sad. No doubt it had been difficult for him to attend Fannie's marriage to Alvin Fisher five months earlier. To top it off, Jonah now had to endure seeing the couple together at their church and social gatherings, gushing over each other as newlyweds were prone to do. If that were the case, Jonah must still love the girl, a thought that bothered Lovina even more, though she couldn't say why.

Fannie's gaze swept over the sleeping baby. "*Ach*, what a sweet little cutie-pie. Whose *boppli* do you have there?"

Autumn's small face was turned slightly toward Jonah as she breathed between parted rosebud lips. Lovina explained what she'd carefully rehearsed about the baby, then endured several minutes of endearments as Fannie admired the tiny girl.

"*Ach*, she's so precious. I hope her *mudder* feels better soon," Fannie said.

"*Ja*, I hope so, too," Lovina agreed.

There was a long pause after Lovina asked about Fannie's *familye*. Jonah continued to sit in silence.

"Everyone is *gut* at home, except Alvin has a terrible head cold," Fannie said.

"*Ach*, are you sure it's a cold? It might be allergies. Ragweed and sage are bad this time of year," Lovina said.

Fannie shrugged, looking a bit helpless. "I have no idea. I don't know what to do for him. He's so miserable. His throat is sore and his nose runs all the time."

Lovina reached out and placed a comforting hand on Fannie's arm, trying to offer reassurance. Everyone in their *Gmay* knew Fannie was normally a bit nervous. Some people were naturally higher-strung than others. But she also was one of the first to volunteer to help when the need arose.

"Give him lots of liquids and have him gargle with salt water. That might help. I hope he's feeling better soon," Lovina said.

Fannie's eyes widened. "Do you think so? *Ja*, I'll try that. *Danke!*"

"We'd best be moving on now." Jonah spoke low and started the buggy moving while Fannie still leaned against the side.

Taking the hint, she stepped back. "*Ach*, of course. See you at church then."

With a curt nod, Jonah slapped the lines against the horse's back and the animal moved off at a quick trot. As she closed the window, Lovina watched Fannie in the rearview mirror. The young woman turned toward the open field bordering her husband's property and finally disappeared from view. Lovina frowned. She noticed a dark scowl tugged at Jonah's forehead as he took the turn leading to the Schwartzes' farm where they would buy the goats.

After a moment, Lovina spoke. "That was rude and unkind."

Jonah just grunted, knowing full well what she was talking about. "I thought we should get on with our day."

"It never would have worked out," she said.

"What?"

"Marrying Fannie. She was never the right girl for you," she said.

He glanced her way, his eyes flashing with annoyance. "Why not?"

Lovina waved one hand in the air. "The two of you aren't compatible. You have completely different personalities."

"What do you mean?" he asked.

Oh, dear. He sounded peeved and Lovina wondered if she should end this conversation right now. And yet something spurred her onward. As if her own future happiness relied upon what she was about to say.

"You obviously still harbor harsh feelings toward Fannie," she pointed out.

He didn't respond, just glowered at the road.

"The Lord wants us all to have a forgiving heart. It brings us lasting peace," she continued.

She wasn't sure but thought she heard him release a low growl. And rather than frighten her, she almost laughed out loud.

"Fannie is pretty and sweet but remember how she fell to pieces at the fall social when she saw a spider?" Lovina couldn't forget the girl's high-pitched screams.

They still rang in her ears. "On the other hand, you're quiet and solemn all the time. The two of you are completely wrong for each other. You're not compatible."

He shrugged one powerful shoulder. "I don't know. I've heard that opposites attract. Maybe that's why we became a couple in the first place."

Lovina had her doubts but didn't voice them.

"And anyway, what makes you such an expert on the topic of matchmaking?" he asked.

She'd touched a raw nerve. The last thing she wanted was to hurt his feelings.

"You're right. I'm no expert. Please forgive me and forget I ever mentioned it," she said.

He pursed his lips and tossed her a frown that could have shriveled onions. They rode in silence for several long minutes. Then...

"You really think I'm solemn?" Jonah asked.

Lovina nodded. "*Ja*, I do. You rarely smile and sometimes your expression looks hard as a block of stone. It wouldn't hurt you to laugh once in a while, you know?"

Her comments won her an even stonier expression.

"I'm a grown man, not a child to run around laughing all the time. I've got heavy responsibilities," he said.

"True, but you should still smile now and then," she said.

Yes, he was definitely a grown man. And the meticulous way he took care of his farm told her that Fannie's penchant for constant reassurance would have grated on his nerves before too long. And though

Lovina didn't say that, she sensed he knew it already. She hesitated, her brain churning for something positive to say.

"The Lord wants us to have joy, but being sober isn't all bad either," she said. "You strike me as a serious man who is calm and self-assured. You know who you are and what you want, and you work hard to get it. Your farm is a prime example of that. But Fannie is rather, um…"

He dipped his head in acceptance. "*Ja*, she can be a little bit…" He hesitated, as if searching for the right word.

"Fussy? Fearful?" Lovina offered.

He snorted. "I was going to say anxious. But she's rather fastidious, too. Her *heemet* is quite tidy. I like that."

Yes, he would. But Fannie was also high maintenance. She seemed to need a lot of reassurance. Some people were inherently like that. But Lovina didn't say anything else. It wouldn't be kind, especially since Lovina had so many faults of her own. It was enough that Jonah recognized these things. And if he couldn't see that Fannie was completely wrong for him and would have made him unhappy, it wasn't Lovina's place to point it out to him. Especially since the girl was now married to someone else. But maybe this conversation would help Jonah feel better about the breakup. Or maybe it would make him feel worse. Lovina wasn't sure. And as they drove into the narrow yard at the Schwartzes' farm, she wondered why she even cared.

* * *

Jonah pulled the horse and buggy to a halt just in front of Mervin Schwartz's big gray pole barn. The man stood in the middle of the driveway with his wife, Hannah, and one of their teenage daughters. Good! Mervin was at home. Jonah had feared the farmer might be out working in his fields.

Mervin waved and walked toward them. Jonah climbed out of the buggy and hurried around to assist Lovina and the baby. As he helped them down, he thought about what Lovina said about Fannie. He didn't agree with her assessment of his ex-fiancée at all. Yes, Fannie could be overly sensitive and excitable at times but she was also sweet, kind and considerate of others' needs. And she made the best schnitz apple pie he'd ever tasted. No one was perfect all the time, including him. But as he walked with Lovina to meet Mervin and Hannah Schwartz, Jonah couldn't help wondering if maybe his love for Fannie had caused him to overlook a few of her flaws that might have irked him over time. But wasn't that what love was supposed to do? Jesus Christ's entire mission was to forgive all failings, if only we would repent of our sins. And yet Jonah couldn't help wondering about Lovina's assessment.

You're not compatible.

Jonah had never heard anything so outrageous. He'd grown up believing love could conquer all. What did it have to do with being compatible? If they both loved and served the Lord and loved each other, that was enough. Wasn't it?

"*Hallo*! What brings you out to our place this fine day?" Mervin boomed in his energetic bass voice.

Jonah inwardly smiled. He'd always liked this gregarious man. Mervin was just as loud and boisterous as his wife was quiet and meek. And Jonah longed to point out to Lovina that the Schwartzes were complete opposites, too, yet they'd made a fine marriage with lots of active children.

"*Guder nummidaag.*" Lovina wished them a good afternoon, her voice filled with eager anticipation. "I'm hoping you might have some goats you can sell me."

Mervin jerked a thumb toward his wife. "*Ach*, that's Hannah's area. She takes care of the goats on our place. I just keep them fed."

Hannah stepped forward, gravitating toward Autumn. "*Ja*, I've got goats you can buy. But first, who is this little one you're holding?"

Lovina quickly explained and soon handed the baby over to Hannah for her to hold.

"*Komm* and I'll show you the goats I have to sell." Carrying Autumn securely in her arms, Hannah headed over to the expansive pen where the active animals were kept.

Jonah and Mervin followed as Lovina studied the herd milling around the feeding troughs. From past experience, he knew the goats were pint-sized dynamos that stood no more than twenty-five inches tall and came in an assortment of gold, chocolate, black and multicolor. They bleated and hopped around the yard, their ears long, their short tails held high like mini flags. Though Jonah liked sheep and lambies, he loved goats and their happy zest for life. And a part of him was glad Lovina liked goats, too.

"My goats are great workhorses," Hannah said. "They give lots of milk, make lots of compost for your garden, and they're friendly to *kinder*, too. How many do you need?"

"Could I buy two?" Lovina asked.

Hannah nodded and waved a hand at the herd. "Certainly! Take your pick."

The woman opened the gate and let Lovina step inside the pasture. Jonah and Mervin followed but Hannah stayed back and closed the gate since she was still holding Autumn.

Jonah waited as Lovina studied the goats. He wanted to see which ones she chose. He would soon know if she had a good eye for healthy animals or not, which was important to a farmer like him.

He watched as her gaze scoured the herd. There were several young animals with soft coats, bright, inquisitive eyes, trimmed hooves, slim and friendly. Lovina seemed to be focused on a black-and-white female and a golden one, which impressed Jonah. They were the exact two goats he would have picked.

Lovina pointed. "How about those two? Whoa!"

Before he could react, Lovina was thrown fully against Jonah's chest. In an automatic response, he reached out to steady her. An older, obstinate goat had butted her from behind and knocked her forward.

"Oof!" he grunted, his arms wrapped around her so she didn't fall.

"Oh!" she cried.

She slumped against him, trying to regain her footing. And when she did, he found himself staring down
into her brilliant blue eyes. She stood there for several pounding seconds, locked in his embrace. For
what seemed an eternity, he felt transfixed by time.
He couldn't move. Couldn't breathe. Finally, he forced
himself to inhale, desperate to regain his composure.
And in those scant moments, he was conscious that she
smelled of lemon soap and fresh-baked bread, a com-
bination he found strangely attractive and exhilarating.

"I... I'm sorry!" she exclaimed, taking a step back.

He let her go, his face hot. Out of the corner of his
eye, he saw Mervin and Hannah watching them and
smiling.

"*Ach*, are you *allrecht*?" Mervin asked Lovina.

"*Ja*, I'm fine. I guess the goats got the better of me,"
Lovina responded with a laugh, her voice sounding ab-
normally shaky as she rubbed her posterior where the
goat had struck her.

"They'll do that when you least expect it," Hannah
said, still wearing a cheery smile. "You know, I just
have to say that you two make such a darling couple.
Dare I hope for another wedding soon?"

Lovina's mouth dropped open in shock. Her face
mirrored what Jonah felt. After informing him that
he and Fannie were completely ill-suited, he wasn't
in the mood to hear such a thing. Not when he considered Lovina to be the most incompatible woman in
their *Gmay* because of her past.

"Oh, we aren't... I mean...we're not..." Lovina stammered, as if she were unable to complete a coherent thought.

Hannah shared a knowing look with her husband, then nodded her head. "Maybe not now, but you two sure are cute together."

Cute! Jonah took a sharp inhale.

Mervin glanced at him. "*Ja*, you should ask her out sometime. You don't want her to get away."

Jonah coughed. He'd never heard such an absurd idea in all his life. Lovina was the last woman he wanted to date. But he wasn't about to let this topic continue. Turning toward Lovina, he pointed at the two goats he thought she wanted to buy.

"Are those the ones you like?" he growled, irritated beyond words.

"*Ja*, I… I'll take them," she stammered, looking as dismayed as he felt.

Walking to the gate, she let herself out of the pasture and reached to take Autumn from Hannah's arms. Jonah forced himself to act pleasant as Mervin helped him catch the two goats. With a rope tied around their necks, Jonah stoically led them out of the pen and tied them behind the buggy. With the patience of Job, he waited for Lovina to pay Hannah the required fee. The two women laughed and chatted for several minutes. A part of him admitted it wasn't Mervin and Hannah's fault he was annoyed and bewildered right now. But inside, he was screaming. There wasn't one single woman in this *Gmay* that he would consider marrying. And he didn't have to look twice at Lovina's expression to know she felt the same about him. Which suited him just fine. Because he was leaving this place as soon as he could sell his farm and was never coming back.

Chapter Five

Three days later, Lovina pushed open the screen door and stepped out onto Abby Fisher's front porch. Birds twittered in the tall poplars lining the front yard. The tree limbs had dropped their leaves. Jakob, Abby's husband, had raked two hours earlier and the air smelled of damp, loamy soil. This was Lovina's second and last prenatal visit of the day, and she was eager to get home to the chores waiting for her there. Holding her medical bag, she shielded her eyes from the late-morning sun.

"*Danke* for coming to see me today." Abby, one of Lovina's expectant mothers, followed her outside.

"You're *willkomm*," Lovina said.

She paused as Abby let the screen door clap closed behind them. Lovina had arrived at the farmhouse forty minutes earlier for a prenatal visit for a new pregnancy. As usual, Jonah had driven her here. She'd visited Norma Albrecht earlier. Now that the new mother was out of the hospital, it was time for her postnatal follow-ups. Soon, Lovina would be finished with her rounds and could take Autumn home.

"And you take these little clothes. They no longer fit my Christine. Maybe you can use them for Autumn."

Abby handed Lovina two bags of baby clothes. Though they were used, they were almost like new and Lovina was more than grateful.

"*Ach*, that's so kind of you. I'll return them as soon as she doesn't need them anymore," Lovina promised.

A spear of delight pierced her chest. She'd been planning to make more clothes for Autumn and wondered when she'd find the time. Then she thought she might need to ask Jonah to drive her into town to shop for some little garments. No doubt he would just loooove making another trip with her. That thought brought a smile to her lips. He always obliged her even though he didn't seem to like it. Thankfully, Abby's generosity saved him the trouble.

"I heard Norma Albrecht is out of the hospital. But I guess you already know that," Abby said.

"*Ja*, I saw her this morning, right before I came over here. Her baby boy is awfully sweet and so alert," Lovina said.

"Have they decided on a name for him, yet?"

Lovina nodded. "Ephraim."

"*Ach*, that's a fine name." Abby smiled, then glanced up. "I wonder where our men have gone off to."

Our men! A flush of heat suffused Lovina's face. Jonah wasn't her man. But pointing that out to Abby would only make the moment more uncomfortable.

Lovina scanned the yard, searching for some sight

of Jonah and Abby's husband. While Lovina had given Abby a prenatal exam and drawn some blood for lab work, Jonah had remained outside with Autumn. It was warm enough that she didn't need her coat but Lovina knew that wouldn't last. Any day now, they could get their first snowstorm of the season. The fact that Jonah had offered to tend to the child while Lovina was occupied had impressed her. But now she felt a bit anxious, knowing Autumn would need a bottle soon.

Stepping off the porch, Lovina walked toward the graveled driveway where Jonah's horse and buggy stood waiting beneath the expanse of several willow trees. Abby accompanied her, the ribbons to her white prayer *kapp* fluttering in the light breeze.

"There they are!" Abby pointed toward the trees.

The two men stood on the far side of the buggy. Jakob was holding Christine, his two-and-a-half-year-old daughter. The child was dressed identical to her mother, her tiny white prayer *kapp* indicating she was a girl.

Jonah had his back turned toward the women. As usual, he swayed gently back and forth as he cradled Autumn in the crook of his arm. His head was tilted slightly as he listened intently to what Jakob was saying. From that gesture alone, Lovina could tell he was actively involved in the conversation. If he held his head aloft and looked away, she knew he was distracted and wanted to be somewhere else. And she couldn't help wondering how she'd learned that about this man.

Seeing the two women, Jakob smiled wide. "*Hallo*! Is all well?"

Abby went to stand beside her husband. He gazed down at her, a look of concern and adoration in his eyes that spoke volumes. It was clear this man dearly loved his wife.

"*Ja*, all is well," Abby spoke in a shy whisper and nodded. Christine reached for her mommy, and Abby took her into her arms before kissing the girl's forehead.

Fearing the bit of breeze was too much for Autumn, Lovina tugged a corner of the blanket up to protect the baby's face. Then she reached into the buggy and took out a small brown paper sack, which she handed to Abby.

"These are the red raspberry leaves I told you about," she said. "I dry them myself every year. Just put a table-spoon or so in your herbal tea to steep and then drink it all down. I think it should help ease your morning sickness."

Abby took the bag and rested one hand briefly over her flat stomach. She was barely two months along. "*Danke*, I appreciate it. I didn't have a bit of sickness with Christine. Jakob's *mudder* thinks this new *boppli* must be a boy to make me feel so unwell all the time."

"Boys will do that," Lovina quipped.

Abby gave a nervous laugh, but Lovina saw a flicker of doubt in the woman's eyes. While the young mother had an active toddler at home, she had suffered a mis-carriage last spring and was eager to carry this new child to term.

Jakob smiled at Lovina, his expression one of grati-tude. "If not for your help, I don't know what we would have done. You've been there with us through it all."

His words touched Lovina's heart. Coming from a father, the compliment was extra special. Lovina didn't speak but merely slanted her head, forcing herself not to feel pride. As Abby's midwife, it was Lovina's job to look after her, including her emotional and psychological needs. But perhaps because she had lost a child of her own, Lovina had taken Abby's miscarriage quite personally, and she desperately wanted this new pregnancy to be a success.

Jakob put a protective arm around his wife's shoulders and leaned closer to her. Without a word, he conveyed his sympathy and loving support. Lovina watched the caring gesture with eagle eyes. And though it was against her faith to feel envy, Lovina couldn't help being a little jealous of the couple's caring relationship. How she wished there was one man somewhere in the world who loved her the way Jakob loved Abby.

Reaching out, Lovina squeezed Abby's hand with warm affection. "*Ach*, your morning sickness should pass within a few weeks. And while I know it makes you feel awful, the nausea is a symptom of a healthy, viable pregnancy. So as long as you're able to keep enough food down and retain your strength, I take this as a *gut* sign."

"Do you really think so?" Abby asked, her eyes filled with uncertainty.

Lovina thought about the medical studies she'd read recently on the topic but she didn't mention them to Abby. The Amish didn't teach science in their parochial schools or put much store in the subject. Rather, they put their faith in *Gott*.

"I know so," she said. "There is definitely a lower rate of miscarriage with women who suffer from nausea in their early months. I have every reason to believe you'll carry this *boppli* to term."

Abby breathed a little sigh and showed a smile of relief. "Oh, *danke*, Lovina! That's the best news I've heard all week." She tilted her face toward her husband. "Isn't that *wundervoll*, Jakob?"

"*Ja*, it's tremendous news," he said, returning her smile.

Lovina felt the love between them. There was such adulation in their gazes that Lovina's chest tightened. Again, she longed to experience such a caring relationship. A husband and *familye* of her own was all she'd ever wanted. But after what she'd done, she doubted any man could forgive her actions. So, hoping for something that could never be was torturous to her heart and she pushed it aside.

"And if you run out of raspberry leaves, just let me know. I've got plenty more," she said.

Abby nodded and their conversation lagged. Jonah shifted his weight, a movement that told Lovina he felt a bit uncomfortable with this intimate conversation. The married couple didn't seem to notice Jonah's unease but Lovina did. She was getting to know him quite well and was highly aware of his moods. He stepped back and shaded his eyes as he peered up at the gathering clouds.

"*Ach*, we may awaken to snow in the morning," he said.

The change of topic was obvious to Lovina. She

knew both men must feel a tad uncomfortable to be talking about Abby's condition. Normally, the Amish didn't verbally acknowledge pregnancy until the baby was born. But Jonah was an EMT and Lovina was Abby's midwife, so it was her job to discuss such personal matters with this married couple. The loss of their last child had been a difficult blow for Abby to bear, and Lovina knew the couple was inordinately pleased by today's good news.

So was Lovina.

"*Ja*, we'd best get going and let you move on with your day," Lovina said.

Abby reached up and gently patted Autumn's small back. "I know you'll take *gut* care of this little one until her *mamm* is feeling well enough to be back with her soon."

A part of Lovina hoped so but another part prayed the missing mother was never found. She just nodded as Jonah opened the buggy door and she climbed inside. He handed Autumn up to her, then walked around to the driver's seat. With a wave of his hand, Jonah urged the horse into a trot down the lane. Abby and Jakob stood there watching them go, their arms twined behind each other's backs with little Christine cuddled between them.

Jonah had turned onto the county road leading home before either of them spoke.

"Did Abby ask you any questions about where Autumn came from?" Jonah asked.

"*Ja*, she wanted to know who the baby belonged to," Lovina said.

"And?"

Lovina shrugged. "And I told her what we'd agreed to say. That Autumn's *mudder* isn't feeling well and I'm looking after the *boppli* for the time being."

He nodded his approval and, though Lovina knew he was just looking after Autumn's best interests, his questions irritated her. It was as if he didn't trust her judgment. After all, she was a strong, independent woman and didn't need Jonah's approval for anything. She could handle this situation on her own. But she realized needing someone had nothing to do with the deep desires of her heart.

"Did Abby want to know anything else about Autumn?" Jonah asked.

"Ne," she snapped a bit too harshly, and quickly softened her tone. After all, it wasn't Jonah's fault people were curious about the baby. "Abby accepted my explanation without objection or any overt curiosity. In fact, you're asking me more questions than she did."

That won a quick look from Jonah. He blinked, as if surprised by her waspish tongue.

"I know you're a highly capable midwife," he conceded, his voice conciliatory. "I didn't mean offense. I'm just trying to protect you and the *boppli*, as the bishop asked me to."

Great! Now Lovina felt rotten for letting her temper get the better of her. She told herself she was being overly sensitive, and yet this man made her feel like she needed to defend herself all the time. He made her feel…angry and resentful. And that was contrary to what *Gott* wanted from her. She must be more patient, long-suffering and slow to take offense. There was absolutely no reason for her to be defensive every time she was around Jonah. None at all.

"I'm sorry. I didn't mean to bite at you like that," she said.

He ducked his head and stared forward, navigating the road as he drove them home. They rode in heavy silence for several minutes, and Lovina felt at a loss for words. She longed to tell Jonah how bad she felt that they weren't better friends. There was so much she wanted to say to him. Things she wished she could confide. If only she knew what to say to help them get past the invisible brick wall standing between them. But what good would that do? Jonah must accept her for who she was. Because she couldn't change her past and there was nothing she could say to alter his opinion of her. And that was that.

"I didn't mean to upset you," Jonah spoke several minutes later.

He didn't look at Lovina but kept his gaze on the road. He sensed his questions made her angry, though that had never been his intent. Only her tart response gave him any clue as to what she was thinking.

"Forget it," she said, her small jaw locked in a stubborn scowl.

Hmm. If only he could forget. It certainly wasn't Lovina's fault his mother and Fannie had left him. Lovina's past wasn't his business, either. It was between her and the Lord. And yet he found himself wishing he could trust her. Wishing things could be different between them. But that didn't diminish his resolve to sell his farm and move back east.

"*Ach*, look!" Lovina pointed at the side of the road.

Jonah jerked his head in that direction, expecting to see some amazing sight. But he saw nothing more than a thatch of burdock plants lining the fence. Their bright pink flowers and prickly heads waved in the morning breeze.

"*Schtopp*, please," she cried.

He did so, thinking he must not see what she found so interesting. What on earth did she want with common burdock plants?

When he put on the brake, she handed him the baby. "I'll be right back," she said.

Pulling a paper sack out of the large bag she'd stowed on the back seat, she got out of the buggy with quick agility. As she neared the field, she hopped over a trickling stream of water and daintily picked her way over to the barbed wire fence. Cradling the baby in his arms, Jonah watched Lovina's every move, just in case she needed help. But if anything, he'd learned this woman was quite self-sufficient and dynamic. The complete opposite of Fannie. And though he didn't expect to feel this way, Jonah kind of liked that about Lovina.

She approached the patch of burdock. The plants were over four feet tall and had large, heart-shaped leaves the size of his outstretched hand. The pink flowers and cockleburs were in full bloom. Though they could appear quite pretty, he hated the obnoxious plants and watched in horror as she began to pluck the leaves and carefully stow them inside her sack.

"Leave them! What on earth do you want those for?" he called through the open window, thinking she'd lost her mind.

As a farmer, he had no use for the nasty weeds and was grateful he had none to contaminate his farm. Over the years, he'd spent hours pulling the irritating cockleburs off the eyelashes, tails and hides of his livestock after they'd gotten into the irksome plants. He could say nothing good about them. Why Lovina wanted the deep green leaves, he had no idea.

Having quickly filled her bag, she headed back toward him, lifting her long skirts out of the way as she again jumped the stream. As she ran toward the buggy, he couldn't help thinking she was a spunky little thing. So determined and full of life.

She fell! She disappeared completely from sight.

Jonah gasped and sat up straighter, holding the baby a bit tighter. He waited for Lovina to stand but she simply sat up. Through the thick weeds and brush covering the side of the road, he could see no more than her head and shoulders.

She turned toward him, a grimace of pain covering her pretty face. And Jonah waited no longer.

Bundling the baby up, he flipped an edge of the blanket over her head to protect her face from the chilly air and climbed out of the buggy. With long strides, he reached Lovina's side.

"Are you *allrecht*?" he asked.

She sat in the middle of the sedge grass, rubbing her ankle with both hands. Her sack of burdock leaves lay forgotten at her side.

"I… I think so. I twisted my ankle." Her voice trembled and he knew she was in pain.

Kneeling down, he handed Autumn to her. "Here! Hold the *boppli*."

He didn't wait to explain as she took the child into her arms and buried her face in the warmth of the blanket. Jonah hoped she wasn't crying. More than anything, he hated to see a woman cry.

With both hands, he gently inspected Lovina's ankle. He squeezed and checked the soundness of the bone. Through her black stockings, her skin felt warm against his palms.

"I don't believe it's broken. Do you think you can stand?" he asked.

She lifted her head and nodded readily. As he helped her up, he noticed her eyes were red and she bit her bottom lip, as if refusing to cry. She was a gutsy gal, he'd give her that.

"Oh!" she cried out when she tried to put weight on her foot. She winced and stumbled. He shot out his arms to steady her, making a snap judgment right then and there.

"Hold tight to the *boppli*," he said before reaching toward her.

"*Ach*, please don't forget my sack of leaves!" she cried, and pointed to where it lay upon the ground.

Shaking his head in annoyance, he quickly snatched up the bag and handed it to her, then he picked her up. She inhaled a sudden breath, but he ignored her look of surprise and carried her toward the buggy. With the baby in her arms, she couldn't very well refuse him.

She felt light and warm in his arms, and he caught her fragrance of fresh baked bread and baby lotion. As long as he lived, he would associate those two aromas with Lovina. And for some reason, that made him feel bright and happy inside.

"I... I can walk on my own two feet." She spoke with outraged indignation.

"*Ne*, you can't. You've injured your ankle, and I can't leave you sitting out here all day long. It's getting colder, and I need to get you and the *boppli heemet*," he insisted. He refused to meet her gaze, but out of his peripheral vision, he caught her exasperated expression.

As he carried the two of them, he felt Lovina's breath against his cheek. Holding her this close made him feel a sense of purpose he didn't understand or even want to contemplate. Never had he felt so strong and invincible. Like he could do anything. A surge of protective strength rose up within him, and he thought there was almost nothing he wouldn't do to keep this woman and baby safe from harm.

Thankfully, Lovina stopped fighting him. It didn't take long until he had both her and the baby safely inside the buggy. Jonah could just imagine what the bishop would say if he heard that he'd had to bring Lovina and Autumn up the embankment. But Jonah figured that was better than making Lovina walk and possibly injure her ankle more. Since Bishop Yoder had assigned him to protect Lovina and Autumn, he was determined to use his best judgment and do just that. And right now, that meant he had to carry Lovina when she couldn't walk on her own.

Reaching to the back seat, Jonah retrieved a heavy quilt he kept there for emergencies.

"Wrap this around yourself and the *boppli*. I don't want either of you to get cold," he said.

Lovina didn't argue as she did just that. Though the baby seemed fine, Lovina was shivering. Her cheeks and nose were red and her teeth clacked together. The baby began to fuss and Lovina offered her a bottle as Jonah slapped the lead lines against the horse's rump and they continued on their way home.

"*Ach*, thanks for rescuing me," Lovina said after a few minutes of silence.

"You're *willkomm*. But what was so important about burdock leaves that you had to put yourself through that?" Jonah asked.

Lovina shrugged, her voice vibrating from the cold and excitement. "I dry the leaves, then store them for a later time when they can be useful."

He snorted. "Useful for what? Burdock isn't *gut* for anything, except snagging onto the hides of my cattle and horses."

She laughed, the sound high and sweet. "*Ja*, the cockleburs do stick to everything."

As a case in point, she plucked several of the burs from her long skirt and rolled the window down a teensy bit so she could toss them out.

"Some people use the roots to make an herbal tea," she continued. "I use the leaves to ease the pain of burns and help wounds heal faster."

He stared in awe as she stashed the bag of burdock leaves in the back, then tucked a burp rag beneath the baby's chin to catch the milky drool. Lovina hummed a wordless tune as she rocked the little girl. Autumn gazed up at her, sucking fiercely on the bottle.

Jonah felt a bit foolish. He was an EMT, after all. He knew quite a bit about the natural remedies his Amish people used on a daily basis for simple aches, pains and bruises. But he'd never heard of using burdock leaves for burns. Lovina had taught him something new today. Not surprising, since he was quickly learning this woman had a vast knowledge of many things. She had an uncanny way of caring about other people. And he realized he liked that about her.

"Is there anything you don't know?" he asked before he thought to stop himself.

She snapped her head up and stared at him with shock. "Of course. I would never presume to know everything. Not at all. Only *Gott* knows all things. I learn something new every day."

So did he, but he wasn't going to admit she'd become one of his greatest teachers. Instead, he merely nodded, impressed by her skills and abilities in spite of his preconceived biases. But that didn't mean they could be any more than friends.

Chapter Six

A light dusting of snow blanketed the ground the following morning. Frost glimmered around the windowpane over the kitchen sink. It was Church Sunday and Lovina was up early, hobbling around the room to feed Autumn and get ready for the long drive out to the Burkholder farm for services. After her accident yesterday, she was moving rather slow.

Thinking about the tumble she'd taken caused her face to flush. When Jonah had carried her and Autumn to the buggy, she'd felt odd and trembly inside—feelings she'd never experienced before. Not a scary thing but rather the opposite. Like everything would be all right, because Jonah was there looking out for her. And now as she contemplated it, she realized she'd felt strangely...

Safe.

Which was something she hadn't felt in years. Especially with a man. And that didn't make sense. Jonah didn't like her. Not really. She sensed it every time he was around. Yet he always made her feel secure, a thought that made her wonder if she was seriously losing her mind.

Reaching inside the fridge for a bottle of goat's milk, she stashed it and several sterilized baby bottles in the diaper bag and turned.

"Oww!" she cried softly as she put too much weight on her injury.

She sank into a chair. Last night, she thought she was fine after placing ice-cold rags against the area, but her ankle had swelled in the night. Though it wasn't broken, it was quite painful. She'd probably torn the tendons and ligaments. How would she get through this day with a baby?

Autumn lay wide-awake in her portable seat on the table. She waved her little arms and made endearing cooing sounds, growing more alert every day. Her pain forgotten, Lovina reached out and rested her hand against the girl's chest. The baby gazed at her with complete trust. So sweet. So innocent and precious. Once Bishop Yoder found her mother, Lovina wondered how she was ever going to give this baby up.

She heaved a weary sigh. So much for making it to church on time. She could barely walk today. And sitting here dawdling didn't help. If that wasn't bad enough, a knock sounded on the back door. The tall shadow through the glass pane told her it was Jonah. Rather than getting up, she called to him.

"*Komm* in!"

He did so, stepping onto the rag rug just inside as he wiped his feet and closed the door to cut off the chilly draft. In a sweeping gaze, she noticed he wore his best pair of black broadfall pants and Sunday church coat. His hair was damp and carefully combed and his face clean-shaven. She could tell he'd even dusted his black felt hat and shined his boots. And though he worked hard, she liked that he knew how to tidy up when the occasion warranted it.

In a glance, he took in the entire room. Lovina felt uncomfortable beneath his astute gaze as he took in the disorder. She was normally tidy, but not today. A fluffy towel from the baby's bath lay piled in a heap on the table, and Lovina hadn't yet put away the lotion bottle and tiny brush she used to comb Autumn's fine hair. Pans and dishes from processing the morning milk were still stacked in the sink, waiting to be washed. Sterilized bottles and nipples lay air-drying on a rack. At least Lovina was dressed and her hair brushed and pinned beneath her prayer *kapp*, though she doubted she looked very nice since she hadn't slept well.

"*Ach*, are you *allrecht*?" Jonah asked, taking a step forward.

A frown crinkled his brow and she hated for him to see her like this. He already thought the worst of her.

"Of course. I'm fine." She looked away, bracing her hands against the tabletop to help her stand. In doing so, she couldn't contain a slight wince.

"*Ne*, you're not. Your ankle is still sore."

It wasn't a question. As he took her arm and gently pushed her back down into the chair, she wondered why he always seemed so in tune with her feelings.

"Sit. The best thing for you is rest," he said.

"I'm not missing church today. If I don't show up, everyone will talk. You know how they are. They'll all start showing up on my doorstep and then ask even more questions about Autumn," she spoke fast, wishing he'd just ignore her for once.

"Would that be so bad? It seems to me you need help today. You're injured, so why not take it easy?"

"I don't have time for that right now."

"I can help." He stood towering over her, his hands on his lean hips as he looked down at her with an expression that told her he could be stubborn, too.

Lovina frowned. It wasn't within her to show weakness like this. She hated relying on him, or anyone, for help. Life had taught her to keep to herself. To never trust anyone. Right now, she wished he'd just go away and leave her alone.

"I'm going to church and that's that," she insisted.

His lips twitched and, once again, she thought he might smile. But he didn't.

"*Allrecht*, what needs to be done so we aren't late?" He removed his coat and draped it over the back of a chair. Rolling up the long sleeves of his blue chambray shirt, he stepped over to the sink.

Oh, no! He wasn't going to wash her dishes, was he?

"I can do that later," she said.

Too late! He flipped on the water faucet with a twist of his wrist. Then he reached for the shavings of dish soap she kept in a jar beside the window ledge. Within moments, he'd scattered some into the hot water and whipped them around with a brisk movement of his hand. Sudsy bubbles formed on top.

"I'll get this done for you now. We'll be eating at church, so you won't have to cook today. Then when we come *heemet* this evening, you won't have it waiting for you. Has Autumn eaten yet?" He didn't look at her as he spoke but reached for a pile of plates and pans and submerged them in the soapy water.

"*Ja*, I saw to her needs first." Lovina watched as he washed her dishes with proficient swipes of the dishcloth.

When he was done, he rinsed and stacked them neatly in the drain where they would air-dry. Then he turned, drying off his hands on a dish towel as he scanned the kitchen. "I've already fed your goats and *Dawdi* is gathering the eggs now. What else must be done?"

"Really, you don't need to do any more," she said.

"Of course I do. The bishop asked me to."

The bishop!

A feeling of disappointment rose in her chest. Jonah was simply fulfilling an assignment from the bishop, nothing more. A part of her wished he was helping her because he wanted to and for no other reason.

Lovina licked her lips, her mouth feeling suddenly dry. Of all the men in her *Gmay*, she didn't want to be beholden to this one, mainly because he didn't appear to like her much. But it couldn't be helped now.

"That's it. There's nothing else. *Danke*. You've taken care of everything, it seems." As she reached for the baby's bath towel and draped it over another chair so it would dry, she couldn't help feeling grateful. Fifteen minutes earlier, she'd felt overwhelmed. Now a modicum of order had been restored to her home. But what must he think of her?

"*Gut*! We can go now. You rest here while I get the buggy," he said.

"You're not carrying me again," she said.

He blinked at her. "I don't think that will be necessary."

Rolling the sleeves to his shirt down his long forearms, he shrugged into his coat, then headed out the door, leaving behind a brief blast of chilled air.

Lovina groaned and buried her face in her hands. Of all the stupid things to say. But sitting here feeling sorry for herself wouldn't help. While he was gone, she stood and hopped on one foot as she crossed the room and retrieved her heavy winter shawl. True to his word, Jonah returned moments later with a narrow wooden cane and *Dawdi* Noah. The elderly man was carrying a basket of eggs.

"Jonah told me your predicament. You poor girl. Twisted your ankle, did you?" *Dawdi* glanced at her feet, which were encased in warm black stockings and practical shoes.

Right now, Lovina wished she dared wear her soft slippers instead but figured that would only raise eyebrows at church.

"*Ja*, but I'm sure it's nothing to worry about. I'll be fine tomorrow," Lovina said.

Shaking his head, *Dawdi* simply made a *tsk*ing sound as he opened the fridge door and slid the eggs inside. Lovina made a mental note to clean them later that evening when she got home.

"This is a spare cane *Dawdi* uses sometimes. I think you might need it today." Jonah handed her the sturdy piece of hickory. Without waiting for permission, he reached for the baby.

Heaving a sigh of resignation, Lovina gripped the smooth hilt of the cane as she gingerly put slight weight on her sore ankle. Though it wasn't perfect, the cane did help diminish the pain and she was able to hobble to the door.

"I think this will help me a great deal. *Danke*!" She showed a slight smile and took a quick inhale. Because, wonder of wonders, Jonah smiled back. And the expression lit up his face like nothing else could. For a fraction of a moment, she thought him the most handsome man she'd ever seen. Then his smile dropped away and he turned toward the door.

"*Gut*! Now we can get on with our day. What should I put on the *boppli* to keep her warm?" he asked.

"Her bundling is right there." Lovina pointed to where the fleece bunting with a warm hood was draped over the diaper bag.

Laying the baby gently on a blanket, Jonah leaned over her and slid her down into the bundling bag. He spoke to her sweetly as he tucked her tiny arms and legs inside, making sure her little ears were covered by the hood. And once more, Lovina was impressed with his gentleness toward Autumn.

"There, Itty-Bit. We don't want you to get cold on the long drive to church," he said.

Gazing up at him, the baby wriggled in response. When he had the child wrapped in a warm blanket for good measure, he picked her up and glanced at Lovina. "Do we have plenty of bottles and goat's milk to last through the day for her?"

Lovina nodded and jutted her chin toward the diaper bag. "*Ja*, I've already put that and plenty of extra nappies in her bag."

"*Gut*! We're ready to go." Jonah clasped the bag and headed for the door. At the last moment, he flipped a corner of the blanket over the baby's face to shield her from the crisp air.

Dawdi took Lovina's arm. "Let me help you. I know what it's like to have pain. I deal with it every day. We can be invalids together."

He chuckled as he helped her shuffle toward the door. He was limping almost as much as her, and she sympathized with the elderly man. It was bad enough to be in discomfort for a day or two because of an injury. She didn't know what she'd do if she had to cope with this all the time.

"I suppose this is a case of the lame helping the lame to walk," Lovina quipped.

Dawdi laughed. "We can only do the best we can do. No more, no less. But at least we can do it together."

Together. She liked that. And for a moment, she wished this man was her real grandpa.

They stepped out onto the porch. Jonah held the door for them, seeming to have no trouble as he juggled the baby and diaper bag with ease.

After securing the door, he accompanied them to the horse and buggy waiting in the driveway. It seemed Jonah had everything ready and in control. A capable man.

As they walked, Lovina saw puffs of their frozen breath on the frigid air. She noticed the snow had been cleared away from the porch and walk paths.

"Do I have you to thank for shoveling the snow for me today?" she asked Jonah.

He merely looked away and opened the door to the buggy.

"*Ja*, Jonah did it," *Dawdi* supplied. "He wanted to make sure you and the *boppli* were taken care of."

Hmm. Just following the bishop's orders again, no doubt.

"How kind," Lovina said, trying to have a humble heart filled with gratitude.

"It's nothing. You'd do the same for someone in need," Jonah said.

Yes, she would certainly try. It was their way. The Lord had taught them to love one another, no matter what. But as she slid into the back seat of the buggy, she looked at him. Their gazes locked briefly and he handed her the baby. Then he turned away and helped his grandfather. The two men sat in front and within moments, the buggy jerked and they were on their way.

As expected, they arrived late, just after the meeting started. Ever solicitous, Jonah helped Lovina to her seat among the women, then joined *Dawdi* with the other men. Everyone in the congregation turned to look and Lovina's cheeks flamed hot as road flares. They sat on backless wooden benches inside the Burkholders' spacious barn. An old black stove piped out heat from the fire. With approximately eighty occupants, the large room was soon toasty warm.

People glanced at Lovina and the baby, but they didn't look surprised. No doubt, Bishop Yoder had already told most of them she was tending to Autumn until her mother could return. It worked that way among the Amish. Word spread like wildfire. They all knew each other's business, which was both bad and good. They had few secrets, but they could always rely on one another for help.

The preacher's exhortations to love one another as yourself touched Lovina's heart and she chastised herself for feeling grouchy today. The long, drawn-out hymns sung a cappella soothed her nerves. The meeting lasted several hours and the time allowed her ankle to rest. Midway through, she stood to go change Autumn's diaper. It was difficult to carry the baby and hobble with the cane as she tried to take Autumn into a private area where she could care for her. Sarah Yoder, the bishop's wife, was right there to help without saying a word.

Soon it was time to set out lunch for the men and children. Lovina wasn't much help. She sat and fed the baby, feeling absolutely lazy and useless. To make matters worse, in all the confusion, she'd forgotten to bring the two pumpkin pies she'd made for the event. Which meant she had nothing to contribute to the meal.

"I'm so sorry you hurt your ankle. I brought you some lunch." Sarah held out a plate filled with a thick slice of homemade bread spread with peanut butter and marshmallow, a thick wedge of ham, beets, pickles, and cheese.

Though she felt miserable, Lovina pasted a bright

smile on her face and accepted the offering with thanks. "*Danke*, that's so kind of you. I really appreciate your help today."

Jonah approached and reached for the baby. "Can I tend to her for a while?"

Looking up into his dark eyes, Lovina saw no censure there. Only an earnest desire to help. Nodding her head, she handed Autumn over. As he walked away, Lovina soon found herself surrounded by women asking after her welfare.

"The bishop told us you were caring for a *boppli* until her *mudder* is feeling better," Rebecca King said.

"That's so kind of you," Sarah said.

Lovina merely nodded. As the bishop's wife, Sarah probably knew the entire story, but since she wasn't sure, Lovina thought it best to say as little as possible.

"*Ach*, look at that. Aren't they cute together?" Hannah Schwartz pointed at Jonah.

In unison, they all lifted their heads and stared at the man. He sat at the long tables with the other men, holding Autumn with one hand while he ate his noon meal with the other.

"He's a natural with children, don't you think?" Norma Albrecht stood just behind Lovina, cradling her own newborn son in her arms.

"I think he is. Look how easily he tends to that *boppli*. He'll make a *gut* husband and *vadder* one day," Sarah said.

Unaware that he was the topic of discussion, Jonah bit into a ham sandwich, seeming deep in conversation with Jeremiah Beiler and Darrin Albrecht, their deacon. The baby promptly spit up on Jonah's pristine shirt. Without missing a beat, he laid his sandwich down, picked up a burp cloth and wiped the milky spittle away. He laughed at something Darrin said. He actually laughed! Lovina stared at the sight, not knowing what to think.

"It's indecent for a man and woman to live together when they're not married," old Marva Geingerich said.

The women stared at her. At the age of ninety-one, she was the matriarch of their congregation. Since she was an Old Order Swartzentruber Amish from Ohio, she disapproved of almost everyone and everything. Prim and proper, she wasn't shy about voicing her opinion.

"But Lovina doesn't live with Jonah," Sarah objected. "He lives out back in the *dawdi haus* with his grandfather."

"Hmph! Close enough. It's not proper, if you ask me," Marva said.

Uncertainly washed over Lovina. She hated to be the topic of gossip but couldn't really do anything about it at this point. As the women looked at her, she saw the suspicion in their eyes. Lovina tried to ignore it and focused on consuming her food. But she had little appetite and thought perhaps she should have stayed home after all.

She tried her hardest not to look at Jonah but her gaze kept drifting back to him. She tried to tell herself it was so she could check on Autumn. But deep in her heart, she knew it was something more. Something she didn't understand.

Yes, Jonah did seem comfortable with the baby, considering he wasn't married and had no children of his own. But Lovina sensed something in Norma's and Sarah's words. She'd seen this happen time and time again. Women in her *Gmay* would frequently point out the attractive attributes of some eligible bachelor, hoping to push them into marriage. But it wouldn't work with her. At the advanced age of twenty-six, Lovina was determined to remain an independent old maid.

Instead of taking their bait, she turned toward Norma so she didn't have to look at Jonah and his handsome, smiling face.

"How are you feeling this week? It can take time for your body to recover after having a *boppli*. Is the fatigue easier now?" she asked the new mother.

Having successfully changed the topic, she was grateful to be discussing something other than Jonah or Autumn. But throughout the day, her gaze kept straying to Jonah and the baby. And for one brief moment, she let herself imagine that they belonged to her and they were a happy *familye* attending church. But that wasn't her life. It wasn't her truth. And she'd do better to remain grounded in reality.

The women were watching him again. Jonah felt it without even looking up. They laughed and he shifted Autumn's weight in his arms, feeling nervous and self-conscious. No doubt Lovina and the other women were discussing him. And as he wondered what they were saying, he didn't like being their hot topic. Not one bit.

"Can I hold her?"

He looked up and found Fannie and her husband, Alvin, standing beside him. Lunch was winding down and he scooted back his chair as he stood. A fissure of nerves pulsed over him. Since their engagement had ended, he'd avoided Fannie like the plague. She'd done the same and he wondered why she'd approached him now.

"Of course." He handed the baby over, looping his thumbs through his suspenders while she cuddled the child against her throat.

Pressing her face close to Autumn's chubby cheeks, Fannie released a chuckle. She inhaled deeply, as if breathing the baby in. "*Ach*, she smells so sweet."

"Um, that's Lovina's doing. She has this special lotion she rubs on the *boppli* every day after her bath," Jonah said.

Fannie laughed again, a shrill, girlish snicker that made Jonah cringe.

Funny. Her laugh never grated on him before. But it did now. And he wondered why.

She didn't seem to hear him as she tilted a shy, side-long look at her husband. In response, Alvin wrapped one arm around her shoulders. Jonah caught a look of devotion in the man's eyes. A sear of pain burned Jonah's heart as he stepped back, feeling like an intruder. Fannie wasn't his fiancée anymore. She was another man's wife. But then Jonah overheard Alvin whisper words that pierced him to the core.

"Just think. In seven months, we'll be holding our own *boppli*. It won't be long now," he said.

Fannie nodded and released another set of girlish giggles.

Jonah turned away, blinking at the intensity of emotion burning through his veins. Fannie was pregnant! With Alvin's child! It was to be expected. After all, they'd married five months earlier. But it still hurt Jonah.

And that's when a thought occurred to him. This couple was truly in love. Fannie hadn't loved Jonah. Not the way a woman should love a man. Not for richer and poorer, for better or worse. And maybe Jonah had never really loved her, either. But their breakup had stung his pride, something he didn't like to admit. The Lord taught that he should be humble and shun pride. But that was easier said than done. And in that moment, Jonah couldn't help comparing Lovina's calm maturity with Fannie's silly outbursts. It took a lot for him to admit to himself that Lovina was right. He never would have been fully happy with Fannie. Maybe their breakup had been for the best. But her rejection—one of many he'd experienced over his lifetime—cut him deep. He'd been hurt too many times to ever let his guard down again.

"Jonah, would you join Lovina and me for a moment?"

He looked up and saw Bishop Yoder beckoning to him.

"I'll watch the *boppli* for you," Fannie said.

Grateful for the distraction, Jonah nodded and crossed the barn to where Lovina sat waiting. The bishop quickly led them to a corner where they could have a moment of privacy. Lovina used her cane to hobble along. Seeing her awkward movements, Jonah quickly pulled up a chair for her.

"Sit and rest yourself," he said.

Nodding her thanks, Lovina sat.

"I just wanted to update you two," the bishop began. "I've sent letters to all the bishops in the area and am waiting for a response. You haven't heard anything, have you?"

They shook their heads, then he frowned.

"If we can't find Autumn's *mamm*, we'll need to place her in a permanent Amish home with both a *mudder* and a *vadder*," he said.

Lovina's delicate eyebrows drew downward and she released a gasp of dismay. "So soon? When are you planning to do that?"

Bishop Yoder held up a hand to reassure her. "Not yet. We've got time. Thanksgiving is coming soon and may delay things for a while. I'll wait until I hear from all the bishops before I make any changes, so rest at ease."

The bishop's words upset Lovina. Jonah could tell by the way she twined her hands nervously in her lap. He looked away, focusing on what the bishop was saying, trying to ignore Lovina and her beautiful blue eyes. Because he was not interested in her or any woman. He told himself he didn't care what she was thinking. He didn't care that she was hurting over the thought of giving up little Autumn. But he knew that was a lie. Because the idea upset him, too.

The bishop talked with them several more minutes,

asking about the baby's health and how she was sleeping. From everything Jonah had seen, Lovina took excellent care of the child, even when she'd sprained her own ankle. Finally the bishop left to speak with other members of their congregation. Lovina sat there, staring at her hands. Silent as a stone.

"Geht es dir gut?" Jonah asked after her welfare.

Lovina looked up at him, her eyes sparkling with tears. "*Ja*, I'm fine. But Jonah, I don't know what I'll do if the bishop takes Autumn and gives her to someone else. I love her so much. She deserves to have caring parents raise her. And the thought of losing her to strangers... It would be like giving up my son all over again. I just don't think I can stand it."

She bit her bottom lip and looked away, as if she realized she'd said too much. She quickly wiped her eyes with the backs of her hands. "I'm sorry. I... I shouldn't have said all that."

No, she shouldn't have. Because it reminded Jonah that Lovina had given away her own child, just like his mother had walked away from him. And her regrets didn't soften his heart toward her. She'd made her choice. The fact that she felt bad about it now was a little late for her child.

He stood there like a great lump of coal, not knowing what to say. He hadn't expected her confession at all. Her words surprised him, especially since he loved Autumn, too. He hated to lose the baby when he'd grown so attached to her. A part of him hoped the bishop never found her mother. But the tenets of his faith dictated that he must be married in order to keep the baby. And that was not something he was prepared to do. Not now, not ever. Autumn could not stay with him and Lovina indefinitely. He knew that. Okay, fine! But it would break his heart once more when Bishop Yoder finally took the baby away.

"The bishop is trying to do what's best for Autumn," he said. "He won't give her to just anyone. She'll be loved by her new *familye*. Everything will work out fine. We have to believe that and put our faith in *Gott*."

Jonah didn't know why he bothered to reassure Lovina. Maybe he said the words out loud because he needed to hear them, too. But when she looked up at him, her eyes so wide and filled with doubt, he found himself longing to wrap his arms around her and kiss her tears away. A totally ridiculous idea if ever he'd heard one.

"Do you really think so?" she asked, her voice a trembling whisper.

"*Ja*, I know so," he said, forcing himself to believe it.

She nodded and showed a sad little smile. She looked so forlorn that it was on the tip of his tongue to say something kind. Something to buoy her spirits. But he knew that would only bond them closer. And right now, he wasn't prepared to take the risk. His heart couldn't stand it. So before he could speak, he clenched his teeth, turned and walked away.

Chapter Seven

Lovina stared after Jonah. Surrounded by members of her church congregation, people laughing, eating and chatting all around her, she'd never felt more alone in her life. What on earth had possessed her to divulge those things to Jonah? She felt stupid and foolish. Of all the people to confide in, he was the last person who cared what she thought. And yet she'd opened a teensy corner of her heart and told him things she'd barely admitted to herself.

For years, she'd worked hard. To never let down her guard. To build an independent life where she didn't need anyone else. And it worked…for a while. She hadn't been hurt in a long, long time. But then little Autumn had fallen into her life. And now she'd cried and blabbed her innermost thoughts to a man who didn't approve of her. Yet she felt so comfortable with Jonah. Too comfortable. She'd grown overly accustomed to being near him.

Oh, no! The awful truth reared its ugly head. She'd

come to rely on him. To anticipate his morning visits and even enjoy working with him.

Well, that was the end of it. Something hardened inside her. She must pull back and keep her thoughts and needs to herself. The bishop had asked Jonah to look out for her and Autumn. To keep them safe. But Lovina didn't need Jonah or anyone. And she certainly should not have told him her innermost feelings. She must not ask him for help ever again. Sprained ankle or not, she would rely on herself and no one else. But when the time came, how could she face losing Autumn? She was so attached to the baby. One day, she knew she'd have to let go. Eventually, the bishop would take Autumn away. Lovina tried to tell herself once the bishop found Autumn's mother, the baby would go home and be happy. Everything would return to normal.

Or would it?

An hour later, Autumn was back in Lovina's arms as Jonah assisted the men in cleaning up the barn. He helped stack the benches and tables in the church wagon—a large black enclosed wagon with a red "slow-moving vehicle" triangle on the back. It would be driven over to the Hostetlers' farm so they could host church in two weeks. And from the looks of things, Jonah and the men were almost finished with their chore.

Lovina rocked Autumn in her arms, gazing at the sleeping baby's delicate features. Memories washed over her as she thought about her own little boy and the few times she'd been able to hold him like this. Daggers of regret and guilt pierced her heart. She often thought of returning to Pennsylvania where she had aunts and uncles and cousins. But she couldn't go back. Not after what she'd done. They all knew her shame. And her child's father was living there still. She'd had a letter from her great-aunt several years earlier. He'd married some cute Amish girl and now had a passel of kids. She could never live there again and see him regularly at church and their other gatherings. He'd moved on, so why couldn't she? She must press forward. She was absolutely certain it was what the Lord wanted her to do. And yet she couldn't seem to.

"Lovina, are you ready to go *heemet* now?"

She jerked and glanced up. *Dawdi* Noah stood several feet away, leaning heavily on his cane. His kind smile brought her cheer. Over the past few months, he'd become more of a father to her than her own dad. Without waiting for her answer, he reached down and picked up the diaper bag.

"*Ja*, I'm ready when you and Jonah are," Lovina said.

Dawdi turned, lost his footing, dropped the bag and reached out to brace a hand against the wall before he fell. Lovina jumped up and would have hurried over to help him but he held out a hand to stop her.

"I'm *allrecht*!" he insisted.

Lovina wasn't so sure. His cheeks were bright red and his breathing heavy from his exertions. Cradling the baby with one arm, she ignored his rebuttal and pulled a stool over for him to rest on.

"Here. Sit a moment. Jonah doesn't look like he's quite ready yet," she said.

Dawdi's bushy eyebrows twitched as he slid onto a chair. "Have you had a nice day, or has it been difficult for you?"

She looked down, fingering the smooth edge of Autumn's fleece bundling bag. "It's been okay. I haven't done a single thing to help the women. People have been kind, and Jonah has tended to Autumn most of the afternoon. I feel lazy but my ankle isn't hurting now. And the *boppli* has been *gut* as gold."

They both gazed at the baby. She looked so innocent and sweet, completely reliant upon their care. She had no idea how precarious her situation was.

"*Ach*, the poor *kind*," *Dawdi* said.

Thinking he was referring to the baby, Lovina nodded in understanding. "I know. But don't worry. We'll take *gut* care of little Autumn."

He whipped his head up and his eyebrows lowered in confusion. "Of course you will. But I was speaking about her *mudder*."

"Oh." Bewilderment fogged Lovina's mind but she liked that *Dawdi* felt compassion for the young woman. For whatever reasons, she'd felt desperate enough to give her baby to strangers.

"She must feel completely alone. Why else would she give her *boppli* to you?" *Dawdi* asked, as if reading her mind.

It touched her heart that *Dawdi* seemed to understand. She longed to confide her inner feelings about marriage to him but wasn't sure she dared trust him. Not with something so personal.

"I don't know what her situation is but I hope she somehow finds her way," Lovina said.

Dawdi pursed his lips together and nodded in agreement. "*Ja*, we mustn't judge. The poor *maedel*. She must be so frightened to give away her *boppli* like this."

That was true. Maybe *Dawdi* grasped more than she realized.

"It's possible her *familye* doesn't even know she had a *boppli*," he continued. "That's what happened to my *dochder* when she gave birth to Jonah. We didn't know she was expecting and she was afraid to tell us, so she ran away. Then when she went into labor, an *Englisch* midwife brought her home to us. We were shocked but tried to figure everything out. She left three days later in the middle of the night. All she left us was Jonah and a note saying she didn't want to be Amish anymore. We searched for her but never heard from her again."

Really? Lovina hadn't known that. And how did that make Jonah feel? She couldn't help but wonder.

"Perhaps Autumn's *mudder* kept her pregnancy a secret, too," she said.

That's what Lovina had done. No one knew, except her boyfriend. It was winter and easy for her to hide her condition.

Dawdi reached out and patted her hand, his palm calloused from years of hard work. "It must have been difficult for her. And for you."

Lovina blinked. It was no secret when Lovina moved to Colorado that she'd had a child out of wedlock. Before he'd left their faith and divorced her mother, Lovina's dad had told almost everyone in their *Gmay* about her pregnancy. Because of the tenets of their faith, her mom could never remarry as long as her father was alive, because it would be considered adultery. It wasn't something Lovina was proud of. But *Dawdi* and Jonah were newer to their community. She could only wonder who told them about her past.

"*Ja*, it was very hard," she said, unwilling to talk about it more than that. It was too embarrassing. Too painful. And she'd already confided way too much to Jonah.

Yes, she'd kept her pregnancy secret. But in the end, when she'd finally confessed to her father that she was expecting a child, he'd been furious. He'd promptly sent her to Kansas to live with strangers until her baby was born a month later. After the birth, she'd had two glorious days alone with her little boy...until her dad showed up and stole the baby away like a thief in the night. Now she wondered if Autumn's mother had faced a similar situation at home.

"Jonah's still angry at his *mudder* for leaving him all those years ago," *Dawdi* said.

Lovina heard the pain and regret in the elderly man's voice. She squeezed his hand tight, offering silent support. In all honesty, she was surprised he was confiding so much to her. But the two of them seemed to have a connection.

"I'm sorry, *Dawdi*. I know it must have been difficult for you. I... I was only fourteen when I found myself in a similar situation. I just wish I could go back in time and change the outcome. I wish I could have raised my son."

He showed a slight smile. "Fourteen is awful young to try to raise a child. There's nothing for you to be sorry about in giving him up."

"That's just it! I didn't give him up. My *vadder* took him from me." She blurted the words before she could stop them. Her voice and hands trembled. It brought her a lot of shame to speak badly about her father. With her upbringing among the Amish, it wasn't appropriate, and she clamped her mouth shut. She'd said enough already.

Dawdi gazed at her for several pounding moments. "I'm sorry for that. You're a *gut* woman, no one can deny that. No doubt your *vadder* thought he was doing what was right for you and your *boppli*."

Lovina doubted it. Looking back, she thought her father was one of the most self-serving men she'd ever met. And if she saw him today, she'd give him an earful. No matter what, she still felt culpable. At least for her own errors. Her greatest fear was that her own son might grow up like Jonah, believing she'd abandoned him. And she hadn't! But she could do nothing about it now. Instead, she put her trust in *Gott* and prayed He cared for her little boy all the days of his life. She prayed he felt happy and loved by his parents.

"Jonah is a kindhearted man, too. He'll find his way," she said, hoping it was true.

Dawdi shrugged and breathed a sad little sigh. "He is kind, but I think he's been hurt too many times. He has difficulty with trust. He doesn't let down his guard easily. I worry about him, especially since Autumn has *komm* to live with us. I see how it eats him up inside. The anguish and pain. He never knew his *mudder*. And none of us know who his *vadder* was. An *Englischer*, that's all we know. But I don't think Jonah can ever be truly happy until he's able to forgive his *mamm* for leaving him."

That made Lovina sad. What if her son felt the same? She hated the thought that he'd go through life resenting her for something she hadn't wanted. She couldn't stand to think about it and purposefully pushed it aside. She must have faith the Lord would make it all right one day.

They sat in silence for several minutes. Lovina didn't know what else to say. No wonder Jonah seemed to dislike her so much. *Dawdi*'s words confirmed her suspicion. Jonah probably thought she'd abandoned her baby. But what good would it do to tell him differently? He was still angry at his own mother. And though he didn't know Lovina's full story, she had no doubt he harbored resentment toward her, too. She tried to tell herself she didn't care but it still bothered her. A lot!

Poor Jonah. He'd grown up not knowing his own mother. And then Fannie had broken off their engagement. Gaining perspective into his past made Lovina wish she could help him somehow. But if she tried, he'd resent her even more. It wasn't her business anyway. She must protect her own heart. She couldn't get involved with Jonah any more than she already was. But that didn't stop her from feeling sympathetic toward him.

Finally, they were on their way home. Jonah released a silent sigh, grateful they'd made it through the day.

He sat in the front seat of the buggy with *Dawdi* beside him in the passenger seat. Lovina rode in back with Autumn. The little girl fussed as Lovina made a bottle. Within moments, the baby's loud sucking sounds could be heard and Jonah hid a smile. It seemed odd that this child wasn't of his making, yet she'd wormed her way into his heart anyway. From what Lovina said, she felt the same. Though caring for the child wasn't a permanent arrangement, Jonah didn't want to give her up any more than Lovina did. They both loved Autumn, which seemed strange and personal since it was something they shared with no one else.

They were all quiet, lost in their own thoughts. Night was coming, cold and dark, with just a bit of moonlight gleaming in the sky to show the way. Jonah flipped on the battery-operated headlights, peering through the blackness as he turned onto the county road. They'd lingered too long at church, catching up on everyone's lives and tidying up the barn after service. If Lovina hadn't hurt her ankle, he knew she'd have been in the kitchen, washing dishes with the other women. It was their way. To help one another all they could.

Most of the men and women in their congregation were kind to Jonah and *Dawdi*. The Amish were just like any other people. In spite of their religious beliefs, some were harsher and more judgmental than others. But after four years, Jonah and his father were part of the group. Aside from the constant matchmaking, Jonah liked this *Gmay*. And for the first time since he'd decided to move back east, he realized it would be difficult to leave this area when the time came. Even though his farm was too small, he tried to tell himself he didn't want to leave because he'd put so much work into the place. But now he wondered if that was the only reason he thought about staying.

Jonah slapped the leads against the horse, spurring him into a faster trot. The black pavement loomed before them. At least it was clear of ice. Even with the lights on the buggy, Jonah didn't feel safe. Too many trucks and cars zipped along the road at a frantic pace, and it wasn't secure for them to be out so late.

"Nice news about Fannie and Alvin, don't you think?" *Dawdi* broke the silence, speaking in a cheery tone.

Out of his peripheral vision, Jonah caught the movement of Lovina sitting forward a bit.

"*Ja*, it's tremendous news. She asked if I'd be her midwife," she said.

"When is her *boppli* due?" *Dawdi* asked.

"In the spring."

Jonah kept silent, listening to every word. In his mind, he still couldn't help thinking Fannie should have been his wife. This should be his baby. And they weren't.

In the faded light, Lovina looked at Jonah, as if assessing his mood.

"What do you think about the news, Jonah?" *Dawdi* asked.

Jonah paused, taking a deep breath and letting it go before he spoke. "I think it's to be expected. Fannie and Alvin are married. They're bound to have *kinder*."

Both *Dawdi* and Lovina stared at him through the

shadows, as if disappointed in his answer. And during the lull in conversation, he took a moment to ask himself what he thought. Honestly, he felt torn. On the one hand, he was delighted for them. But on the other hand, it ripped his heart to shreds.

"I think it's *wundervoll* news. I'm happy for them," he finally said.

Yes, he was genuinely pleased for Fannie. Anything else would be uncharitable. Though she'd broken his heart, he was glad she was in love. Glad she'd found happiness and peace. Her husband seemed to actually care for her. Her childlike manners didn't seem to bother Alvin. And she seemed much calmer and happier with him than she'd been with Jonah. Maybe Lovina was right…he and Fannie weren't well suited. Maybe he'd dodged a bad marriage after all. But that didn't change his mind about moving back east. *Dawdi* just wanted Jonah to be happy and would do whatever he liked. It was bad enough seeing Fannie share her good news with everyone in their congregation. He couldn't stand the thought of sticking around to watch her raise a passel of kids while he remained single. He still wanted out of here as fast as he could go.

He glanced at his grandfather, who stared at him without flinching.

"What?" Jonah said, wondering what the old man expected.

"Are you sure you're okay with it?" *Dawdi* asked.

Jonah looked away, focusing on the road. He shrugged, trying to keep the resentment from filling his voice. "I don't really have a choice, do I? I certainly don't want to be married to a woman who doesn't love me. I told you, I'm better off being alone the rest of my life."

"*Ach*, you're better off being married to a woman who loves you, but you're not better off being single. It's time you found someone else to wed. We have many eligible young women in our *Gmay*. You need to look harder," *Dawdi* said.

In the rearview mirror, he saw that Lovina was overly quiet, listening to this exchange, her eyes bright and wide. And though she was always around lately, Jonah reminded himself she wasn't part of his *familye*. She didn't belong in this moment. Not when he was discussing something so private with his grandfather.

"I don't want to talk about it right now, *Dawdi*. Marriage isn't for everyone. Not all of us find that special someone we want to grow old with." Jonah spoke low.

Lovina sat back on the padded seat with a little bump. In the quiet that followed, Jonah was almost certain he heard her mumble under her breath.

"I agree with you there."

He tilted his head toward her. "Did you say something, Lovina?"

"Nothing of importance," she said.

Maybe not but he knew he'd heard her correctly. And her words startled him. Did Lovina prefer being single, too? By Amish standards, she was definitely considered an old maid. But why didn't she want to marry? He'd never thought about it before. Was she still single because she preferred it that way? Or because she'd had her heart broken like him? It didn't make sense. She was a beautiful, proficient woman who would make any Amish man an ideal wife. And yet she'd never married.

Why?

The even clip-clop of the horse's hooves filled the air. *Dawdi* released a sigh and leaned his head back against the seat. After a few moments, Jonah thought he'd fallen asleep.

He was wrong.

"After church services, I saw the two of you talking with the bishop," *Dawdi* said. "Did he have any news about Autumn's *mudder*?"

Jonah paused, purposefully letting Lovina respond.

"*Ne*, nothing new to report. He wondered if we'd heard anything, too. He mailed off the letters to all the bishops in the area quite some time ago but no one has responded back. I guess we're waiting to hear," she said.

Dawdi sat up straighter. "But what happens if none of them know who the *mudder* is?"

"He said he knows a *gut* couple who can raise Autumn as their own," Lovina said.

Jonah turned in her direction. He caught the note of anxiousness in her voice.

"Autumn's *mudder* may not be from around here," Jonah said. "She may be from another state. The Amish talk and word spreads. Someone may have told her about our midwife. But for her to abandon her own child the way she did, we may never find her. It's what she wanted, after all. To dump her responsibility on Lovina and be left alone."

That old feeling of resentment surged inside Jonah. He tried not to sound condemning or unkind but it didn't quite come out like that.

"You're being judgmental again," Lovina pointed out in a rather tart tone. "We don't know what Autumn's *mamm* is going through or what her motivations are. From the note she left us, she wants only the best for her *boppli*. And it's not becoming of you to be so unkind."

Jonah gripped the lead lines harder. Lovina had just put him in his place. She had a way of making him feel small and unfair. And yet she was right.

"I'm sorry," he said.

And though he meant it, he still couldn't help feeling angry at Autumn's mother just as he felt angry at his own mom.

They rode in silence the remaining miles to his farm. And when they arrived, he hopped out and helped Lovina gather up the diaper bag and escorted her inside with Autumn.

He switched on the gas-powered light in the kitchen, then turned. As Lovina limped across the room, he noticed the weary slump of her shoulders. She was tired and probably in pain. Yet her own needs were forgotten as she spoke to Autumn in a soothing, sweet voice while she removed the babe from the warm bundling.

A surge of compassion rose within him. What call did he have to be so critical of others when he had so many failings of his own? The Lord asked that he forgive all men and women. That he not judge. And yet that's exactly what he'd done since he'd become aware that his mom had left him behind.

"Is there anything else I can do for you?" he asked.

Lovina shook her head, placing the used bottles in the sink for washing. "*Ne*, we're going up to bed now. Since she's having a *hoppli*, I'll need to pay a prenatal visit to Fannie tomorrow."

He didn't say anything for several moments. The last thing he wanted was to drive Lovina over to his ex-fiancée's house. But like Lovina, he would do his duty.

"What time do you want to leave?" he asked.

She turned and faced him, and he saw the fatigue in her eyes along with a strong sense of responsibility. After all, she knew the bishop wanted him to accompany her on her rounds. "I'd like to leave around ten o'clock, if that works for you. The visit shouldn't take long. You don't need to come inside the house, unless you want to."

Hmm. She was making this easier on him. And why didn't that surprise him? Lovina was always so kind. So in tune with what other people were feeling.

"*Allrecht*. I'll be ready with the buggy by then." He turned and stepped outside on the porch.

"*Gut nacht,*" she said, closing the back door firmly behind him.

He stood there for several moments, his fingers cold inside his leather gloves, his breath a puff of steam on the frigid night air. So much had happened at church today, and yet nothing out of the ordinary. But as he walked toward the barn, he didn't feel very good about himself. He knew he needed to forgive and forget. To love others. He must figure out a way to let go of the anguish that filled him every time he thought about his mother and Fannie. He just wasn't sure how to go about it.

Chapter Eight

"Congratulations! I believe you're about ten weeks along," Lovina said.

She sat at a small table in Fannie Fisher's bedroom. Picking up a pen, she jotted several notes on the chart she'd just created for the new mother-to-be. Late-morning sunlight gleamed through the window as Fannie sat at the foot of the bed. She waited as Alvin knelt in front of her and tied the laces to her practical black shoes. Finished with the chore, Alvin stood and stared at his wife with doe-eyed fondness. Lovina looked away.

"Everything is okay, then?" he asked quietly.

Lovina knew his question was for her, though his gaze remained fixed on Fannie. He'd been here while they'd listened to the baby's heartbeat for the first time. It had been a happy experience, to say the least. The couple was practically glowing, filled with the warmth that only new parenthood could bring.

Lovina set her pen down and nodded. "Both *mudder* and *boppli* appear to be just fine."

"You're absolutely sure the *boppli* is *allrecht*?" Fannie asked, smoothing her hands over her long skirts as she stood.

"As far as I can tell, everything looks great. The *boppli*'s heartbeat is strong and appears normal," Lovina said.

She quickly labeled and stowed the vials of blood and urine she'd taken from Fannie in her medical bag. They'd be sent to a lab to check for Rh factor, blood type, anemia, sugar, protein and any possible infections.

"And what about me? Am I okay?" Fannie asked.

Lovina glanced at the young woman, wondering what she meant. Then Lovina noticed a hint of fear in the young woman's eyes.

"*Ach*, sure! Your blood pressure is right where it should be. Once I get the results back from your labs, I'll know more. But I see nothing that alarms me. Nothing at all," she said.

"But my *mamm* had an awful time birthing her six *bopplin*. And I'm built narrow, just like her." Fannie's voice trembled and she clutched Alvin's hand until her knuckles whitened.

Feeling confused, Lovina glanced at the young woman and saw how her forehead creased with worry, her eyes wide and uncertain. She looked almost terrified. In all her years as a midwife, Lovina had never encountered so much anxiety in a new mother. Fannie seemed to need extra reassurance.

Stepping over to the girl, Lovina reached out and squeezed her arm. "Don't fret, Fannie. From your exam, I don't think you'll have trouble giving birth.

I believe you'll do just fine. Try to enjoy this experience. Think about your *boppli* and have fun with this special time in your life!"

Fannie blinked at her for several moments, as if she didn't understand. Then she nodded. "*Allrecht*, I'll try."

Inwardly, Lovina took a deep, relaxing breath. Motherhood could be a bit unsettling, especially with the first baby. As Fannie's midwife, Lovina was in this for the long haul and determined to make it as joyful and easy as possible for the new mother.

Lovina met Fannie's gaze without flinching. "Just remember to eat right, take a brisk walk every day and focus on your *boppli*. If you have any concerns whatsoever, no matter how small, you contact me right away. Alvin and I are both here for you."

She glanced at Alvin, who nodded with deep sincerity and stepped even closer to his wife, if that was possible. Lovina tried to sound as upbeat and positive as she could. But in her heart of hearts, she wondered what had induced Jonah to propose to this girl. Fannie was so different from him. The complete opposite. Jonah seemed so solid and down-to-earth whereas Fannie was a huge worrywart. Alvin was more suited to her. He seemed to relish doting on her. Anyone who looked at the couple could tell they were in love. And even when Jonah had been engaged to the girl, Lovina had never seen that kind of devotion between them. If only he could realize their breakup was for the best, he might feel happier.

Lovina packed her fetal Doppler, pregnancy wheel to determine a due date, blood pressure cuff and stethoscope into her medical bag. She noticed Alvin retrieved a clean hanky for his wife to blow her nose, then poured some water for her from a pitcher beside the bed. As he handed her the glass, he spoke gentle words of comfort. Lovina couldn't imagine Jonah fussing over Fannie like this. And yet when she thought about it, Lovina realized Jonah had his own way of caring. Whenever she needed wood for the cookstove, she found the bucket in her kitchen always filled. And since baby Autumn had come to stay with them, Jonah tended to the little girl like any father. He frequently fed and milked Lovina's goats while *Dawdi* gathered the eggs. Of course, Lovina wouldn't call that doting on her, but they were her chores. And though the bishop had assigned Jonah to look after her and the baby, Lovina liked to pretend he did it because he wanted to and not because he felt compelled.

"I'll want to see you again in four weeks," Lovina said as she shrugged into her warm shawl and picked up her bag.

"*Allrecht*. I'll *komm* to your place next time," Fannie said.

"That would be great." It would save Lovina a long trip.

She had no idea if Autumn would still be living with her then. It was easier to tend to the baby in her own house. Right now, Jonah was home with little Autumn…that was the only way he would agree to let Lovina drive herself over here to Fannie's place. Lovina knew he dreaded this prenatal visit with his ex-fiancée, so this morning she'd asked if she could come alone. Even though he had his own work to do, he'd willingly agreed to watch the baby while she was gone. And though Lovina dearly loved Autumn, it felt nice to get away for a change. On the way home, she was going to make a quick detour to the general store in town to buy supplies. She'd be home by lunchtime and Jonah could return to his farmwork.

Lovina stepped out of the room and headed downstairs. Fannie and Alvin followed.

"*Danke* for coming. I'm so excited. We're really going to have a *boppli* of our own." Fannie smiled as she and Alvin accompanied Lovina outside.

A brisk wind blew from the north and Lovina shivered. "You're so *willkomm*. Now, you go back inside where it's warm. I'll see you soon."

Fannie nodded and turned to go inside. Alvin wrapped his arm around his wife's shoulders and opened the door for her, leaving Lovina to climb into her buggy alone. As she stowed her bag in the back, Lovina glanced at the house one last time. The door was securely closed and she was on her own. Taking the lead lines into her gloved hands, she released the brake and urged the horse forward. As the buggy jostled into motion, it felt good to be by herself for the ride into town. A part of her pretended she was out running errands and her *familye* was waiting for her back at home. How she wished it was real. But it wasn't and she shook the feeling off, focusing on the damp road ahead. Thankfully, it was a warmer day with no black ice.

Within an hour, she'd finished her shopping in

town, paid her bill and loaded her purchases into the buggy. As she stood on the boardwalk and lifted the last heavy box, Vance Anderson, one of the three real estate agents in town, reached to help her.

"Here, let me get that for you, Mrs. Lapp. It's too heavy for you." He stashed it in the back, then turned to smile at her with big white teeth.

Mrs. Lapp!

"Thank you," she said. But she didn't correct his error. He was *Englisch*, after all, and probably didn't know the Amish very well.

Dressed in blue jeans and a long wool coat with a red scarf around his neck, Vance slid his hands into his pockets and hunched his shoulders against the cold. A middle-aged man with dark hair and a touch of gray at the temples, he wore a full beard and mustache.

"Fancy meeting you here today. I'll be coming out your way tomorrow. Where would you like me to put the for-sale sign?" he asked.

"For-sale sign?" Lovina tilted her head, feeling confused.

"Yeah, Jonah came to see me two days ago. He's selling your farm. I thought you knew. You're his wife, aren't you?"

She shook her head. "No, I just rent the farmhouse from him. We're not married."

Vance took a step closer. "Ah, so you'll be looking for a new place to live once he sells the place, won't you?"

Lovina didn't know what to say. Feelings of uncertainty, anger and disappointment rose up inside her.

She shoved them down, forcing herself to remain calm. Jonah wouldn't sell his farm. Would he?

"I… I think you must have me mistaken for someone else," she said.

Vance frowned. "Jonah Lapp. He lives at 4514 County Road 113. That's the place. I listed it on the market just this morning."

Yes, that was Jonah's address! It was Lovina's address, too. Her mind whirled in a melee of chaos. Jonah wouldn't sell. He loved that place. She could tell from the way he tended his livestock, fields and buildings. It was a small farm but he took meticulous care of it all. And what would he do if he sold it off? Where would he go?

Where would she go?

"I've got some great rentals I can show you," Vance persisted. "Or if you're interested in buying your own home, I can show you a few reasonable options. Great asking prices."

Reaching into his pocket, he whipped out a business card and handed it over. She took it, staring at it in frozen silence.

"Um, I don't think so. But thank you, anyway." She hurried to climb inside the buggy.

As she pulled away from the store, Vance waved farewell. Lovina pasted a smile on her face, urging the horse into a quick trot down Main Street. But inside, she was screaming. It couldn't be true. Could it? Jonah wouldn't put his farm up for sale. Not without telling her. She'd only been renting from him about four months now. Her midwifery business was doing well.

She didn't want to move again. Surely Jonah would warn her first. Wouldn't he?

She passed the edge of town, her heart beating like a drum. A surge of panic rose upward in her throat. She loved where she lived. It was the first place that felt like a real home. She could never get such a nice setup for her business somewhere else. But in her heart of hearts, she knew it was more than that. It was Autumn, *Dawdi* and Jonah working together with her that made her feel like she had a real home. For the first time in years, she had folks who depended on her. People who really needed her.

And she needed them.

She blinked, wondering where that thought came from. But there it was, rising in her mind like a summer sunrise. No matter how remote and independent she'd tried to be, she still needed others. She needed to feel loved and wanted. Yet she didn't belong to anyone. Not at Jonah's farmhouse, not anywhere.

As she drove home, she told herself not to fret. Surely Jonah had a reasonable explanation. She sensed he was unhappy. No doubt Fannie had broken his heart. So where did that leave Jonah? Even if he forgave Fannie, it couldn't be easy for him to stand back and witness her wedded bliss with Alvin. But Jonah would get over it. Eventually. He wasn't the first, or the last, to suffer a fractured heart. But she could hardly believe he would leave Riverton and all that he'd worked so hard for. At least, not without giving her fair warning that she needed to find a new place to live. Or would he?

* * *

Jonah twisted the socket wrench hard in order to remove the rolling cutter on his seed planter. It gave way and he took the cutter, careful not to drop the cushings out. The quiet barn smelled of fresh straw he'd just spread in the animal stalls. Earlier, he'd fed Autumn and put her down for a nap. *Dawdi* was inside the farmhouse with her, reclining on the sofa in case she woke up. No doubt he was fast asleep, too. But he'd hear the baby if she woke up and alert Jonah.

It was early afternoon and Lovina should be home soon. To avoid driving over to Fannie and Alvin's place, Jonah agreed to look after Autumn…a much more pleasant chore, he must admit.

When he had the new cutter safely in position, he tightened it down. Reaching for the latch on the seed box, he lifted it off. This planter had come with the farm when he'd bought the place four years earlier. It was ancient and needed to be replaced but so far, he'd kept it going with careful maintenance. Maybe in another year, he'd have enough money to buy a new one.

What was he thinking? He'd be gone next year. He'd sell the place and wouldn't be here for early planting in the spring. Which led him to wonder why he was performing this upkeep now.

As he lifted the seed tube up, he discovered lots of dried dirt inside. Knocking it out with a screwdriver, he coughed at the cloud of dust. What if he couldn't sell his farm? It could take a long time. He might be forced to stay here another year, and he told himself it was best to be prepared.

"Jonah?"

He turned, dropping the screwdriver in the process. It bounced off his boot and hit the dirt floor. Glancing up, he saw Lovina standing inside the double barn doors. She pulled them closed, shutting off the frigid breeze.

"You're back." Bending at the waist, he picked up the hand tool and set it aside.

She came to stand beside him, no more than an arm's reach away. He turned aside, forcing himself not to look at her flushed cheeks. She wore her black traveling bonnet over top of her white prayer *kapp*, her blue eyes sparkling, her nose red from the cold. Absolutely lovely.

"The *boppli* should still be asleep. She was tired after her bottle," he said.

"Can I speak with you, please?" Lovina asked.

Something in her voice caused him to swivel around. In a rush, he noticed how she lifted her chin a couple inches higher, her lips pressed in a tight, disapproving line.

Oh, no! What was wrong now?

"What is it?" He gestured to a large wooden crate where she could perch and chat in comfort. He sat on a bale of hay, forcing himself to focus on her pretty face.

"I… I just came from town. Vance Anderson stopped me on the street and…"

"And he told you I'm selling the farm," he finished for her. He clenched his eyes closed, wishing he'd told her first.

"*Ja.* He said he'll be out here tomorrow and wanted

to know where we want him to put the for-sale sign. Is it true, Jonah?"

He looked at her, seeing the rigid set of her shoulders and the angst in her eyes.

"*Ja*, it's true. I've asked Vance to put the farm on the market," he said.

Her back stiffened. "And when were you going to tell me?"

A flush of regret filled his chest. "Later this evening, once you got *heemet*."

"But why? Why would you sell your farm?" she asked, her voice filled with incredulity.

"Because there's nothing for me here." The words burst forth before he could stop them.

"Nothing? You have this farm. You have people who care for you. I wouldn't call that nothing," she said.

Though there was a pleading tone in her words, he thought she was doing an admirable job of maintaining her temper. It was something he admired about her. If this was Fannie, she'd be in hysterics by now. But not Lovina. No, she was always steady and calm. So strong. So reliable.

"I'm sorry, Lovina. You have every right to be upset. But I didn't realize you would feel so strongly about me selling the place. I figured you'd just rent a room from one of our other Amish families in the area. Forgive me for not telling you sooner." He meant every word but his apology seemed rather hollow now.

She looked at him without flinching, without blinking. But in her eyes, he saw a glimmer of moisture. She was near tears and that tore him up inside.

"Of course I forgive you. But what am I supposed to do now?" she asked.

He couldn't answer. He didn't know what to say.

"*Ach*, do you know when you'll sell the place? Have you had any offers?" she asked.

He stood and took two steps toward her even as she stood and took two steps back. "*Ne*, I have no offers yet. I only just listed the place a couple of days ago. Vance said it could take a long time to sell or no time at all. The market is pretty depressed, so I don't know."

"I'll… I'll have to move again. This is the first place I've felt happy in years and…and now it's being taken from me."

Her voice trembled. Her confession opened a part of her that she'd kept hidden from him until now. A part that told him she was as lonely as him. And that's when he realized she wasn't as strong as she appeared. He opened his mouth to express regret once more but she turned and swept across the expanse of the barn so fast that he felt frozen in place. Without a word or backward glance, she left with a chilling gust of wind, quietly securing the doors behind her.

Jonah sat there and stared after her for quite some time. He thought about running after her. To apologize and plead with her to understand. He had to go. He must! But all at once, the thought of moving away and never seeing her again left him feeling sad and empty inside, and he couldn't for the life of him understand why.

Thanksgiving was just days away, followed by Christmas soon after. But in the frame of mind he was in right now, Jonah couldn't seem to find a lot to feel grateful for. Instead, he felt as though he'd just lost his best friend. A silly notion if ever he'd heard one. Because he and Lovina weren't friends. They couldn't be.

Why hadn't he told her he was selling the farm? The question made his thoughts scatter. He wasn't sure. He should have done so. She deserved that much honesty. After all, she needed time to find another place to live and run her midwifery business. But he hadn't wanted to alarm her. He'd planned to tell her but kept putting it off for some crazy reason. He wasn't sure why. Yet he'd dreaded it. Because as soon as she knew, she would start packing her bags.

Maybe, just maybe, deep down in his heart he was hoping the farm wouldn't sell. But that didn't help him now. Because he had listed the property. He would sell the place and move back east with *Dawdi* and they would start anew.

"Jonah, what did you say to Lovina? She just ran into the house and I think she's upstairs crying."

He looked up and found his grandfather standing just inside the door.

Oh, no! This kept getting worse and worse. Lovina was in tears. And he hated the thought that he'd made her cry. But right now, he didn't want to hear a lecture from his grandpa.

"I told her I'm selling the farm," Jonah said.

Dawdi's bushy gray eyebrows lifted in surprise and he slipped his thumbs through his black suspenders as he came to stand beside Jonah. The old man chewed his bottom lip, as if mulling this over.

"I thought you told her several weeks ago, like you said you were going to do," *Dawdi* said.

"I know, but I put it off. I was going to tell her tonight but she found out from my real estate agent in town."

Dawdi nodded in understanding. "You should have told her, *sohn*."

"I know, I know. But honestly, *Dawdi*, I don't know why she's upset. It's not like this was ever going to be a permanent *heemet* for her. She must have known she would have to find another place eventually."

Heaving a labored sigh, *Dawdi* sat beside him on the bale of hay. "Jonah, everyone has their own grief. Even Lovina. No one is immune to the hardships of life. You know I felt heartbroken when your *mamm* abandoned you as a new *boppli*. She gave up her faith and walked away from her *familye* and everything she'd ever known so she could become *Englisch*."

He said *Englisch* as if it was a dirty word.

"*Ja*, I know. It must have hurt you and *Grossmudder* very much when she left," Jonah conceded.

"It did. For a long time, we thought we must have been horrible parents. We wondered what we'd done wrong. Maybe we didn't teach our *dochder* well enough. Maybe we didn't love her enough. Otherwise, why would she do the things she did?" *Dawdi* asked.

"It wasn't your fault, *Dawdi*. My *mudder* made her own choices," Jonah said.

Dawdi pointed a finger at him and narrowed his eyes with determination. "That's exactly right. You hit the nail on the head. Your *mudder* chose for herself, just as we all must choose."

"You mustn't blame yourself," Jonah insisted.

"I don't. Not anymore. But I still have many re-grets," *Dawdi* said. "Everyone has their freedom to choose how they'll live, but our decisions can hurt oth-ers. The best we can do is love and serve one another as Jesus Christ taught us to do. It's the greatest com-mandment of all."

Jonah nodded, feeling guilty for thinking only of himself. Until now, he'd never really thought about how his mother's actions must have hurt his grandparents. "*Ja*, I know that. And I'm sorry for hurting Lovina. I'm grateful you were there to raise me."

Dawdi clapped a hand against Jonah's back with fondness. "It was my pleasure. But remember some-thing. Lovina's *vadder* abandoned her, too. Knowing her the way we do, I don't believe it was easy for her to give up her *boppli*. She told me she was only fourteen years old at the time. Little more than a child herself."

Jonah frowned. This was the first time he'd heard how young she was. "She was only fourteen?"

"*Ja*, very young. We must not be unfair or judgmen-tal toward her. From what I've observed over the past four years that we've known her, Lovina is a pious, hardworking woman with an overly generous heart. We mustn't be unkind to her. Especially when we each have many faults of our own to deal with."

Jonah was very quiet, especially when his grand-father quoted a well-known scripture from the book of Matthew. *Dawdi*'s voice sounded low and quiet but filled with a deep richness that Jonah couldn't deny... like the rushing of many waters.

"Why beholdest thou the mote in thy brother's eye, but consider not the beam that's in thine own eye? First, cast out the beam out of thine own eye and then shalt thou see clearly to cast out the mote out of thy brother's eye."

With those words, *Dawdi* stood and left the barn. Jonah sat there, speechless and ashamed. He'd felt so angry over the wrongs he perceived that had been done against him over the years that he never stopped to realize he was being so critical and harsh of others. And suddenly, he started thinking deeply. It was as if a window opened to his heart. He saw Lovina with a fresh set of eyes. Her rights or wrongs were not for him to judge. Who was he to find fault with someone else when he had so many of his own failings to repent from? But recognizing this didn't change his mind about selling the farm. In fact, it made him even more determined to leave the area as soon as possible. He needed a fresh start somewhere else, far away from his heartache.

Chapter Nine

The week of Thanksgiving, Lovina avoided Jonah like the plague. Not easy to do, considering they lived on the same farm. Though she was able to slip in and out of the barn to milk her goats, he still brought her firewood every morning. But she used the baby as an excuse to not be in the kitchen when he came inside the house. And rather than have him accompany her to visit her expectant mothers, she'd arranged at church for the moms to come to her. That meant very little travel... and a bad case of cabin fever.

Stepping outside on the front porch, she put weight on her injured ankle, testing its strength. It wasn't perfect but it was getting better every day and she could manage without help.

She folded her arms and inhaled the crisp air as she bid farewell to her last client of the day. It was late afternoon and Autumn was still down for her nap. If Lovina hurried, she might have just enough time to start supper and whip together pumpkin pies for Thanksgiving dinner in a few days.

She glanced at the for-sale sign planted smack-dab in the middle of the front lawn. A constant reminder that she would soon have to leave. So far, no one had come to view the property. A part of her hoped no one would. And yet another part of her wanted Jonah to be happy. And that meant he needed to sell the farm and move away.

Back in the kitchen, she glanced at the local newspaper and rental ads spread across her table. She'd circled several possibilities with a bright red marker. Though she'd mailed off a few inquiries to find a suitable place, nothing appealed to her. She wanted to stay right here.

She reached for a mixing bowl, fighting off a feeling of deep frustration. Who knew how long she had before Jonah sold the place? Thanksgiving was upon them and she felt anything but cheerful. The holidays had always been a source of sadness for her, probably because she had very little *familye* to celebrate with. But this year, she felt even more morose than usual. She reminded herself that Christmas was about the Savior's birth. And because of Him, she was never really alone. But she couldn't help wishing for more.

As she cubed raw carrots and potatoes for a stew, she forced herself to count her many blessings. Maybe she would invite Jonah and *Dawdi* to share Thanksgiving dinner with her. It was logical, after all. She certainly couldn't eat an entire turkey on her own. And she had no doubt the preparation of a big meal was beyond *Dawdi*'s culinary skills. Then again, maybe they had been asked to join one of the many families in their *Gmay*. Since she'd had no such invitation, she could very well find herself spending the day alone, which would be awful.

Within an hour, she had a bubbling pot simmering on her stove, fresh corn bread in the oven and batter for several pumpkin pies ready to pour into the crusts. A thin cry came from the back of the house, and she quickly wiped her hands as she went to get Autumn.

The baby lay on her back, waving her little arms in excitement. She'd kicked her blanket off, but Lovina didn't think the room felt too cold.

Leaning over, Lovina smiled and spoke lovingly as she tried to coax a smile out of the tiny girl. Autumn was almost two months old and it was time to reach this milestone. But in spite of her best efforts, the baby merely gazed at her with sober intensity. No matter. Lovina kissed the girl and continued talking as she changed her diaper.

"You're such a *gut* girl. Are you hungry? I'll get you fed soon enough." She lifted the baby to her shoulder.

In the kitchen, Lovina quickly prepared a bottle and sat in a chair to feed the child. Autumn sucked ravenously, her big blue eyes never wavering from Lovina's face.

As she burped the baby, Lovina heard loud voices coming from outside. She stood, peering out the kitchen window to see what was amiss.

Jonah was hurrying away from the *dawdi haus*, his long legs moving fast as he headed toward the barn. He wore no coat but had on oven mitts as he carried

a frying pan that billowed black smoke. *Dawdi* Noah
followed on his heels, gesturing wildly and looking
miserable as he limped heavily on his wooden cane.
Without glancing his way, Jonah doused the sizzling
pan in the water barrel.

Oh, dear. It looked like *Dawdi* had burned their
supper again.

"I'm sorry, *sohn*. That old stove is just too hot. I'm
afraid it got the better of me," *Dawdi* exclaimed in a
rather loud, regretful voice.

Lovina didn't catch Jonah's reply. His words were
too soft to overhear. But she saw him turn and remove
the oven mitts before he placed a calming hand on his
grandfather's shoulder. Even from this distance, Lovina
saw his kind gesture as he lifted a hand to placate the
elderly man. Rather than yelling at his grandpa, Jonah
offered him reassurance. Jonah's mellow empathy impressed Lovina like nothing else could. And in a moment of compassion, she broke her own promise not
to invite them in for another meal.

Placing Autumn in her bassinet beside the table,
Lovina walked to the back door. She stepped outside
onto the porch and lifted a hand to her mouth as she
yelled to the two men.

"It looks like you're in need of a hearty supper,"
she called.

Both men jerked. Jonah whirled around and stared
in surprise.

"*Komm* inside and share my meal. I've got plenty
of food here," she said.

Dawdi immediately smiled and waved, his expression one of utter relief. Jonah just frowned. For a moment, Lovina thought he might refuse. In a stubborn gesture, she decided it was too cold to stand out here and argue with him. If he wanted to eat, he could come inside. If not, he could suit himself.

Turning, she returned to the kitchen and busied herself with her work. She was facing the gas-powered stove when she heard the creak of the screen door. It clapped closed and the chilly breeze was shut off. Forcing herself not to turn around, she glanced at Autumn. The baby was restless and let out a squall but Lovina didn't pick her up. Instead, she spoke to the girl as she poured the pumpkin mixture into her pie crusts.

"You're *allrecht, liebchen.* Give me a few minutes and I'll get you," she said, reaching for a pot holder.

"I'll tend her," Jonah said.

The clatter of boots on her hardwood floors told her both men had come inside. Still, Lovina ignored them.

"Sit anywhere," she called without looking their way.

Out of the corner of her eye, Lovina saw Jonah step over to pick up the fussy baby. She pulled a pan of steaming corn bread out of the oven and set it aside on the counter to cool. Then she slid the pies in and set a battery-operated timer for forty-five minutes. So the crusts wouldn't get overly brown, she'd covered the edges with tinfoil.

"There, Itty-Bit. I've got you," Jonah spoke low.

Lovina shivered as that old feeling of safety and comfort washed over her. She couldn't understand the impact Jonah's presence had on her. It didn't make sense.

"This is kind of you," *Dawdi* said.

"It's no problem. We'll be ready to eat in just a moment," she said.

She turned and saw Jonah staring at all the papers and classified ads still spread across her table. The heat of awkwardness rushed up her neck and she quickly gathered them and stashed them in the other room. Now that she was being evicted, she didn't want Jonah to know her business.

Jonah cradled Autumn in the crook of his arm as he sat in one of the wooden chairs. Lovina quickly washed, then set the table, noticing how the baby stared up at him with rapt attention. He tilted his head, looking directly into the little girl's eyes as he spoke in that conciliatory voice of his.

"Have you eaten yet, little girl? Or are you starving again, as usual?" he asked.

"I just fed her," Lovina said.

"*Ach*, is that right?" Jonah asked, still gazing at the baby. "So you're trying to fool me into giving you another bottle, is that it?"

In response, the baby smiled. She actually smiled! Lovina stared in shock. At first, she thought she must have imagined it. But no! Jonah had done what she hadn't been able to do. He'd cajoled Autumn to smile.

"*Ach*, you're such a sweet *maedel*," he said.

To which the baby smiled a second time. Oh, this was too much!

"*Ach*! Will you look at that?" *Dawdi* whispered.

Jonah gave a soft chuckle, the sound pleasant and surprising to Lovina. But inside, she felt deflated. For several days now, she'd been trying to get Autumn to smile, with absolutely no success. In walks Jonah, and the baby smiles twice for him.

He looked up at Lovina, his grin still firmly in place. "Did you see that, Lovina? Did you see? The *boppli* just smiled at me."

Lovina could only stare at him. His words and the way he said her name made her quiver inside. It was as if he wanted to share this important milestone with her. Like she mattered to him. Like she was his friend and companion. And how could she be angry with him when he acted like that?

She stood transfixed. Unable to move. Barely able to breathe. She wanted to smile at him, too. Yes, it was wonderful that little Autumn had finally smiled for the first time. But Lovina was more fascinated with Jonah. Because he was smiling, too. She'd seen him do it before, at church and other gatherings when he'd been speaking to someone else. Usually from far across the room. Not up this close and personal. Not at her. But this time, his smile was for her alone. And for just a few moments, she felt as though they were the only two in the room. That no one existed in the whole wide world but them.

"Um, *ja*, I saw. That's amazing," she said, feeling awed by the event and completely unable to take her eyes off him.

Dawdi scooted closer, peering at the baby in anticipation. "See if you can get her to do it again."

Jonah turned and gave Autumn his full attention.

"Can you smile for me again, sweet one?" he asked in his softest, most enticing tone.

A vision of the serpent beguiling Eve in the Garden of Eden flashed through Lovina's mind. Without intending to do so, she found herself smiling, too. And at that moment, she thought she might do anything for Jonah. Then she remembered who she was and who he was and that they weren't friends. Not really.

The baby rewarded Jonah for his effort, smiling so sweetly it brought tears to Lovina's eyes.

She turned away. The men's sudden laughter startled Autumn. Her eyes widened and her little chin quivered. Looking over her shoulder, Lovina wondered if the baby might cry.

"*Ach*, none of that, Itty-Bit. Everything is *allrecht*. There's no need for tears," Jonah soothed.

The baby settled right down, tracking Jonah's face as he reached for a burp cloth to wipe away a bit of drool from the corner of her mouth. Mesmerized, Lovina watched his movements.

"What a sweet *maedel*. It's too bad you can't keep her," *Dawdi* said.

Lovina's balloon popped. As if being propelled through a dark tunnel, she found herself back in reality. The future loomed before her like a great, hulking beast.

"*Ja*, it's too bad," Jonah said.

And Lovina realized she dreaded giving up the baby more than anything she'd faced yet.

"*Ach*, I better get this meal on. And you might as well join me for Thanksgiving dinner on Thursday, too.

Unless you've been invited elsewhere?" She glanced at them, wondering what had possessed her to make the offer.

"*Ne*, we haven't been asked elsewhere. Most folks think you'll cook for us, so they don't invite us over for dinner anymore," *Dawdi* said.

Oh. No wonder old Marva Geingerich disapproved of Lovina living here on the farm. A single woman alone with two men. Even if they lived in separate houses and *Dawdi* was here to chaperone, it did seem a bit improper.

"I was planning to throw something together." *Dawdi* gave a little snicker but had the good grace to look a tad embarrassed. "We all know how that will work out. I'm not much of a cook but my Bertha could make anything. The best feasts I've ever eaten. We'd love to accept your invitation. It's awful kind of you to think of us, Lovina."

She merely nodded and stepped over to the stove. As she flipped off the burner and reached for the pot, she took a moment to wipe her eyes and gather her composure. Now she'd done it. Jonah would be here in her home on Thursday, but she'd rather eat with Jonah and his gentle grandfather than spend the holiday alone.

As she cut huge chunks of golden corn bread and placed them on the table, she couldn't help wondering what had just happened to her. A myriad of emotions coursed through her, and she couldn't make sense of it all.

She ladled stew into each of their bowls, realizing she'd shared something special with Jonah that most married people enjoyed with their own child. But they weren't married and never would be. Autumn was not their child. And against her better judgment, Lovina had invited these two men into her home to share Thanksgiving dinner with her. It was a time of peace, hope and gratitude. Yet she was filled with uncertainty. If she could have her Christmas wish, it would be for a *familye* of her own.

That thought brought a flood of warmth to her chest. How she longed to belong to someone. A *familye* who cared for her. Someone she could shower her love upon. But that wasn't possible. Not for her. Not ever again. She didn't deserve such exquisite joy. Especially not with a good, hardworking man like Jonah Lapp.

Oh, no! Not again! Jonah never should have let *Dawdi* drag him here to Lovina's kitchen for another meal. And now they were going to have Thanksgiving with her, too!

As he ate the hearty beef stew, his stomach rumbled with satisfaction. He couldn't deny she was one of the best cooks in the county. In fact, she seemed so good at everything she did. But he sensed something else was going on between them. Something he didn't understand. Because every time he was near Lovina Albrecht, he found himself feeling incredibly...

Confused!

An odd notion if ever he'd had one before. Lovina especially made him feel nervous. He had so many reservations about her. He told himself it wasn't because of her past. After all, *Dawdi* was right. Jonah didn't know all the details and wasn't in a position to judge her. Rather, he told himself that his misgivings were because of his own past. He didn't dare trust again. More than anything, he feared letting down his guard. He could never take that chance again.

"While I was working my EMT job this morning, I saw the bishop in town," Jonah said.

Lovina lifted her head and gazed at him.

"He said he'd received letters from three of the bishops in our region, and they know of no unwed *mudders* who might have run away. He hopes to hear from the other two bishops soon."

"What do you think is taking them so long to respond?" she asked.

Jonah shrugged. "I have no idea. Maybe they're making inquiries among their congregations."

Lovina frowned and he knew what she was thinking. The baby's mom obviously knew Lovina was a midwife. Only the Amish in their region would know who she was...unless word had traveled through the grapevine. The Amish were great letter writers and had lots of *familye* members they wrote to all the time. There were Mennonites but no Amish in New Mexico, Arizona or Utah that Jonah knew of. If Autumn's mom was from Kansas or Oklahoma, they might never find her, and Bishop Yoder would be forced to give the baby to another *familye*.

"We'll wait as long as it takes." Lovina ducked her head over her bowl.

They continued their meal in silence. Not unusual since they'd all worked hard and were hungry. Jonah held the baby easily with his left arm, listening to her little coos and gurgles as she waved her tiny arms. She smelled nice and he realized Lovina took excellent care of her. He worried what would happen to her when she left. Would her mom take as good care of her as Lovina did? Would her other *familye* protect her as they should? Would they love and teach her right? Oh, how he was going to miss her once Bishop Yoder took her away.

Likewise, he fretted over Lovina, too. He'd seen the newspaper and rental ads spread across her table when he'd come inside the house. From the big red circles drawn around several listings, he knew she was actively looking for another place to live. And where would that be? Maybe she could rent a room from another Amish *familye* in their *Gmay*. Without an examination room and nursery, that would make it difficult for her midwifery business. She might rent a house in town, which wasn't to his liking. She was a woman alone. Though she was independent and strong, she was also vulnerable. He didn't want someone to take advantage or hurt her. He wouldn't be there to protect her. And though it wasn't his business, he still worried about her. And that realization shook him to the core. Because caring led to an open heart that could be hurt.

"I… I better get out to the barn. I've got a few more chores I need to take care of." He scraped his chair back and stood, placing the baby in her bassinet.

Lovina looked up in surprise, holding her spoon aloft. "I've got pumpkin pies coming out of the oven in a few minutes, if you'd like a slice for dessert."

He shook his head. Though his mouth watered at the thought, he'd already consumed two huge bowls of tasty stew and chunks of buttered corn bread and his stomach was full. It was time to get back to work. He needed to put some distance between him and Lovina. Right now!

"What chores do you need to do? I thought we were through for the evening," *Dawdi* said, his forehead crinkled in a bewildered frown.

"I… I forgot to check the water troughs. Ice might have formed over the top, which will keep the horses and pigs from being able to drink."

Okay, it was a lame excuse but still very true.

"I checked them and everything's fine," *Dawdi* said.

Jonah's mind scattered. Both Grandpa and Lovina were sitting there, gazing at him with confused expressions.

"*Ach*, I also need to chop more firewood for the morning," he said.

There! That was good.

"Can't you do that in the morning?" *Dawdi* asked.

Yes, he could.

"It's nice to have it done and ready to go," he said.

Like him, Lovina was an early riser and he wanted to keep her supplied with kindling. After all, she had a new baby to tend. If nothing else, he was fastidious and took his work seriously. He rarely left things undone and liked to get a head start.

He stood at the back door, his hand on the knob as he threw a quick glance at Lovina. "*Danke* for supper."

"You're *willkomm*."

Her voice sounded quiet and subdued. Maybe she was uncomfortable with him here and wanted him to leave, too.

Conscious of the chilly breeze on the baby, he opened the door just a bit and stepped outside. He hurried and closed it tight again, then hustled over to the woodpile. It was dark outside but the round moon provided enough light for him to split several chunks. Even though he wasn't wearing his winter coat, he didn't feel the cold night air. He'd been well-warmed by Lovina's delicious stew and cheery kitchen. Although the farmhouse belonged to him, he'd started thinking of it as her place. Her home. She seemed to have settled right in, and it was obvious she didn't want to leave. And for the first time since she'd moved in, he found himself wishing she could stay. That they could keep Autumn for their own and be a real *familye*.

Ah, that would never work. They both had complicated pasts that haunted them. He didn't know Lovina's full story, but he was astute enough to see the pain in her eyes whenever she talked about her life. She'd been hurt deeply, just like him. But he didn't dare let down his guard with her. It was less painful to remain a bachelor. And yet the thought of Lovina moving away and never being able to see her bothered him greatly. Instead, he wished he could tell her that Autumn would stay with them forever. That everything was going to be all right. But it wasn't. And he didn't dare get involved. He couldn't make this right for any of them.

Chapter Ten

Lovina knocked forcefully on the front door of the *dawdi haus*. It was just past one o'clock in the morning and she should be fast asleep. Thick darkness gathered around her, the frigid air enfolding her quaking body. She was fully dressed but had forgotten her warm shawl. Yet she didn't feel the cold. Standing on Jonah's doorstep, all she could think about was little Autumn.

She pounded hard. "Jonah! Please, help!"

The door jerked open and she reared back in surprise. He stood before her wearing his pants and shirt. His feet were bare, his sand-colored hair askew. Obviously he'd dressed fast. He blinked his eyes, which were filled with sleep. She had no doubt she'd woken him.

"What is it?" he asked, his voice low and groggy.

"It's the *boppli*. Can you *komm* with me, please?" she asked.

She hated to disturb him. Hated to beg for help. If she wasn't in dire need, she never would have asked.

"What's wrong?" *Dawdi* called.

Lovina winced. Through the open doorway, she saw the older man standing in the threshold leading to his bedroom. It looked like she'd roused him, too. He was just pulling his black suspenders up over his shirt. His silvery hair was ruffled as he pushed his spectacles up on the bridge of his nose. Like Jonah, his feet were bare. Not so odd, considering it was the middle of the night.

Jonah raked a hand through his tousled hair and called over his shoulder. "Something's wrong with Autumn."

"Oh! You better go, then." A note of urgency filled *Dawdi*'s voice.

"*Ja, komm* quick. She's so sick," Lovina said, her voice sounding breathy and anxious to her own ears.

As she said the words, her heart skipped a beat, then pounded madly in her chest. The baby was ill and Lovina didn't know what to do. She couldn't lose another child.

"I'll be up at the farmhouse," Jonah called to his grandfather.

He reached for his boots sitting beside the front door and stomped his feet into them without socks. Grabbing his coat from the hook on the wall, he shrugged into it as he hurried into the night. Having completed her mission, Lovina literally sprinted back to the house. She hated leaving Autumn for even a moment and was eager to get back to the little girl. Jonah kept up with her all the way.

"What's the matter with her?" he asked when they stepped into her warm kitchen.

Lovina closed the door, then scurried to the back

of the house where the nursery was located. "She's running a high temperature and has a deep, hacking cough. Over the past couple of days, I noticed she had a sniffly nose, but I didn't think it was serious. Now I'm worried."

Jonah was hot on her heels as they reached the baby's room. Lovina had turned on several gas-powered lamps. Autumn lay wheezing on her back in her rocking cradle. She was fussy, moving restlessly and flailing her tiny hands against her face, as if she didn't feel well. Now and then, she let out a miserable squall. And when she coughed, it sounded like a little dog barking.

"*Ach*, you poor *maedel*," Jonah said.

Lovina leaned over the child, resting a hand against her tiny chest. She felt an edge of uncertainty. Thankfully, the baby's color looked good, and she seemed able to breathe well enough. But she kept coughing, a deep watery sound that Lovina knew was not good. As a midwife, she worked mainly with prenatal and postnatal issues. The babies she tended were usually newborns. She'd never had to deal with something like this and had no idea what was wrong.

"I don't know what to do," Lovina said.

"Here, let me."

Jonah crouched over the crib. He wasn't a doctor but as an EMT, he was called out on emergencies like this. While Lovina stood by, he quickly examined the baby from head to toe, then wrapped her up warm and lifted her to his shoulder.

"There, Itty-Bit. We're going to take *gut* care of

you." His deep, soft voice seemed to calm the baby. And knowing he was here soothed Lovina's nerves, too.

"She's definitely hot to the touch. Have you taken her temperature in the last twenty minutes?" he asked.

Lovina nodded, filled with trepidation. "*Ja*, it's one hundred degrees on the dot."

"*Ach*, not too high yet."

Not too high? Considering Autumn was two months old, Lovina thought it was in outer space.

Autumn coughed again, a heavy, crackling sound. What if she had pneumonia?

"What do you think is wrong with her? Is it just a bad cold?" Lovina asked. She twined her hands together, wishing she could do something.

"I think she has croup."

"Croup?" Lovina's voice squeaked with dismay.

"*Ja*, haven't you ever dealt with a croupy *boppli* before?"

"*Ne*, I help *mudders* with birthing issues. If their *boppli* is sick, I refer them immediately to a medical doctor at the hospital."

Also, Lovina had no children of her own. Though she had given birth once, she hadn't been able to raise her son.

"Where on earth would she have gotten croup from?" she asked.

Jonah shrugged. "Most likely from church. She is rather cute and everyone was oogling over her last Sunday. It's contagious among *kinder* and she could have easily picked it up then."

Oogling over her? If the situation wasn't so dire,

Lovina would have laughed at his made-up word. Jonah was so serious all the time, except when it came to this baby. Then he was a giant teddy bear. And Lovina liked that about him, though she would never admit it out loud.

"Should we take her to a doctor?" Lovina asked.

Jonah frowned. "*Ne*, not yet. They'd ask questions about her parents, and we still don't want the *Englisch* involved. If all else fails, we could take her to Eli."

Eli Stoltzfus was an Amish paramedic in their *Gmay*. While an *Englisch* EMT drove the ambulance for them, Jonah frequently rode with Eli during their work shifts at the hospital. He was a nice man and Lovina trusted him. She had no doubt, if they were forced to take Eli into their confidence, he could be discreet and would help them protect Autumn and her mom from the *Englisch* authorities.

"I'd rather not involve more people in Autumn's situation without Bishop Yoder's permission. Let's see what we can do for the *boppli* on our own first," Jonah said.

Lovina didn't question him. They were Amish, after all. Self-sufficient and separate from the world. Even though they were certified as an EMT and midwife, they went to a doctor as a last resort. They also didn't want to lie when the *Englisch* medical staff asked them to fill out admitting paperwork. No doubt the form would include a place for the names of Autumn's parents, which meant they'd have to tell the truth and possibly lose the baby for good. But it was more serious than that. If the *Englisch* authorities discovered they'd had a baby abandoned into their care and hadn't turned her in, they could both lose their jobs. They might even face jail time. But worst of all, they would lose Autumn for good.

"What can I do?" Lovina asked.

"Have you got a warm hat for her?" he asked.

Filled with confusion, Lovina handed him a white yarn cap she'd knitted a week earlier. It was soft and warm for when she took Autumn with her to visit her expectant mothers.

"It's important we keep her as calm as possible." Jonah spoke as he tugged the cap onto Autumn's head. Then he bundled the baby up nice and warm with blankets, tucking her little hands and legs into the folds.

Carrying the *boppli* to the back door, Jonah spoke over his shoulder as Lovina followed. "Right now, I think we need some cool air to ease the swelling in her air passages."

"What? You mean, you're taking her outside? But it's freezing cold out there," Lovina said.

She couldn't believe he wanted to take Autumn outside. It was late and officially Thanksgiving Day. Christmas was right around the corner. Lovina didn't believe the cold night air was good for anyone, much less a young baby. She took Autumn's care quite seriously. If something happened to her, how could Lovina live with herself or explain it to Bishop Yoder?

"She's dressed warmly. The cool air will help diminish the inflammation in her air passages. We'll only go outside for a few minutes," Jonah said.

Determined not to let Autumn out of her sight,

Lovina reached for a woolen shawl and dragged it over her shoulders as she stepped out onto the back porch with Jonah. The heavens above were black as coal, not a single star or moon to offer them light. They might have rain or another snowstorm by morning.

Jonah stood and rocked Autumn back and forth, comforting her. As he leaned his head over her, Autumn stared up at him with her wide eyes. So sick and vulnerable, yet so trusting. Now and then, she released a tight, low-pitched cough.

"We don't want her to get overly excited. That will only trigger more coughing spasms," Jonah explained, speaking quietly to Lovina.

Ah. Now she understood his whispers and slow, methodical movements. Jonah was so calm, so confident. He always seemed to know just what to do.

They stood there in the dark, their puffs of breath looking like gray smoke on the air. A dim light glimmered in the *dawdi haus* window, and Lovina knew *Dawdi* must have lit a kerosene lamp. She was sorry to wake everyone, but it couldn't be helped. After a few minutes, the baby closed her eyes and a blaze of panic gripped Lovina.

"Is she okay?" She reached out and touched the baby, searching for life.

Autumn jerked and began to fuss again but Jonah shushed her gently. "There, Itty-Bit. It's *allrecht*. You're going to be just fine. *Mammi* Lovina is just overly worried about you," Jonah said.

Yes. Lovina felt like a very worried mommy.

The baby settled again, and Jonah offered Lovina

a reassuring smile. "You see? She's fine. She was just falling asleep. Notice she's stopped coughing? The cool air has helped quite a lot."

Lovina stared at him, her pulse racing, her legs feeling weak as noodles. How could he remain so relaxed when she was frantic with fear?

"We can't stay out here in the cold much longer," she said.

"We won't. We'll take her to the bathroom and run hot water to get some nice moist air for her to breathe. It will help relax her vocal cords," he said.

"But what if it doesn't work? What if…?"

She couldn't finish. Absolute terror gripped her heart. She wasn't Autumn's mother but she felt like she was. For the past weeks, she'd been tending to the baby as though she were her own. And like any worried mom, Lovina feared the worst. She loved this baby. Heaven help her, she did! She knew Jonah did, too. And for one insane moment, she thought it was a shame they weren't Autumn's parents. That they weren't a *familye* for real.

"Lovina, stop worrying. She's going to be *allrecht*," he said again.

The way he said her name made her feel special for some odd reason. Like she could do anything as long as he was by her side.

He nodded at the door. "Let's take Autumn inside and run some hot water."

Lovina opened the screen for him, then stood back as he carried the baby inside. She scurried ahead to the bathroom and turned on the hot water. It took a moment for the water to warm up. She didn't have a humidifier, so this would have to do.

Sitting on a stool, Jonah pulled the shower curtain so it would hold the mist around the baby. With his strong arms, he held the girl close to the faucet as she breathed in the moist air.

"Let's keep the door closed as much as possible, to hold the steam in," he said.

Lovina nodded and closed the door before sitting on the edge of the bathtub. Soon, the condensation built up and water droplets ran down the sides of the walls and clung to every surface. She gazed at Jonah, drinking in his confidence. Letting his cool demeanor calm her frayed nerves. Then she studied the baby's face, ensuring herself that Autumn was still breathing. That she wasn't turning blue from lack of oxygen. Though Lovina had always taken pride in her calm, deliberate movements as a midwife, she now felt frenzied and out of control. She tried to quiet herself. To have faith and trust in the Lord. And as they sat there, she prayed, asking *Gott* to bless Autumn and help them know how to care for the little girl.

Over the next few hours, they took turns holding the baby over the tub. Though the girl was small, Lovina's arms gave out after some time. Jonah seemed to know exactly when to take Autumn from her. With his strong arms, he held the child easily, showing no fatigue. His kind patience impressed Lovina. She realized with a bit of dismay that if Jonah wasn't here, she wouldn't have a clue what to do. She'd be lost without him. And that's when she knew she loved him, though she didn't know how it had happened. She loved him and he was leaving and her heart would be broken once more.

Before sunrise, she took the baby's temperature again. It was still high.

"I'm afraid this isn't enough," Lovina said.

"If her fever hasn't broken and she's not breathing easier by daybreak, I'll get the buggy ready and we'll take her to Eli or the hospital. A doctor would probably give her a steroid to help her fight the illness," he said.

"Can't you give her the steroid?"

Jonah shook his head. "I don't have any here at the farm. Eli might have some but his farm is seven miles away. It'd be quicker to take Autumn to the hospital in town. Either way, she's a very young *boppli*. I'd rather not administer medications unless we must."

Lovina nodded. They'd done everything they could for the child. Now it was up to *Gott*. But the stakes were high. To save the baby's life, they would visit Eli or an *Englisch* doctor…and possibly lose their jobs in the process.

"How long will this croup last?" Lovina asked.

She was holding Autumn at this point and cradled the child close against her chest while keeping the baby's face turned toward the warm, moist air. In a moment of dismay, she realized the steam had wilted her hair and clothes, and she had damp tendrils sticking to her face. With her hands occupied, she couldn't even push them back. Jonah must think she looked a sight.

Jonah shrugged. "Two or three days. But I think we're making progress already."

"*Ja*, she's not coughing as much."

And what a relief. Obviously Jonah knew what he was doing, but Lovina didn't believe they were out of the woods yet.

Throughout the night, they kept their vigil over the baby. At one point, Lovina passed the child back to Jonah and went out to the kitchen to make them a cup of hot chocolate. She offered Autumn a bottle, but the baby wouldn't take it.

Hours later, the hot water tank was drained and Autumn's fever finally broke. She was breathing easy and sleeping peacefully.

Lovina carried the baby into the living room, satisfied the danger had passed. Jonah was slumped awkwardly in a nearby chair that was way too small for his long frame. His handsome face softened in sleep, his full lips parted as he breathed in repose. Like her, he must be exhausted.

Dawdi Noah lay sprawled across the sofa, his soft snores filling the air. Lovina had no idea when the elderly man had come inside the house. Jonah must have let him in and explained what was going on. Though both men were asleep, it brought Lovina a great deal of comfort having them near. Against her better judgment, she'd grown fond of them both.

A faint spray of sunlight gleamed through the wide picture windows. Lovina had made plain brown curtains and hung them there just a month earlier. When she'd moved into this house, she'd known it wasn't forever but she had adopted it as her semipermanent home. Now she wondered where she would go. Previous to living here, she'd rented a room from the

Schwartz *familye*. But Hannah was expecting again and they needed the space for their own kids. The Burkholders' eldest daughter had just married and moved to Westcliffe. Maybe they had room for her. But Lovina dreaded another temporary home. She wanted a place of her own.

A glint of sunbeams landed squarely on Jonah's angular profile. A lock of hair hung over his forehead and she was tempted to reach out and push it back. She resisted the urge, knowing the movement would awaken him.

For several minutes, she gazed at his relaxed face, unable to understand the warm feelings cascading through her heart. And though it made her feel all mushy inside, she forced herself to think about the baby instead. She couldn't let down her guard. She'd fought too hard for her independence to lose it now. Jonah was selling his farm. Soon Lovina would find a new place to live. And once Jonah moved back east, they'd never see each other again. And yet she couldn't help wishing for more.

By late afternoon, Jonah sat in Lovina's kitchen, watching her mash potatoes in a tall cooking pot. The air smelled of roast turkey, stuffing and fresh yeast rolls. In spite of being up all night with a sick baby, she'd managed to cook them a Thanksgiving feast.

Holding Autumn in his arms, Jonah saw she was asleep. He was tempted to put her in her cradle and help Lovina, yet he was loath to do so. He wanted to keep the child close until he was positive she was safe. The baby's fever had finally broken and her cough diminished quite a bit, yet he was worried. What if it flared up again? What if she had pneumonia?

A loud clatter in the sink caused him to snap his head up. The baby jerked and her eyes fluttered open, then closed again. She didn't even cry, indicating how badly she needed rest.

"I'm sorry," Lovina said.

She looked over her shoulder at him, her hands gripping the potato pot. The slump of her shoulders and black circles beneath her eyes attested to her exhaustion. Last night, she'd done everything he asked without hesitation. And her trust touched his heart like nothing else could. For just a moment he imagined Fannie in the same situation and doubted she would have handled the baby's illness as well as Lovina.

Standing, he stepped into the living room and laid the baby in her cradle. He'd moved the tiny bed there last night. She'd be close enough that they could hear her breathing and check on her often, yet not so close that the noises in the kitchen would disturb her.

Lovina struggled to lift the heavy turkey out of the oven. With three of them for dinner, he wondered why she'd baked such a large bird. His mouth watered in anticipation of the yummy leftovers. Then he reconsidered. Until he sold the farm, this was Lovina's home. Her kitchen. Her turkey. He doubted he'd get to enjoy the remnants later tonight or tomorrow.

"Let me." Brushing her hands aside, he took the oven mitts and lifted the bird over to the counter for her.

"Danke," she said.

He inclined his head. Working side by side, they drained the drippings into another pan. While Lovina stirred together a tasty gravy, Jonah sliced the juicy meat.

The back screen door creaked and Jonah looked up. *Dawdi* came inside, carrying a bucket of firewood.

"*Ach*! It's a cold one. I had to chop ice off the watering trough so the cows could drink." The old man limped over to the far wall and set the bucket down. There was no resentment in his cheery voice.

"I'm sorry, *Dawdi*. I should be out there working. You should be inside where it's warm," Jonah said.

He reached for his jacket. He'd been so wound up helping Lovina and the baby that he'd almost forgotten his responsibilities on the farm.

Dawdi waved a gnarled hand in the air. "Don't worry yourself. There's nothing left to do today. I got all the livestock fed and the cows milked. I even gathered the eggs and put them in the fridge. We can clean them later, after we've had our Thanksgiving dinner."

Jonah glanced around the kitchen. Lovina had spread a plain white tablecloth and set out the dishes. In the center of the table, she'd laid small orange pumpkins and white and yellow gourds. Simple, yet colorful for the season. It added a festive look to the table and pleased him for some odd reason.

"How's the *boppli*?" *Dawdi* asked, keeping his normally loud voice low as he peered into the living room.

"She's doing *gut*, thanks to Jonah," Lovina said.

Setting a large drumstick on the meat platter, Jonah blinked in surprise. He appreciated Lovina's trust, yet it was a confidence he didn't feel. Last night, he'd kept it together for her and the baby's sake. After all, he was an EMT and it would do none of them good to panic. But inside, he'd never been so afraid. What if Autumn had died while in their care? How could he ever live with himself if he lost that little girl? How could he explain himself to Bishop Yoder?

Setting the meat on the table, he hurried into the other room to check Autumn. She was sleeping and breathing easy. Nothing to be alarmed about.

When he turned, he bumped into Lovina. She leaned over his shoulder, her eyebrows pulled together in concern. She stood so close that he caught the subtle fragrance of her coconut shampoo. Their eyes met and her soft breath brushed against his chin. For several pounding moments, he felt suspended in time.

"Is she *allrecht*?" Lovina whispered.

"*Ja*. She's fine. I just wanted to make sure before we start our meal," he said.

A movement caught his eye, and he turned toward the doorway. *Dawdi* stood there smiling softly, his eyes filled with knowing curiosity.

Lovina nodded and turned back to the kitchen, wiping her hands on the apron around her waist. Jonah followed, feeling warm and flushed.

"I think we're ready to eat," Lovina said.

She set a bowl of steaming gravy beside the potatoes and corn along with two kinds of homemade preserves and a colorful fruit salad. They each took their seats and waited for *Dawdi*, who was the eldest and would fill the role of head of the household.

"*Danke* for this great feast, Lovina. It looks *wundervoll*. Let us pray and give thanks," *Dawdi* said.

Lovina smiled graciously and they all bowed their heads. After a few moments, they ate quietly. Jonah figured they were too tired for much conversation. He couldn't help feeling grateful. They'd had a frightening night but Autumn was doing well. They had plenty of food on the table and a warm home to live in. Surely the Lord had blessed them. So why did Jonah feel anxious and nervous? Why couldn't he find peace in his heart?

Why did he want to leave?

The question made him pause. Since Fannie had broken their engagement, he'd longed to escape. To live anywhere but here. But now he wasn't sure.

The baby coughed and they turned toward the doorway, their eating utensils suspended in midair. Lovina immediately popped out of her chair but Jonah held out a hand to stop her. She hovered there, looking anxious.

"Her cough sounds looser. I think she's over the worst of it," Jonah said.

Autumn quieted and Lovina sat down again, releasing a little sigh. Like him, she was worried and unwilling to leave anything to chance. Yet he knew that right now the baby needed sleep more than anything.

They resumed their meal, rounding it off with thick wedges of pumpkin pie and sweet cream. After so much preparation, now came the cleanup.

Sitting in the rocking chair in the living room, *Dawdi* fed a little milk to Autumn while Jonah helped Lovina wash the dishes.

"*Danke* for all your assistance last night and today,"

she said as she rinsed another plate and set it in the drain.

Wielding a clean dish towel, Jonah dried a glass and set it aside. "It's no problem. I'm just happy it's all worked out. I was just doing what the bishop asked."

She glanced at him, a slight frown on her face. For a fraction of a moment, he saw some emotion in her beautiful blue eyes. Doubt or regret, he wasn't sure which. Maybe a little of both. Then she looked away, and he thought he must have imagined it. But he couldn't help feeling as if he'd said something wrong. Something that bothered Lovina. A lot.

He gazed at her soft profile. A lock of golden hair had come loose from her prayer *kapp* and lay against her soft cheek. The curl trembled slightly with every exhale she took. He was tempted to reach out and touch that silky texture. To gently tuck it back behind her ear. But he didn't dare. Because it was much too personal and might give her the wrong idea. After all, he was selling the farm and would be leaving the area soon.

For several minutes, Jonah gazed at Lovina's sweet face. He forced himself not to give in and tell her what he was thinking. Over the past few months since she'd moved into his farmhouse, they'd worked together. Caring for Lovina's expectant mothers and little Autumn. He couldn't deny they'd grown close. But that was just one more reason for him to distance himself from her as fast as possible. He could never tell her his thoughts. Never confide in her. That would only make him vulnerable to being hurt again.

Once the kitchen was tidy, he stepped toward the back door, eager to flee.

"I better check on the livestock. If you or Autumn need anything else, anything at all, just call," he said.

Lovina blinked, seeming surprised by his sudden departure. Today was a day for eating too much, giving thanks and visiting. Not a day for work. But Jonah felt if he didn't get out of here right now, he might explode.

"*Ach*, I know we're all tired. *Danke* again. You've been such a great help," she said.

Looking away, he hardened his heart and purposefully pushed aside his riotous feelings of frustration and regret. He wanted to smile and talk and stay right here with her, but that would only prove fatal to his peace of mind. Instead, he focused on his goals. He was going to sell this farm and move back east where he could forget his broken heart once and for all.

Chapter Eleven

Ten days later, Autumn had recovered from her croup and was doing well. It was the second week of December and two inches of snow blanketed the ground. Long icicles clung to the edges of the farmhouse gutters. The early-morning air was brisk, a chilly breeze blowing from the north. The sun blazed brilliantly in the sky. Little Autumn was down for her morning nap, and Lovina had taken advantage of the good weather. Standing in the backyard, she had just finished hanging her clean laundry on the line, knowing the icicles would melt and her clothes would be freeze-dried by late afternoon. That would give her enough clean diapers for Autumn to last several days.

As she finished the chore, a horse and buggy came down the lane. After dropping the unused clothespins into a plastic bucket, she picked up her laundry basket and skirted the house. As usual, Jonah had shoveled the paths and they were almost dry.

Bracing the basket against her right hip, she stood

there and waited. David Troyer, one of her expectant fathers, pulled his buggy to a halt beside the house and jumped out in an energetic bound. His black felt hat was askew and he wore a warm winter coat, scarf, black leather gloves and boots.

Lovina's senses perked into overdrive. "David! What are you doing here? Is everything *allrecht*?"

"*Ach*, Lovina! I'm so glad you're here. It's Millie's time. You've got to *komm* with me," he said.

Lovina forced herself to remain calm. This was Millie's first baby and she wasn't due for three weeks. It could be a false alarm.

"How often are her contractions?" Lovina asked.

"Every three to five minutes. I timed them, just like you showed me," he said.

"And how long are they lasting?"

"About sixty seconds."

Yes, it was time to go. Carrying the basket, Lovina walked briskly toward the house. Whether Millie was really in labor or not, Lovina would hurry to her side. She spoke over her shoulder as she hurried along. "I'll get my medical bag and be right with you. Jonah should be working out in the barn. Can you get him for me, please?"

Since she had to travel to the Troyers' farm by buggy, she shouldn't delay. During her husband's absence, Millie's contractions would have increased. Millie's mother was staying with her, so she wasn't alone, but the baby might be coming early. Lovina needed to get there and ensure everything was all right.

But what should she do with Autumn? If Millie's

baby really was coming, Lovina wanted Jonah to accompany her, just in case there were complications. He could tend to Millie while Lovina cared for the premature baby.

Autumn was doing great since her illness but Lovina hated to take her out into the cold air quite yet. Maybe *Dawdi* would be willing to keep an eye on her.

Inside the farmhouse, Lovina set the laundry basket on the kitchen table. Opening the fridge, she scanned the baby bottles she'd prepared earlier that morning and did a quick assessment. There was plenty of milk for Autumn to last through the day and night. Hopefully, she'd be back by morning to prepare some more. If not, *Dawdi* would be on his own to milk the goats and process the milk for the baby. It wouldn't be ideal but Lovina knew he could do it. She'd learned that *Dawdi* and Jonah did what had to be done without grumbling about it.

In the living room, she gathered up her medical bag, which she always kept packed and ready to go at a moment's notice. As she turned toward the kitchen, Jonah knocked, then entered the back door already dressed in his warm winter clothes. *Dawdi* Noah and David accompanied him.

"David says Millie's gone into labor and you wanted to see me," Jonah said.

Lovina set her bag on the table. "*Ja*, she's three weeks early. Can you accompany me? I want to ensure we provide the best care possible, in case there are difficulties."

"Of course. I've already harnessed the horse and

buggy and can leave the moment you're ready." Jonah dipped his head in acknowledgment.

"I can look after Autumn while you're gone," *Dawdi* offered.

Lovina stepped over to the older man and gripped his hand with affection as she gazed into his eyes. "I was hoping you'd offer. I don't want to take the *boppli* out so soon after her illness. There are plenty of bottles of milk already prepared in the fridge. She ate about an hour ago. I don't know how long I'll be. It could be a long birth. And if there are complications, I'll need to stay with Millie."

Dawdi straightened his sagging shoulders and nodded, no hesitation in his eyes. "I understand. I can do it. I know how to warm up a bottle for Autumn. I raised my own *kinder* and I've watched you do it often enough."

She smiled, her heart filled with love for this kind old man. "I have no doubt you know what to do. But if Millie's labor is long and keeps me away until tomorrow, you might have to milk the goats."

"Don't worry! It's no problem." The man looked perfectly serious and ready to accept this assignment.

It occurred to Lovina at that moment that *Dawdi* liked being included. And she didn't ask why. No matter how old a person got, they still liked to feel loved, wanted and needed.

"The *boppli* is down for a nap and should sleep another hour. I've got more diapers drying on the clothesline and some leftovers from a nice chicken-

and-dumpling casserole in my fridge. Help yourself," she said.

Dawdi smiled wide at that. "*Ach*, that's kind of you."

No doubt he was pleased with the prospect of not having to cook today.

"You're *willkomm, Dawdi* I really need your help right now, and I so appreciate your willingness to do this for me," she said.

"It's my pleasure."

"Let's go then!" An anxious-looking David opened the back door.

Jonah picked up Lovina's medical bag. She stepped outside and he took her elbow, as if he feared she might slip and fall. And though she was surprised by the gesture, she didn't shrug him off as he accompanied her to their buggy. David climbed into his own buggy and they followed him.

The journey took forty minutes. While Jonah put the horses in the barn, Lovina hurried into the house with David. Since she'd been here many times before, she went straight to the back bedroom. Millie sat up in the narrow bed, a plethora of pillows supporting her back. Her mother, Iris Miller, stood beside the bed, wringing out a wet cloth.

"Lovina! I'm so glad you're here," Millie cried, her face damp with sweat.

Lovina went right over to the young mother and squeezed her hand, giving her a warm smile of encouragement as she checked her pulse. "*Ja*, I'm here. How are you doing?"

"I'm okay but it's too early. I told David I couldn't be

in labor yet. It's just those early contractions you warned me about. Isn't it?" Her voice sounded rather breathless.

Opening her medical bag, Lovina took out her blood pressure cuff, fetal Doppler and stethoscope. "Let's find out."

After checking Millie's blood pressure, she waited for the young mother to have another contraction, then checked the fetal heart tones. A quick exam confirmed that the baby was in the right position to be born.

"*Ja*, you are definitely in labor. You are going to have a sweet little *boppli* in the coming hours," Lovina said.

Iris reached to hold her daughter's hand. "What can I do to help?"

Lovina patted the older woman's shoulder. "If you can continue to swab Millie's face and neck, I think that will provide her a great deal of comfort right now."

David stepped to the other side of the bed. A sweet feeling washed over Lovina as she watched him lean over and kiss his wife's forehead and whisper gentle words of encouragement to her.

At that moment, Jonah stepped into the room, carrying his own medical bag.

"Is there anything I can do?" he asked quietly.

His gaze rested on the loving couple but he hung back, as if he didn't want to intrude. After all, Millie was giving birth and he was somewhat of an outsider.

"Could you heat some hot water for me?" Lovina asked.

Iris frowned. "I'll do that."

Tossing Jonah a disapproving glance, the older

woman bustled past him and hurried into the kitchen. Obviously she didn't like him being here. Even though she knew he was an EMT, for some Amish, childbirth was a woman's art and not to involve a man.

Taking the hint, Jonah shrank back, speaking in a quiet tone. "I don't want to interfere. I'll wait out here. If you need anything at all, just holler."

Lovina nodded. This was her area of expertise, yet she still liked having him around. Especially if something went wrong.

She went to work laying out her instruments and preparing the room just as she liked it for a birth setting. Iris returned minutes later and Lovina kept her busy. Though he stayed out of the way, Jonah anticipated Lovina's every need. While she laid out extra under-pads and clean sheets, she asked him to set up the oxygen and accessories, then hang a plastic trash bag on the door handle. Though he wasn't a father, he knew what to do and she was impressed by his knowledge and sensitivity to the process.

David focused on his wife, seeing to her comfort, offering support through each contraction. And in between, he offered Millie a few crackers to eat and sips of water as Lovina directed. Millie panted through each painful spasm, the couple working together like a team. The tender way David massaged his wife's shoulders and back reminded Lovina there were still good men in the world.

Kind men like Jonah.

She assessed the baby's heartbeat every half hour. Everything proceeded like clockwork...until Millie felt like pushing. Then she gasped and spewed through the first agonizing contraction and the next. At this rate, Lovina realized Millie would become too exhausted to last.

"Let your body do the work and try to breathe gently through your nose. Don't let air escape your lips. Put that energy into pushing. That will make the process easier on your *boppli*," she encouraged.

Millie nodded obediently, then her face was torn by another painful grimace. As instructed, she kept her mouth closed, her face contorting with focused pain. Over the next few hours, the young mother labored to bring her child into the world. And though everything appeared to be proceeding as it should, Lovina became concerned. Millie's labor was not progressing. There was no movement. And that could take too great a toll on both Millie and her baby.

"I had all my *bopplin* fast," Iris kept saying. "I popped them right out."

Lovina let the woman talk, using it as a distraction for poor Millie. But she stepped over to the doorway and quietly gestured to Jonah.

He glanced into the room. He ducked his head as he listened to her quiet whispers.

"Millie's heart rate is strong but I'm concerned about the *boppli*. I'm seeing signs of distress in the fetal heart rate," she explained.

He nodded. "What would you like me to do?"

Because she'd already done her homework, Lovina knew the nearest telephone was only one mile down the road at the Watson farm. The Watsons were *Eng-*

lisch but they were good neighbors and knew Millie was expecting. If Jonah showed up on their doorstep, they had already said they would gladly let him use their phone to call an ambulance.

Darkness filled the top of the windowsill, telling Lovina it was late at night. No doubt the road was dark and slick by now. She hated to send him out before morning but they both would do what was necessary for the safety of Millie and her baby.

"I'm going to give it another twenty minutes, and if Millie's labor hasn't progressed by that time, I'll ask you to go to the Watsons' farm and call an ambulance," she said.

She didn't feel the need to explain. With his training, Jonah knew exactly what to expect and how to proceed. After all, they'd been in situations like this before and she knew she could depend on him.

He nodded. "I'll be ready the moment you give me the word."

She took a deep inhale and offered a silent prayer. But as she swiveled around to return to Millie's side, Jonah did something completely unexpected. He squeezed her hand.

"It'll be *allrecht*," he said.

She looked at him, feeding off his kind words. How did he always know exactly what she needed to hear? It was as if he knew her thoughts and feelings.

"Danke," she said.

As she worked with Millie to coax her baby into the light, Lovina took comfort in knowing *Gott* had a plan for each of them. She felt Him in that room, guiding her every move. Another fifteen minutes passed. Finally, in a mad rush, the baby slid into David's capable hands.

"It's a *maedel*," he crowed with delight, a grin as big as Kansas plastered across his face.

Both Millie and Iris laughed out loud. Then Millie wept tears of absolute joy.

"*Ach*, she's so beautiful," Lovina said.

She instructed David to deliver the squalling newborn to her mother's chest. Millie clutched her baby close and kissed the top of her daughter's head.

"She's lovely," she said.

"She has a *gut* pair of lungs, that's for sure," Lovina said.

Her pronouncement was meant to put the new parents at ease but was also an assessment of the baby's health. Since the little girl was born early, Lovina was watching for any signs of distress.

"There, there," Millie cooed, trying to calm her child.

Iris stood close by, admiring the little girl's fine features. "She looks just like Millie when she was born. Not a bit of hair on her head."

They all laughed, and Lovina took several minutes to appreciate the miracle of life. While she unobtrusively tended to Millie's needs, she let the *familye* talk and bask in the joy of new parenthood. And soon, the child calmed as she quietly nursed.

"Since it's Christmastime, we'll name her Mary in honor of the Christ child's *mudder*," David said.

Millie looked up at her husband with complete devotion and smiled with pleasure. "Mary. *Ach*, that's a fine name."

Lovina thought so, too. Looking up, she saw Jonah standing in the doorway, a soft smile curving his fine mouth. Their gazes met and held for several profound moments. And just then, Lovina basked in the soft glow of love filling the air. She also felt a sudden and deep sorrow in her heart.

She looked away. This was her work. It was Jonah's work, too. They were both trained to deal with situations like this. Lovina was glad to share the joy of a successful delivery with him, and yet a dark cloud hung over them. Because she was soon moving out of his farmhouse. They wouldn't be working together anymore. Especially when he sold his farm and moved far, far away. And that thought left her bereft.

"I hope Dawdi is doing okay with Autumn. Do you think the two of them are *allrecht*?"

Jonah jerked his head to the side and glanced at Lovina. She sat beside him in the buggy. They were headed home after a successful birth at the Troyers'. The soft glow of sunrise filtered over the Wet Mountains and glimmered off the surrounding snow-covered fields in a cascade of sparkling diamonds. Though they'd been up all night, he wasn't tired at all. Instead, he felt light and victorious. Like he could conquer anything in the world.

"*Ja*, I'm sure they're both fine," he said.

Spindly tree limbs, devoid of any leaves, outlined the county road. The cold December morning was crisp but clear. To fight off the chill, they'd bundled up beneath two warm quilts. Hunkered securely within the confines of the buggy, Jonah could see the frost of their exhales, yet it felt quite warm. The cheery sound of sleigh bells filled the air with each step of the trotting horse. *Dawdi* had put the bells on the harness several days earlier. The bells reminded Jonah that Christmas was just a few weeks away. This season marked the Savior's birth. A time of hope and joy. But Jonah had never cared for the holidays much. And yet he'd just shared an amazing experience with Lovina. The miracle of birth. Something he'd participated in a number of times before. But this time, it seemed more personal and real.

"You're awfully quiet this morning. What are you thinking about?" she asked.

"I… I was just pondering little Mary's birth and how appropriate it was for this time of year. It was a nice reminder as we prepare to celebrate the birth of Jesus Christ," he said.

Okay, maybe he shouldn't have said that, but he was feeling a bit sentimental today.

"You're so right. I'm glad everything worked out *allrecht*," Lovina said. "Little Mary is eating and breathing well on her own and seems perfectly healthy. Even though she was born three weeks early, she weighs a *gut* six pounds and two ounces."

"*Ja*, that's a sound enough weight for a newborn," he agreed with a laugh.

"I weighed just under five pounds when I was born," she said.

He quirked his eyebrows up. "Really? That's quite tiny."

"Uh-huh. My *mamm* said I came two weeks early. How much did you weigh?" she asked.

He shrugged, the question taking him off guard. "I have no idea. My *mudder* wasn't around to ask."

Lovina was quiet for a moment. "I'm sorry, Jonah."

"Don't be. It's not your fault. I just wish she'd stuck around. There's so much I want to ask her. So many things I'd like to learn. As it is, I still don't know what she was like or anything about her. I have no idea why she left. I don't even know who my father was."

"*Dawdi* doesn't know either?" she asked.

He gripped the lead lines tighter. "*Ne.* My *mudder* told him my *vadder* was *Englisch* and didn't want us. That's all she would say. But none of us know where she went. It haunts me, you know? Wondering about her. And more than anything, I hate the thought that Autumn might suffer the same fate."

Okay, he'd just confided too much. And yet Lovina was so easy to talk to. Right now, he felt as though he could tell her anything. But he mustn't. He'd been hurt enough and didn't want to open up his heart again.

"I'm sorry for your heartache," she said. "But you're a *gut* man, Jonah Lapp. You serve the Lord willingly. Your *dawdi* and *mammi* loved and raised you. You're a hard worker and have a nice farm. You're a member of our Amish faith and have so much to be grateful for. Your *dawdi* is so proud of you."

She was right, of course. Yet he still felt deficient

somehow. There was an emptiness inside him that couldn't be filled.

"My farm is too small," he said.

She shrugged. "Maybe so, but it is beautiful."

"You really think so?" he asked.

"*Ja*, I do. I've never been happier than while I've been living there."

Her words stunned him to the core. "But I can't grow enough feed for my own livestock. I have to work at the hospital to make ends meet," he said.

The confession was difficult for him. He'd never forget how disappointed Fannie had been when he'd told her. Though they'd been engaged to marry at the time, she'd gotten real quiet and wouldn't look at him. When he'd taken her home, she'd avoided his kiss good-night. Three days later, she'd broken off their engagement. She'd married Alvin a month after that. Alvin, whose *familye* owned the largest farm in the area, with plenty of money to go around.

"But you're making ends meet, right?" Lovina asked. "You've overcome the obstacles and made your place a great success. Besides, you're so talented that you have other options to earn a living. That's why you're an EMT. And you provide a great service to our community. Your farm is where you live but you're able to bring money in from other places, too. And anyway, you don't want to put all your eggs in one basket. It's best to have income from several different sources."

He stared at her, stunned to the tips of his toes. Her optimism was insightful. He'd never looked at it like that, but she was right. Instead of seeing the bad, he should focus on the good.

"And don't worry about Autumn," she continued. "We're going to ensure she grows up feeling loved and wanted. She's not alone. She'll always have us," she said.

Us. The word seemed so final. So united. But once the bishop took the baby and gave her to another *fami-lye*, she wouldn't have them anymore.

"I wanted to keep my *boppli*," Lovina said, her voice a broken whisper filled with longing. "My boyfriend was barely fifteen years old…way too young to support us. But after the birth, I was determined to keep my *sohn* anyway."

"Why didn't you?" Jonah asked.

She didn't look at him. "I was too young and it was a difficult birth. I was exhausted. If only I hadn't fallen asleep. My *vadder* took my child away in the middle of the night. And when I awoke and discovered what he'd done, I was beside myself. I tried to find my *sohn* without success. But to this day, I still mourn his loss. I have no idea if he's growing up feeling loved and wanted or sad and neglected. I can only have faith that *Gott* is watching over him. I have to put my trust in the Lord. And that's what you should do, too."

Jonah stared straight ahead. He was surprised and torn by her words. They were the last thing he'd expected to hear.

"I didn't realize you wanted to keep your *boppli*," he said.

"Of course I did! I would have raised him," she

cried. "He'd still be with me now. If only my *vadder* hadn't taken him away. But my *daed* was so angry. I was young and stupid, Jonah. Too young to realize the pain and trouble I caused with my actions. My *daed* said I'd brought shame to our entire *familye*. He took my little *bu* away and refused to tell me where he'd gone. Then my *vadder* left us, too."

Lovina's words made Jonah feel rotten inside. She'd been abandoned just like him. His heart gave a painful squeeze when he thought of the grief she must have suffered. The loss and humiliation she must have felt. Jonah's grandparents had never made him feel ashamed or unwanted. He could only imagine what Lovina had gone through at the hands of her disapproving father.

"Like a hypocrite, my *vadder* left our faith and joined the *Englisch* world and married some *Englisch* woman," Lovina said. "And the worst part about it was that my *mudder* could never remarry. You know the tenets of our faith. Even with a divorce, it's considered adultery to marry as long as your ex-spouse is still alive. I watched my poor *mudder* work herself into an early grave so she could provide for me."

He glanced at her. "Surely our *Gmay* helped her?"

"*Ja*, as much as they could. But she refused charity. I think she died of a broken heart."

Lovina buried her face in her hands, her shoulders trembling with silent tears. Jonah hesitated. Then he reached out and rested a hand on her arm, trying to comfort her.

"You've suffered so much, Lovina. More than I ever

knew. And I… I've judged you unfairly. I'm so very sorry," he said.

She sniffled and lifted her head. Her nose and eyes were red "It's okay, I've learned to live with it. I've moved on and tried to make the best of what *Gott* has given me. I don't usually cry about it but I'm overly tired today, so my guard is down."

"Have you really gotten over it? Losing your little *bu*, I mean?" he asked.

She glanced his way and he saw the trickle of tears as they ran down her cheeks. She shook her head. "*Ne*, I don't think I'll ever get over losing my *boppli*."

Ah, how he hated to see her cry. She'd been victimized by her father. It wasn't her fault. She'd wanted to do what she thought was right. To make things good and raise her baby on her own. But her dad wouldn't let her. And knowing this filled Jonah with the desire to protect Lovina and always keep her safe. He knew he could change the future for them both. The two of them didn't have to be sad and lonely anymore. They didn't have to let the bishop take Autumn away. Not when he could do something about it.

"We need to talk," Jonah said.

In a spontaneous act, he pulled the horse and buggy over to the side of the road. The sun was burning the frost off the asphalt. No doubt *Dawdi* was weary after caring for Autumn all night long. Jonah needed to get home and take care of his farm chores so *Dawdi* wouldn't feel obligated to do them. But first…

"What are you doing?" Lovina asked as she wiped her eyes.

He faced her, reaching to gently clasp her upper arms. She met his gaze without flinching, her lips parted slightly, her eyes tired and damp from tears.

"Marry me, Lovina. Marry me and we'll adopt Autumn as our very own. We can make a *familye* together, you and me. All you have to do is say yes," he said.

Her eyes widened and she stared at him like he'd just sprouted a second nose. She chewed her bottom lip and didn't say anything for several pounding moments.

"I'll admit I don't want to lose Autumn. But if I ever marry, it will be for love or not at all. And you don't love me, Jonah," she said.

Her voice sounded small and wounded. And oh, how he wanted to tell her what she so desperately wanted to hear. What they both needed was someone to love them. But she was right. He didn't love her.

Or did he?

Oh, he didn't know anymore. He cared for her. A great deal. He knew that without hesitation. But love? He thought he'd loved Fannie and look how that turned out. Now he realized he'd been more in love with the idea of marriage and having a *familye* of his own. He'd never really loved Fannie. Not for herself. In fact, the woman now grated on his nerves every time she was near. He wasn't a good judge of what love was. How could he ever know for sure that he loved Lovina? Really loved her, the way a man should love a woman. He didn't think he could know for sure.

So where did that leave them now? Here he sat with Lovina, and he couldn't say the words out loud to her.

He wanted to but didn't dare. Because he would never lie to her.

She pulled free of his grasp. "Please, Jonah, no more talk. Just take me *heemet* now."

She faced forward, her lips and shoulders tight, her little chin hard as granite.

He took hold of the lead lines and did as she asked. When they pulled down the lane to his farm, the only sounds were the buggy wheels churning over the graveled driveway and the horse's low nicker of relief. Finally they were home. And yet neither of them belonged here. They were both alone in the world, and it appeared they always would be.

Lovina didn't wait for his aid. Without a word, she tossed aside the heavy quilts, threw open the buggy door and hopped out, dragging her medical bag with her. He sat there and watched as she disappeared inside the farmhouse. Soon *Dawdi* came out, his shoulders bent with fatigue as he limped on his cane toward the *dawdi haus*. The old man saw him and waved but kept on going. And still, Jonah sat there for some time, his heart just as frozen as the winter breeze blowing down from the mountains.

Chapter Twelve

The week before Christmas, Lovina sat at her kitchen table, filling out paperwork for her midwifery business. By law, she had ten days after baby Mary's birth to file her birth certificate with the state of Colorado. Lovina had met that deadline but needed to catch up on her bookkeeping. Each invoice for her services was hand-written and mailed or hand-delivered to her clients, who always paid in a timely fashion. It was painstaking work, but each envelope was a fulfilling reminder that she had a livelihood and could sustain herself.

A pot of ham-and-bean soup bubbled on the stove, filling the kitchen with a scrumptious aroma. Little Autumn sat in her bassinet on the table, wide-awake and kicking her legs like there was no tomorrow. It was late afternoon and she'd just had a bottle. With her tummy full, she was filled with energy and joy. Her little coos were a sweet distraction that Lovina couldn't resist and she set her pen down.

"You're happy today, aren't you, *liebchen*?" She rested her hand on the tiny girl's chest.

The baby smiled and chortled in response, completely melting Lovina's heart into a puddle.

She thought about the night not so long ago when Millie Troyer had given birth to little Mary. It had been a special time for all of them. Not only had Lovina participated in the miracle of birth but she'd received her first and only marriage proposal. She'd never forget the hurt in Jonah's eyes when she'd refused him. Oh, she'd been tempted, make no mistake about it. For just a moment, she'd allowed herself to believe he could love her the way she loved him. But then she'd shaken herself.

More than anything, she longed to experience the joys of being Jonah's wife and a mother to his children. But at what cost? She wouldn't accept his offer when he didn't love her. She'd had enough heartache in her life. Too much, in fact. She could never live in a loveless marriage. And Jonah couldn't love her. So she must leave. As soon as possible.

The rattle of a buggy drew her attention. Keeping an eye on the wriggling baby through the doorway, she stepped into the living room and peered out the window. Thin white candles surrounded by a green bed of pine boughs glimmered on the windowsill. It was the only Christmas decoration she ever put out. Not overly ostentatious but part of nature. Simple yet elegant. A reminder that Jesus Christ was the light of the world.

Bishop Yoder parked in front of the barn and stepped out to greet Jonah in the yard. It had rained heavily in the night, melting the remaining snow on the ground and leaving wide mud puddles along the lane. Frozen pools of ice lined the driveway, and she figured Jonah would be forced to break through the animal's water troughs so they could drink.

The two men turned her way, and she snapped back from the window. She didn't want to be caught spying on them. Through the filmy curtains, she saw them heading toward the house.

Her heart thudded. Maybe the bishop had some word about Autumn's mother. Maybe he'd come to take the girl away!

Hurrying to the kitchen, Lovina picked up the baby and walked to the back door. She opened it wide as she greeted the two men.

"*Guder mariye*, bishop! *Komm* in. What brings you out to our place?" she asked.

Our place. She'd said the words before she thought better of it. Because this was Jonah's place. Not hers.

She tried to appear casual but inside, her heart was pounding and her mind was screaming. *No! Please don't take my baby from me. Not again.*

Both men doffed their black felt hats and wiped their damp boots on the rug. Lovina's gaze briefly locked with Jonah's. For a moment, she saw her fears mirrored in his eyes. Then he looked away.

"I've got some news for the two of you," Bishop Yoder said.

From his sober expression, she didn't think it was good. Lovina forced herself to remain calm.

Lifting one hand, she gestured toward the living

room. "*Komm* in and sit down. Can I get you something to eat or drink?"

"*Ne*, I can't stay. I've been gone from my farm all day. I just wanted you and Jonah to know what has happened." He headed into the living room and plopped down on the sofa, holding his hat in one hand.

Jonah stood in front of the coffee table, his legs slightly spread in that commanding stance of his, as if he was self-assured and in control. He folded his hands behind his back and waited quietly. Though he appeared completely calm, an energy pulsed from him... an anxiousness she felt. And in his eyes, she saw a flicker of uncertainty.

"Yesterday, I received a letter from the bishop in Westcliffe," Bishop Yoder began.

Westcliffe was a neighboring town fifty miles away. Like Riverton, it had a population of around five thousand people with a small Amish community.

"His congregation has a teenage runaway girl who reportedly gave birth about three months ago. She's joined the *Englisch* world," he continued.

"Is she a minor?" Lovina asked.

"*Ne*, she is eighteen and a legal adult, though she was never baptized into our faith. Her name is Beth Gascho and her *mudder* died about a year ago. Beth had been living with her *vadder* and four elder brothers, but I'm afraid they've had a falling-out. It seems her *vadder* disapproves of her."

Lovina's hands tightened around Autumn. Even though the Amish believed in repentance and forgiveness, she'd been treated the same by her own father.

People weren't always perfect and frequently hypocritical. Because of her own experience, she had instant compassion for Beth.

"Apparently Beth ran away a year ago during her *rumspringa* and took up with an *Englisch* boy," the bishop said.

Rumspringa, that rite of passage during adolescence when Amish teenagers experience freedom of choice without the rules of the *Ordnung* to hold them back.

"Beth's *vadder* didn't know until recently that his *dochder* had given birth out of wedlock. I've spoken to him and found him to be rather unforgiving. He wants nothing to do with Beth or her *boppli*," the bishop said.

The room suddenly whirled around Lovina. She reached to clasp the armrest of a chair and slid into the seat so she wouldn't fall over and drop Autumn.

"Lovina, are you *allrecht*?" Jonah was instantly by her side, leaning down to take the baby from her trembling hands. His look of concern only made matters worse.

"*Ja*, I'm fine." Her voice sounded hoarse as she averted her gaze from his caring face. But she wasn't fine. Not at all. It felt like she was reliving her own childhood trauma all over again, right alongside Beth.

"Beth is now living in Pueblo," the bishop said.

Pueblo was yet another neighboring town that was no more than sixty miles away but it had a much larger population of over one hundred thousand people. It would be easy for an Amish girl to get lost there.

"Wh-what is she doing in Pueblo? How is she living?" Lovina asked.

"She's waitressing at a restaurant and lives with another *Englisch* girl in a rather dowdy apartment," the bishop said. "Early this morning, I hired a driver to take me there. I first visited Beth's *vadder* and then I went and found her. I have only just returned from my journey."

The bishop had gone and met Beth!

"Do you think she is Autumn's *mudder*?" Jonah asked.

The bishop nodded. "I have no doubt. Before I revealed any information, she confirmed Autumn's name and birthdate and all the details of how you found the *boppli*. Beth wasn't happy I'd found her. She still has no idea where the *boppli*'s *vadder* is and believes he has left the state. Apparently she hasn't spoken with him in nine months, since she first told him she was expecting his child. I asked her to return here to Riverton with me and even offered a roof over her head until she can figure out how to support herself and her *boppli*."

"And what did she say?" Lovina prompted, her voice wobbly.

"She flatly refused."

The bishop's face looked severe. Lovina figured the encounter must have been highly unpleasant for him, especially since he'd offered to help the young woman.

"Beth insists she doesn't want to be a *mudder* or Amish anymore. But she did agree to one thing," he said.

"And what is that?" Jonah asked.

The bishop's gaze rested on Lovina like a leaden weight. "She has agreed to sign her parental rights over to Lovina in a formal adoption."

Lovina gasped. "Me! But why would she do that?"

Bishop Yoder lifted one shoulder. "It seems your reputation as a kind and caring midwife has filtered through the Amish community to Westcliffe. Beth thought by giving her *boppli* to you, she was providing Autumn with a *gut* home. I agree, except for one problem."

Lovina held perfectly still and waited. She didn't dare move. Didn't dare breathe.

"I will never agree to let Autumn remain with you permanently as long as you remain unmarried. The tenets of our faith dictate that a *boppli* deserves both a loving *vadder* and *mudder* to raise them. You are unmarried," he said.

A horrible, swelling silence followed. So loud that Lovina thought her ears might burst. She understood only too well. If she were *Englisch*, she could adopt Autumn and think nothing of it. But she was Amish and they lived by a different set of rules. And though she loved her faith and saw the benefit of raising a child with both parents, she couldn't help wishing her situation could be different. But she would never go against the doctrines of her faith.

Jonah opened his mouth and took a step forward but Lovina held out a hand, cutting him off. She knew what he was going to say. He would offer again to marry her. To sacrifice himself on the altar of matrimony in order to keep Autumn safe. But Lovina couldn't do that. Not even if it meant she could keep this precious baby girl as her own.

"I understand what it's like to give birth out of wedlock," she said. "I know how it feels to have a heartless *vadder* who won't help you. Perhaps if I spoke with Beth, I might be able to convince her to *komm* here. Once I move to my new *heemet*, she and Autumn can live with me."

The bishop leaned forward, his eyes filled with warmth as a kind smile tugged the corners of his mouth upward. "My dear, I thought you would offer that, so I posed the idea to Beth and still she refused. If she had agreed, I would let you do that. But I fear your generous efforts are wasted. You see, Beth was furious I'd found her. She has such an ugly spirit of resentment about her. She hates our faith and refuses to live it again. I don't want you to become the brunt of her anger. Not with your kind heart."

Oh, dear. That didn't sound good.

"At Beth's request, I paid a visit to Carl Nelson right before I came here to see you," Bishop Yoder said.

Jonah tilted his head to one side, his eyebrows pulled down in a quizzical frown. "You mean the attorney in town?"

The bishop nodded. "*Ja*, a few of our Amish people have used his legal services in the past. He is friendly to us Amish, and I believe he is trustworthy."

Lovina's mind swam with confusion. "But what does he have to do with Autumn?"

"I asked his legal advice, and he has agreed to help us with an adoption for Autumn," he said. "I know of a loving Amish couple whom I believe would cherish and raise her as their own. The *boppli* would want for nothing and would grow up Amish and learn to love the Lord."

Yes, that was what they all wanted for Autumn.

Looking down at her lap, Lovina folded her shaking hands. She swallowed hard, knowing she could not prevent the inevitable. The bishop would take the baby from them and give her to another *familye* to raise.

"It sounds like you've got everything worked out nice and tidy," Jonah said.

Lovina glanced up. Had she detected a trembly note of anguish in his voice? She wasn't sure because he turned away and dipped his face down to the baby before Lovina could see his expression. But she didn't need to. Just the fact that he was snuggling Autumn and holding her tight told Lovina all she needed to know. He didn't want to let go of this baby any more than she did.

"When the time comes, we know what to do," Bishop Yoder said. "But I need to make a few more inquiries first. I'm now working with the attorney to have Beth sign over her parental rights."

"But what about the *vadder*? What if the man returns and tries to take Autumn?" Jonah asked.

"Since Beth doesn't know how to find the man, Carl said the adoption must be published in the local newspaper," the bishop said. "It will take some patience but the attorney knows what to do legally. In the meantime, I would ask that you keep Autumn here a while longer, until I can put everything in order."

"Of course, as long as it takes," Lovina spoke without hesitation.

Anything to delay Autumn's departure. But Lovina knew it was a stay of execution. Eventually, the bishop would take the baby away.

The bishop stood. "*Gut*! I'll let you know as soon as everything is settled."

"But one more thing," Lovina said.

The two men looked at her with expectation.

"I… I'll be moving soon," she said. "Jonah is selling his farm, and I've been making inquiries for new living arrangements. I've found a small house in town that I can rent for a reasonable price and run my midwifery business from there."

The bishop frowned. So did Jonah.

"You found another place already?" Jonah said, his voice low and nervous.

"*Ja*. It needs heavy cleaning and a lot of paint but the rent is quite low," she said.

"I'm sorry to hear you're moving again," Bishop Yoder said. "I knew Jonah was planning to sell but hoped the present situation might have changed his mind."

The bishop looked at Jonah as he spoke. Jonah didn't say a word, and a heavy silence filled the room. The older man's gray eyes seemed to pierce a hole right through Jonah's head. But it made no difference. Not for Lovina. Jonah could take his farm off the market and stay here forever, but she must go. The sooner, the better. Because she loved him. Heaven help her, she truly loved him beyond anything she could comprehend. And staying here would only bring her more pain.

Living so near to him. Seeing him every day. Working with him. She couldn't do it anymore.

"But there is still time. Perhaps you'll both change your minds," the bishop said as he walked to the front door and left without another word.

Lovina didn't think so.

She stared out the living room window, waiting until his buggy pulled away from the farm. She longed to call him back. To tell him she would accept Jonah's offer just so they could keep Autumn. But she couldn't do that. And nothing would change her mind.

"Lovina, I know you're upset," Jonah said.

He stood beside her in the living room as they both stared out the wide picture window and watched the bishop's buggy fade from view. Although Jonah had expected this news, it wasn't what he'd wanted to hear. He was still holding Autumn. As if sensing the morose mood in the room, the baby began to fuss and wriggle in his arms.

Lovina turned and took the baby from him, then walked into the kitchen, where she retrieved a bottle for the little girl. Jonah followed, his ears echoing with all the things the bishop had told them. There was so much Jonah longed to say to Lovina but he didn't dare. She'd only reject him again.

"It's all settled," Lovina said. "Soon, the bishop will return to take Autumn to her new *familye*. There will be a formal adoption, which will make things nice and legal. We don't want Beth or the *Englisch vadder* to show up years later and try to take Autumn after she's bonded with her new *familye*."

"*Ne*, we don't want that," he said.

"And I'll be moving soon. You'll sell your farm and go back east. Everyone can return to the lives they've chosen."

Jonah blinked, her words striking him as hard as a fist to the gut. But she was right. How they lived was a choice they each made. They could choose the path they wanted to take. And right now, he didn't want to lose Autumn. He didn't want to lose Lovina, either.

She sniffed and he realized she was crying. Standing at the stove, she had her back to him. The baby had become very quiet, peering over Lovina's shoulder at him with her big blue eyes. It was as if she were telling him to do something about this. Right now!

Letting his heart guide him, Jonah stepped over to Lovina. He gripped her arms gently and turned her around. She hung her head, staring at the floor as she wiped her eyes. The baby waved her arms and grabbed a handful of Jonah's hair, pulling him closer. He placed one finger beneath Lovina's chin and lifted her face so she was forced to meet his gaze. Her eyes swam with tears and were filled with so much hurt and betrayal that all he wanted was to see her smile again.

"Please don't cry, Lovina. It's all going to be okay," he whispered, drawing nearer.

Before he realized what was happening, he kissed her. Or she kissed him. He wasn't sure which. He only knew how it made him feel. Happy, wild and free. The kiss was so gentle, like a soft caress. And for that moment in time, emotion overwhelmed Jonah. Surely there was no better place on earth than right here in his kitchen. Lovina's kitchen. Their home. This was where he wanted to be.

Wasn't it?

Lovina exhaled a little sigh and he felt her warm breath against his face. The baby rested her hand against his cheek, as if showing her approval. For several profound moments, the three of them stood there in a close huddle. Then Lovina drew her face away, and he realized he had enfolded her and the baby in his arms.

"Jonah, don't." Lovina pressed one hand against his chest, pushing him away.

He stepped back, his mind scattering. What had he done?

"Marry me, Lovina. We will do well together. It's the only way," he whispered low.

"*Ne*, I will not," she said.

She moved over to the fridge, as if she were desperate to put some distance between them. Autumn immediately began to cry.

Jonah's gaze followed them as Lovina prepared a bottle for the baby.

"I care for you. I do," he said.

Lovina stared at him, her eyes filled with outrage. "You care for me?"

He nodded, his mouth dry as chalk. "I do. Very much."

She snorted. "*Ach*, we each care for lots of people, Jonah. That doesn't mean we want to marry them. Marriage is for keeps. It means living together, sharing the *gut* and the bad forever. Caring isn't enough. Not for me."

She turned her back on him. As usual, he'd said the wrong thing at the wrong time. But how could he make her understand? They had to be together. They must!

"You know our church elders will never agree to let you keep Autumn without us being wed. The bishop made that clear today," he said.

"I will not marry you and that's final," she said. She turned and met his gaze, a somber, resolute expression on her face. "Instead, why don't you sell the farm to me?"

He tilted his head to one side, thinking he must have heard her wrong. "What?"

"You want to leave and I need a place to live. I have a little money saved and a *gut* income from my business. What is your asking price? Perhaps I can qualify for a loan and buy the place," she said, her voice firm.

His mouth dropped open in surprise. She wanted to buy his farm? She must be teasing. But as he stared at her unwavering expression, he realized she was dead serious.

As if through a fog, he named his price. The very amount he'd given to the real estate agent in town. It wasn't high. Just enough to pay off what he owed and move him and *Dawdi* back east where they could start anew.

Lovina frowned and reached for the bottle, giving it to the baby. Autumn latched on and sucked furiously, as though she didn't like this conversation any more than Jonah did.

"I'm afraid I can't afford that much. Would you be

willing to sell me just the farmhouse?" Lovina asked without looking at him.

He leaned against the wall and looped his thumbs through his suspenders. "*Ne*, I'm afraid the house would have to go with the farm. Otherwise, I would never be able to sell the acreage. And without a house, *Dawdi* and I would have no place to live if we can't sell and are forced to stay and work the land."

Her shoulders sagged in resignation. It seemed they were at a deadlock.

"Then I will move to town as I planned. I... I have things to do. If you don't mind, I need to get back to work," she said.

Okay, he could take a hint. She was bluntly inviting him to leave.

Nodding, he turned toward the door. He rested his hand on the knob, his mind churning with what he should say. But nothing came to mind. His hand trembled. He couldn't leave but he couldn't stay.

As he stepped outside, a blast of frigid wind struck him in the face. He knew what was at stake. Soon, Autumn would be taken away. Lovina would go live somewhere else. Jonah would eventually sell his farm and move back east with *Dawdi*. They would never see each other again and that thought crushed Jonah's heart like nothing he'd experienced before. Now that he was really faced with losing Lovina for good, a flash of insight speared his icy heart. With perfect clarity, he realized how deeply he loved her and he knew he couldn't let this happen.

Finally. Finally, he understood what his own mother

must have felt when she'd abandoned him years earlier. The fear and uncertainty must have caused her to run away and seek another life. Anger, hurt, shame and dissatisfaction with herself must have caused her to run. She'd made some bad choices but was too young and inexperienced to see how to make it right. And knowing this, Jonah was finally able to let go of his anger at her. Now that he understood her motives, he could forgive her.

But now he had a new dilemma.

How could he convince Lovina that he loved her and wanted to be with her forever? If he told her now, she would laugh in his face. She would think he was saying what she wanted to hear just so they could keep Autumn. It was too late to make this right between them. Or was it?

Chapter Thirteen

The very next day, Jonah drove one of his big Percheron draft horses into his spacious driveway and headed for the barn. Though it was bitter cold outside, he'd taken advantage of the clear weather to clean out the stalls and haul the manure out to his fields. The ground was frozen but he'd spread the fertilizer across the barren land, knowing it would benefit the summer crops.

Stepping to the back of the horse, he unhitched the wagon. The afternoon sun glinted off the metal roof of the shed, and he lifted an arm to shield his eyes as he glanced at the farmhouse. Christmas was just a few days away, yet his heart felt heavy as he considered paying a visit to Lovina. He'd made a final decision that would impact his life forever and had gone into town earlier that morning. There was no going back. Now they needed to talk.

Gripping the halter on the Percheron, he led the gentle giant into the barn. He'd tossed the animal some hay and rubbed him down when *Dawdi* burst into the stall.

"Jonah! I'm so glad you're back."

He turned as *Dawdi* hobbled toward him on his cane. The old man was dressed in his warm winter coat and black boots. He sounded breathless and anxious, his bushy eyebrows drawn together in an urgent frown.

"What is it? What's wrong?" Jonah asked.

"It's Lovina. Just after lunch, she packed a bunch of boxes into her buggy and drove into town. She took Autumn with her. She's gone," *Dawdi* said.

Boxes! Was she moving already? She'd told the bishop she'd be leaving soon but Jonah thought he had more time. But no. She'd left!

A flash of panic blazed through his chest. He'd spent the last twenty hours trying to figure out how to convince her that he loved her and wanted to marry her. But now he was out of time. She was gone!

"Here!" Jonah handed a small bucket of oats to his grandfather, knowing the older man would feed it to the Percheron.

Scrambling out of the stall, Jonah hurried over to his road horse, Bob. Without a glance at his grandfather, he tossed a blanket and then an old dusty saddle onto the animal's back.

"I've got to go after her. Can you take care of things here for a while?" he asked.

Standing nearby, *Dawdi* took hold of the halter to steady the horse. "Of course. I've got this. You go bring them *heemet.* And don't take *ne* for an answer this time."

Jonah had told his grandfather how Lovina had refused his proposal. He paused a moment as he looked at the older man. *Dawdi* nodded and smiled. It was the only reassurance Jonah needed.

In a single bound, he swung up onto Bob's back and kicked his heels. The Amish rarely rode horses. The animal wasn't used to this and danced around nervously for several seconds, then sprang out the barn doors like a racehorse breaking from the starting gate.

As he sped away, Jonah leaned low over Bob's neck and held on tight. Needles of cold lashed his face but he barely felt it. One thought pounded his brain. He had to find Lovina. He had to see her, speak to her and convince her he loved her. He must bring her back home. Now that he was faced with losing her for good, everything became so clear in his heart and mind. He loved her. More than anything else on earth. He couldn't lose her or Autumn. Not now, when he'd finally realized what they meant to him. His future happiness depended on his success.

For several minutes, he clung to the horse, with only the sounds of the winter breeze and thudding hooves striking the road. Finally, he saw the outskirts of town. Only then did he realize he had no idea where to go. Lovina hadn't told him where she was moving. But surely it wouldn't be difficult to find an Amish buggy in this small town. He'd scour every street searching for her. And if that failed, he'd pay an urgent visit to the real estate agent. Jonah would beg for her address. He'd find her. Whatever it took…

There she was! Parked on the main street, right in front of the general store. She stood beside her buggy, reaching inside to lift a heavy box out of the back. She set it on the boardwalk.

He pulled Bob to a skidding stop. As he jumped out of the saddle, Lovina whirled around in surprise.

"Jonah! What are you doing here?" she cried, her eyes wide, her cheeks flushed.

"Lovina, I had to find you," he said, looping the reins around a post that supported the covered portico overhead.

"Why? What's happened?"

He scanned the area, then peered inside the buggy. "Where's Autumn?"

Lovina jerked a thumb toward the store. "She's inside with Mrs. Maupin. Why?"

Berta Maupin owned the grocery store. She was a kind, elderly woman who'd always treated the Amish well.

"*Gut*! We need to talk," he said.

Lovina snorted. "*Ne*! The time for talking is over. I've got work to do."

As she reached to take another box out of the buggy, Jonah stepped in front of her, impeding her progress.

She sighed. "Jonah, please…"

"I love you, Lovina. I do!"

"Don't say things you don't mean."

"I do mean it. With every beat of my heart. When I got *heemet* and *Dawdi* told me you'd left, I… I couldn't stand to lose you. I raced after you. I've got to bring you back, Lovina. Please, listen to me," he said.

She stared at him with disbelief. A car zipped past on the street and their horses shifted restlessly.

Lovina shook her head. "It's not going to work and we both know it. You're selling your farm."

He saw the hurt in her eyes as she turned away.

"I'm not selling the farm."

She whirled around. "What do you mean?"

"I rode into town first thing this morning and visited my real estate agent. I took my farm off the market. I'm not selling it after all. I'm staying right here, in Riverton."

She blinked those beautiful blue eyes at him, her lips parted slightly. "You're not selling? You're staying?"

He nodded, letting it sink in. Then he reached out and pulled her toward him. He expected her to jerk free but she didn't fight him. Not one bit.

"But why? I... I thought you wanted to leave?" she said, her voice a breathy whisper.

"That was before I fell in love with you," he said. "I spent a restless night trying to figure out how to convince you that I love you and want to make a *familye* with you for real. And I realized it might take me a long time, but I'd do whatever it took to make you trust me."

Her eyes narrowed suspiciously. "You couldn't change your mind that fast. Why should I believe you?"

"Because it's true. When *Dawdi* told me you were moving today, I was panic-stricken with the thought of never seeing you again. I can't lose you, Lovina. I love you."

She took a step closer. "But I'm not moving today."

He squinted in confusion and gestured toward the boxes. "Then what's all this?"

She gave a low laugh, the sound soft and sweet to

his ears. "It's the annual food drive. For a month now, the women in our *Gmay* have been bringing canned goods to me. Most of them pay regular visits anyway for their *boppli* needs, so I was assigned to bring it all into town. Mrs. Maupin is the chair of the food drive and will see that it gets delivered to people in need throughout the community."

Ah, now he understood all the boxes. She wasn't moving after all. At least not today.

Before he could stop it from happening, a smile of relief spread across his face. Though the Amish took care of one another, they also frequently participated in works of service with their *Englisch* neighbors. Lovina wasn't moving. Yet. But that could soon change. Unless he convinced her otherwise.

"I can't tell you how happy that makes me," he said.

She heaved a disgruntled sigh. "I don't understand, Jonah. Sometimes you make me so crazy."

He laughed. He couldn't help himself. Because she made him crazy. Crazy in love.

"I've been confused, too. But right now, I've never been filled with more clarity. I know we both could go on and live our lives without romantic entanglements. We'd have a perfectly safe and very lonely existence, Lovina. But we'd also never know the joy of love we could have together. And that isn't what *Gott* wants for us. I don't want to go through life without you. I can only hope and pray that, one day, you can love me as much as I love you. Please say you'll marry me and make me the happiest man in the world."

As he waited for her answer, his breath was shallow

in his chest. He couldn't say another word. He'd done what he'd vowed he would never do again and laid his heart bare, giving her the power to shatter it into a thousand tiny pieces once more. Now it was in her hands.

Lovina stood in front of Jonah, gazing at his earnest face. She couldn't believe what he said. After all they'd been through, how could she trust him now? He loved her? Unthinkable. Something she'd only dreamed of. And yet he'd said it several times.

"*Ach*, Jonah! Your timing is terrible. But in my heart, I so want to believe you," she said.

Oh, dear. Maybe she shouldn't have said that. But if he really meant what he said and could gather the courage to say it out loud, then so could she.

He stepped closer, the tips of his scuffed boots touching the toes of her clean, practical shoes. She gazed up into his smiling face, lost in the translucent depths of his eyes.

"Believe me, Lovina. You know I wouldn't say it if it wasn't true."

Oh, she couldn't fight him anymore. Not now when he was saying what she'd wanted to hear for so long.

"Oh, Jonah!"

He took her hands into his and she didn't resist. Their noses touched and she thought he might kiss her. She even hungered for it.

"Ahum!"

Someone cleared their throat behind her and she snapped back.

"Bishop Yoder!" she exclaimed.

Yes, the bishop stood right beside her on the boardwalk. The heat of mortification burned her cheeks. She had no idea how much of their conversation he'd overheard. Out here on the open street, for all the world to see. What must he think of them?

"Wh-what are you doing here?" she asked before she could stop herself. She didn't want to sound rude. Not to this kind man.

"I was looking for you two," he said.

Bundled in his warm winter attire, he smiled broadly. "I was just out at your farm, and Noah told me you were here."

Lovina stepped away from Jonah but he didn't release her hand. And that touched her heart like nothing else could. It was a blatant, physical declaration that she belonged to him. That they were a couple and he wanted everyone to know.

"What did you want to see us about?" Jonah asked.

The bishop stepped down into the street, standing close. "I overheard Jonah's proposal and I feel I must intercede. I have news for both of you. It seems the elderly *Englisch* farmer who owns the land bordering Jonah's property died two days ago."

"He did?" Jonah said.

"*Ja*, and his *kinder* don't want his farm. Instead, they want to sell it off as soon as possible. It would give Jonah thirty more acres of land, which is plenty to make his farm prosper."

Jonah's mouth dropped open, and he gaped at the bishop. A zing of happiness ripped through Lovina's heart. She knew this was what he wanted. And it looked like he would get it.

"That's great news!" Jonah said.

"*Gut*! Because I told them you wanted the property. Our *Gmay* will ensure you have the funds to buy it immediately," Bishop Yoder said.

"I have some money saved and would love to invest it in our farm. Together, we can afford to buy the extra land," Lovina said.

Jonah blinked at her. "Our farm? Together? You mean...you'll marry me?"

She smiled, her heart overflowing with joy. "How can I not when you're the love of my life?"

"Oh, Lovina. That's more than I ever dared hope for. Now it will truly be our *heemet*."

"*Ja*, it will." She gazed at him with elation.

The bishop chuckled. "There's just one more thing you two ought to know. That couple I've had in mind to adopt little Autumn..."

"*Ja?*" Jonah urged.

"It's you two," the bishop said. "I always knew you'd come around eventually, though you took your sweet time realizing how much you love each other. But I'm glad to hear you've finally arrived at the decision to wed." He looked between the two of them. "You are getting married, right?"

Jonah gazed adoringly into Lovina's eyes...the way so many of her expectant fathers looked at their wives. Lovina searched Jonah's face for any doubts, any reservations at all, but saw nothing but hope and love.

"You will marry me, won't you, Lovina?" he asked softly, enticingly.

She nodded her head, no longer willing to fight against the feelings in her heart. "*Ach*, of course I will. Because you see, Jonah, I love you, too. So very much!"

With a loud whoop, Jonah pulled her into his arms and whirled her around until she was dizzy. He kissed her right there on Main Street, in front of the bishop and anyone who chose to look. And when he finally set her on her feet, they all laughed.

The bishop cleared his throat. "Um, I think I'd better go now. I'll talk with you again on Christmas Day and you can be married soon after. But I believe Autumn has found her permanent *familye*. She belongs with the two of you. I'm glad to say I won't have to search for another *familye* to take her after all."

He turned and walked away, the heels of his boots thudding against the planks of the boardwalk lining the street. Watching him go, Lovina couldn't believe their good fortune. It had come so unexpectedly. So magnificently. Love and *familye*. The best Christmas gifts of all.

"As the bishop suggested, I'd like to get married right after Christmas," Jonah said.

His arm was still firmly around her back, holding her tight against his side. She nodded, feeling suddenly shy with this newfound closeness between them.

"*Ja*, I'll marry you. Just as soon as we can."

He kissed her once more, then let her go and turned toward the buggy. "*Gut*! I'm going to get the rest of these boxes out and then we're going to retrieve our *boppli* from Mrs. Maupin and go *heemet*. We have a lot of plans to make."

Lovina smiled, more than pleased by his words. After all, she'd just gotten the desire of her heart. A loving husband and sweet baby daughter. What more could she ask for?

Epilogue

One year later

Lovina stepped out of the county courthouse in Cañon City, Colorado, and glanced up at the gray sky. Another snowstorm was coming in tonight but she had no doubt they'd be safely home before then.

Tugging the warm blankets tightly around Autumn, she noticed someone had spread pellets of ice melt across the slick sidewalk. She was extra careful as she carried the little girl toward the parking lot. Autumn was over a year old now and toddling all around the place, getting into everything. But Lovina didn't mind one bit.

It was the week before Christmas and they had so much to celebrate. It seemed the year had flown by. So much had happened in the past twelve months that she could hardly contain her excitement.

An *Englisch* driver waited for them in his parked car. Lovina held back, giving Jonah time to join her. She didn't have long to wait. He emerged from the tall double doors, accompanied by *Dawdi* Noah, Bishop Yoder and Carl Nelson, their attorney from Riverton. Lovina watched as the four men talked together for several minutes. She didn't mind, knowing they were finalizing the adoption. She cherished the few moments she had alone with Autumn.

The baby held out a chubby hand and waved at the drifting snowflakes that were starting to fall. Lovina smiled and snuggled the girl close.

"You like snow, don't you, *liebchen*?" Lovina said.

Autumn babbled incoherently in response, her sweet voice filling Lovina's heart with so much happiness that she thought it might burst. The baby looked so cute, bundled in her warm blankets and wearing the miniature white organdy prayer *kapp* Lovina had made especially for this occasion.

"*Ach*, how are my two *maed* doing?"

Lovina turned as Jonah slid an arm behind her back and pulled her in close. Upon seeing her daddy, Autumn gave a gleeful laugh and clapped her little hands.

"*Dat*," she cried.

He smiled wide. "*Ja*, Itty-Bit, I'm your *daed*."

After assuring herself no one was watching, Lovina snuggled against him. Though the Amish rarely showed open displays of affection, this was a special day and she couldn't resist his charm.

"We're *gut*, and I'm glad to have all this legal stuff behind us. All I want to do is glory in this *wundervoll* day," Lovina said.

He leaned close, brushing the baby's face with a gentle caress before he kissed Lovina's brow. "*Ja*, we have much to celebrate. I thought we could enjoy lunch at the restaurant down the street before we go *heemet*."

A pleasant fissure of surprise pulsed over Lovina. They rarely ate out. Leave it to Jonah to make this day even more memorable.

"I thought we might like to walk together and have a few moments to ourselves. Ted is taking *Dawdi*, Bishop Yoder and Carl in the car and we'll meet them over there."

Ted Calhoun was their *Englisch* driver. Since Cañon City was fifteen miles from Riverton, it was too far to drive by buggy. Ted frequently drove the Amish in those situations.

"We'll have a real celebration with all of us there," Lovina said.

She glanced at the parking lot and noticed Ted had pulled his blue sedan into afternoon traffic. *Dawdi* sat in the back seat, waving to them. Lovina lifted Autumn's hand and waved back.

"Say bye-bye," she coaxed the girl.

"Bye-bye," Autumn mimicked in a tiny voice.

They laughed, delighted by their sweet little daughter.

"*Allrecht.* Let's go." Jonah took the baby from Lovina, and she held tight to his solid arm as they headed down the street.

"Isn't it a beautiful day?" Lovina breathed a sigh of relief, grateful the adoption was finalized.

Over the past months, there had been moments when she'd wondered if Autumn would ever really belong to them. But Beth Gascho had been as good as her word and signed over her parental rights. Finally, Autumn was legally and lawfully their child. No one could take her away. They were truly a *familye* now. The best Christmas gift Lovina could ever hope for.

"Lovely, indeed," Jonah said, gazing at her.

Lovina knew he wasn't talking about the day. She smiled, feeling suddenly out of sorts. Jonah had a way of making her feel so special. Like she meant everything to him. And she loved him for it.

They walked for several moments in silence, each of them lost in the thrill of the day. Then...

"Lovina, you don't have any regrets about marrying me, do you?" Jonah asked.

She glanced at him. They'd been married ten months now but even she could hardly believe how blessed they were.

"*Ne*, not ever! The Lord has been so *gut* to us. I never thought I could be so happy," she said, speaking the truth.

"How about you? Do you have any regrets?" she asked.

"Just one. I wish I'd asked you sooner. I was a dolt for taking so long," he confessed.

They both laughed.

"Not a dolt. Just a man who needed to figure out what he really wanted," she said.

"And I want you." He was looking at her again, so intently her face flushed.

"It was soon enough. But I'm afraid we'll have to make room for more. I may need a midwife of my own," she said.

He frowned and threw her a quizzical look. "What do you mean?"

She slowed and finally came to a halt on the sidewalk. When she rested her free hand across her abdomen, she looked up and hoped he caught her meaning. She delivered babies but it wasn't the Amish way to speak openly of pregnancy. Especially not out on the street like this.

"Lovina!" he whispered. "Am I going to be a father again?"

She nodded, speaking low so no one would overhear. "In the summer."

He released a pent-up laugh and hugged her tight. "That's *wundervoll* news! Maybe we'll have a little *bu* this time. *Ach,* how I adore you."

"And I love you," she whispered.

"*Lub* you," Autumn echoed their words.

They stared at their daughter, then burst into laughter. She was starting to say more words every day but these were the best of all.

As they continued on their way, they discussed their farm, the extra crops Jonah would plant in the spring, their EMT and midwifery work, and possible names for their new baby. Their life was so full and busy. Lovina loved listening to Jonah talk. Like her, he was happy and animated today. She breathed a contented sigh and enjoyed their walk together. Her heart was so full as she looked toward the future with her husband, and she couldn't ask *Gott* for anything more.

* * * * *

A PRECIOUS CHRISTMAS GIFT

Patricia Johns

To my husband, the best choice I ever made!
And to our son, who makes our family complete,
I love you both.

For I know the thoughts that I think toward you,
saith the Lord, thoughts of peace, and not of evil,
to give you an expected end.
　　　　　　　　　　　　—*Jeremiah* 29:11

Chapter One

The wind was bitingly cold this December morning, and Noah Wiebe hunched his shoulders against the probing chill as the Englisher snowplow ground on past Redemption Carpentry. The driver—a man in a baseball cap with cold-reddened ears—nodded at Noah in a silent mutual acknowledgment as the giant blade scraped across the asphalt, snow accumulating in a tumbling avalanche in front of the vehicle. Noah nodded back and headed across the street toward the town center roundabout where Redemption Carpentry had built a nativity stable to collect donations for a local family in need.

Wollie Zook's family, more precisely. Noah had known Wollie since they were both boys, and they'd been good friends. Wollie left the community when he fell in love with an Englisher girl, and when their house went up in flames a week ago, he'd asked for help. He and his wife had four *kinner*, the youngest of which was still a toddler. He was doing his best to provide, and he had a decent job and some insurance, but he needed help to get through the Christmas season. Wollie had been talking to his parents about returning to the Amish life, but whether or not he could make that happen with an Englisher wife and children was anyone's guess. This one had hit Noah hard—but no matter how much Noah liked to get things organized and into line, he wasn't going to be able to help Wollie without the town's cooperation. And Noah had a personal investment in bringing ex-Amish home again.

Noah carried a clapboard sign under one arm, and he stepped aside and politely nodded as an Amish woman with three little girls in tow passed him on the sidewalk. The clapboard had the times that the nativity would be open written in black paint so that passersby would know when to bring the donations that might be in danger of being stolen so that they could be brought back to a safe location. If the Zooks were going to get settled again, they needed everything from forks and spoons up to beds and furniture.

Noah stopped at the top of the street, and then jogged across, ahead of an Amish buggy, heading to the nativity stable in the center. This was his handiwork, and he was proud of it—a traditional looking stable with a locking door and animal silhouette cutouts that decorated the snowy ground in front of it. There was a firepit, too, usually used during street festivals as a source of heat where people could warm up. But today there was no fire in it—just some blackened logs.

Noah paused at the door—it wasn't locked—and when he opened it, he looked into the simple interior and found a woman standing with her back to him, sorting through a box. She looked up as the door thunked open, and when she partially turned, he saw that she was heavily pregnant. She wore a thick, dark gray shawl that seemed to make her creamy skin glow in comparison, and her *kapp* was gleaming white against her dark hair. Her eyes were bright, but she didn't smile. Instead, she turned her attention back to the box.

"Good morning," Noah said.

"Good morning." She pulled out a broken dish and tossed it into another cardboard box, presumably the garbage.

"I'm just here to drop off the sign," he said.

"Oh… Okay. I'm just going through some donations. It's not all good enough to give away." Who was she? She had an interesting face—dark, expressive eyes and a strong jaw. Her lips were pink and they looked perpetually ready to smile, even though she looked at him with a completely solemn expression.

"You're new around here," he said. "Aren't you?"

He was only being polite. Obviously, she was. He knew everyone in their Amish community, and he'd remember meeting a woman like her.

"*Yah*, just visiting," she said.

He nodded. "I'm Noah Wiebe. I work at Redemption Carpentry. I know Wollie Zook, the man we're helping with this charity drive, from our growing up years."

"He's a cousin…on my *mamm*'s side," she said. "A distant one, but still family."

"Oh." Noah nodded. "Well, we'll do our best to get them back on their feet. And you are…"

She blushed slightly. "Sorry. I'm Eve. I'm Lovina Glick's niece."

Noah started. Lovina Glick's niece... His heart sped up as the details clicked into place. Lovina owned Quilts and Such, the shop next door to the carpentry shop, but that wasn't what made his heart skip a beat. This hit his family more personally than even Wollie.

"Wait—" He cleared his throat. "Are you the niece who is...uh...who is..."

Eve turned toward him, her expression wary. Noah now knew exactly who she was. His brother Thomas and his wife Patience were hoping to adopt a baby...

"I'm Thomas Wiebe's brother," he added. "Thomas and Patience Wiebe are... Well, they know your aunt quite well, and..."

How was he supposed to say this? Or had he already said too much? The color drained from Eve's face, and she ran her fingers over her stomach protectively. She suddenly looked different—sadder, even a little smaller.

"*Yah*, that would be me," she said. "I'm the one they're probably hoping to meet."

Noah dropped his gaze. He'd heard a little bit about the mother—a girl who got pregnant outside of wedlock and who had come to give birth to her baby and give it to a good Amish home. There wasn't much more information than that, but Lovina Glick had told Thomas about her niece's baby, and that she hadn't decided on which family she would give her child to. Patience couldn't have any children of her own, and this was a chance to grow their family. It felt like a

Christmas answer to prayer...if Eve would choose them, that was.

"Are there any other families you're considering?" Noah asked.

"There is one. They're willing to take the baby, but—" She shrugged. "I don't know. I haven't made up my mind yet."

"Being willing to take a child and longing to take one are two different things," he said.

"Yah." She nodded.

"My brother and his wife—they're longing for another child," he said. "My brother had a child before he met his wife, but they aren't able to have any *kinner* together. They desperately want another baby to grow their family."

She nodded. "It is different, I agree."

Noah smiled at that. Maybe he could put his brother in a good light—help the cause a little bit. Because he knew how deeply Thomas and Patience desired to grow their family.

"I wasn't even going to come here," Eve went on. "Aunt Lovina heard that I was staying with strangers the last few months, and she insisted I come be with family. And when I got here and Wollie's house burned down, I wanted to help him somehow. Wollie was older than me, but he visited us once to help my *daet* with the corn shocks, and he was a good man. I don't know if it's too much to hope he might come back."

"We prayed for him last Service Sunday," he said. "His parents told us that the last time they visited with him, he said he wished he could find a way to come back."

"Really?" Eve's eyebrows went up. "I don't know his *mamm* and *daet* personally. Wollie only visited the once, and he came alone. But that's something to fuel some hope, isn't it?"

"Seems like," he agreed.

Their gazes met and Noah smiled. "Now, I don't like to blame house fires on *Gott*, but I do believe that *Gott* can use this calamity for good."

"Maybe He will," she agreed.

Noah glanced around. There didn't seem to be anyone else out here. And this was a particularly cold day. Eve rubbed her hands together and blew on her fingers.

"It's cold," he said.

"Yah." She turned back to sorting through the box.

"Are you sure you should be out in this cold—I mean, this close to…" How could he put this delicately?

"Noah…" She paused and turned back. "I could try to be coy about this, but we both know the biggest reason why I'm here in Redemption. I came out here to have my baby and to leave it in the arms of another woman." Her voice shook, and she sucked in a breath. "I've tried not to love this baby—I really have. But I couldn't help it. I love this child, even though I know I have to give it up. So while I wait for that miserable day, I'm trying to make this time count for something—maybe make a difference for Wollie's family in their time of need. This is very likely the hardest thing I will ever do in my lifetime, and the day is coming very quickly. So while I wait, and I dread, are you wanting to take away the one thing that might make this time in your town be about more than my own heartbreak?"

Noah blinked at her. She wasn't like other Amish women—there was no quiet deference to him as a man. But she had a point. He shook his head. "No. I wouldn't do that."

Eve turned back to the box. "Good."

She obviously wasn't looking for permission, nor did she seem overly concerned over his opinion. And yet, looking at her standing there with a donated pot in one hand, she looked very much alone. This was Christmas, and the women would be gathering in warm kitchens to cook together and laugh and talk—

Noah eyed her for a moment. Maybe she didn't have anything more to lose here in Redemption, because she wasn't going out of her way to be friendly, either.

"I know that Thomas and Patience are looking forward to meeting you," he said.

"I'm not ready for that," she replied with a quick shake of her head. She put the pot aside on a folding table and pulled out a teapot next, turning it over as she inspected it.

"Oh..." He wasn't sure what to make of that. Was she perhaps changing her mind about giving up her baby?

"I just need some time," she said, glancing up. "I don't want to meet them until I'm ready."

"No, that's understandable," he said quickly. "And there is no pressure. I promise. In fact, if you need anything at all, you can ask me. I'm Thomas's brother, *yah*, but I'm not quite so directly involved." He cast her a smile, hoping to charm her into relaxing a little bit.

"You're only offering because you want me to choose your brother," she said bluntly.

Noah paused. "Maybe. But I'm going to be around— either at the carpentry shop, or here. And we both want to help Wollie out the best we can, so while we're doing that, if you need anything, tell me."

She licked her lips, then sighed. "Thank you. It's a kind offer. In the meantime, let's do what we can for Wollie."

If she wasn't ready to meet Thomas and Patience yet, he could understand that. Noah opened the door again to go arrange the sign. He'd start up a little fire in the brick-lined firepit while he was at it, too. But he couldn't help but glance in the direction of the woman with those dark, expressive eyes. There was something about her that tugged at him—and he pushed it aside. This wasn't about him.

Maybe, if *Gott* was willing, this woman could be the answer to Thomas and Patience's most earnest and heartfelt prayers.

Eve sorted through the last of the box—some ladles, three tea towels, a box of matches and a pair of gloves. The rest would be useful, and she pulled out a list her aunt had given her and wrote the items down. They had to keep track of the donations so they would know what else was needed.

But Wollie needed more than household items—he needed to come home to his Amish roots. Just before

Wollie jumped the fence, he'd come to help her *daet* with the corn, and she'd been too talkative as a teenager when she'd been doing all the regular adolescent questioning of the Amish ways. When she learned that he'd left the Amish life, she'd been stunned. He seemed so...normal. She'd determined then that she'd never flirt with that line—she'd be good. She'd stay Amish, and have the Amish family she'd always dreamed of.

Her baby shifted and stretched inside her. This far along, there wasn't any room for proper kicks anymore, and she paused her work and put a hand over the spot where the baby was pushing. She could feel something pointy—an elbow?

A wagon came clattering along the road, and she heard the driver's jovial voice as he reined in the horses. Eve looked out the window as Noah headed over to the wagon that was piled high with firewood.

"Hello, Elmer!" Noah called. "Cold enough for you?"

"*Yah*—it's plenty cold," the other voice replied, and when they were close enough, their voices lowered and she could no longer make out what they were saying.

Eve hadn't decided on a family for the baby yet. There were families that would accept another child, but simply being willing to feed and shelter an unwanted baby wasn't what she was hoping for. This baby should be wanted—by someone.

Thomas and Patience seemed like an ideal choice, even though she wasn't ready to admit that to Noah. They wanted this child desperately. And that had made her feel almost competitive with the woman who longed for her baby. It stoked an instinct inside her to fight the woman back. And she knew it wasn't rational. It was maternal instinct—an instinct that she'd have to tamp down. She'd meet this couple eventually, she knew, but she'd been putting it off because she didn't know how she'd feel to look at the woman who might be *mamm* to this baby. She'd rather imagine the baby's adoptive *mamm* like a faceless doll—an idea rather than a real woman who would be everything that Eve could not.

She looked out the window again, watching as the men unloaded wood from the back of that wagon, carrying it over to the firepit and stacking the wood neatly beside it. Noah was taller, broader, and he carried himself with the latent strength of a man accustomed to physical labor. He was distractingly handsome—something that seemed almost silly to be noticing in her present condition—and he might be uncle to this baby.

Adoption was no longer just an idea…she'd be handing her child over to very real people. There would be family, extended family, a whole community—and none of it would include her. So strange to even think that! She'd spent the last eight and a half months being the physical protection for this little one, and when she gave birth, other people would take over. The thought brought a lump of anxiety to her throat.

Noah and Elmer came back to the stable, and when they came in, the older, lanky man looked at her in mild surprise as he saw her figure for the first time. She dropped her gaze and turned away.

"Your husband isn't going to like you being out here in the cold in your state," Elmer said glibly, bending down to pick up a package of matches and kindling that had been stored in a wooden crate in one corner of the small room.

"Let her be," Noah said gruffly. He didn't look up, or explain, but Elmer closed his mouth into a firm line and didn't say anything else.

The men went back out to start a new fire, and the door clattered shut behind them again, leaving her in silence.

She heaved a shaky sigh.

Yes, most Amish assumed she had a husband, because that was how a proper Amish family began—marriage and then babies. She hoped to have that very thing in the next couple of years. She hoped to meet a nice man, marry him, and start a family the respectable way. This child inside her that she was trying so very hard not to get too attached to wasn't even fully Amish. This baby was half-Amish, half-English, and the best way for this baby to grow up would be in a proper Amish home, without the blight of her reputation. To be adopted was in no way shameful. It was a blessing. But to be raised fatherless with an unmarried mother? That was different—that kind of stigma clung.

Outside, she could see that the fire was now started, and Noah hunkered down and poked some wood into the new, crackling flames. She heard the muffled farewell and the clop of horses' hooves as the wagon pulled away.

Eve was done sorting through the latest donations that had been left overnight, and she came back outside toward the fire, leaving the boxed items in the stable for now. She didn't mind admitting that she was cold.

"What did you tell him?" Eve asked, coming up to the flickering warmth.

"That you were visiting your aunt and it was a complicated situation," Noah replied, standing up.

Complicated—that could cover a lot of ground. Was it wrong of her to want people to believe a lie? Because she did! She wanted them to see her as a respectable woman instead of as a warning to the younger girls.

Eve licked her lips. "What are they like?"

"Uh—" Noah looked over at her. "My brother and his wife, you mean?"

"Yah."

"They're very nice. They're newly married—and very much in love. My brother works with me in the carpentry shop. He's very skilled, and his work is in demand with Amish and English alike." Noah crossed his arms over his chest. "My brother had no idea how to be a *daet* when his daughter ended up on his doorstep, but he threw himself into it. I was impressed, really." He glanced toward her. "And it wasn't his fault that he didn't know Rue—that's his little girl. The Englisher *mamm* didn't want him in her life, and what was he supposed to do?"

Eve held her hands out toward the crackling fire. She understood that dilemma well enough, and her aunt had explained Thomas's situation. He'd fathered a child during his *Rumspringa*, and then he and the Englisher mother broke up. The Amish life was separate from the English life—and Amish didn't go about suing others in courts. Thomas would have made his mistake that resulted in a child, and he'd have to live with the painful consequences—much like she would.

"Anyway," Noah went on, "Patience is teaching school until Christmas break, and then her replacement will come and take over. She takes Rue with her some days—so Rue is getting an early start with her reading and writing. She's smart, that little girl. The other days Rue is with her *mammi*, but Patience wants to raise Rue herself, and she wants the girl with her, so…"

"She sounds like she's accepted Rue, then," Eve said. This was a detail that mattered to her.

"Completely."

"Are they strict?" she asked.

Noah paused, then shrugged. "Not overly. Rue managed to keep them from eating a crotchety rooster, just because she loved it."

Eve smiled at that. "That's rather sweet."

"They're good people," Noah said, straightening to look at her. "And you could be an answer to their prayers—I promise you that. They love *kinner*, and they want nothing more than another baby to raise with Rue."

Eve glanced up as a car sped past. "Lovina said the same."

"Are you… Are you sure that you're willing to give your baby up?" Noah asked.

Was she sure? Not on an emotional level, but she'd thought this through over and over again, and she always landed on the same conclusion.

"I need to find a family for this baby," she said, her throat feeling tight. "That's already decided."

Noah gave a nod, then smiled with a look of relief. "They're good people," he repeated.

And from what she'd heard of them, they were. They'd be loving and stable and faithful. What more could she ask for?

"I will meet your brother and his wife, of course," she added. "Eventually. But right now, I want to find a way to help my cousin."

"Of course." He met her gaze, and her stomach fluttered in response. She looked down.

"I should get back to my aunt's store," she said. "I'm sure she needs some extra help."

Eve just wanted out—away from here. Whatever it was about this man, she was talking too much. She needed to just survive these next couple of weeks—that was all. She could sort out her emotions later, when her future was secured once more. She wrapped her shawl a little more snugly around herself.

"I'd better go," she repeated.

"I'm glad you're here—" he said, then cleared his throat. "With the charity drive, I mean. I'm glad for another person who sincerely wants to bring Wollie home."

"Yah," she said with a weak smile. "We'll do our best."

Eve met his gaze, and then turned away without any further goodbye. She picked up her pace as she headed across the street and stepped up on the opposite sidewalk, the tiny, icy snowflakes whipping through the air around her.

Noah seemed nice, and he was oddly comforting, but she knew better than to get herself entangled with new friendships while she was here. Eve was in the town of Redemption for one reason, and the Amish community here wasn't going to be any part of her long-term solutions. She was very much in *Gott*'s hands.

Chapter Two

Noah gathered up the box of garbage from the nativity stable and then headed in the same direction Eve had gone, toward Redemption Carpentry. His mind was still on the young woman he'd just met. She wasn't what he'd expected.

In fact, he wasn't sure what he'd expected… Maybe someone who looked more rebellious, but Eve had looked every inch a proper Amish woman. He'd never known anyone in her situation before, and he was personally rather cautious by nature. His brother had had a fairly wild *Rumspringa*, but Noah had all but skipped his own.

He wondered how difficult it must be for Eve being pregnant and single. She seemed like a strong young woman, her personality one that tugged at him in spite of himself. She reminded him a little bit of his own *mamm*, Rachel Wiebe, ironically enough. Not that his *mamm* had ever been in that predicament, but in personality. She hadn't been a typical Amish woman. She used to tell them jokes while she was cooking in the kitchen, and her laughter used to ring through the entire house. Amish women were quiet, and *Mamm* hadn't been quiet at all. But it had been wonderful, and he remembered how happy he used to feel listening to her laughing at her own jokes, completely oblivious to the fact that his own *mamm* was an example of the kind of woman not to marry because she wasn't going to stay.

Rachel Wiebe left the community when he was just a teen, coming back to visit only once a month, and *yah*, he was angry about that. Her weekly letters didn't take the place of her presence, and he hadn't been willing to go join her with his aunt and English cousins, no matter how many times she begged him to. But it wasn't just his *mamm* going English that was so upsetting. He was angrier still that the way she'd raised them had stuck—both the Amish teaching and the laughing and joking, and he found himself drawn to Amish women with a similar personality. That was problematic, because while he'd learned later just how un-Amish his *mamm* had been, he couldn't help the type of woman who drew him in. Like the pregnant woman in the stable—outspoken, direct. And that wasn't helpful to him at all.

Noah let himself into the carpentry shop showroom and took off his hat, slapping it against his thigh to shake off the snow. The customer side of the shop was empty, and his brother was leaning over some paperwork at the counter.

"You'll never believe who I saw in the charity stable," Noah said.

Thomas raised his eyebrows questioningly.

"Eve," Noah said. "Lovina's niece. She's arrived."

"Eve... The mother?" Thomas asked, straightening. "She's in the stable?"

"She was. She's in Quilts and Such with Lovina at the moment," Noah said.

"Did you talk to her?" Thomas asked.

"*Yah*, we chatted a bit," Noah confirmed. "I made sure to talk you up a bit, tell her what a great *daet* you are."

"I should go say hello," Thomas said, wiping his hands down the sides of his pants. "Patience should be with me for this, but—"

"Look," Noah said. "She said she isn't ready to meet you yet."

"Why?" Thomas asked. "Lovina says she's due by Christmas."

"I don't know," Noah replied. "And she said it's hard to think about giving up her baby, and she needs some time before she meets you."

"Is there another family she's considering, or something?"

"There is one other that she mentioned," he replied.

"I didn't know there was another one." Thomas rubbed a hand over his short, reddish beard, then looked up at Noah. "I thought we were it."

"*Yah*, that's the impression I got from Lovina, too," Noah agreed. "But I guess there is one more."

Thomas sighed. "When Lovina said she'd told her niece about us, you should have seen Patience's face. She just...glowed. I don't know... I just know that Patience and I are going to have more *kinner* in our home, and Patience deserves a baby in her arms. She does. She's a wonderful *mamm*, and…maybe I shouldn't have gotten her hopes up. I really thought this was more certain than it seems to be."

"Yah…" Noah didn't know how to answer that.

"I don't want to overstep with Eve," Thomas said. "And I can appreciate how difficult this would be for her, but maybe she'll need something that we can provide. I don't mean it as pressure, but as Christian charity."

"I offered, actually," Noah said. "I hope I wasn't going too far on your behalf, but when she said she wasn't ready to meet you, I thought maybe she'd accept it from me. I'm not quite so personally involved."

Thomas hooked his thumb into the front of his pants and sighed. He looked worried.

"Sometimes the *mamm* changes her mind," Thomas said after a pause. "It happens, you know. The *mamm* decides to keep the baby, or she chooses a different family."

That was the fear—Noah knew it. Thomas and Patience had already gotten their hopes up, and it had all felt a little too perfect. It had felt like *Gott* was moving… A half-Englisher baby in need of an Amish home.

"Thomas, she said she's looking for a family for the baby, so…" Noah shrugged helplessly. "Besides, I'll be seeing more of her. She's one of Wollie's distant cousins. So she's invested in helping his family right now."

The door to the shop opened again, and Amos Lapp, the owner of Redemption Carpentry, came into the showroom. He wiped some wood dust from the hair on his arms and looked between them curiously. Amos was nearing forty, and there was some gray at his temples and just a few strands in his beard, but he was tall and strong.

"What?" Amos asked. "You both look like something's happened."

Noah retold the story of his brief encounter with Eve in the charity stable, and Amos blew out a slow breath. Amos had taken Noah and Thomas into his home when they were teens, and of anyone in Redemption, Amos understood them best.

"Should I just go introduce myself?" Thomas asked. "I mean…if she sees me and meets Patience, maybe it will take away her anxiety. We'll love her baby. We've already gotten attached, I think. If she could see—"

"Don't push her," Amos interrupted.

"I'm not suggesting I overstep, exactly—" Thomas began.

"I didn't think I was overstepping with Miriam, either," Amos replied.

Noah froze and exchanged a glance with his brother. Amos didn't talk about his wife often. All they knew was that they had broken up after less than a year of marriage. She'd gone back to her hometown, and they'd both continued with their lives alone. It took a lot to break up an Amish couple, because there was no remarriage for them unless their spouse died. But Miriam Lapp had gone home, and she'd never returned to her husband.

"What happened between you and Miriam, exactly?" Noah asked.

"You could say she was stubborn and unyielding. You could say I was just the same. But one of the mistakes I made, looking back on it, was that I didn't take her seriously enough. When a woman looks you in the eye and says something, she means it." Amos shuffled his feet uncomfortably. "Women are...different. They're both stronger than us and more fragile. So if she's said that she isn't ready to meet Thomas and Patience yet, my humble advice is that you take that woman at her word. Give it a few days."

"Yah..." Thomas licked his lips. "That makes sense. I should ask Patience what she thinks, all the same, but you're probably right."

It wasn't like any of them had a wealth of experience when it came to women. Amos had been estranged from his wife for nearly ten years. Noah was single, and Thomas had been married for all of three months. All combined, they weren't exactly experts in the female mind. Waiting for Patience to give an opinion was probably the smartest thing to be done. She had just as much at stake as her husband, after all.

Thomas went back into the workshop, and Noah exchanged a look with Amos.

"You never told us much about Miriam," Noah said.

"I don't want to scare you off of marriage," Amos said. "Choose a quiet, hardworking woman, and you'll be fine. Don't overreach. That's all. It's simple enough."

Noah smiled ruefully. "Have you ever thought of going to get her? Bringing her home once and for all?"

"I tried," Amos replied. "It didn't go well."

Amos didn't look amused, and Noah let his smile fall.

"We should get back to work," Noah said.

"*Yah*. There are orders to complete," Amos agreed.

There was one complete bedroom set that needed sanding still, and three different hutches that had been ordered in the last few weeks that were still in the beginning stages of the work. Redemption Carpentry was known for its quality work, but also for keeping to its promised delivery dates.

When the bell dinged from the customer showroom, Noah had just finished rubbing oil into the side of a newly finished bedside table, and he dropped the rag on his workbench and headed toward the door, letting Amos and Thomas continue undisturbed.

When Noah stepped into the showroom, it wasn't an Englisher client as expected, but Lovina Glick. Noah looked at her in surprise.

"Hi, Lovina," he said.

"Hello." Lovina smiled. "Is it a busy day today?"

"Well, we keep pretty steady," Noah replied. "It is Christmas."

Lovina nodded knowingly. "It's the same with my shop, and add in trying to organize the charity drive for Wollie's family…"

"*Yah*, I saw your niece there today."

"I'm glad it's you who came out." Lovina lowered her voice. "You see, I need to go check on my mother. She and my aunt have been working on more quilts for me to sell, and we need to pick them up. I'm a little worried—my aunt was supposed to bring them to the shop first thing in the morning."

"Do you think they're sick, or—"

"I'm sure they're fine, but I won't feel better until I check."

"That's understandable," Noah agreed.

"Eve is minding the shop for me while I'm gone, but if I don't come back in time, I was wondering if you might be able to drop her off at our house when you leave for the day. I don't want her to be too tired out in her condition."

"*Yah*, that wouldn't be a problem. It's on the way," Noah replied.

"I…" Lovina smiled apologetically. "She isn't ready for a proper meeting with Thomas yet."

"She mentioned that, and Thomas understands."

"Good." Lovina smiled again. "Thank you. I do appreciate it, especially at this busy time. And don't worry about Eve not wanting to meet your brother just yet. She just needs some time to adjust."

"What are neighbors for?" Noah asked.

"Thank you," Lovina said again. "I'd better go, then."

"*Yah*—say hello to your *mamm* for me."

"I will. She'll be tickled you thought of her." Lovina smiled, her eyes crinkling at the corners and her entire face softening.

With a wave, she swept back out the front door, the bell dinging over her head. As Lovina headed out, an Englisher woman came inside, pulling her gloves off. She was dressed in blue jeans and a bright red coat that matched her lipstick.

"Hello!" she said. "I'm looking for something for a Christmas gift for my mother—"

Yes, Christmas brought out the urgent requests for

everything from quilt racks to full shelving units. And staying busy was a blessing to any business.

Noah glanced toward the door once more, his mind moving to the young woman in the shop next door. Eve was vulnerable, but she seemed so determined to take care of herself. At a time like this, a woman needed a husband to be caring for her…

"…I was hoping for a medium-size one," the woman was saying, and Noah realized he'd tuned out.

"Sorry," he said. "Could you repeat that?"

"A spice rack, but I wanted something with an Amish flair to it, you know?"

Noah blinked at her. "Maybe some Pennsylvania Dutch on it?"

"Yes, that would be perfect! How do you say 'kiss the cook' in Pennsylvania Dutch?"

Not exactly an Amish flair. Noah swallowed. "How about something like '*Gott* bless this home'?" he asked.

"Oh…yes, that might do," she replied. "How long will that take to make? I need it in time for Christmas. Did I say that already?"

Christmas. It brought out the Englishers, but it also brought out thoughts of friends, family and goodwill. There was his brother, Thomas, and his hopes for another child. There was Wollie, who had lost everything in that fire, but who was still in *Gott*'s hands. And there was Noah's *mamm*, who had returned to Redemption as an answer to his own prayer…but in spite of all of *Gott*'s goodness, Noah was missing some necessary element in his life to make him feel rooted and satisfied, and he knew what he needed. A wife. He needed a family of his own, like his brother now had. But he wasn't sure he trusted himself to find a woman who wouldn't break his heart.

Marriage was for life, and if a man married the wrong woman, heartbreak was for life, too. Just ask Amos.

Gott, help me stay on the narrow path.

Eve looked at her watch. It was time to close up Quilts and Such, and Aunt Lovina still hadn't returned. The last few customers had been Amish, and they'd asked a few questions about where she was from. This visit would be simpler if Eve could just keep to herself, spend time with the Glick family and not see another person, but *Gott* wasn't leaving her with that option. She had to admit that sitting by herself, feeling the nudges and movements of her baby inside her, wouldn't make these last few weeks any easier. Part of her wanted to get this over with—have her baby, and just face the pain of giving the child up. And another part of her wished she'd never have to face it— that she could go on forever with this little one inside her, feeling those jabs and movements with no one to separate them.

But nothing lasted forever, especially not a pregnancy.

The shop had been picked over today—a few rolls of fabric had gone from fat and full to nearly empty, and almost all of the Christmas crafts that women from the community made and brought to the quilt shop to sell had been purchased by one of the many Englisher shoppers. There had been little log cabin tree ornaments, snowflake-decorated aprons, embroidered oven mitts, and one enterprising Amish family had been making little Amish Christmas villages that sold for a very good price. There had only been four of them, and more than one customer had asked after them once they were sold.

The most difficult part of the evening was the questions—not from the Amish customers, but from the English. *Oh, when are you due? Boy or girl?* And then added with a lowered voice, *Do you people find out the gender, or is that considered Fancy?*

Eve flicked the sign in the frost-laced front window from Open to Closed. It was a painted sign that was made to look like the words had been cross-stitched. She turned to the front door and was about to flick the lock, too, when Noah appeared on the other side of the glass. She startled—she hadn't seen him come up in the winter evening darkness and he materialized all at once, his thick woolen black coat and rimmed hat blending into the darkness behind him. He held a pair of gloves in one hand, and he smiled hesitantly. Eve pulled the door open and let him inside. He eased past her, and she noticed how tall he was next to her, and broad. She turned the lock behind him.

"I was just closing up," Eve said. "Thank you for the ride home. I really appreciate it."

"So Lovina didn't make it back?" he asked.

"Lovina said that her *mamm* might need help with a few things," Eve replied. "She thought it might take some time."

"Right." He nodded, glanced around. "Are you ready to leave?"

"Almost." Eve didn't know how to deal with the cash or do the paperwork for end of day, and Lovina had told her not to worry about that since they could take care of it in the morning. She straightened a bin of thread spools and ran a duster over the counter. Noah stood to one side, fiddling with his gloves, and she noticed as she glanced around the store one last time that his dark eyes were locked on her. When she met his gaze, he dropped his immediately.

Eve had a coat—one she was borrowing from Lovina's husband—that was big enough to cover her belly. She reached for it, and when she fumbled with the heavy woolen garment, Noah stepped forward and caught it, holding it open for her to slide her arms into.

"Thank you." She felt her cheeks warm. "It's heavy."

"Yah." He caught her eye, and she saw warmth in that smile—something she wasn't used to lately. In the last community where she'd been staying, the Amish there all knew she was "one of those girls," and there wasn't much friendliness. Kindness, yes, but friendliness was a different sort of thing. Even the older woman she'd stayed with had been emotionally removed—offering food, clothing, shelter and spiritual guidance, but not friendliness.

Eve's feet were sore. Lovina had provided a chair for her to sit in, but it didn't seem to take much to make her feet ache in these last few weeks. She took off her indoor shoes and slipped her feet into her winter boots, then she picked up a bag of scraps her aunt

had said she could have. They headed for the back door
that lead through the storage room and then out into
the brisk cold air. Eve paused to lock the door with the
key Lovina had entrusted to her, and then they headed
to the waiting buggy. Noah had already hitched up the
horses, and she accepted his work-roughened hand as
he helped her up into the buggy. He didn't let go of
her hand in his tight grip until she was seated, and
then he released her and headed around the horses to
the other side.

Eve picked up a lap blanket and tucked it around
her knees. Dresses, even with lots of layers underneath them, were cold this time of year. She let out
a slow breath that hung in the air in front of her. The
stars shone bright, and a full moon illuminated the
sky. Streetlights lit up the parking lot, and the horses
shifted their hooves on the snowy asphalt. As Noah
hoisted himself up into the seat beside her, he gave her
a reassuring smile.

"Was it busy today?" he asked as he flicked the reins,
the horses starting forward and heading toward the road
without any further encouragement from Noah.

"*Yah*—lots of shoppers," she said. "Lots of questions
from them, too."

"You mentioned keeping the adoption discreet," he
said. "Have people pieced it together?"

"I'm not sure. Maybe a few. I'm only saying that I'm
here to see my aunt, and most have been too polite to
pry much further. The thing is, I'd like a life still when
I go home. I'd like a chance at marriage and being a
proper part of the community."

He didn't answer, and she thought she knew what he was thinking—it was the very thing she'd be thinking, too, in his shoes. Did she even deserve that second chance? They rolled out onto the street and through the downtown, the horses plodding along through the sound-dampening snow on the roads. Eve pulled the blanket up a little higher and put her hands under the woolen folds.

"This wasn't my fault," she added. "This...pregnancy. I didn't do wrong, you know."

Noah looked over at her, perplexed.

"It was a party," she said, saving him the discomfort. "I took my *Rumspringa* late. When I was seventeen, I was taking care of my *mamm* while she battled cancer. When she died, I took my *Rumspringa*, and it wasn't a rebellious one, either. But I went to an Englisher party with some other Amish girls, and someone must have put something in my drink, because I woke up the next morning on a couch and I couldn't remember what happened."

"Your friends left you there?" he asked.

"They thought I'd left early. I said I was going to. It was too wild. It scared me. But then I accepted a drink, and... I don't know. I must have passed out."

"I've heard some boys can do that," he said gruffly.

"An Englisher taxi brought me home for free—the driver was a woman and she felt sorry for me, I guess. When I found out I was pregnant, I knew where it had happened, but I couldn't even remember what those Englisher boys looked like. It was all so fuzzy."

"That's horrible!" Noah's tone hardened. "No one went to try to figure it out?"

"My *daet* and I had a long talk, and we decided that we'd deal with things as they were rather than try to get some justice."

"Your community would understand, though," he said.

"As much as they could." Because while they might not blame her, she would certainly be in an outside circle. She'd gone to the party, after all, and she hadn't done the right thing and left immediately for home. She'd lingered, wondering if she was overreacting. She'd talked to the Englisher boys, and she'd enjoyed that strange feeling of freedom she'd never experienced before.

No, if she'd told her community what had happened, they wouldn't have blamed her, but they'd never forget, either. She certainly wouldn't have been marriageable when there were so many other girls available without babies already.

"It would be complicated, though," Noah said, and she was glad to have him see that fact instead of having him argue with her about it. It wasn't like she hadn't agonized about this choice for the last several months.

Noah flicked the reins, and the horses picked up their pace, the buggy moving slowly around the roundabout and the little nativity stable that sat in the center. There were some bags placed in front—more donations since they'd last been there, it seemed. With the animal outlines in front, the blanket of fresh snow surrounding it, and the warm bath of a streetlight beaming down, the scene looked so simple and festive that it brought a wave of nostalgia for her own Christmases past. But those happy times when her *mamm* was alive weren't coming back.

"What was your *Rumspringa* like?" she asked.

"Uneventful," he replied. "I was working at the shop, and I was wanting to build my career, not take a break from it."

She nodded. That was the ideal, actually—a *Rumspringa* that allowed an Amish young person to see the English life without too much drama involved. She'd wanted to enjoy herself, though—see what all the fuss was about. She'd never dreamed she'd be in this position.

"You're a hard worker," she said.

"Yah," he agreed. "It seems like a good use of time."

She shot him a rueful look. Yes, she knew his type well. He was the kind of man who got ahead, and who could be relied upon to stand by his word. But he was also single—she knew it from his shaved face. Maybe there was a girlfriend.

"Are you saving for a wedding?" she asked.

He looked over at her, and color touched his cheeks. "No."

"Okay." She chuckled. "I didn't mean to overstep, it's just—you seem to have your life in order, and most men are moving on to finding a wife."

"A wife isn't so easy to find," he said.

"Around here? I'm sure there are plenty of single girls," she replied. "Even Wollie found one."

But Noah didn't smile.

"He married an Englisher. And it's ruined his life," he replied.

"*Yah*... I was...joking," she said feebly.

"Oh." He shrugged and gave her an apologetic look. "Sorry. I can get too serious sometimes. I guess I'm just being careful. That's a decision you have to get right the first time."

And somehow she didn't doubt him. He would be cautious—and he *could* be. He had a lot to offer a woman in these parts.

"I'm sorry about your *mamm*," Noah added.

Eve looked over at him in mild surprise. She'd told her story in the other community, and Noah was the first one to say that. Everyone else had been too fixated on her pregnancy and what it would mean for her future.

"*Yah...*" she said quietly.

"When did she pass?" Noah asked.

"Just after Christmas last year. She was sick for about three years. She fought hard, but..."

That was another reason she just wanted to get past this Christmas—she'd lost her *mamm*, and in a very real way over the next few months, she'd gone from cherished girl to woman in an awkward, jolting dash. Normally, that milestone happened with marriage for an Amish girl, but enough heartbreak could have the same effect, she realized. She'd grown up, just not in a way her community could acknowledge.

They'd moved outside of the town center, and the streetlights grew farther apart as they headed toward the dark, rural streets. The headlamps illuminated the backs of the horses and the road ahead, the horses' shadows stretching out in front of them. A car slowed and passed them, giving a good distance around the buggy, but it still made Eve's heart jump.

"You had to grow up fast," he said.

"Yah," she agreed. "When *Mamm* got sick, I had to take over most of the housework for months at a time. I was keeping house on my own, helping *Mamm* take her medication and selling extra produce plus anything that wasn't nailed down so we could get extra money for *Mamm*'s treatments."

"That's not easy," he said.

Before she died, her mother had tried to tell her something. Eve could still remember the earnestness in her mother's gaze, the way she'd clutched at Eve's fingers. It was like she wanted something from Eve—a promise? "I did my best, Eve," her mother had whispered. "I did." Did she somehow know what was to come—her daughter's pregnancy out of wedlock? Those last words now felt like an accusation. This was not the life her mother had wanted for her.

"Did you envy the girls who didn't have to grow up so fast?" Noah asked, and she pushed the memory back.

"Yah." She looked away. "Maybe that was why I went to that party to begin with. I wanted a break from all the pressure. I wanted to just have fun for a change..."

"That's understandable," he said.

"Is it?" she asked softly, and she ran her hand over her belly.

"I understand having to grow up really quickly," he said. "My *daet* died when I was fifteen."

"I'm sorry. That's a tough age to lose your *daet*."

"It was hard," he said. "And I became the man of the house overnight. I had just graduated from the eighth grade, and I had to start giving my *mamm* the money I made at Amos's shop to pay the bills. I was expecting to work full-time, but I didn't realize how fast the money went once you had to pay for everything."

"So you grew up fast, too," she said.

"Yah," he agreed. "But I still think back on what it was like when *Daet* was alive and we had our family. Those were more precious times than I realized back then."

"What were your parents like?" she asked. "Together, I mean... Were they happy?"

"Yah," he said, thinking back. "They laughed a lot when they were together. And when they felt uncomfortable in any way, they leaned toward each other. Like, physically. You could see it. Both of them. When *Daet* died, my mom had no one to lean toward anymore."

Eve smiled sadly. "They sound like they were well matched."

"How about yours?" he asked.

"Not so well matched," she admitted. "There wasn't much laughing. At least not when they were together."

"There's nothing wrong with being more serious," he said.

"Well, *Daet* is serious—very stoic and pious," she said. "He insisted upon family worship at the same time every evening, no matter what was happening. *Mamm* was the fun one. She told jokes and found the light side of life, but that only seemed to irritate *Daet*.

He thought she was pulling us *kinner* away from more serious concerns."

"My *mamm* was like that, too," he said.

"But your *daet* liked her humor," she countered.

Noah seemed to consider a moment, then nodded. "*Yah*, he did. But yours—they weren't happy?"

"I think they tried to be," she said. "But they were too different. She drove him up the wall with her jokes and how she could be late sometimes. And he exasperated her with his refusal to budge, even an inch, on something he'd told us *kinner* to do." She let out a slow breath. "They were *so* different."

"That's too bad," he said.

"It got better, though," she said. "I don't mean to make it sound like we weren't a happy family. When *Mamm* got sick, *Daet* softened up a lot. I think he appreciated her more when he knew he was going to lose her."

"Is he softer now?" Noah asked.

"He's…" Eve tried to find the words to describe her father. "Let's just say that he's trying."

It made her guilty to even think it, but they were happier when *Mamm* was sick. Everyone worked harder at being kinder to each other and making sure that *Mamm* was comfortable and didn't need to get upset about anything.

"I think that trying matters," Noah said.

"It does, but it's not always enough," she said quietly.

Noah nodded. *"Yah…"*

"But enough about my family," she said, forcing a smile. "What do you do for fun around here?"

"Me?" Noah smiled faintly. "Like I said before, I work."

"That's it?" she asked.

"Well, I like what I do," he replied. "And there's always more that needs to be done. Since I don't have a family of my own, I have the time."

"You're the stoic, pious one, aren't you?" she asked with a soft laugh.

"I think I am," he said, but a smile tickled his lips. "It's just my personality, I'm afraid."

"That can't be helped," she replied.

Eve turned her attention to the snowy fields—the glitter of moonlight reflecting off the crust of snow. Barbed-wire fences cut through like stitches on a patchwork quilt.

"When Wollie married that Englisher girl, none of us could see why he did it," Noah said quietly. "I still wonder... What was he thinking?"

Everyone at her home had asked the same question—why would he do that? But Eve knew something that most of them didn't...

"He came to help my *daet* with the corn shocks just before he jumped the fence," Eve said. "And I used to follow him around and talk to him. One of the things he told me a few times—enough times that I remember it today—was that it was important to do the right thing, even when you'd made a mistake. He said that two wrongs didn't make a right. And three wrongs just made it all worse. So I know he was noble, and honest. I've thought about what he said a lot over the last few months."

"Doing the right thing, even after a mistake?" Noah asked quietly.

"*Yah*. I think this is right—giving a family a child to raise. It hurts deeply to do it, but the right thing often does, doesn't it? I made a mistake in not leaving that party right away, but compounding that mistake with my own selfishness will only punish this child. An unwed mother… Can you imagine growing up Amish with that stigma?"

"I can't answer that for you," Noah said.

"My *daet* overpaid Wollie by a few dollars when it was time for him to leave, and Wollie counted it out and handed back the extra. My *daet* was impressed with him. Wollie was…a good man. When he left the Amish life like that, everyone thought he'd just succumbed to temptation, but I don't. Sometimes there's more to the story—I know that better than most."

"He left for an Englisher girl," he said. "That's what we all assumed, at least. He married her shortly after."

"That wouldn't have been noble, though," she said. "Do you think I'm naive for still believing the best in him?"

Noah shrugged. "I think it says more about you than it does about him."

They fell silent, and Eve looked out the side of the buggy, watching the snowy fields glisten in the passing light of their headlamps. What did it say about her— that for all her quick growing up, she was still very much a girl in some ways? She wasn't sure. Maybe she just wanted to believe that people could be good at heart, even after a big mistake. Maybe she wanted to believe in redemption.

"I like you," Noah said after a moment. "You're honest, too."

She smiled at that—his confession had been unexpected. Well, she liked him, too, in spite of all his seriousness, but she wouldn't tell him that.

"This is my last chance to be completely open," she said, attempting a joke. "Maybe I'm relishing it a little. After this I'll have nothing but secrets."

Chapter Three

The Glick house was only a couple of miles away from the house Noah shared with Amos and Amos's elderly grandmother who they fondly referred to as *Mammi*. He guided the horses down the drive, leaving the cold, dark road behind. They pulled up to the warmly lit house, and he could see the white *kapp* of a girl in the window—her back to them. The windows that he could see were all decorated with evergreen sprigs, red ribbons tying them together, and candles that flickered on the windowsills. It was homey, and festive in the Amish way.

"Here we are," Noah said.

"Yah." Eve leaned forward to look at the house. "Thank you for the ride."

Noah brought the horses to a stop and tied off the reins. Eve moved toward the side of the buggy, the plastic bag in one hand, then hesitated.

"I can't see my feet anymore," she said with a low laugh.

"Wait—just wait." Noah hopped down into the crunchy snow and headed around the horses to her side of the buggy. Eve's face looked so pale, even partially lit by the golden glow of the buggy's headlamp. She must be tired, he realized belatedly. Should he have picked her up sooner to bring her home?

"Here—" He held his hand up and she caught his fingers in hers, then leaned into his shoulder as she maneuvered herself down. There was something about the softness of her in his arms—even though she was all coat, and all he grabbed were her arms, but still... She smelled like the nutmeg and cinnamon scent that filled the fabric store this time of year mingled with the soft scent of her hair. That plastic bag rustled against his coat. He waited until she had her balance on the snowy ground, then let out a breath.

"Sorry," she said, pulling free of his grip. "I feel so ungraceful."

"Don't be sorry." If things had been different for her, this would be a husband's role. She didn't have that, and it wasn't her fault. At least he knew that now. He still felt an angry tangle of emotions knowing what had happened to her. Someone should have paid for that—even if making your enemy pay went against everything he believed in.

"I do appreciate the ride home, and the conversation. But you don't have to do this, you know," Eve said.

"What?" he asked. Helping her down?

"Being friendly, entertaining me," she replied. "I don't need to be someone's Christian duty."

"You're not. You're… Well, you're connected to us, in a way," he said.

"If you're being kind to me because you want me to choose Thomas and Patience—"

"*Yah*, I do hope that you choose them, and I'll probably tell you how great they'd be as parents a few more times yet, but…this isn't about my brother."

"No?"

He'd already opened up more on this ride home than he ever had with a girl before. It had started as wanting her to be comfortable with their family, but…

"Honestly? Christmas isn't an easy time for me," he said. "You aren't the only one trying to get through, although you've got it worse than me, I'll readily admit."

"Are you saying you…need a friend?" she asked uncertainly.

"I wouldn't turn one down," he replied.

A smile came to her lips, and for the first time she seemed to relax, and the smile transformed her face from pretty to downright stunning. He caught his breath.

"I'm going to be dropping off some food at the hotel where Wollie is staying tomorrow," he added. "Do you want to come along?"

"Uh—" She hesitated. "*Yah*. I do. Thank you."

"Great. I'll come by and pick you up, then."

Eve turned toward the side door, and Noah followed her. When she opened it, the sound of laughter and the scent of baking wafted out together to meet him. One of Lovina's daughters waved at him with a smile.

"Hi, Noah! Why don't you come in for some apple crisp? We have it fresh from the oven."

The sweet aroma curled around him where he stood on the step, but he shook his head. Eve wanted to get in and get warm, and he needed to get home. *Mammi* would have a meal waiting.

"Thanks for the offer," Noah said. "But when I get home, *Mammi* is going to be deeply offended if I don't eat dinner. I'd better get going."

He waved at the teenage boys who looked out to see who was there, and then he looked back at Eve and met her gaze.

"Thank you," she said so quietly that he didn't hear it, but he could see the words formed on her lips.

He didn't answer, but gave her another nod. Now that he'd seen that smile, there was no forgetting it, and as he headed back to the buggy, he had to remind himself that this was supposed to be about Thomas and Patience, and their hope for a baby. Because they all did hope that she would choose Thomas and Patience, after all. Dropping her off to her family's home, waving to her cousins and seeing himself off again—*yah*, all of that had felt a little too familiar, and it left him with an unsettled feeling in his stomach.

Noah turned the buggy around and the horses took him back down the drive to the road, and they headed in the direction of home.

Right now, in the midst of the Christmas bustle, Noah was looking for a little bit of peace of his own. He was hoping that Wollie would find a place in their community again, and that Eve would give her baby to Thomas and Patience. And he was hoping that he'd find what he was looking for, too—some peace that seemed so elusive lately.

The winter wind whisked into the open buggy window, nipping at his ears and nose. The Glicks' Englisher neighbors had their Christmas lights up along the eaves of their house, and there were plastic reindeer in the yard, lights coiled around their bodies.

This Christmas his *mamm* was properly back in the Amish life for the first Christmas season in a very long time, and he found himself working his fingers to the bone at the workshop, in the charity drive for Wollie, and even to gain the good opinion of this young mother—anything but face his own feelings surrounding his mother. His prayer of the last ten years had been answered. He was supposed to be happy, but Noah hadn't counted on forgiving his own mother being quite this difficult.

Aunt Lovina came back home in time to eat dinner together as a family, and then the boys went to the sitting room to talk and read *The Budget*. Uncle Hezekiah, who was working a night shift at the canning plant, headed upstairs for an early bedtime since he'd be up in a few hours to get to work.

Eve had been thinking about Noah, and how he was oddly comforting in his own gruff, serious way. It wasn't just his kindness or his good looks, either, she realized. He was more familiar than she'd realized at first—he was a lot like her father. *Daet* was serious and dedicated to doing the right thing, too. He was the kind of man a neighbor could count on—the kind of man who made an Amish community work. But he'd also opened her eyes to what a good man wanted in a wife.

"When I was courting your *mamm*," he'd told her, "I was watching for her character. I knew I wanted to marry her, but I also wanted to make sure she was the woman I thought she was. Before we announced the engagement, a man from another community came to ours to look for a wife, and he set his eyes on your mother. He even told me that he thought she was beautiful, and I didn't tell him she was mine."

"That wasn't fair, *Daet*," Eve used to say with a laugh. "The poor man! Making a fool of himself..."

"I wanted to see what your *mamm* would do." He always told the story in the same way. "And she told him straightaway that she was spoken for, and she wished him well. I knew then that she was a woman I could trust with my heart and my good name."

Good men were looking for good women, and they had a lot to lose if they miscalculated. As did a woman, for that matter! If her mother had entertained that other man's attention, Eve's *daet* would have called the engagement off. That was all it would have taken.

What about a girl with a baby? Who would take a chance on that? Not a good man. The good ones would be careful—much like Noah was doing.

It was times like this that her mother's last words would come back to her... *I did my best, Eve...* And Eve had let her mother down.

Whatever warm feelings he'd brought up for her on that buggy ride back, she'd best quash them now. Her situation was too complicated. When she went back home again, when her secret was safely tucked in another woman's arms in Redemption, then she could allow herself to enjoy a good man's company.

After dinner, Eve had helped her two cousins, Ruby and Rebecca, along with Lovina in cleaning up the kitchen. With four of them working, it went quickly. The girls were kind enough to Eve, but there was a careful refusal to even mention Eve's condition.

That was the most tiring part of this whole ordeal— the humiliation of her pregnancy. Her cousins chatted with her cordially enough, but they never asked about the baby, or about how she was feeling, or even asked to feel the baby kick. If Eve stopped drying dishes and put her hand over a spot where the baby was kicking, they'd turn away and pretend not to see as if it were shameful, somehow.

But they were young—fifteen and sixteen respectively—so they were doing what they'd been taught to do, namely, keep to the narrow way. If anything, Eve was an example of what to avoid—a cautionary tale for their own upcoming *Rumspringas*, but ironically enough, Eve was not allowed to tell her own story. She could only stand there as a swollen representation of all their fears, and Eve hated it. But what could she do?

When the counters were wiped down and the last dish had been put away, the girls went to join their brothers in the sitting room, leaving Eve alone with her aunt.

"Have you seen Wollie at all?" Eve asked. "I mean, recently."

"*Yah,*" Lovina replied. "Their insurance company

is paying for them to stay in a hotel for now. I think there is some tension between Wollie and his parents, so I invited the family to come stay with us for the holidays, but the hotel is…more comfortable for an English woman, I suppose."

Eve could sense her aunt's hurt feelings.

"How is he?" Eve asked. "I mean, besides the fire."

"He's the same old Wollie," Lovina said. "I mean, he looks English now, but he's the same in the ways that matter."

Looking English—even thinking of Wollie dressed like that made her uncomfortable.

"And his wife?" Eve asked.

"His wife is overwrought by everything," Lovina replied. "And she seemed wary of us. I know that Wollie said he was thinking of coming back, but there is no changing one mind in a couple. You have to convince both, or give up."

There was wisdom there, but it made Eve's heart sink. Had things gone too far for Wollie to return?

"Noah offered to bring me along to drop off some food at the hotel tomorrow," Eve said. "Can I trust Wollie to keep my secret?"

Lovina was silent for a moment, considering. "He's English now. He isn't passing gossip around with the community at large."

"I know, but—" This was sensitive—more than that, this secret was about her chance at a future.

"If you can trust me, then I think you can trust Wollie," Lovina said. "Besides, who knows? Maybe you're the one Wollie needs to see."

Eve nodded. Maybe her aunt was right—there might be more divine design in the timing of her visit and his time of need.

"I thought you'd be tired," Lovina said, hanging up a tea towel. "When I was as pregnant as you are, I'd crawl into bed just as soon as I could."

"I am tired," Eve admitted. "But I wanted to do a little bit of quilting tonight."

"For Wollie's family?" Lovina asked. "I think I have enough quilts set aside for them, but you know it is winter—an extra blanket is always useful. Don't worry about making it too intricate—"

No, this one would be more personal. Eve licked her lips.

"I wanted to make something for the baby," Eve said.

Lovina froze, then slowly pursed her lips. "You've changed your mind, then?"

Eve blinked, then shook her head. "No…"

"Then why are you making something for the baby?" Lovina asked.

"Because I wanted to make something to go along with him or her—something from me. Maybe this little quilt would end up being my child's favorite blanket, and it would get dragged all over the house and outside, and—" Her voice cracked as tears rose in her eyes. Maybe there could be some tangible way that her love could go along with this baby to a new home. Maybe this welling of love she felt for the squirming baby inside her needn't be wasted.

"Sit." Lovina gestured to a kitchen chair.

"Lovina, I'm not in the mood to be lectured," Eve

replied with a shake of her head. Yes, she was unmarried and pregnant, and yes, she was in the very situation that Ruby and Rebecca were being warned about constantly, but Eve was the one who would have to bear the heartrending consequences of her assaulter's actions, and that was punishment enough.

"I said, sit." Lovina raised her eyebrows, and Eve couldn't resist the command in the older woman's voice. She pulled out a chair and sat down. Lovina sighed, then pulled out the chair next to her and sank into it. "I know it's hard."

Eve looked over at her aunt uncertainly. "And this is where you tell me that I'm doing the right thing and I need to just toughen up and do it, right?"

Lovina shook her head slowly. "Not at all. I just know that this is hard. And maybe I haven't had the chance to tell you that yet."

Eve hadn't wanted a lecture, but sympathy might be worse. She wiped at a tear that escaped her lashes. "Have you ever given up a child?"

"No," Lovina said quietly.

"It's harder than you'd even imagine it to be," Eve said, her voice thick. The baby squirmed, and she ran a hand over her belly tenderly.

"If you want my humble opinion, sending a gift along with the baby is a kind gesture, but it won't make it easier for the child. Let the baby go to that family fully and completely. Let the *mamm* raise this baby as her own. What do you want to happen—have your child come looking for you? Get another chance at being a *mamm* to that child in fifteen or twenty years?"

Eve had to admit that thought had crossed her mind. If her child knew that she'd loved him...would he come find her one day?

"Maybe?" she whispered.

"And what happens then? Your husband will have a rather large shock when he finds out that the girl he married had already given birth to a baby. That sort of secret has a way of rocking a marriage, my dear. From what I understood, you wanted to give this child up to another Amish family so that you could get married and have more *kinner* with a husband."

"*Yah*, that's true..." Eve sighed.

"Then do that," Lovina said. "If it's what you want, then stop feeling guilty!"

"You're really telling me that?" Eve demanded. "No guilt?"

"This child is half-English," Lovina said softly. "And you had no choice in getting pregnant. Eve, *no guilt.* That Englisher took not only your innocence, but he took your ability to live a good Amish life. This was not your choice, and if you still want that good Amish life, then I don't judge you for it. I promise you that. And this family that you're considering—Thomas and Patience Wicbe—they can't have more *kinner* of their own, and adoption is the only way for them. You'd be doing something beautiful for that family."

"I've been told that," she agreed, swallowing hard. "But the other family—they have six *kinner* already."

"Then your child would have older siblings to learn from," Lovina said. "Do you want your child to have a good, Amish upbringing?"

"*Yah.*"

"Then let go. And let the woman you choose be the *mamm* to this baby. It won't be easy, but it's better than causing a ruckus later to your own life. Sometimes love means doing the hardest thing possible."

Eve nodded. Letting go had been easier to imagine earlier in her pregnancy. When the baby was just a little poke and flutter, she could imagine letting go. But now—

"Unless you've changed your mind," Lovina said. "Or if you're unsure about this. I'm not trying to push you in any direction. I just want to make sure you know what you're doing."

"*Daet* wants me to give this baby up," Eve said.

But what would her *mamm* have said if she'd lived? Likely the same thing, but kindlier. *Mamm* would have helped her through this. *Daet* had never been the most eloquent when it came to emotions and feelings.

"Your *daet* wants you to be as happy as possible in your life, and he's furious about the man who took the life you wanted from you. It's different than him simply wanting you to give this baby to another family."

Her father loved her as much as she loved this baby inside her, and he wanted her to have a life. But what kind of life would she give her child if she brought him home with her? She'd never marry—the competition was rather fierce when it came to landing a marriage partner, and a single mother wasn't going to win. Her child would have the stigma attached of being born outside of wedlock—but worse, being the result of that kind of trauma. No, a life with her would not be sweeter for this innocent baby.

"I've gone over this in my head a thousand times," Eve said. "My baby will have a better life with another family."

Lovina nodded. "That's a loving choice."

"I hope so."

"And I know you've been feeling unready to meet this couple, but Eve, this is not going to get easier. It might actually help to see them—to be able to imagine the kind of life your baby will have growing up. You're due in two weeks—and babies have a way of defying those due dates. You could have this child any day now."

Eve sucked in a slow breath. "Meeting them makes it feel final."

"Maybe that's what you need."

Eve was silent.

"And I don't want to put the weight of other people's expectations onto you, dear," Lovina went on, "but Thomas and Patience are on pins and needles right now. They want a baby desperately, and it isn't very often that a child arrives in Redemption in need of a family. If you don't want to give your child to them, it's kinder to just tell them. This is agony for them, too."

While Eve wanted this to be about her alone, it wasn't. In a community, everything affected everyone else. This would affect her father and her sisters at home. It would affect Thomas and Patience here in Redemption. Maybe it felt good to stay on the sidelines, hold back her firm decision and allow herself to wonder what it would be like to keep this baby, but it wasn't fair to anyone else.

Would she keep this baby? If she had to be brutally honest with herself and cut past the emotion and her own longing, then she'd have to admit that no, she wouldn't. It would hurt, but she'd give this child up because it was better for the baby, and it gave her a chance at a life, too. That Englisher had taken her innocence, but he wouldn't take the rest of her life away from her.

"I should meet them," Eve said, her voice firming.

"That's a good idea," her aunt replied.

"I'd like to see their home, actually," Eve added. "I'd like to see where my baby would grow up if I choose them."

"Should I see if you can go to their home for dinner, then?" Lovina asked. "Set a date, make this firm? I can go see them myself, tonight."

"*Yah.* If you'd be willing to do that for me," Eve said with a quick nod. "Thank you."

Lovina leaned over and slid and arm around Eve's shoulders. "*Gott* will get you through this, too, you know."

"I know…" Eve swallowed. *Gott* was here with her, and she could still feel His presence. Her mistakes hadn't taken that away from her. She'd made a mistake, and everything had changed except for that one constant certainty—*Gott* was still by her side.

One day, she'd like to get married, and for some reason when she imagined a husband now, he was looking an awful lot like that Noah Wiebe—strong, handsome and capable of making her stomach flutter with a single look.

She pushed him out of her mind. She wasn't here to find a marriage match—she was here for a goodbye.

Chapter Four

When Noah came into Redemption Carpentry the next morning, peeling off his coat and hanging it on a hook, Thomas looked up from the lathe and turned off the gas-powered engine. Thomas grinned at him, a sparkle in his eye.

"Where is Amos?" Noah asked, glancing around.

"He went to square up his tab with Wayne at the dry goods store," Thomas replied. "It's not fair to leave it hanging, especially not at this time of year."

"*Yah*, of course," Noah agreed, and he eyed his brother. "You look cheery."

Noah headed to the woodstove that was already piping heat into both the display room and the shop, and he rubbed his hands in front of it.

"Lovina came by last night," Thomas said. "She wanted to set up a visit with Eve. Lovina said that Eve is ready to meet us, and she wanted to see our home."

"*Yah?*" Noah smiled. "That's great."

"I suggested she come for dinner tonight," Thomas

said. "Patience is a nervous wreck. She started scrubbing the minute Lovina left. She wants everything to be perfect."

"Have you told Rue about it?" Noah asked.

"We didn't tell her, exactly," Thomas replied. "She overheard us talking about it, and she came bursting into our room, so overjoyed at the thought of having a baby brother or sister, and…we couldn't just lie to her, could we?"

Noah grinned at the thought of his little niece's rambunctious nature. She'd been ecstatic to have Patience as a new mother, and she'd very solemnly accepted Noah as her uncle, and it seemed her enthusiasm was going to bridge this, too.

"Wait…you were talking about it in English?" Noah asked.

"It would appear that Rue has picked up enough Dutch to know the words for new baby, mom and dad, big sister, and a few other things that let her piece it all together," Thomas said with a sigh. "I should be proud that she's learning the language so fast."

"You *are* proud of that," Noah countered with a laugh.

"Fine, I am," Thomas admitted. "But I'm also seeing the difficulty in keeping conversations private from *kinner* when you can't just speak in a language they don't understand."

Noah chuckled. Rue had arrived as a little Englisher girl who stubbornly refused all things Amish. And now, she looked the part of an Amish child, except for her hair that had bangs in the front and kept getting into her eyes. But there was still that wild, free part of Rue that would not be tamed, except, possibly, by a younger sibling.

"So she's excited, too?" Noah asked.

"Yah..." Thomas sobered. "I now have a little girl with her hopes up, too. We told her that we weren't sure what would happen, and that maybe, just maybe, Eve would pick us. But then Rue got it into her head that if we prayed for that baby, *Gott* would give it to us. And she wanted to pray right then and there, in the middle of our bed."

"Oh, dear..." Noah felt his stomach sink. "And she's only just learned about *Gott*. If this doesn't go as we hope—"

"I'm afraid of it shaking her faith," Thomas agreed. "But Patience is brilliant. She told Rue that we mustn't pray only for ourselves. We have to pray for Eve, too, and for the baby, and for *Gott* to work things out for the best for everyone."

Noah sighed. "It's tough."

"Incredibly tough," Thomas agreed. "But all the same, tonight we'll meet her over dinner. And *Gott* willing, she'll be impressed with our family and want to leave her baby with us. I don't think there was any way of introducing Eve to Rue without Rue figuring it out anyway."

"I'm sure it will go well," Noah said. "Just relax. You're a loving family. Eve will see that."

"Do you want to come?" Thomas asked.

"Me?" Noah shook his head. "Why?"

"Because you're part of this family, and she already seems to like you," Thomas said. "I think having you there might help, actually. Besides, I don't feel right keeping secrets. This baby is due very soon, and I want her to know exactly the kind of family we are—all of us, *Mamm* included. I won't feel right about it otherwise."

Noah blew out a breath. This was a delicate time, and while Thomas seemed to think this was a good idea, he didn't want to have to face Patience if Eve didn't choose them for her child… What if he said something stupid? He already seemed to talk a whole lot more than he should around that woman.

"I'll tell you what," Noah said slowly. "I'll ask Eve if she wants me there. That's probably the safest thing to do. She's the one who needs to be comfortable, right?"

"Probably wise," Thomas agreed.

The door opened again, and this time Amos came inside along with a rush of cold air and a swirl of icy snowflakes. He slammed the door shut and pulled off his gloves.

"It's cold out there!" Amos said. "I gave all the horses some extra feed. I think they'll need it." Amos rubbed a hand over his beard and looked between them. "What's going on?"

They brought him up to speed, and Amos nodded sagely.

"All right. Good!" Amos shrugged. "Thomas, this is a good thing! It looks to me like *Gott* is working in this. It's all perfect. She needs a family for her child, and you'd love nothing more than to be that family. *Gott* brought her here. Let's trust that *Gott* can finish what He started, shall we?"

"Yah..." Thomas said with a sigh. "I suppose part of my problem is that it's not just Patience and Rue with their hopes up. It's me, too. I'd love nothing more than to raise a baby. I didn't get to do that with Rue, and I missed out. But to start fresh—to raise a little one from a babe in arms and be the *daet* that child always knew... I'd like that."

Noah's heart gave a squeeze. Thomas didn't talk often about what he'd missed out on when Rue's Englisher mother kept him away. But it had hurt him deeply—Noah knew that much. If he could help his brother, he would. One thing was certain—this baby was going to come into this world deeply wanted by more people than could do the raising.

Noah rubbed his hand through his hair, and then reached for his hat.

"I'm going to bring some food over to Wollie's hotel room," he said.

"Yah, of course," Thomas replied. "Don't be too long, though. I need you to help me finish up that tall cabinet. I can't move it alone."

"I won't take too long," he promised, and he headed out into the cold street and next door to Quilts and Such. He'd promised Eve that he'd take her with him, and he found himself feeling a little thrill of anticipation at seeing her again.

Noah paused when he entered the fabric shop, and then he spotted Eve refilling a display of Amish Christmas tree decorations—tiny knitted red mittens, crocheted snowflakes and little cardboard barns that lit up on the inside with battery-operated lights.

Eve saw him at the same time and she smiled. He headed over to her. Lovina was chatting on the other side of the store with her brother-in-law, Bishop Glick, so they had some privacy for the time being.

"Are you ready to come see Wollie?" he asked.

"Yah." She nodded, then licked her lips. "My aunt and I put together a few items for them—some blankets, towels, sheets, that sort of thing. If Mary Lapp baked, we know she'll have done justice to it."

"Yah, there's a lot of food," he said with a chuckle. "Where is it? I'll carry it out—the buggy's hitched."

It didn't take long to get the buggy loaded up, and when Eve came out back to where he was waiting, she looked cheerful. He helped her up into the buggy and then got up beside her. The day was bright and sunny, and he was telling himself that his cheeriness was due to the weather, but he knew that wasn't entirely true.

"I heard that you've got plans for dinner at my brother's place tonight," he said.

Eve tugged the blanket over her lap. *"Yah.* I thought I should. My aunt pointed out that Thomas and Patience are on pins and needles waiting for my decision, so drawing this out is more painful for everyone." She raised her gaze to meet his. "Will you be there?"

"I could…if you wanted me there," he replied.

"The thing is," she said, lowering her voice further, "my aunt is connected to everyone in this town—even the bishop!"

"Yah, I know," he said with a small smile.

"Anyway, Lovina has a strong personality, and I don't want to be pushed into anything, you know? I don't think she'd mean to because she really is trying to be supportive, but if she drives me to your brother's home, there is a better than average chance that she'll stay to dinner because she's the family I have here. And—" Her cheeks flushed. "I'd rather she didn't."

"Ah, I see," Noah said. "I'm happy to drive you. I don't have to stay to dinner, either. I can just drop you off and pick you up later."

"No, you should stay," she replied, and then a smile tickled her lips. "If I want a quick exit, I'll need you."

Noah chuckled at that. "Okay... I could see that."

"I'm only halfway joking about that quick exit," she said. "Would you be offended if I asked you drive me home early...should I need it?"

"Not at all," he replied. "You're in full control of this, Eve. I promise. When you want to leave, I'll drive you. No questions asked."

"That's kind," she said.

"It's only right," he replied. "I can take you after work is done—we can go straight there, if that's okay."

Eve nodded. "*Yah*, thank you."

The hotel where the Zook family was staying was on the far end of Redemption, away from the Amish tourist section of town. It was a one-story affair with plenty of parking, and while the parking lot wasn't exactly Amish friendly, Noah knew the area well enough and parked his buggy next to a car. Eve looked around uncertainly.

"It'll be fine," Noah said. "I parked here last time. We won't stay long anyway."

He put his horses' feed bags on before helping Eve down onto the salted driveway.

"When did you see Wollie last?" she asked.

"I dropped off some food earlier this week," he said, then he headed around to the back of the buggy and pulled out the covered basket that contained *Mammi*'s baking—whoopee pies, cinnamon buns, cookies... even a chocolate pie. He was about to grab the plastic bag containing the linens Lovina was sending, but he looked over at Eve, standing there in the patchy snow.

"I'll come back for it," he said, and he offered her his arm.

Eve put her hand into the crook of his arm, and he found that he liked the way this felt—being the strong arm for a woman to depend on...and maybe even for this particular woman. He led the way to the last room at the far end of the strip. That was where the Zooks were staying, but before he knocked, he glanced down at her. Eve was looking determinedly at the door, her jaw tense and her cheeks pale.

When Noah knocked, the door opened a moment later revealing Wollie dressed in jeans, a long-sleeved shirt, and sock feet. Wollie looked between them, his face registering shock, and it was only when Noah saw his friend's bewildered expression that he realized how this looked.

"Noah...and Eve?" Wollie laughed, and then bent down to give his cousin a brief hug. "I had no idea! Noah, you've kept a rather good secret, my friend!"

And for just a single moment, Noah felt what it

would be like to introduce a wife to an old friend...
and it felt better than it should.

"No, no—" Eve's pallor suddenly turned pink.
"We're not—it's not—" She looked up at Noah. "Maybe
you go get that linen?"

Right—she'd need some privacy for explanations.
He should have thought of that. He handed Wollie
the basket of food with a rueful smile and wordlessly
headed back toward the buggy. He took his time about
gathering up the cloth bags that Lovina had set out for
the Zooks, and when he returned to the hotel room, the
explanations seemed to be out of the way, because both
Wollie and his wife were looking at Eve with sympathy in their eyes.

"I'm back," he said, carrying in the last of the bags.

"It's good to see you again," Wollie said, coming
over to shake his hand. "And thank you for bringing
my cousin. It's been...eight or nine years?"

"Something like that," Eve agreed. "You look the
same... I mean, English, but..."

Noah knew what she meant. Wollie still had a certain Amish quality about him, no matter what an Englisher barber did to his hair, or what clothes he wore.

The hotel room was cramped for a family with four
children. There were two queen-size beds, a TV playing in one corner, and not much else. Wollie's wife,
Natasha, had her toddler daughter on her hip, but the
little girl's fingers were in her mouth and her attention was locked on the television that a brother and
sister were watching from one of the beds. The older

boy, who looked about eight, stood next to his mother, watching them curiously.

"I'm Noah. I'm one of your *daet*'s friends," Noah said. "And you've met Eve? She's your..."

"She's my cousin," Wollie said with a smile. "And Noah's a friend from a really long time ago. We played together when we were your age, Caleb."

"Wow." Caleb looked properly impressed, and he stuck out his hand and Noah shook it. It looked like Wollie was raising his *kinner* with some Amish manners—that was nice to see.

"Do you like whoopee pies?" Noah asked.

"Yeah!" The boy grinned, and Noah couldn't help but smile at the fact that this English boy loved Amish desserts. "Well, we've got whoopee pies and more in that basket over there. We hope it makes things a little cheerier."

"Thank you for this," Natasha said. "We do appreciate it. You've all been really wonderful."

"We're putting together as much as we can," Noah assured them. "And in January, my brother and I will give you some bedroom furniture of your choice, too."

"That's too much," Wollie said, his voice firming. "I know how much you sell your work for, and that's a hit to your bottom line. I've got insurance to cover that."

"We're still here for you," Noah replied. "And you know there's a place for you if you come back to the Amish life."

Wollie and Natasha exchanged a look, and she slipped away, carrying the basket to the bed for the kids to come look through. Eve followed her and sank on the edge of the bed. She glanced over her shoulder once toward the men.

"And if we don't come back?" Wollie asked, switching to Dutch for privacy. "For Natasha—it's not what she was raised to do, you know."

"We heard that you might want to," Noah said.

"Wanting to do something and having the ability to make it work—" Wollie shook his head. "Natasha isn't Amish. I knew that when I married her. I can't push this."

"Whatever you decide to do, we're providing you with bedroom furniture," Noah said firmly. "I'm standing by it."

Wollie's face colored and he nodded. "You're a good man, Noah. I may have spoken too enthusiastically when I saw my parents last."

Looking around that hotel room at the Zook family, he could see exactly why it would be complicated. These *kinner* weren't Amish, and neither was their mother. Natasha looked even more English next to Eve's somber clothing and neat *kapp* in her hair.

"And my cousin?" Wollie asked, lowering his voice further. "Is she going to be okay?"

"*Yah*, I think so," Noah replied. "Did she tell you why she's here?"

"To have the baby and…give it up?" Wollie asked sadly.

Noah nodded. *"Yah."*

"Natasha and I aren't in a position to take in another child," he said.

"I don't think she's here for that," Noah said. "She

cares about you and wanted to make this time here about something more than…the baby."

Wollie met Noah's gaze. "She was a sweet kid—smart, kind. I really liked her."

"I think she felt the same way about you," Noah replied. "From what she's told me."

"She's Amish—I probably won't see much of her," Wollie said. "You'll look out for her, won't you?"

"For as long as she's here," Noah agreed. "Of course."

"Thank you." Wollie pressed his lips together. "I appreciate that."

And here Noah and Eve were trying to do the same for Wollie. He was more part of their Amish community than he thought, even now. This was what community was for—for the hard and worrying times.

"How are you doing otherwise?" Noah asked.

"I've still got a job," Wollie said. "And the insurance agent is getting things cleared away so we can get some money to restart. It'll be okay."

"I'm glad to hear that," Noah said. "And your parents?"

"They're fine." Wollie smiled weakly. "Still deeply disappointed in me, but fine."

"*Yah*, well… Amish parents, right?" Noah said—it was an old joke, and Wollie chuckled, too.

"Amish parents…" he agreed. "Funny. I always thought I'd end up being an Amish *daet* one day. Didn't turn out that way."

"You're more Amish than you think, Wollie," Noah replied.

"I've actually got to get to work soon," Wollie said. "My shift starts in about an hour."

"We'd best get back, too," Noah said. "But just to let you know, we're collecting household items for you— the whole town is pitching in, and we'll get you back onto your feet. That's a promise."

"Like I said, I have insurance," Wollie said.

"You also have us."

"I do appreciate it, Noah." Wollie shook his hand firmly, and his eyes misted. "You're a good friend. Just make sure my cousin is taken care of, too."

"You can count on it," Noah said.

They said their goodbyes, Eve gave Natasha a smile and a nod, and then they headed back out to where the buggy was waiting. But something from this visit had stuck in Noah's heart. Wollie had a family—and seeing that family struck home how much a man changed with marriage and *kinner*. This wasn't Wollie's choice to come back—it would have to be a family decision... like his own parents had made. His parents had taken on the challenge of joining the Amish life together. For all the things that frustrated him about his mother, Rachel Wiebe was a brave woman to do it.

It was very likely too much to hope that Wollie and Natasha could do the same.

"What did you think of his wife?" Noah asked as he flicked the reins and they headed back out to the street once more.

"She's nice," Eve said. "I can see why he loves her."

Noah looked over at Eve and smiled faintly. *Yah*, a

man could fall in love with the right woman rather easily. But making a life with her wasn't always so simple.

Wollie went English for a very nice woman, and he may very well have to stay that way.

Chapter Five

That evening after the sun had set, leaving the town of Redemption aglow with streetlights that reflected cheerily off the Christmas decorations, Lovina flicked the sign to Closed and locked the door. The fire in the potbellied stove had burned down, and Eve pulled on her uncle's heavy coat, wrapping it around herself.

"The sales were very good today," Lovina said, opening the till. She pulled out the first batch of bills and began to count them, her lips moving silently as she worked.

"*Yah*, it looks that way." Eve perched on the edge of a stool, watching her aunt flick through the stacks of bills.

"Are you sure you don't want me to come with you tonight?" Lovina asked, pausing in her counting. "I'd be happy to offer moral support. This is a difficult time, I know, and I'd just feel better knowing that I was there for you. I think your father would feel better, too."

"I appreciate it," Eve replied. "And you have been wonderful, Aunty. I just think it's better if I see their home alone. I have to be able to look back on this later and feel confident in my choice, and that will be easier to do if I go by myself."

Lovina nodded and made a note on a bank deposit form, and moved on to the next pile of bills. "I do understand that, dear. This is an incredibly personal choice."

"Do you have any advice, though?" Eve asked. "Anything I should be looking for?"

Lovina was silent for a moment, her brow furrowed.

"Just pray for *Gott*'s guidance," Lovina said. "And... maybe expect to feel some conflicting emotions when you meet Patience."

"Is there something off-putting about her?" Eve asked, straightening. "Anything I should know?"

"Nothing." Lovina made another note on the bank slip, wrapped it around the bills, slipped the money into a plastic bank bag and sealed it. "It's just... I'm only thinking about how I might feel in your situation, and I imagine it would be hard to meet the woman who might be your baby's *mamm*. There would be some very natural feelings attached to that... Some jealousy, maybe. Some protectiveness."

That was sage advice, Eve had to admit. She wasn't looking forward to seeing Patience. She would be a lovely woman, no doubt, but even the thought of seeing her had Eve's stomach in knots.

There was a tap on the front door, and Eve turned to see Noah through the window.

"He's here," Lovina said with a reassuring smile. "It will be okay. I know it."

Eve exchanged a look with her aunt, then she rose

to her feet. There was no use putting this off—if she was looking for a family for her baby, she'd just found a very good match. So why didn't she feel more peace about this?

"I'll be praying for you," Lovina said. "And I'll wait up for you." Lovina gave her a nod.

There was something reassuring about having someone wait up for her, and Eve said a silent prayer for guidance this evening. She needed to know, beyond any shadow of doubt, that she was making the right choice.

Eve and Noah headed back out into the street, pulled the door shut behind them, and when Eve looked in through the window, she saw her aunt's troubled gaze following her. Was Lovina uncertain about this choice in family, or was her concern something deeper?

But it wasn't Lovina's concern that should be influencing her tonight—tonight was about meeting a family without the benefit of her aunt's opinions to steer her.

Noah had the buggy ready to go, the horses stamping impatiently in the icy snow.

"Let me help you," Noah said, and Eve pulled herself out of her thoughts. She accepted his hand and hoisted herself up into the buggy.

There were two folded blankets on the seat, and while Noah got into the buggy next to her, she arranged the blankets over her legs. He flicked the reins and the horses started forward, the wheels crunching over the packed snow.

The few Englisher businesses along this street had Christmas lights circling their windows, and the streetlights had large green wreaths with shining red berries. The sky was clear, but the stars weren't visible here in town—just the silvery moon that hung low in the sky.

That morning, Eve had been reading the Christmas story in her Bible. It was a solitary feeling to be carrying a child without a husband to support her, or a community to celebrate this baby. In years past, Eve hadn't appreciated how difficult Jesus's birth would have been for Mary. In Bible stories, Mary seemed different from people today—holier, stronger, braver. But now, pregnant with her own child outside of her society's approved boundaries, Eve wondered how frightened Mary might have been. Because Eve was terrified.

"You know, Wollie asked me to look out for you today," Noah said.

"Did he?" She smiled at that. "He always was a nice, older cousin."

And neither of them had ended up with the proper Amish life, had they? She might be determined to stay Amish, but she had a hard road ahead of her.

"He's worried about you, I think," Noah said.

"Well, I'm equally worried about him," she replied frankly. "I still have a chance at an Amish life. I'm not sure he does."

"*Gott* knows," Noah said.

"*Yah...*" Only *Gott* knew what was in store for any of them, and there were some problems that only *Gott* could fix.

"My brother is so excited to meet you," Noah said. They came to the end of Main Street and turned onto a smaller road, past Englisher houses with front yards covered in children's boot prints, windows lit from within and Christmas trees sparkling.

"Yah?" she said faintly.

"He could talk about nothing else all afternoon," Noah said. When she didn't answer, he added, "I know this is a hopeful evening for my brother, but for you—I imagine it's different."

"Yah," she admitted. "I hate this—every step of it. But we can't refuse to do what we have to, can we?"

"I'm sorry," he said. "I wish I could make it easier somehow."

"I don't think you can," she said. "I'm doing this for a reason, though. That Englisher boy took away more than he ever knew, I'm sure. He took away my ability to have a proper, Amish life. I want a husband and a houseful of my own *kinner*. The truly sad thing is that I want what your brother and his wife want—I just can't have it yet. I want to cook breakfast for my own family. I want a husband to drive me to church, and I want all the trials and challenges that come with raising and loving a large family. I've always wanted that."

"And your chance at that beautiful life was taken from you," he said.

"Yah. Without my consent. Against my will." She sucked in a deep breath. "If I'd had a boyfriend, and I'd made the mistake, I might be less angry. But I didn't! I was in the wrong place at the wrong time! That Englisher destroyed *my life*." Her voice trembled. "Is it fair to ask me to give up the rest of my life because of something I didn't choose?"

"I agree," he said quietly. "You don't deserve this."

"My *daet*… If you'd seen his face." Eve sighed. "He wanted more for me. If I stay single, and never get married, I'll be his responsibility to care for. I'll stay a dependant. I'll likely be a hindrance to him remarrying one day."

"I'm sure your *daet* doesn't see it that way," Noah countered.

"But I do."

She hadn't sat by her mother's bedside, listening to her last bits of advice, for nothing. Eve wanted to be a good daughter, and eventually, a good wife. She wanted to live out her beliefs with her Amish community, and she wanted to pass down her love for *Gott* to her own *kinner*.

Rebellion isn't worth it, her *mamm* had told her. *Be a good girl, and you'll reap the rewards of having made solid choices. Going a little wild might feel good in the moment, but there is only regret at the end of that road. Trust me, my dear girl.*

And Eve had promised *Gott* that she'd follow her *mamm*'s advice. She'd stay to the narrow path, and she'd embrace all of *Gott*'s best that He had waiting for her.

For it to be taken from her like that? To have a child out of wedlock and become completely unmarriageable, all because of one despicable Englisher who tricked her? Could she lose *Gott*'s best for her just as easily as that?

"My *mamm* told me stories about girls who made unwise choices," Eve said. "She even told me about Wollie—how he went English and all he'd given up for an Englisher girl. She didn't want me to do the same thing—fall in love with an Englisher and have no path home again." Eve sucked in a breath of frigid air. "Maybe *Gott*'s best for me will have to change, too, now."

"I don't have the answers," Noah said quietly. "Maybe the bishop has more than I do, but I just can't imagine that we're powerful enough to thwart *Gott*'s plans. *Gott* is still working, Eve. He has to be."

Eve fell silent for a few beats, mulling over his words. But she'd had enough of talking of her own sadness.

"Tell me about your niece," Eve said instead.

Noah looked over at her uncertainly.

"Please," she added. "I'd like to hear about her."

For the rest of the ride, Noah chatted on about his little niece, whom he seemed very attached to. It was good to see that the girl in that home was surrounded by a devoted extended family. If her child joined them, her half-Englisher baby would be equally loved.

Would Thomas and Patience's home be enough to give *this* child a reason to stay Amish, too?

Chapter Six

Eve sucked in a wavering breath as Noah steered the horses into a driveway and they plodded toward a little one-story house. This was an acreage, obviously, and she could make out a stable in the darkness, illuminated by the light coming from Noah's headlamps. The house looked snug, and it glowed cozily into the frigid night. Her stomach clenched in nervousness, as Noah reined in the horses in front of the house, and she felt his hand touch her sleeve.

"You okay?" Noah asked, his voice low.

"Uh—" She tried to force a smile but wasn't sure it was successful. "I'll have to be."

"They're very nice people," he said.

The door opened, and a young man appeared in the doorway. He had a short russet-colored beard and a kind face. She could see the family resemblance between the two men, so this must be Thomas. He pulled on a coat as he stepped outside, and dropped a hat onto his head. He came out onto the steps with a nervous smile.

"Hello!" he said. "Noah, I'll help you with the horses."

"*Yah*, thanks," Noah replied, and he looked over at Eve again, and lowered his voice. "They're very nice. I promise."

A woman appeared in the doorway behind Thomas, and a little girl who was only barely being restrained.

"Is it her?" the girl asked, a little too loudly in English.

The woman bent to talk to her, and Noah hopped to the ground. He held out his hand, and then stepped closer to help her descend. She managed to get down with a little more dignity than the last time he'd helped her out of a buggy, and she glanced up to see Thomas Weibe looking at her hopefully. He put out a hand.

"It's a pleasure to meet you," Thomas said.

Eve shook his hand, and Thomas gestured behind him. "That is my wife, Patience, and our daughter, Rue. If you want to go in where it's warm, Noah and I will join you in a few minutes."

"*Yah*, I'll do that," Eve said, and with one last glance at Noah, whose gaze was locked on her almost protectively, she headed toward the open door.

"Come in," Patience said as Eve came up the steps. "You must be freezing. I have tea on, if you want some."

Eve came into the house, the welcome warmth enveloping her. She slid off her coat and Patience hung it up for her with a smile.

"My name is Patience," she said, and the introductions were made.

After having said a polite hello, Eve glanced around the entryway. It wasn't quite a full mudroom—but it did give some space from the kitchen, which she could see directly into from where she stood. A big, black stove dominated one side of the room, and a bank of tall white cupboards flanked the other side. The floor was a polished dark wood, and the solid kitchen table was the same color as the floor.

An older woman sat at the kitchen table. She had graying hair and a neat dress. She stood up as Eve came in and gave her a smile. Who was this, in the family circle?

"This is my mother-in-law," Patience said.

Noah and Thomas's mother…it was nice to see her, actually. This would be her child's grandmother if Eve chose the Wiebe family.

"It's nice to meet you. I'm Rachel," the older woman said. "Come, sit down. Do you want some cookies? I'm just going to get the pot of tea ready."

"No, I'm not hungry," Eve said, and she felt heat rise in her cheeks. "I mean—" She was there for dinner, after all.

"You're nervous, too," Patience said.

"Yah," she admitted with a shaky smile. "I am."

"I think we all are," Patience replied.

"What are you saying?" Rue whispered to Patience.

"This is Rue," Patience said, switching to English. "She doesn't understand very much Dutch, but she's learning, aren't you, sugar?"

"Yah, I'm learning," Rue said proudly. "I can ask for the bathroom in Dutch. Do you want to hear it?"

The women laughed, and Patience smoothed a hand over the girl's straight blond hair.

"Not just now," Patience said gently.

Eve sank down into a kitchen chair; the little girl sat down next to her and put a hand on the side of her belly.

"Rue, you can't just—" Patience started.

"It's okay," Eve said. In a way, it was nice to have someone, even a very young someone, react to her pregnant form with some spontaneous happiness. "Can you feel that? That's the baby moving."

"I can feel it!" Rue's eyes lit up. "Is that my baby brother or sister?"

Eve hesitated, meeting the little girl's expectant gaze. Rue's breath was bated, and her little hand rested on Eve's stomach hopefully. Even this little girl was hoping for this baby...and that was almost heartbreaking.

"We talked about this, Rue," Patience said. "We don't know yet. We have to ask *Gott* to do what's best for all of us, and we don't know what that answer is yet."

What was best for all of them... That was a tall order that Eve wasn't even sure could be answered this side of glory.

"I'm sorry," Patience said, switching into Dutch again. "She's very young, and she overheard us talking. Apparently, she understands more Dutch than we gave her credit for. We would have tried to be more discreet. Please don't take this as pressure from us."

"No, of course not," Eve replied.

Such polite discussion over the future of her unborn baby...

"Have some tea?" Rachel asked, coming back to the table with a teapot. She put it on top of a cork pot holder, and then headed back to the counter for teacups.

"Thank you," Eve said. It was something to do with her hands, at least.

"Patience here is a wonderful teacher," Rachel said, returning with a teetering pile of cups. "She's not teaching at the schoolhouse anymore—she just finished the semester—but there are a few boys that come by for some extra help with their reading after school. She's got a real gift with *kinner*."

"Oh?" Eve said.

Rachel poured Eve a cup of tea and nudged a sugar bowl toward her.

"This home is a loving, supportive home for a child who is half-English," Rachel said in Dutch. "Rue has come such a long way in a short period of time. Her Englisher mother had bought her all sorts of clothes that weren't appropriate for an Amish girl to wear, and as you can imagine, it was very difficult for Rue to let go. She'd lost her mother, and those clothes were a connection to her."

"Poor thing," Eve murmured, looking down at Rue, who now had her elbows planted on the table.

"Yah..." Rachel agreed. "But Patience was the one who had the idea to turn that Englisher clothing into a quilt for her, and Rue sleeps with it every night now."

"Are you talking about my quilt?" Rue piped up.

"See? She understands more Dutch than we think!" Rachel chuckled.

"My *mammi* is teaching me to talk like everyone

else," Rue said soberly. "And that's because she was born regular, just like me."

"Regular?" Eve asked weakly.

"She means English," Rachel replied, some color coming into her cheeks. "I was born English, and my husband and I converted when our *kinner* were very young."

This was information that hit Eve like a wet slap. Eve gave Rachel a second look. Come to think of it, the older woman did lack a few of those Amish facial characteristics.

"And *Mammi* even went back to live regular for a while, too!" Rue added with a bright smile. "But then she came back again."

"About the same time that Rue arrived, actually," Rachel said uncomfortably. "I apologize, Eve. This wasn't quite how I intended to tell you about my history."

"Were you going to tell me at all?" Eve asked, her voice tight. Because up until now, there had been plenty of opportunity for both Lovina and Noah to fill her in, and neither of them had said a word.

"Yes, I was going to tell you," Rachel said. "Of course! Why do you think I'm here tonight? We aren't the kind of people who ask to adopt a baby without giving all the information."

Englishers... The very thought made her stomach turn and her heart speed up. She'd had very limited contact with the Englishers in her life. Wollie going English had been a shock to the entire family—one so terrible that they only talked about it away from other people. She'd never worked at a store or dealt with tourists directly until she'd come to Redemption, but she had discovered what kind of people the English were at that party nine months ago. And this woman—Thomas's own *mamm*—was English born, and had even reverted to English ways rather recently. She could hear her own heartbeat thudding inside her skull.

"I can see that this has been a shock," Rachel said softly. "And I'm very sorry about this. You see, I thought it might help if you met me directly, if you could see that I'm no different from you—"

"But you *are* different from me," Eve said, and Rachel recoiled.

"Am I?" Rachel asked. "If I hadn't said anything, would you have guessed?"

"The English are different from us. They're raised differently. They see the world differently! They see *Gott* differently!"

"We aren't a different species," Rachel replied. "We're all human. And I'm as Amish as you—I was baptized into the church, and I raised my *kinner* in the faith, too."

"*Yah*, all human," Eve agreed. "But you aren't as Amish as me. You were raised with different expectations in behavior and in…everything. I was raised to want *Gott*'s way and to be satisfied with my role. Were you?"

"I was raised Mennonite," Rachel said tersely. "I didn't exactly come off the bottom of someone's shoe. And I've loved *Gott* all my life. You can't assume that because I wasn't born on one of these farms that I didn't know *Gott*. Is He so narrow that He can only be found here?"

"So you're saying that the Amish life isn't necessary?" Eve asked. "It's all the same—Amish, English..."

"No!" Patience interjected for the first time, and her face flushed red. The room fell silent, and even little Rue stared up at Patience in shock. "No, she isn't saying that!" Patience closed her eyes, and then lowered her voice. "The Amish life matters—and we are a devoted Amish family. Our faith, our way of life, our language—it's what makes us who we are and draws us closer together as a community and closer to *Gott*. No one here is suggesting that there is no difference."

Tears rose in Rachel's eyes, and she looked toward her daughter-in-law, stricken. "I didn't mean that," Rachel said, and then turned to Eve. "It's just...sometimes when you weren't born in the Amish faith, you get treated differently when people find out. People can act like you're lower, almost. I just mean that on a human level, we're the same. It's our choices that matter, that change us. I didn't mean to get testy. I was just being overly sensitive. I'm sorry."

Rachel's Dutch was flawless. If she hadn't told Eve, she wouldn't have guessed...and that scared her, too. Because this family was offering her child an Englisher grandmother.

Even if that Englisher grandmother spoke excellent Dutch.

The door opened just then and the men came back inside. They pulled off their boots and washed their hands, then came into the kitchen. Thomas hesitated, looking around the room.

"I'm hungry," he said, a little too cheerfully.

Noah met Eve's gaze, and he winced. Did he guess at what she'd just discovered?

"We were—uh—just discussing your mother's history," Patience said weakly.

"Oh…" Thomas nodded. "We wanted my *mamm* to be here so that you could meet her properly."

"*Yah*, she mentioned that," Eve replied.

Patience and Rachel exchanged a look, and Eve noticed the silent apology passing between them. Rachel might have been born English, and even returned to her English life for a while, but she was a part of this family.

Noah came into the kitchen and when Thomas gestured for him to have a seat at the table, he pulled out a chair next to Rue and sat down. Noah glanced around the table, then his warm gaze landed on Eve. His eyebrow flicked up, and she sensed the question. She smiled faintly in response. She was fine—she wasn't leaving yet.

"Since this is out now," Eve said, "I have some questions. Rachel, why did you leave the Amish life after converting? If you chose the Amish way, what made you leave again?"

Rachel looked uncomfortably toward Thomas and Patience.

"You'd best just talk about it," Thomas said. "We're here to be honest, aren't we?"

"I lost my husband," Rachel replied quietly. "And it was a difficult time for me. I missed my family—my sister, mostly. I missed who I used to be."

"Englisher, you mean," Eve said.

"No, I missed being young," Rachel said. "You won't understand that at your age. But when I lost my husband, I was suddenly a different person than I was with him. Marriage does that—it changes you fundamentally, especially the longer you're together. And when he died, I missed who I was when I was a young woman, before I'd married and had *kinner*. And having lost my husband, I had to discover who I was again—on my own."

"And who were you?" Eve asked warily.

"Me, just lonelier." Rachel dropped her gaze. "I thought I could find some part of myself that I'd laid aside, and it turned out that I couldn't. I found the old Mennonite church very comforting, and I'd missed my sister desperately. I didn't want to have to marry again to keep myself as I would with the Amish, so I got a job. I was a janitor at a school, actually. And for a little while I worked at a retail store, and then I got a job at the company my sister works for, in the mail room…" She smiled faintly. "You don't care about that, though, do you?"

"But you came back…" Eve said.

"*Yah*. The Amish life isn't an easy one, but it's the right one for me. It turns out that I had changed too much during my marriage to be able to fully embrace an English life again."

"How long were you gone?" Eve asked.

"Nearly ten years," Rachel replied. "I know that sounds terrible, but I did visit every month, and I wrote my sons letters in between those visits."

"What took so long?" Eve asked.

Rachel lifted her shoulders. "It was a process to find myself again and to come full circle. But now that I'm here, I'm here to stay."

"And what will keep my little one Amish, if this family has so many connections to the English?" Eve asked.

The room was silent for a moment, and Eve looked around at them daringly. What did they think they could give her child, with all of this rebellion in their own ranks? Was the other family better, perhaps? The solidly Amish family that would accept another child without having longed for it? Maybe so.

"We'd give your baby love," Patience said, breaking the silence. "We'd love your baby with all our hearts. And we are an Amish family—we just aren't hiding anything from you. We're being open and honest with you because we don't believe that *Gott* can bless anything less."

"What other English family members do you have?" Eve asked.

"None we have much contact with," Thomas replied. "My mother's siblings come by once every few years, but we don't keep up with them much. It's just how things worked out."

"And Rue's family?" Eve pressed.

"Her mother was all she had," Thomas replied. "Rue's *mamm* had a tragic life of her own, and she grew up in the foster system. So there wasn't any other family to try to gain custody of her."

Eve let out a shaky breath, and she instinctively put

her hand across her belly protectively. This baby was already coming from tragedy...

"I want this child raised Amish," she said. "And I don't want him or her to even know that they have any English family."

"We don't have to tell the child about—" Thomas paused, licked his lips "—about your difficulties. We could simply say that you wanted him or her to have the best life possible, and you weren't able to provide that."

And she did want her child to have the happiest, most fulfilling, most secure Amish life available—that was why Eve was here. She wanted her child to grow up happy, loved and unapologetically Amish. She wanted her child to be free from any stigma attached from a single mother.

"Why don't we eat?" Noah said, speaking for the first time. "I don't know about all of you, but I feel better with food in my stomach. We've all been working all day."

"Yes, good idea," Patience said. "The food is ready, so let's get it onto the table."

Eve instinctively started to stand up to lend a hand in the kitchen, and Patience waved her off.

"No, Eve, sit. Be comfortable. I've never been pregnant myself, but I've seen enough pregnancies with my sisters and my friends to know that these last weeks aren't an easy time. Dinner won't take a minute."

And Eve sank back down into her chair and looked over at Noah. Rue had come up with a carved rooster and was making it walk up Noah's arm. He looked over the top of Rue's head and smiled faintly.

This was the Wiebe family—a husband who'd had an Englisher child out of wedlock, a grandmother who was Englisher born and had only recently returned, and a little half-English girl who seemed to relay all of the family secrets when she chattered.

Her child's birth story wouldn't remain a secret long in this home; she could already tell. And here, it seemed, being English wasn't something to be ashamed of.

Was that a good thing, or a bad thing? She wasn't so sure. Because in her experience, the English were not to be trusted.

"Cookie?" Noah murmured, nudging a plate toward her.

There were shortbread cookies on the plate, all in the shape of little trees. She accepted one and took a bite. It was buttery and perfectly baked.

Patience came to the table with a platter of roast beef, and she put it down with a smile. She was pretty, slim and seemed very loving to the family around her... She was the perfect Amish mother. Or was she? What else was this family hiding?

And yet, if Eve had met Patience under different circumstances, she would have liked her. Eve watched Patience as she brought the food to the table. Thomas gave his wife an encouraging smile, and there was a tenderness between the couple that Eve couldn't help but envy. What would it be like to have a man love her the way Thomas loved Patience? It was wrong to envy, she knew that, but she couldn't help the pang all the same. One day, hopefully soon, Eve wanted this very scene for herself—a husband, a family, *kinner* that she could proudly claim as hers… Patience Wiebe was the wife and *mamm* that Eve longed to be.

For all appearances, at least.

The baby wriggled inside her, and Eve ran her hand over her stomach, feeling the baby settle at her touch. Could Eve pass the baby into this lovely woman's arms and let her be the *mamm*? Could she trust them?

The problem was, now that she'd met her, Patience was no longer an ideal to be jealous of. She was a very real woman who wouldn't be perfect…and that might be even harder to accept.

Noah sat across from his mother, and her gaze flickered toward him. There was red in her cheeks— she was embarrassed. Somehow that stabbed at his heart worse than anything else. His *mamm* might have wronged him, and he might have his own issues with her, but seeing her embarrassed…

Mamm pushed her chair back, then left the table, heading into the kitchen. Noah swallowed against the tightness in his throat. This was their family—and their private problems. He knew it was only right to be open with Eve about all of it, but it still felt like an invasion.

And yet seeing his mother's back to them, pretending to arrange buns in a bowl, but taking far too long to accomplish the task, he felt his chest constrict in sympathy. She was still his *mamm*, and she'd been hopeful that she could help in this adoption process…

Beside him, Eve nibbled at the food on her plate, as she listened to Thomas tell a story about Rue. What did Eve think of them now?

Noah pushed his chair out and stood up. He angled around the table and headed over to where his *mamm* stood by the bowl of dinner rolls.

"Mamm?" he said quietly.

She wiped her eyes hurriedly. "Yes, son?"

"Are you crying?" he asked hesitantly.

"No." But the tears in her eyes said otherwise, and he stood there awkwardly, unsure of what to do.

"Mamm, all you could be was honest," he said, putting a hand on her arm.

Rachel sucked in a breath and checked her hair with her hands.

"It's what you told me and Thomas over and over again when we were *kinner*—after we made a mistake, we had to confess and be honest."

"That wasn't a confession," *Mamm* said softly. "That was judgment."

"She doesn't know us…" Noah said. "And we're asking her to choose us—"

"I'm being judged by an unwed mother," Rachel said, and her lips wobbled.

"You were right to tell her the truth," Noah said. "I think it was…brave of you, actually. You're doing all of this to help Thomas, and I know he appreciates that."

"You didn't hear the way she spoke to me…" Rachel licked her lips. "She thinks I'm beneath her—"

"She's terrified of Englishers," Noah said. "She was taken advantage of by some Englisher boys—that's how the baby was conceived. It wasn't by choice on her part."

Rachel blinked, then darted a look back at the table. "What?"

"That pregnancy isn't her fault, and I dare say that her reaction was based on those fears," Noah replied.

Rachel nodded. "That does change things. The poor girl…"

"*Yah.*" Noah swallowed. "I'm sure that's private information, though. And she never wants her child to know it."

"I can understand that," Rachel said, and she shook her head slowly.

"Are you okay, *Mamm*?" Noah asked.

Rachel turned toward him and gave him a nod. "I'll be fine, son. Tonight isn't about me—or it shouldn't be. Anyway, let's try to make your brother look good."

At the table, Rue was up on her knees and Thomas told her to sit down properly. Patience sat faced away from them, but from the set of her shoulders, Noah could see her tension. He knew what Thomas had been hoping for from this evening—a chance to put Eve at ease and show her they were a loving family—but Eve seemed just as tense as Patience was. She'd stopped pretending to eat, and the fork lay on her plate.

Mamm returned to the table ahead of Noah with the bowl of rolls in her hands, and Noah followed. This Christmas, they were all hoping for a special gift… a tiny bundle of joy. But that gift would come with a price for Eve, and only now was Noah realizing how steep it would be.

Rue left the table, carrying her plate to the sink, and Noah took his niece's chair next to Eve. For the next few minutes everyone talked, pretending that this was just a normal dinner.

"And how was work today, Noah?" *Mamm* asked.

"Uh—" Noah shifted uncomfortably. "It was busy."

"Did you finish that sleigh bed you were working on?" *Mamm* pressed brightly.

"No, not yet."

"Oh…"

The conversation seemed to be at a lull, and Noah felt a touch on his knee under the table. He looked over to see Eve's gaze flicker toward him, her cheeks flushed.

"I'm actually getting tired," Eve said quietly.

The table fell silent.

"Right," Noah said. "I can give you a ride home, if that's what you want."

"Please."

"I'll just go hitch up," Noah said, and he scraped his chair back and headed for the door. This was what he'd promised her he'd do…even though they hadn't succeeded yet in showing Eve the family they wanted her to see—the family they *were* beneath all the mistakes.

All the same, he didn't think Eve's decision was going to come down to how united and happy the Wiebe family appeared to be over a dinner. It might not even come down to Rachel and her past mistakes. This decision was going to be made by Eve's personal accounting of things…and even Noah wasn't sure how that would turn out.

The question that hung almost palpably in the air was, *What does she think of us now?*

When Noah got the buggy hitched up, he brought it around to the side of the house. The door opened and Eve came out.

"Good night!" Patience called.

"If you need anything at all—" Thomas began, but he didn't finish the offer, the words hanging in the air with the cloud of his breath.

"Thank you." Eve turned toward Thomas and Patience. "I appreciate it. Good night."

Noah got down and helped her up into the buggy. Once they were both settled in, away from the winter wind, he flicked the reins and they started off. Noah looked back to see his brother standing in the doorway, his hands limp at his sides. They'd failed—Noah could feel it, too.

The evening was clear and bright, the stars twinkling overhead and the moon spilling silvery light over snow-cloaked fields. The snow seemed to absorb the sound around them as the horses plodded forward, their tack jingling in the icy air.

"They seem nice," Eve said after a couple of minutes of silence.

Noah looked over at her uncertainly. "Did you think so? You didn't seem comfortable."

"It isn't a matter of liking people," Eve replied. "This is a different kind of decision, isn't it?"

"*Yah*, you're right," he agreed.

"I was wondering about your *mamm*," she said.

Noah nodded. "I thought you might want to know more about her."

"They converted to our lifestyle?" she asked.

"*Yah*. My parents were both Mennonite, and my *daet* was working on a book about Amish life. He stayed with a bishop and his wife in a nearby community, and then *Mamm* joined him there. I guess they fell in love with our ways. The bishop in that district had some connections here in Redemption, so when my *mamm* and *daet* decided to convert, and once they understood the ways well enough, they settled into the community here. But no one really knew them from their Englisher days, so their secret was safe, for the most part."

"They came to Redemption for a fresh start," she said.

"I guess. I never knew about it growing up. I was a toddler at the time, and my brother was just a baby. They raised us as if we'd been born Amish, and we never knew any different."

"When did you find out?" she asked.

"When *Daet* died," he said, and his throat tightened. "*Mamm* told us then. It was a huge shock. We hadn't even met any of the Englisher family at that point. We knew we had some, but we also knew they thought we were crazy for living like we did, so we had nothing to do with them. My grandparents were dead. In fact, I honestly thought the bishop and his wife in the other district were our relatives until *Daet* died and *Mamm* told us differently. It was a lot to take in."

"Then your *mamm* left you?" Eve asked.

"She asked us to go with her," he replied. "She asked us to leave the Amish life behind and go back to the life she'd had before. She said she could get a job and take care of us. And we refused."

"Were you angry?" Eve whispered.

"Furious," he replied. "We'd been lied to all our lives, and then asked to leave everything we believed in behind. I was angry at *Daet* for dying, and I was angry at *Gott* for allowing it to happen. But mostly, I was angry at *Mamm* for not being strong enough. She raised us to choose the right path, no matter how hard it might be. But she didn't do that, did she? *Daet* died, and she gave up."

"Did you ever go see her life—the English one?" she asked.

"Not me. My brother did. But I didn't want to see it. She came to visit once a month, but it wasn't enough. I remember being a big, strong, teenage boy and crying alone in my bed at night because I missed my *mamm*." He laughed uncomfortably. "That's probably more than I should admit to—"

Eve slid her hand into his, and he looked down at her.

"That would have been terrible," she said. "In a way, you lost both your parents."

"In a way," he agreed. "Then she'd come to visit, and I'd be so angry that I would barely talk to her. It wasn't helpful. It didn't make me feel any better. I just didn't know any other way to deal with it." Noah cleared his throat. "I'm sorry, I'm not sure that's helpful for my brother—"

"It helps me know you better," she said quietly.

Did he dare show her more of what was inside him? He was supposed to be building his brother up, not exposing his own personal pain.

"Do you think your *mamm* will ever leave again?" she asked.

Noah let out a slow breath. "I hope not. I'm not sure I could take it."

That was all he had—a truly sincere hope that his *mamm* was back for good. She said she was, but was he confident of that? *Mamm* still wasn't like the other Amish women. She didn't have that quiet, unshakable confidence that other Amish women had, because she had been shaken.

Noah looked down at Eve's hand in his. The wind was cold, and he flipped the blanket over their entwined fingers.

"I'm afraid I'm making our family sound less devoted than it is," he said quietly. "You've seen the worst of us—I promise you that."

Eve didn't answer, but she did lean into his shoulder, the pressure of her arm against his feeling like an undeserved comfort. He wasn't supposed to be taking this from her...he was supposed to be the strong one. He was supposed to be doing this for Thomas.

"We love each other," he added earnestly. "And we care enough to stick around and work it out. I think that should count for something."

"It does."

He could sense the hesitation in her words, though.

"What do you think of us Wiebes now?"

Eve looked over at him, then sucked in a breath. "I thought I'd prepared myself to feel some jealousy."

"Yah?" He looked down at her.

"Do you know what it's like to look at the woman who might be the *mamm* who raises your baby? To look her in the face and know that your child will run to her with a skinned knee, and cry for her after a bad dream at night…"

"No," he breathed. "I guess I don't."

"My aunt warned me about how it might feel, and I thought I may be ready to face my own jealousy and pettiness." She dropped her gaze. "It turns out that it's scarier to see real people who might make mistakes, just like I would. Much scarier. I want my child to be insulated from anything that might hurt him. If I'm giving this baby up, that guarantee would make it easier. But instead I have to choose from very real, imperfect people."

"I'm sorry we aren't more perfect," he said quietly.

She smiled at that, but didn't answer. For a few minutes they rode in silence, their hands clasped under the blanket. He ran his thumb over her soft skin and looked over at her. He wished he could put his arm around her, tug her a little closer, but he was already overstepping by holding her hand, and while he should let go of her, he couldn't quite bring himself to do it.

They were quickly approaching the Glick house, and he let the horses slow just a little.

"You don't have to choose them," Noah said, looking over at her.

Eve's face was pale, and the headlamps reflected off her face, making her eyes look bigger. She was beautiful—distractingly, heart-stoppingly beautiful.

"But you want me to," Eve whispered. "Even my aunt wants me to choose them."

Everyone wanted the ultimate sacrifice from Eve, and Noah had to wonder if there was anyone in her

life right now who wasn't wanting to take this child
from her…

"I want you to do what's right for you," he said earnestly. "And I mean that. *Yah*, my brother and his wife
want to grow their family, but I want you to make the
choice that feels right in your heart. I want you to find
some peace—if you can."

"You won't try to convince me?" she asked.

"No. I know I've been talking my brother up, and he
is a good man, but this isn't about how good or proper
Thomas and Patience are. This isn't even about our
family and what we can offer…or what we can't! It's
about you—what you want."

Eve smiled faintly, and she looked like she was
about to say something; her lips parted, but then she
shut them and a strange little smile turned up the corners. He wasn't sure what had pleased her, but at least
he'd been a part of it. Eve turned forward. He wished
she'd look at him again, but the Glicks' drive was right
ahead, and he pulled his hand back to take full control of the reins as he guided the horses into the turn.

"I know we keep saying that if you need anything,
you should ask us," Noah said as they rolled toward the
house. "But I'm here for you—me, personally. I mean,
regardless of your choice. If you said right now that
you'd chosen another family, I still want you to tell me
if I can make any of this easier for you."

He reined in the horses just shy of the house lights.
He wanted just one more minute with her. There was
so much to say, and yet he didn't have the words to say
it. There was something about Eve that tugged at him,

that hinted at more just beneath the surface, and even though he knew that whatever friendship they formed would be cut off the minute she left Redemption, he couldn't bring himself to stop yet.

"What do you need?" he asked softly.

"I don't know…" Eve's eyes sparkled with unshed tears. "I think I need a friend."

"You have that," he said earnestly. "If I count at all…"

"We are very unlikely friends," she whispered.

He reached up and moved a tendril of stray hair off her forehead.

"I didn't expect to feel what I do when I'm with you—" He swallowed the words. He didn't know how to name what he felt.

His gaze dropped to her lips, and for a brief, insane moment, he imagined what it might feel like to kiss them. He touched her soft, chilled cheek with the back of one finger, and then let his hand drop—afraid to give in to any more temptation. What was it about this woman that drew him in this way? She was the mother of the child his brother hoped to adopt. Noah wasn't supposed to complicate her life!

"What do you feel?" she whispered.

"Like I want to be the one to take care of you," he said.

She dropped her gaze. What did she think of that—was it laughable?

"If I weren't expecting a baby, and if I'd met you at a hymn sing, I'd be soaring to hear you say that," she said, and he saw a smile tickle her lips.

"But everything is complicated, and we haven't just come back from a hymn sing," he said.

"No, we haven't." The smiled dropped, and she looked over at him sadly. "I should go in."

"*Yah.* Of course," he said, tearing his gaze from her face. "Let me help you down."

The front door to the house opened, and Lovina appeared in the glowing doorway. The kerosene lamps were lit throughout the bottom story, and candles flickered in the window, illuminating those evergreen sprigs tied with red ribbon.

Noah couldn't waste any more time, and he waited until Eve scooted over and he gave her a hand down. She stayed in his arms for only a moment, and then she stepped aside.

"Thank you for driving her, Noah!" Lovina called from the step.

Any privacy they might have had was spent, and Noah forced a smile and gave Lovina a wave.

"Anytime, Lovina!" he called back.

As if that was all that happened in his buggy tonight, and he hadn't told Eve what was happening inside him. When he looked toward Eve again, she gave him a private little smile.

"Good night, Eve," he said softly.

Eve didn't answer, and she headed toward the front door, following the packed path through the snow. He watched until she got to the step, and then turned away.

Eve had much to discuss with her aunt tonight, and it would be none of his business—none of his family's business. Her choice was going to be an intensely personal one, and all he could do was pray the prayer Patience had suggested—that *Gott* would do right by all of them…especially Eve.

Chapter Seven

Aunt Lovina held the door as Eve went inside the house. The smell of percolating coffee filled the interior, and the sound of chatting voices filtered through the sitting room from the kitchen. Eve paused to slip out of her uncle's coat and hang it on a hook, and then step out of her boots, leaving them on a mat to absorb the melting snow.

She looked behind her at the buggy now disappearing up the drive, the headlamps bopping along with the rhythm of the horses. Noah had said he felt something for her…and the timing was terrible—impossible, really. But he'd said it, and she tucked his words away inside her heart.

"How did it go?" Lovina asked quietly.

"I learned about Rachel Wiebe," Eve said.

"Oh…" Lovina's face pinked and she nodded. "*Yah.* Rachel."

"You didn't tell me?" Eve met her aunt's gaze. "You

said this was a good family, and you didn't share a detail like that?"

"It's complicated, dear," Lovina replied. "Rachel's back. We have to forgive, don't we? If we hold on to anger and resentment—"

"This is the family you recommended," Eve said.

"I know…and I still do. They're good people, Eve. I promise you." Lovina looked over her shoulder hurriedly. "But we don't have time to talk about that this minute—we have company."

Ruby came into the sitting room just then, Rebecca in tow. They were both carrying platters of Christmas cookies, and they smiled when they saw Eve.

"You're in time for cookies," Ruby said. "And mint tea if you don't want to stay awake until the crack of dawn with coffee. Wollie's here!"

"Wollie?" Eve suddenly felt very tired.

"Come, let's get you something to eat," Lovina said quietly. "I have a feeling you haven't eaten much…"

"No, I didn't," Eve admitted. "Thank you."

Wollie, as it turned out, had come in this direction to see a little house that was for rent. He had to find a home now, and this one was available.

After everyone chatted and played some card games, Eve found herself alone with her cousin in the sitting room.

"So will you come back?" Eve asked him.

"I don't know…"

"We heard that you wanted to," she said. "Everyone here has been praying for it."

She'd been praying for it, too.

"It's not so simple," he said. "My wife isn't Amish, and my *kinner* are old enough to remember not being Amish…"

"You think they won't be accepted?" she asked.

"I think they might be angry at me," he said, his voice low. "I think Caleb, my oldest son, might have a few opinions of his own right now."

"He's not even ten," Eve said.

"Don't underestimate a boy's ability to hold a grudge." But Wollie smiled while he said it. "You don't need to worry about me, Eve. You've got enough on your plate."

"Why did you go?" she asked. "You left right after visiting us, and for a few years after that I blamed myself. I thought I'd talked too much about rebellious ways."

"Evie," Wollie said softly, shaking his head. "This isn't something I like to spread around, but Natasha was already pregnant with Caleb at that point. I'd been working with your *daet* because he was paying me, and I needed the money to marry Natasha and support her. It wasn't you. My decision was already made."

Eve shrugged. "I didn't know she was pregnant…but I had figured out it wasn't a thirteen-year-old's flawed logic that chased you off."

Wollie chuckled. "That's good. And for the record, I'm fine, Eve. I promise. And I love my wife and my children. I'm more worried about you right now. You've come here to have the baby and…give it up."

She nodded. "That's the plan."

Wollie was silent for a moment. "Have you considered…other options?"

"Like going English?" she asked bitterly. "It was an Englisher boy who did this—against my will. I'm not going there."

"They aren't all the same," Wollie said. "And a single mother might be able to raise her child."

She met his gaze, but didn't answer, and his cheeks pinked.

"Right…" he said. "That's too far."

"Why did you go English? Just for…her?" Eve asked hesitantly.

"*Yah*, and because I didn't see a life for myself at home," Wollie said. "I wanted options. I felt constrained, like there was only one path for me and I had no choices left."

"But you did say you wanted to come back…"

Wollie blew out a slow breath, then leaned his elbows onto his knees. "I miss it. I miss our way of life, our pace of life… I miss knowing what's right and what's wrong. But now, I'm thinking things through, I guess. I came here to see my aunt, and there is that little farmhouse that came available to rent. They go fast in these parts—if I want it, I have to move quickly. It would be a nice change for us, I think—getting back to the earth again."

"What does Natasha think of that?" Eve asked.

He shook his head. "I don't know. I'm afraid to ask. I love her with all my heart, Eve, but we're very different. I want some space to breathe, some chickens, maybe a cow or two. She wants convenience. And I don't blame her—but even the thought of raising chickens intimidates her. Right now, we might not have a lot of choice, though. We need a home, and this is available. And I can't be cooped up in an apartment with four *kinner*. I'll go crazy."

Wollie and Natasha would be very different—an Englisher woman and an Amish man. Wollie hadn't fully transformed into an Englisher, either. He still had the slow movements, the thoughtful way about him that distinguished him from regular Englishers. It wasn't just about the clothes or the electricity.

"You think it's too late?" she asked.

"I think it might be," he said with a nod. "Right now, I need a home for my family. I'm married now—I made my choice."

Eve's heart might be breaking, but she had a chance at an Amish marriage still. Wollie had taken those vows, and he couldn't try again in the Amish community if it didn't work with Natasha. Marriage was for life for the Amish, wherever that marriage took place. He'd chosen an Englisher life, and even if he longed to return to his Amish roots, it wasn't only about him anymore. He now had a family.

"I can pray for you anyway," Eve said.

"Thank you," Wollie said, casting her a sad smile. "I'll pray for you, too."

For whatever it was worth—because they were both in impossible situations. Maybe *Gott*'s best had changed for Wollie, too. No matter how much wisdom they'd gained along the way, there was no undoing the choices that had led them here.

There was the sound of a buggy coming into the drive, and they both looked out the living room window to see Uncle Hezekiah returning from his shift at the canning plant. It was time for the family to come together and enjoy the time they had. This was what Christmas was all about, wasn't it? Gathering with family and leaving the impossible in *Gott*'s hands.

The next day, Eve went with her aunt and her cousin Ruby into the shop. Rebecca was staying home to take care of the housework, and Ruby brought her cross-stitching with her, attempting to finish the job that morning between helping customers. Rebecca had finished hers the day before, and Lovina already had it on display when she flicked the sign to Open.

"Wollie's very nice," Ruby said, settling down with her needle.

"He always was," Eve replied. "He was always easy to talk to. He's decent."

"What's his Englisher wife like?" Ruby asked.

Eve shook her head. "She's... English."

How to describe a woman that different? She was everything they were not, from the blue jeans down to the way she talked. She was uncomfortably open.

Lovina came past with a bolt of fabric under one arm. She gave her daughter a meaningful look.

"I think it's good that you saw Wollie for yourself, my dear girl. You just remember how hard it is to even visit your family once you've gone English. It's painful, and Wollie has to live with the consequences."

"Won't his parents even see him?" Ruby asked.

"Oh, they will, but they won't be happy with his choices, either," Lovina said. "He visits them from time to time, but there is no warm affection between his mother and his wife. How can there be? They're as different as night and day."

"Maybe in time—" Ruby started.

"Ruby." Lovina fixed her with a serious look. "Can you imagine what it would be like not to see me anymore? Can you imagine not seeing your *duet*, or having babies and having them never really know us? It would break my heart, for sure. And I think it would break yours, too. There are some mistakes that you just can't undo."

Ruby's glance flickered in Eve's direction, and Eve felt her cheeks heat. Like her own situation—that was true, this baby was coming and there was no undoing that.

"I can help with the cross-stitching," Eve offered, eager to change the subject.

"Would you?" Ruby passed it over. "My fingers are in agony. I can hardly hold a needle anymore."

Eve looked at the pattern so far, and then the nearly finished project that was neatly stretched out on a hoop. There wasn't much left to finish—just one piece of holly—and Eve settled in, counting stitches on the pattern, and then on the cloth, before she began to work.

Eve didn't really enjoy cross-stitching, but keeping her fingers busy seemed to be a good distraction, and she worked on the last of the cross-stitching while her aunt and cousin waited on customers.

The day was a busy one—Christmas being right around the corner—and most of the clientele were English looking for gifts for their friends and families. Eve watched the people as they flowed through the shop, stitching until the piece was complete, and when she snipped the last thread, running her fingers over her handiwork, the bell tinkled above the door. She looked up to see Patience Wiebe come into the shop.

Eve's breath caught. Patience...she'd want an answer, wouldn't she?

"Hello," Patience said cheerily. "How are you, Lovina? Hi, Ruby!" Then her gaze swept over to where Eve sat, and Patience's expression shifted to something less confident. "Hello, Eve."

Another customer came up to the counter and Lovina had to serve her. Eve put down the needlework and rose to her feet.

"Hello," she said. "I should thank you for dinner last night. It was delicious."

Did she sound sincere? Eve had all but run for the door the night before, and while it was her opinion of the Wiebe family that mattered in the adoption, she did have enough good character to care what they thought of her.

"I'm here to see you, actually," Patience said, coming toward her. "I don't feel like that dinner went very well, and—" Patience lowered her voice when she noticed Ruby watching them curiously "—I was hoping we could talk, just the two of us."

Eve hesitated. "I don't have an answer for you, if that's what you've come for."

"That's actually a relief, because if you'd made your decision after last night, I feel like it wouldn't have gone in our favor," Patience said. "I just wanted to explain our family, maybe. Or…show you who I am without a meal and a family around me. Just me."

Eve nodded. "All right."

"I was going to pick some lunch up for my husband, Noah and Amos," Patience said. "Would you like to come with me?"

"*Yah*, I suppose," Eve agreed. "Let me get my coat."

Another few customers came into the shop, distracting Ruby, and allowing Eve and Patience to leave without further notice. When they got out into the street, their breath stood in the air in front of them.

"It seems that no one told you about my mother-in-law," Patience said as they headed down the sidewalk. "I thought your aunt might."

"She didn't," Eve replied. "But Noah filled me in a little bit more on the ride home."

"She's a very loving woman," Patience said. "And our family had to deal with a lot of hurt feelings and old grudges when Rachel returned. I think we've done well, though. And we have to forgive."

"*Yah*," Eve said. "And I have to think of my child."

"You do." Patience gave her a sad look. "I understand that. I suppose I was hoping that it might help you in your decision if you got to know me a little bit. Most of that dinner seemed focused on my mother-in-law."

Eve smiled at that. "It was, wasn't it?"

They looked both ways before crossing the street, and when they reached the opposite sidewalk, Eve tugged her shawl a little closer.

"Would you like to know about me?" Patience asked hopefully.

"Yah," Eve replied. "I would."

"My family had eight *kinner* in it," Patience said. "I got sick in my teens, and I had to have a surgery that... it left me unable to have *kinner* of my own." Patience's gaze flickered in Eve's direction, and color rose in her cheeks. "It broke my heart. I loved children so much, and I wanted my own babies. But *Gott* sometimes takes things away, doesn't He? So I decided to teach school. It was partly because it would let me be with *kinner* again, and partly because I had to turn down a man who proposed very sincerely."

"Why did you turn him down?" Eve asked, slowing her steps.

"Because he wanted more children, and I couldn't give him that," Patience replied. "He was very excited at the thought of more children, and while he might have married me anyway, I didn't want to be the wife who let him down."

"I can understand that," Eve replied softly.

"So when I met Thomas, I was convinced it would be the same—he had Rue and he longed to have more *kinner*. Rue needed siblings to help her settle in as an Amish child, and...and once again I couldn't give that."

"Why did you marry Thomas, then?" Eve asked.

"Because I met an older couple who had never had *kinner* of their own, but who had lived such a full and loving life by opening their home to young people who needed love and support, and I realized that there were other ways to live a happy life." Patience stopped and turned toward Eve. She crossed her arms over her chest and shivered. "I think *Gott* works in mysterious ways, and He puts people together for a reason."

"'God setteth the solitary in families,'" Eve quoted the verse from scripture.

"I'm not a perfect *mamm* or wife, and maybe you saw that," Patience said, her voice shaking. "Maybe you don't think I'd be good enough for your little one—"

"No one is perfect," Eve replied. "And that is probably the scariest part. I have to choose a real, honest woman to be my baby's *mamm*. And she'll make mistakes."

"I'd certainly do my best not to," Patience said quietly. "But you're right. I'm only human."

"I hadn't counted on this being so hard," Eve admitted softly.

"Are you giving this baby up?" Patience asked.

"I have to."

"Is there anything I can do to make it easier for you?" Patience asked. "I'd send you letters, if you wanted. I'd send you locks of hair, little handprints—"

"No." Eve cleared her throat. "No. If I do this, it has to be complete. I can't drag my heart after your family. I'd have to let go."

An icy wind wound around them, and they started walking again up the street. Eve couldn't have any emotional connections to the Wiebes if she left this child with them—and that included Noah. Whatever had started to stew between them needed to stop. She was in Redemption for one heartbreaking reason—and she couldn't allow herself to form attachments.

They went into a restaurant, and Patience ordered

food to go. She ordered a meal for Eve, too, and when they had collected the foam containers and were ready to head back, the wind had let up somewhat, and some watery sunlight sparkled through the clouds, warming the air just enough to take the sting out of the cold. They headed back down the sidewalk, each of them carrying two bags of food. A wagon with jingling bells on the horse's harness came past them, the wagon filled with laughing Englishers. The side of the wagon read Eli's Christmas Wagon Rides, and Eve forced a smile in return to a small Englisher boy who beamed at her, waving as they passed.

"You have a lot of connections with the English," Eve said. "I have to admit, that makes me nervous. Especially with this child being half-English, I'm afraid that there will be a pull of some sort, tugging my child back to them."

"I knew a boy once who was adopted from the English and grew up Amish," Patience said. "I went to school with him. He wanted to know about the family that gave him up, and his Amish parents wouldn't tell him anything. They simply said that he was adopted, and they loved him, and what was in the past was in the past."

"That sounds proper," Eve said.

"It wasn't what he needed, though," Patience replied. "He needed to know the truth, to have information. He ended up leaving during his *Rumspringa*, and he went off to find his Englisher mother."

"Did he find her?" Eve asked.

"No, he didn't. And he didn't come back, either. He

came to visit once every long while, but he never came back for good."

Like Wollie? He had been born Amish, but his visits were infrequent, and they seemed to be laced with sadness.

Eve sighed. "Why does that Englisher life tug at people that way?"

"I think it only tugs at people if it stays a mystery," Patience said. "For what it's worth, I have a daughter who is half-English, my husband's daughter from a previous relationship, but she feels like mine. And I'm afraid sometimes of the exact same thing—that the Englishers will tug at some private place in her heart. And I know that telling you this won't help my cause, but it's true. I worry. But I've also given it a lot of thought, and people are drawn to mysteries. But mysteries are only intriguing until they come out into the light. When you learn the full truth about something and are allowed to look at it straight, you realize that it isn't quite so alluring, after all."

"And so with Rue—"

"She remembers her Englisher *mamm*. She knows her *mamm* loved her dearly and that Thomas is her father. She knows I'm her stepmother, and that I love her, too. We talk about Tina—Rue's *mamm*—and we don't make mention of her as something bad or uncomfortable. Tina will always be part of Rue's heart. Always."

"Do you think it will keep her Amish?" Eve asked.

"I hope so. I love her like my own, and I'll continue to love her with everything I have. If love is enough to keep a child in our way of life, she'll have more love in her life than she will know what to do with."

"And if you adopted this baby..." Eve asked softly.

"We would do the same," Patience replied. "We'd tell this child that his *mamm* couldn't take care of him. That it wasn't her fault and she loved him so much that she allowed him to grow up with us. And I'd love him with all my heart."

"And if he came looking for me one day?" Eve asked, and she felt a swell of hope that she couldn't tamp down, no matter how hard she tried.

"Then I would welcome the chance to have you back in my kitchen," Patience said, stopping to meet Eve's gaze. "And you and I would be family in a different kind of way. But you would never be hidden away as a dark secret. You'd be in our hearts—in your child's heart—and I would never compete for that love. Your child would be loved from all sides."

"If I—" Eve swallowed. "If I made a little quilt—"

"I'd let him know that you'd made it for him," Patience whispered. "And I'd let him know that his birth *mamm* prayed for him with every beat of her heart that he'd grow up to be good and kind and honest."

Lovina had thought that sending a little gift would be a mistake, but talking with Patience, it didn't seem like such a mistake. And maybe Patience was right about the mystery.

"Just one thing," Eve said, lowering her voice. "I never want my child to know about the father. To know his father was such a despicable man—"

"I agree there," Patience said with a nod. "That

would be a conversation that you could have with him later, but I wouldn't tell that story."

"Or her..." Eve said faintly.

"Or her." Patience smiled hopefully. "If this child needed more answers to stay decidedly Amish, then I would write to you. We'd do the best we could for this child together, you and me. I'd love this baby well, Eve."

Eve slid her hand over her belly, feeling the shifting of this infant inside her. Of the families she could choose from, even with their very human foibles, the Wiebe family was the best choice. Her child wouldn't be just accepted, her baby would be longed for and deeply loved. And Patience had a heart big enough to embrace the birth mothers of her *kinner*, too. That was more than Eve had expected to find for her child's future home.

"I know I have to make a choice..." Eve said slowly. "And I've put it off because it made it easier somehow to avoid what I have to do, but I know I can't keep doing that. This baby will arrive soon, and when it does, it needs a mother."

Tears welled in Eve's eyes at the thought. She would give birth, and she'd have to say her goodbyes.

"I'm not pressuring you," Patience said softly.

"I choose you," Eve said, swallowing the lump in her throat.

Patience put her bags down on the sidewalk, tears welling in her eyes.

"*Yah?* Me and Thomas?"

Eve nodded, and Patience stepped forward and wrapped her arms around Eve's neck in a fierce hug.

"Thank you," Patience breathed. "Thank you so much, Eve. We'll do well by you, and by your baby—I promise!"

The plane bit into the wood, shaving off a golden curl. With every heave, another one slipped to the floor, gathering in a tumbled heap at Noah's feet. He had always liked the smell of freshly shaved wood, and when he paused to test the surface, he heard the sound of voices from inside the showroom. More customers, no doubt. Thomas was already out there.

Noah hadn't been great company today. He'd been thinking about that buggy ride home—the one where he'd said too much and held Eve's hand as if they were courting. He wasn't being appropriate—on any level! This woman wasn't available, especially not to the brother of the man who hoped to adopt her baby. He'd been out of line, and he felt like a fool for having let himself go there, especially at such a sensitive time.

Noah leaned into the labor again, and as he did so, his gaze moved over to the little cradle Thomas had been working on between customers' orders. It wasn't anywhere near done—still rough, and the pieces had been put together to test the fit, but the next step was to take it all apart again to smooth everything down and sand it.

Thomas hadn't said anything about that little crib, and it wasn't an order—that was for certain—so he didn't have to explain himself. This was a baby's bed, just in case they needed one in the next couple of weeks.

Noah felt a wave of guilt. Thomas and Patience had already fallen in love with this baby—or the idea of the baby, perhaps. Their hopes were soaring up along with their prayers. Was Noah messing this up? He hadn't been talking to Eve on their behalf last night. He'd been opening up because it felt good to talk to her, and somehow opening up to Eve was feeling all too natural. That wasn't helping his brother's cause.

The door to the workshop opened and Thomas stuck his head inside, a beaming smile on his face.

"Noah, come out here!" Thomas said.

Noah put down the plane and grabbed a towel to wipe the wood dust from his hands and arms.

"What's going on?" Noah asked.

"Just come out here!" Thomas disappeared again, and Noah headed for the door. Maybe there was someone he hadn't seen in a long time, or a gift from a neighbor? Noah attempted to put himself into a better mood to be sociable, and when he pushed open the door that led to the showroom, he saw Patience and Eve standing there with bags of food from a local restaurant.

"This is nice," Noah said. "Tell me you aren't just teasing us with all that food."

Eve looked up when he said that, and she lifted a bag in his direction. Her expression was solemn, and he moved over to where she stood.

"Is it okay if we tell our family?" Patience asked.

Noah took the bag that Eve held out to him, his fingers lingering over hers. She pulled her hand back, then smiled faintly. "That would be fine."

"Eve has chosen us to be the family for her baby," Thomas said with a grin, but his smile slipped when he looked back to Eve. "Eve, I can't tell you what this means to us. And we can promise you that we'll love this child with everything we have, and we'll raise him or her to be godly and honest and good. Thank you. From the bottom of our hearts. Thank you."

She had made her decision? Noah's gaze whipped to Eve, who stood as still as a post, her hand now on top of the dome of her belly.

"Love this child well," she said, her voice tight. "That's all I can ask."

For the next few minutes there was some excited talking. Patience and Thomas looked at each other with such happiness in their eyes that Noah had to look away from the intimacy of the moment. This was a happy day for Thomas and Patience, but he could see the way Eve stood—still as stone, but for the flutter of her pulse at the base of her pale neck. She'd made her choice, but that didn't mean it had been easy for her.

Noah touched her elbow and Eve looked toward him.

"I suppose you'll be happy," Eve said quietly.

"Are *you*?" he asked, frowning.

"No," she said. "But it's the right thing to do."

Of course, it wouldn't be a happy day for her, and Noah felt the imbalance in the room—Thomas and Patience's elation compared to Eve's crushing sadness. Could he really expect anything different?

"We should probably keep this quiet for now," Patience said. "Let's keep it to our family only—Amos and *Mammi* included, of course—but other than that, we can tell people after the baby has arrived."

Eve didn't answer, but she nodded, and her face went

just a little bit paler. He put his hand out and touched her elbow again. He could claim that he was afraid she was going to faint, but truthfully, he just wanted to touch her—reassure her that she wasn't alone in this, maybe. Let her know that one person in this room understood how much this hurt her.

What was it like for her to have everyone celebrating the baby she'd have to give up? Noah couldn't even imagine what she must be feeling right now, but when Thomas and Patience turned toward each other again, Noah tugged Eve aside.

"Are you all right?" he asked quietly, searching her face for some deeper feelings—some strength, perhaps, that she was holding in reserve.

"I will be," she said, and tears sparkled in her eyes. "It's good to know this child is wanted by so many people."

She met his gaze, and he could see the clashing emotions swimming there. She looked away and seemed to steel herself.

"I'm going to be seeing your cousin on Monday— I'm dropping off some things when they move into that farmhouse," Noah said.

She looked up at him mutely. He didn't know why he was doing this—it was all he had to offer. He wanted to spend some time with her, and maybe give her some distraction from this painful time. And he had so little that he could offer her...

"Will you come with me?" Noah asked.

"*Yah*, I will," Eve said, and she swallowed hard.

"Are you coming to Service Sunday tomorrow?" Noah asked.

She nodded. "*Yah*, I'll be there."

"Maybe I can get you to take a walk with me. Get away from everyone for a while."

"That would be worth more than you know." Eve seemed to rally herself, standing a little taller.

"Are you sure you're okay?" he asked uncertainly.

"I will be. I just need to be alone for a little bit." She pressed her lips together. "I'm going back to my aunt's shop now."

"Sure."

Eve slipped along the edge of the shop, past the display headboards and footboards, and had almost made it to the outside door when Thomas looked up. Eve didn't stop—didn't explain herself. She just pushed outside, the cold wind billowing her dress behind her as she walked outside, and passed in front of the window before disappearing from sight.

"Was it something we said?" Thomas asked, his expression turned worried.

"I think she just needs to be alone," Noah replied. "As joyful as it is for you two, it's a sacrifice for her."

Noah met his brother's gaze, and Thomas looked back toward the window again. He and Patience leaned toward each other, their arms brushing as they looked in the direction Eve had gone.

"I don't think it's possible to make this any easier for her," Patience said. "But should I go after her, or—"

Thomas looked helplessly toward Noah.

"I don't think so," Noah said. *Let her cry in peace.*

"Let me show you something I've been working on," Thomas said softly to his wife.

As Thomas and Patience went into the workshop, Noah stood in the empty showroom, watching out the window as some people, laden with shopping bags, dashed across the slushy street. This Christmas would be a new beginning for his brother, but it would be a tragic goodbye for Eve.

Her sacrifice was making a dream of a family come true for Thomas and Patience, and while they excitedly got ready for this baby, Eve needed someone to care for her, too.

Until she left them all behind to restart her life, was it terribly stupid if he wanted to be that man?

Chapter Eight

Service Sunday was always a day that Eve had looked forward to in years past. It was a chance to see friends and extended family, to catch up on gossip, and worship. But today, as the buggy rattled down the road and she watched the scenery pass from her seat squeezed in next to her aunt and uncle, the horses clopping comfortably through the winter morning, Eve's mind was on the family she'd left behind seven months earlier when *Daet* sent her to stay with a distant cousin of his. But when *Daet* asked Aunt Lovina for confidential advice, Lovina had insisted that Eve come stay the rest of the time with her. Eve was glad for that now—she felt more emotional support with Lovina than she had in the other community.

How was *Daet* doing on his own? She'd gotten a few letters from him, but he was never one to complain. He just said that all was well and told her of the things he was looking forward to once she was home again. Her siblings seemed to be doing fine—one of her brothers bought a new buggy. Life was plodding along back in her hometown, and when she returned, there would be a place for her again, but she wouldn't be able to breathe a word about the baby she'd left behind.

Maybe she could talk to *Daet*, but she didn't want to put more pressure onto his shoulders. He wanted things to go back to normal. He wanted her to see her friends, to get to know some nice young men and to carry on as if this visit was simply an extended stay with some family.

Could she do it? Would seeing her friends again make all of this seem like a bad dream? She could only hope.

The baby moved. There wasn't as much space anymore for kicks, but she could feel the extension of a foot pushing up into her ribs, and she smoothed a hand over her belly. Everything would be fine—wouldn't it? This baby would be loved, she would get her second chance at a proper Amish life and a family's prayers for another child were about to be answered through her.

It just didn't feel fine. It *hurt*.

Gott, *please make this easier... I'm trying to do the right thing.*

Lately, she'd been thinking about Hannah from the Bible—Samuel's mother. She'd longed for a baby of her own, and she'd prayed for one, but she'd also made a promise to *Gott* that if He gave her a child, she'd give him back to the Lord. How could a mother make a promise like that? But she had—and she'd stood by her word and sent him away to live with the priest when he was just a little boy.

Hannah's heart would have been in shreds—but *Gott* rewarded her with more *kinner.*

Would Eve be like Hannah—a woman whose heart was broken by keeping a promise? If she was, maybe *Gott* would reward her like Hannah, too, and give her the honest home complete with husband and children that she so desperately longed for.

And the price would be this child that had been forced upon her…this child she couldn't help but love with all her heart.

The buggy turned into a drive, and her eyes moved over the familiar scene of an Amish farm set up for Sunday services. A field was already filled with buggies from neighboring Amish homes, and the horses were in the field beyond, a pile of dried silage and a watering trough already set out for them.

In the back of the buggy, Ruby and Rebecca chattered on about someone's handsome cousin who was visiting from another community. From what Eve could gather, the boy was far too old for either of them, and while the girls admitted this, they still wanted a chance to see him themselves.

"Emma said he has red hair." Ruby sighed. "And green eyes."

"I don't know any Amish boys with red hair!" her sister said. "I think that's an exaggeration. But I do know that he's tall and handsome. Naomi Zook said he was at her farm helping with some broken fences, and she talked to him for five whole minutes while he had some pie before he left, and—"

"Enough of that," Lovina said sharply, looking over

her shoulder. "You aren't old enough for courting, so I suggest you leave it to those who are!"

"It's just that we heard there aren't enough girls his age he isn't related to in his community—" Ruby started.

"And you aren't his age, either!" Lovina retorted. "I don't think you're going to be much help to him, are you?"

Eve smiled at the exchange. Her own *mamm* had given her own little lectures when Eve was as young as her cousins were now. Girls were never quite so grown up as they believed themselves to be.

When Uncle Hezekiah parked the buggy and let the horses into the pasture beyond, her aunt helped her get down from the buggy, and then both let out a sigh once her feet were solidly on the ground. Ruby and Rebecca headed off to find their friends, leaving Eve with her aunt.

"I can introduce you to some people," Lovina said.

"I'd rather not, actually," Eve said. "I'll come sit with you when the service starts, though."

"How are you feeling?" her aunt asked. "Any twinges lately? Any discomfort?"

Lovina had given birth enough times of her own to know the early signs. Eve shook her head. "Nothing. I feel...cumbersome, but that's about it."

Lovina smiled wanly. "I know that feeling, too." She looked over toward another arriving family. "Dear, I need to talk to Emma—I'm going to be helping her host a quilting day."

"Go ahead, I'll be fine," Eve said with a smile. "I'm going to go find a washroom at the house."

Her aunt smiled. "I'll see you later, then. We've got a fair amount of time before the service starts."

Eve breathed out a sigh as she escaped from her aunt's well-meant friendliness and headed toward the house. Eve hadn't told her family that she'd made her choice. It wasn't that she thought she'd change her mind, but she hadn't had the heart to discuss it all over again, so she'd simply not mentioned it.

She'd tell her aunt tonight—she'd have to soon. This baby was due any day now, and Christmas was this upcoming week.

Eve didn't actually need to use the washroom—it was just an excuse, a mission to head out on that would let her spend some time on her own before she was squeezed onto a bench with her aunt, cousins and a multitude of women she didn't know.

A few young men came ambling past her—one of whom was rather tall, and if she wasn't mistaken, appeared to have red hair. Maybe Emma Zook was more truthful than they'd thought. The young men didn't take any notice of her, but there was a woman with three preteen girls who looked her over with prim disapproval.

Eve gave a nod and smiled, hoping to disarm her with a bit of pleasantness, but as they passed her, Eve could overhear the woman speaking, even with her voice lowered.

"…and that is why you don't toy with boys too early, girls." More girls mooning over the redheaded boy from another community? Eve couldn't help but smile at that. But the woman's next words drained her humor. "You see that pregnant girl? That's shameful, is what that is. She's here to have her baby because she has no husband. And she'll have to give it up. That's what comes of doing things the wrong way..."

Eve couldn't make out the rest of the woman's words, but tears misted her eyes and she struggled to maintain some decorum. This was precisely why she needed a fresh start of her own—people would never forget, and whether or not it was fair, she'd be used as their walking lessons for their *kinner*, the warning against what could happen to misbehaving young people.

Shameful. She didn't even feel angry at that word, although she'd have every right to it. This wasn't her fault, but even if she'd been the one to make a mistake, was this not punishment enough? That woman would never know the ache of loss that Eve was going to experience. Couldn't that morality lesson have waited until she was at least out of earshot?

"Eve?"

Eve blinked through the tears in her eyes and looked up in surprise to find Noah coming out of the house, dressed in somber black. He was different than she'd gotten used to seeing him around his workplace. He looked so much more proper in his Sunday black with the woolen coat. His gaze moved over her face, and then he looked around them, his attention landing in the direction of the retreating woman with her daughters.

"What happened?" he asked.

"It's—" Eve swallowed. "It's nothing."

"It doesn't look like nothing," he replied. "You're crying."

"I'm being used as a morality lesson for some girls," Eve said hollowly.

Noah's expression clouded and his jaw tensed. "That's wrong."

"I agree, but I can't do a whole lot about it, can I?" What was he going to do, chase a woman down and tell her off? Not likely.

"I promised you a walk," he said.

"Now?" she asked. "Isn't service about to start?"

"It's up to you," he replied. "Whatever will make you feel better right now."

She didn't actually want to go sit on a bench and pretend she didn't feel the eyes boring into her. She didn't want to try not to be selectively deaf to the whispers. She'd wanted to come to Service Sunday so she could worship, but she might have been better off staying home. Noah's offer of a walk was a rather tempting one. A few snowflakes danced through the air, spinning and pirouetting their way to the snowy ground.

"All right," Eve said. "I think I'd like that. But I can't walk very far."

"You tell me how far you want to walk," he said. "And I'll carry you back, if I have to."

She smiled in spite of herself at that mental image. He was joking, obviously, but the thought of being in his arms was a rather cozy one.

"It'll be in sight of anyone who cares to check up on us," he added.

She smiled wistfully. "I don't think I'm any worry

to the unmarried girls right now, Noah. I'm no one's competition."

But the way a smile quirked up one side of his mouth made her stomach flutter.

"You're the only one I'm out walking with," he said.

"Don't tease," she said.

Now was not the time to pretend that they were anything they were not. Her stay here was difficult enough as it was, and she wasn't in the mood for pointless flirting or untruths.

"I'm not teasing," he said, sobering. "I'm serious. I'm not taking anyone home from singing. I'm…very single."

So was she, for that matter, but she was leaving here sooner than later. And when she left, she'd leave her heart behind in a bundle of baby blankets, but she wouldn't be coming back.

"They'll still talk," she said quietly.

"Let them." His dark gaze locked on to hers and he raised an eyebrow. "Not everything that is said is worthy of being heard."

She felt a smile tug at her lips. Was this really the proper Noah Wiebe, unconcerned about gossip?

"All right. Then a walk would be very nice, Noah. Thank you."

A few spinning snowflakes danced in the air, but there was no wind, and as Noah and Eve walked up the drive together, Noah felt warm in his woolen coat. The last of the buggies had already arrived, and he and Eve ambled past some boys who were throwing snowballs at each other. He put up his gloved hand to bat one out of the air that was coming in Eve's direction.

"Sorry!" the boy called after them.

"Aim better!" Noah called back, and the boy who'd thrown the snowball got another one right in the chest. He couldn't help but chuckle. When he glanced down at Eve, she looked somber, though.

"I know that woman from earlier," Noah said. "The one with the three girls."

"I'm sure," Eve said dully.

"No, I mean—" Noah stepped closer to her, his arm brushing hers. "She's warning her daughters because she's had some difficult times of her own. Her twin sister got pregnant before marriage, and no one could figure out who the father was. We never did discover who had done it, and she went English."

"Oh." Eve looked up at him, her brow creasing. "So it was an Amish man who—"

"It seems," he replied. "But he wouldn't step up, and she wouldn't say who he was. She was only about sixteen at the time, and she had her baby, stayed home with her parents, and when the baby was a toddler, she took her child and left."

"What became of her?" Eve asked.

Noah shook his head. "I don't know. She'd be in her forties now. No one told me more than that. But I remember the huge scandal at the time."

"So she's afraid of her own girls making the mistake her sister did," Eve concluded.

"*Yah*. I don't think it's as personal as it feels…if that helps."

Because if he could help to deflect at least some of that insult, he'd feel better, too.

Eve sighed. "It does, actually."

"Do you ever get tempted to leave the Amish life?" he asked.

Eve looked over, surprised. "Why?"

"You could keep your child…" he said simply, and he eyed her, wondering if he'd just planted a seed of rebellion.

"No." She shook her head. "I wouldn't be here if I were willing to do it."

"Has it crossed your mind?" he asked.

"Honestly?" She glanced up at him. "*Yah.* It has. But I want an Amish life, and I love this baby too much to allow him or her to grow up out there with the Englishers. This isn't only for me, it's for my baby, too. I want an Amish life for both of us."

They reached the top of the drive, and a red pickup truck rumbled past with a husky in the back, its tongue lolling out happily. The snow started to fall a little thicker now, dampening the sound around them. They started up the road together, their boots leaving tracks in the newly fallen snow.

"I considered it—" Noah said, his voice low.

"Jumping the fence?" Eve asked, and he heard the surprise in her voice.

"Joining my *mamm*," he said. "A few times, in fact. I missed her so much, and once I even went so far as to pack a bag. I never told anyone that before. Not even her."

He looked down at Eve, and she shrugged weakly. "You're human, Noah. I'm glad you didn't go."

"Me, too…"

Another car came up the road, and as they stepped closer to the side, Eve's foot slipped, and he instinctively put his arm through hers to keep her up. For a moment, they stood like that, arms linked and his feet firmly planted to support them both. She looked up at him, her eyes wide in surprise.

"Careful," he murmured.

She laughed softly. "I almost fell."

"Not with me here," he said.

She straightened and pulled out of his arms. "You shouldn't flirt, Noah."

"I'm not," he replied. "I'm serious. As long as I'm here, I'm looking after you. And not for my brother, or for the sake of community, or anything else. I'm here for you."

Eve looked down, but she slid her hand into the crook of his arm, and the gentle pressure of her fingers against his coat felt good.

"We have a little bit of time together," he said. "And I know it isn't much, but I'm glad I've gotten to know you."

"Even if we can never speak again?" she asked. Her ears were getting red from the cold, but she didn't look up.

"Even then," he said quietly. "You deserve someone who cares, even for a little while."

Ahead, there was a vegetable stall, the little shack painted white and blending into the falling snow if it weren't for the hand-painted words in red on the side of it: Amish Home Grown Produce. In the summer,

Englisher vehicles would park along the side of the road to come buy Amish fruits and vegetables. In the winter, that little shack stayed empty.

A brisk wind picked up, and Eve hunched her shoulders against it, moving closer to his arm. The snow, once falling lazily, whipped in a momentarily blinding haze around them, and Noah slowed.

"We should go back," Noah said, but when he looked the way they'd come, snow was blasting across the road in swirls of white. The wind had picked up faster than he'd anticipated, and it was probably stupid of him to bring a pregnant woman on a walk at this time of year. He'd been thinking of getting her away from the pressure, not dragging her through a blizzard.

"Let's just stop inside the veggie stand until this calms down a bit," she suggested.

"*Yah*, that's smart," he agreed, and they picked up their pace.

He fumbled with the latch, but once he flicked it open, Eve went into the little hut ahead of him, and he followed her, pulling the door shut behind them. Daylight streamed in through cracks in the wall, and a sifting of snow covered the bench along the back wall. Noah brushed it off, and Eve sat down with a sigh.

"I'm sorry to drag you out like this," he said.

"I wasn't dragged." Eve shot him a smile and put her hand over her coat-covered belly. "Everything is harder right now. I can barely take a full breath."

Noah sank onto the bench next to her. "Are you comfortable enough?"

"*Yah*, I'm fine. This is just part of being pregnant."

They were silent for a couple of beats, and Noah heard the rumble of a vehicle passing again. Her time here was short. She'd deliver soon, and then she'd go home, and he found himself feeling an aching emptiness at the very thought.

"What do you want for Christmas?" he asked suddenly.

"What?" She stopped the slow rubbing of her belly.

"I'm serious. What do you want? Chocolate? New embroidery thread?"

"Are you offering to get me something?" she asked with a smile on her lips.

"*Yah*, I am."

Her smiled slipped and she looked away. "I wish I could have a Christmas with my *daet*. I miss him…"

"Is he coming to see you?" Noah asked.

"No." Eve leaned her head back against the wooden wall. "This is a secret. I'm supposed to be helping some ailing family member, and my siblings don't even know what I'm really doing. If he comes to see me at Christmas, it will seem awfully strange to the ones at home, won't it? We have appearances to maintain."

"What do you want for Christmas?" he repeated quietly, and Eve turned to look at him. Her dark eyes sparkled in the low light, and she shook her head.

"I don't know," she whispered.

"I'm going to bring you something," he said.

"I don't have any money to get you anything," she said.

"I don't need presents," he replied, then he chuckled. "Maybe I'd ask for a Christmas kiss."

Her eyes sparkled with humor. "Now?"

Noah's heartbeat sped up, and he dropped his gaze. "If you're offering…"

Eve leaned toward him, her soft lips brushing his chilled cheek, and when she pulled back, he turned toward her again, and their eyes met. There was something in that moment that seemed to warm the space between them, and the teasing evaporated with their breath in the frigid air. A snowflake, blown through the cracks in the opposite wall, landed on a stray tendril of hair, balancing there, perfectly intact.

Noah reached forward and brushed the hair off her forehead, his hand touching her cold cheek, and she turned her face toward his touch, ever so subtly.

What was it about those pink lips, slightly parted, and the way her eyelashes touched her cheeks with each blink… When he leaned toward her, she leaned toward him, too, and their lips came together in a soft kiss.

Her breath was warm against his face, and it was like the storm, the shack, even the wood beneath them melted away, leaving them alone in this tender moment. He reached to pull her closer, but as he did, his hand brushed against her coat-clad belly and he felt a little movement from within—like something rolled against his touch.

He pulled back, and her eyes fluttered open. He didn't know what to say, and she put her hand over the spot he'd inadvertently touched.

"The baby's awake," she said, dropping her gaze.

He'd felt the baby move… He felt a rush of warmth

at the thought—they weren't quite so alone as he'd been thinking, were they?

"I shouldn't have kissed you," he breathed.

"No, probably not," she agreed, looking up again. "All the same, it was very nice."

Noah smiled at that. "*Yah*. It was."

It was more than nice—it was intoxicating, healing, and it filled him with a yearning for more of the same, but he knew he was walking on thin ice already. What was he doing kissing the mother of Thomas and Patience's newest addition? If this felt wrong for him, how complicated must it be for her?

"We can't do this, though," she said, sucking in a breath.

"I know," he said quickly. "I'm very clear on that. I know it's wrong in all sorts of ways, I just…" He searched for the words to explain himself. "I don't go around kissing girls, you know."

"I'm glad… I think," she said, licking her lips.

"You're different," he said, his voice dropping. "You're strangely wise, and you're smart, and sweet and…beautiful. I've never met a girl quite like you."

"It doesn't matter," she said.

"I know."

"I'm leaving as soon as the baby comes, and—" Tears welled in her eyes.

"I know. I'm sorry—for all of it. I'm sorry you have to make this sacrifice, and that I'm connected to all of it, and…" He sighed. "I don't know what to say."

Noah reached out and took her gloved hand in his,

wishing he could feel her soft skin next to his, instead of all this padding between them.

"We have to get back," Eve said.

She was right, of course, and he reached over from where he sat and pushed open the door. The wind had died down again, and they were left with softly falling snow once more.

Surfing through the trees, through the snow and over their mangled hearts, the sound of four-part harmony church singing reached them. It was a Christmas song—"It Came Upon a Midnight Clear"—and Noah's heart lifted with the words toward *Gott*.

Once, long ago, another baby was born to a vulnerable young mother... Noah had no business kissing Eve, he knew that, but his feelings for her weren't just the kind of attraction that sparked between young men and women, either. This went deeper. He cared for her. And somehow that didn't make this easier.

"Let's get back," Noah agreed, and they both stood up and stepped back out into the gently falling snow.

Sometimes the arrival of a baby could bring both hope and heartbreak, and Noah could only pray that *Gott* would grant Eve's deepest hopes for that husband of her own. If Noah couldn't be the one to fill her heart, then she deserved a chance with another good man who would see the true treasure she was.

Chapter Nine

"That was a powerful sermon," *Mammi* said when they all came back from service late that afternoon. The snow had stopped falling, and the sun sparkled on the new white mantle that covered everything within sight.

"Yah," Noah said. "Very."

Noah looked out the window. There would be a fair amount of shoveling to do to make paths to the stable and to the little hay barn that held feed for the horses. Just because it was Sunday didn't mean the necessary work stopped.

"You know, I don't think we hear sermons on the role of men in our community often enough," *Mammi* said, taking off her good apron and replacing it with her kitchen one. Her swollen, knobby fingers worked slowly as she tied her apron behind her. "We hear about the sins we need to combat, and the beauty of marriage, and the important job of raising our *kinner* to honor *Gott*, but we don't hear about men specifically, do we? At least we haven't in a long time."

"Maybe not," Amos agreed. He crossed the kitchen and picked up a muffin from a bowl on the counter. "It was certainly an engaging three hours."

Amos took a bite of the muffin, and *Mammi* took a plate from the cupboard and handed it to him. He accepted it with a rueful smile.

"And when the preacher said that men were put on this earth to protect and provide, I have to say, I felt a shiver," *Mammi* went on. "I've been blessed with strong, kind, patient men in my life. My own *daet*, my husband, my sons who grew up to be so much like their father, and now you boys taking care of me…"

Amos shot his grandmother a smile. "I'm grown, you know."

"Oh, you'll always be my boy, Amos," *Mammi* replied with a chuckle. Then she turned to Noah. "And I'm proud of how you've grown, too, Noah. You stood for what was right when your *mamm* left, and you never wavered."

Never wavered. Not that he'd admitted to, at least.

"I may have wavered a little," Noah said.

"Well, I never saw it," *Mammi* said. "And you're still that honorable young man I've grown so fond of."

She meant well, just loving them as she always had, but *Mammi*'s words cut deep. As a man in this community, it was his role to protect and provide, not to be toying with the emotions of a vulnerable woman who was in this community's care.

"Let's get out and start shoveling," Noah said to Amos. "I'd rather get it done in daylight."

"*Yah*, agreed," Amos replied, pushing the last of the muffin into his mouth.

He'd work—that might help purge his system of the growing guilt that he just couldn't seem to shake.

Noah didn't sleep well that night. He kept thinking of what a relief it had been to finally kiss Eve, which didn't help his guilt at all. It had been more than a kiss—it had been a connection at long last, and it felt like something inside his chest had been reaching toward her and was finally rewarded with a touch. Even remembering that kiss in the cold sped up his pulse. He'd never meant to feel more for her than gallant protectiveness, but somewhere—and he couldn't even tell when it had happened—his feelings had crossed that line.

What would his brother think if he knew what Noah was feeling for this woman? Noah was supposed to be helping Thomas and Patience, not muddling with their hopes of adopting the baby. He couldn't be tangling with Eve's emotions. She was supposed to be preparing to give her child to someone else…and he was kissing her? This was a betrayal to both his brother and to Eve. They were both counting on his strength of character to support them, not to be selfishly giving in to his own feelings.

Obviously, a relationship with her was impossible on too many levels, and he was playing with fire. Whatever this was *had* to stop. So he lay awake late that night praying for strength, for clarity, for whatever it would take to get him to stop tumbling down this emotional path.

Lord, convict me of how wrong that was, and for-

give me for caving to my feelings. Make me into the man You created me to be, because I'm falling short. Protect Eve's heart, too. Bless her. Let me carry whatever burden is right, but lighten hers...

He was still the man *Gott* had put in her path, and it was his job to protect her, even now.

The next day, Noah was tired, but he got up early and helped Amos with the chores before they headed off to Redemption Carpentry together. By the time Thomas arrived an hour later, Noah had already gotten most of a side table stained. He looked up when his brother came in. If his thoughtlessness had ruined this for his brother, he wasn't going to forgive himself.

"You wouldn't believe how happy Patience is," Thomas said, pulling off his coat and hanging it on the wall. He stomped his boots on the mat. "She's already sewing a few little outfits."

"*Mammi* started crocheting a blanket the minute we told her," Noah said. "The women will pull it all together. They always do."

Thomas pulled out the cradle, still a little rough, and he squatted next to it.

"I've never been allowed to be a *daet* to a baby before," Thomas said quietly. "I won't know what to do."

"Patience will show you," Noah said.

"*Yah*, I guess." Thomas rose to his feet and shot Noah a nervous smile. "You know when you've wanted something so badly and you finally get it... I'm half-afraid it won't work out. Something will happen and she'll choose someone else."

Noah dropped his gaze. He didn't need any fresh reminders about what he was toying with here.

"Don't worry about that," Amos said. "She and Patience have an agreement, don't they? This agreement was between women. It has very little to do with you."

Thomas cast Amos an annoyed look. "I'm going to be the father, Amos."

"*Yah*, and you'll have everything to do with the raising of that baby, but this agreement—" Amos paused. "That's what I'm talking about. Eve chose a mother. It's okay."

Hopefully Amos was right and her choice was about Patience, and Noah couldn't ruin it.

Noah stood up and brushed off his hands.

"I promised I'd bring the donations we've collected so far to Wollie's new place this morning," Noah said. "They're moving in today."

"That's great!" Amos said. "Give Wollie our best. It'll be nice to have him around again."

"Eve wanted to come along—see her cousin and all that," Noah added, and he wasn't sure why he was explaining himself, but he felt like he owed Amos and Thomas something, and he wasn't sure what.

"Sounds good," Amos replied. "Thomas and I had better stay and keep working on the orders, though."

"She's close to her due date," Thomas said.

"I'll keep a careful eye on her," Noah replied. "Maybe it will help distract her from...you know."

Thomas nodded, and there were a few beats of silence. It was a difficult topic to discuss, especially as men.

"Wollie and I can handle the lifting between us,"

Noah added, trying to sound cheerier than he felt. "But I'd better head out—moving day is always a little hectic."

"Right," Thomas replied, and the brothers exchanged a look. "Look after her for us."

Because right now, Thomas wasn't worrying about Wollie, he was thinking about the baby. And Noah couldn't blame him for that.

Today, Noah needed to keep his head about him— no more overstepping with Eve.

In fact, if he was going to be really honest, he owed Eve an apology.

Half an hour later, Noah had loaded the last of the donations onto the wagon, and he and Eve rattled down the road toward Wollie's new farmhouse. The day was warmer, hovering just below the freezing mark, and sunlight sparkled off last night's snow. As Noah and Eve left the town's limits, he noticed some deer footprints in the snow beside the road, and a blue jay flitted from post to post along the barbed-wire fence that ran alongside them. It was a perfect winter morning, or it would have been if he didn't feel like he'd let everyone down.

"How are you feeling?" Noah asked.

Eve glanced toward him. "Fine. Everyone keeps asking that." She shrugged. "But I feel no different than I did yesterday. The baby isn't showing any signs of arriving today, at least."

"Okay," he said. "Um. That's good. I was a bit worried after yesterday."

Eve cast him an understanding smile. "It's okay. I'll be fine."

"No, I mean—" Noah had to get this out. "Look, I overstepped—by a lot. I shouldn't have asked you for that kiss—I shouldn't have kissed you, period. And I'm sorry."

"I'm okay," she said quietly.

"I know you're dealing with a lot right now," he said. "I'm adding more complication to your life, and that's wrong of me. That sermon yesterday was awfully convicting. I wasn't being the man I should have been."

Eve looked over at him, her gaze meeting his for a moment, then flickering down to her gloved hands that were resting on top of her belly.

"Do you know what it's like to be pregnant and never have been kissed before?" she asked.

Noah's heart stuttered, and he saw some pink rise in her cheeks.

"No?" He hadn't meant for it to sound like a question, but it had caught him off guard.

"I spent my time with my *mamm*," she went on, "helping her to feel more comfortable, going with her to doctor's appointments, taking care of the housework and the cooking." Eve sighed. "And being so busy with my *mamm*, I wasn't getting to know the boys, going to young people's events, or that sort of thing. I hadn't been out to a hymn sing in ages. That might just be my excuse for not having anyone interested in taking me home from singing, but I didn't have any boys who came calling. That's what I'm trying to say."

Was she saying what he thought she was saying… had he taken more from her than he'd imagined?

"So when I kissed you—" he said, his voice catching.

"It was my first kiss." She raised her gaze to meet his again.

"I feel worse," he breathed.

"Don't feel bad," she said with a sad flicker of a smile. "Like I said, I'm pregnant, and up until yesterday, I didn't know what it felt like to be kissed. And I'm actually grateful to know—especially with someone who seems like he genuinely cares."

"I do care," he said earnestly. "I'm not the kind of man who just… I'm not that kind of man. So I care more than I should. You're quite incredible, you know."

"I think there is something about pregnancy that makes a girl seem like more than she really is," Eve said. "More wicked, perhaps. Or wiser. Or sweeter. I don't know. But I'm still just Eve Schrock, a farmer's daughter who didn't steer clear of that Englisher party."

"Your last name is Schrock?" he asked quietly.

"*Yah.* I'd appreciate you not telling people, though. It doesn't help in keeping secrets."

But she'd trusted *him*, and that tugged at him all the same.

"I don't blame you for that party," he said quietly.

"That's nice," she said. "I do appreciate that. But blame me or not, I still have to live with the consequences, don't I?"

The horses plodded along, and a chill wind blew snow up from the field in a white haze. Noah put his head down against the icy blast, and he reached out to tug Eve a little closer against his side. While she was here, he'd protect her.

"You're going to find a good man," Noah said. "And you'll get that family you want so much. I know it."

"I hope so," she replied.

If Eve could see herself the way he saw her, she'd be a lot more confident in that. She might not have been courted yet back in her hometown, wherever that was, but he had no doubt that when she returned, more than one single man would take notice. She had a certain glow about her, a gentleness, a depth, that Noah hadn't seen before in any other woman. It was drawing him in, too.

"Noah, how come *you* aren't married yet?" Eve asked.

"Me?" Noah laughed self-consciously. "I'm tough to tie down, I guess."

"That's it?" she asked.

Noah sighed. She'd opened up to him, after all. "I have a hard time trusting myself—my ability to choose the right woman. When everything you believed to be true ends up being wrong, it makes it hard to trust your own instincts anymore."

"But your faith wasn't wrong," she said. "Right and wrong doesn't change. You stayed to the narrow path, and that was a good choice."

"My parents weren't what I thought they were, though," he said. "They'd held back a lot, and I guess I'm afraid that if they could hold back that much and keep me oblivious, then anyone could. I'm…less trusting now." He hadn't admitted that before, and he looked down at Eve apologetically. "I don't mean to keep dumping my problems on you, you know."

"I like to hear it," she said. "For what it's worth, I think you should get married. You'd make a good husband."

Noah felt his face heat, and he chuckled self-consciously. *"Yah?"*

"Yah." But there was no teasing in her voice, and when he met her level gaze, the part of him that was supposed to stay resolute trembled just a little.

If only it were that easy to marry. A man couldn't always have everything—his community, his faith and the woman he was most powerfully drawn to. And it was going to be harder to settle down after Eve left, not easier. No one else would be Eve.

They came to a corner, and Noah guided the horses around it. He could see the farmhouse from here—a green SUV parked out front, and some *kinner* running and playing in the snow of the front yard.

"I think that's Wollie's family," Noah said.

Eve leaned forward and shaded her eyes. Wollie waved his hand overhead, and the woman turned and looked in their direction, too.

Wollie and Natasha needed the basics this Christmas—furniture, bedding, clothes. One disaster had served as a reminder of what was really important, and that wasn't an extravagant Christmas.

Noah's Christmas needs weren't extravagant, either. He needed to put these complex feelings for Eve in the background and be the man he knew he needed to be. With *Gott*'s help.

* * *

Eve couldn't help but notice how strong Noah was, easily hoisting heavy boxes, carrying them into the house and stacking them in the empty, echoing living room. The men's boots thunked against the linoleum floor, little Caleb tramping along after them, carrying lighter items, and the youngest boy, Cory, following along just for the fun of it.

Eve sat at the newly set up kitchen table—a recent donation—her baby shifting around inside her as if trying to get more comfortable. The baby wouldn't settle, no matter how much Eve rubbed her belly, maybe reacting to her discomfort. Sitting in a kitchen with an Englisher woman was disconcerting.

Natasha wore close-fitting jeans and had her hair pulled back into a ponytail that drew Eve's gaze. Natasha's parenting style was very different, too—letting the girls do whatever amused them, and when they were naughty, Natasha just rolled her eyes.

"I haven't met much of Wollie's family or old friends," Natasha said, sitting down at the kitchen table opposite Eve. "But Wollie has talked about Noah before—they used to swim together in a creek. Did you know that?" She smiled. "Wollie has the best childhood memories."

There was no tea to share—but there was a box of cookies that Eve had thought to bring, and a larger box of baked goods sitting on the kitchen counter behind them. The Zooks would need some food before they stocked up at a grocery store. Natasha's gaze moved over to where her four-year-old daughter was eating a cookie over a heating vent that was blowing some welcome warm air. The toddler crouched next to her older sister, her fair hair fluttering in the warm blast.

"You're Wollie's cousin, right?" Natasha asked.

"*Yah*. Distant, but we're related. He came to help my *daet* with the corn shocks one year, and we got to know him better."

"The corn shocks?" Natasha asked.

"It's…farming stuff." Eve smiled and shrugged. "But family is family—*Gott* put us all together for a reason. That's what we believe."

Natasha nodded a couple of times. "I'm not close with my extended family. We had a few family reunions when I was a kid, but we've all drifted since my grandmother passed."

"So you don't go visit anyone?" Eve asked.

"Not really." Natasha shrugged. "We don't have much in common, honestly."

Being part of the same family seemed like a rather large thing to have in common. It was sad to think of a family so distant as to not get together anymore. Amish families made a point of gathering as often as possible. What was life without family ties?

"I'm sure you'll see more of his family, living out there," Eve said.

"Maybe. We'll see," Natasha replied noncommittally. "The thing is, marrying me was a big deal, you know? They're still pretty miffed."

"*Yah*, I could see that," Eve replied.

"Can you?" Natasha frowned. "What's the big deal? We're married! We have kids. We're a family—"

"He has more family than just you, though," Eve

said, then sighed and softened her voice. "His parents love him just as much as you love your own little ones."

"I met them a couple of times, but they've never been warm," she replied. "That's all I'm saying. They disapprove, and after four children together, we no longer care."

And what did Eve know about the tensions within Wollie's family? Maybe Natasha was right about her in-laws' attitudes. Still, there was something in the woman's voice that suggested she cared more than she said.

"Besides," Natasha went on, "I don't think I could ever do all the things you Amish women do—cooking from scratch, sewing your own clothes, going without a microwave! I mean—I couldn't do it!"

"Why not?" Eve asked.

"It's—" Natasha met Eve's gaze. "It's terrifying. Wollie tells me about his mother's cooking, and how they'd gather around the stove in the winter, and all these stories that sound so simple and wonderful, like *Little House on the Prairie* come back to life, but he didn't marry me because I could provide that. He married me because I was different."

"I'm not married," Eve said. "So I have no advice on how things are between a husband and a wife, but I can say this… We Amish believe that Christianity isn't about one person's talents or abilities—it's about what we are together as a community. And there are plenty of women who would be happy to show you how to start a garden, and how to sew some clothes, and give you some recipes to try out. Wollie's one of us, and like it or not, you're connected to us, too, now. But you don't have to do any of it alone."

The men came back inside just then with more boxes, and the little girls came running to meet them, nearly tripping them in their excitement.

"Careful now," Wollie said, scooping up his smaller daughter in one arm. "Go on over to your *mamm*."

Eve noticed how Natasha's expression softened at the Dutch word. There was more Amish in her home than she seemed to realize.

"You really think they'd help me figure it out if I wanted to…try?" Natasha asked, turning back to Eve.

"*Yah*, I do," Eve replied. "In fact, Noah's *mamm* was born English, too. I imagine she'd be a big help."

"I'm not sure they're as accepting as you're making out," Natasha said. "You're here to give up your baby—because they aren't so accepting of differences. Right?"

Eve looked away, and her heart squeezed. How could she explain herself to an outsider? This woman wouldn't understand—Englishers never did. They just judged.

"I want to get married," Eve said quietly. "And if I'm a single mother, that won't happen easily. I'd still be part of the community, I'd just…miss out on the things I've longed for all my life." She paused. "And I love our lifestyle. I love how we women pull together and make quilts or bake pies. We women make a home, and I love how the men take care of the farming and the men's work. It's satisfying to do our jobs well…and I love how our Plain life gives us the chance to focus on the things that matter most—loving *Gott*, supporting each other and the raising of *kinner*—children, I mean. I like the cozy warmth of a fire in a woodstove, and the soft light of a kerosene lamp hung over a kitchen table on a winter evening. But more than anything, I want little ones to look at me and call me *mamm* without my reputation being a burden to them. I want a houseful of children of my own, and I want a husband to love, like you have. I want a man to come home to me, to eat my cooking and to hold me close. I love our Plain life so much that I'm willing to make this sacrifice so that both me and my child can have *everything* an Amish life offers."

Natasha was silent for a moment, then she nodded. "It sounds beautiful. I'm sorry it comes at such a price for you."

"We're conservative people," Eve said. "And if you don't like that, you won't like living the Amish life. But that also means that my child would have a fuller, better life with an already established family. It's not perfect, but it's the life I've been raised to love. And I can't think of a better life to give this baby. That's how much I believe in our faith, and our way of living. It's not just words for me."

Natasha nodded. "I can see that."

But more than being a beautiful experience of the simple things, a Plain life meant commitment. It meant giving up conveniences for the deeper beauty of work and family. And that kind of commitment could only be made *as* a family.

The men came back in with the last of the donations from the wagon, and after some polite talking, it was time for Noah and Eve to take their leave. Once they'd said their goodbyes and Eve was settled back up on the wagon seat once more, Natasha came outside, her feet thrust into her husband's boots, and no coat over her sweater. She came up to the side of the wagon.

"Here," Natasha said, handing her something covered in a napkin. Eve peeked inside. It was an apple turnover. "I know what it's like to be pregnant, and I'm always hungry when I am! You'd better bring a snack." She paused. "And thank you—for the food, for the donations... And for the visit. I'm grateful."

Eve met the other woman's gaze, and in that moment, it wasn't about Amish and English anymore. It was about two women who might understand each other just a little bit better now. Eve felt her eyes mist.

"Thank you," she said, and Noah flicked the reins.

"Merry Christmas!" Noah called, and Natasha stepped back, crossing her arms against the cold as Wollie put an arm around her shoulders.

It was strange to be envious of an Englisher, but Eve was. No matter if Natasha realized it or not, she had something wonderful in a husband and a houseful of children. And they might have been reduced to the bare essentials with that fire, but the Zooks were within a whisper of an Amish life, forced upon them. Sometimes the greatest blessings came like that—without a lot of choice. All the same, Natasha had a man to eat her cooking—that was a gift from *Gott*. While He was blessing others, Eve could only pray that He wouldn't forget her.

Noah guided the horses back up the drive as they headed toward town once more. They rode in silence for a few minutes, and Eve took a bite of the sweet, flaky turnover. Aunt Lovina's baking was superb, as always.

"We might see Wollie for Christmas," Noah said. "I suggested he join us, and he said he'd try. We'll see."

"Your *mamm* could be a real help to her," Eve said, but as she said it, a low ache spread across her belly. Eve leaned forward, looking for a more comfortable position.

"Are you okay?" Noah asked.

"Yah..." She put the pastry on the seat between them and shifted again. "I'm just a little uncomfortable."

"Should I stop?" he asked.

She shook her head. "No, no, I'm fine. I was thinking that your *mamm* might be able to show Natasha some plain cooking...some sewing? She's intimidated by the work, but if Wollie wants to come back, he can't do that alone."

Noah flicked the reins to get the horses going a little bit faster, and Eve shut her eyes against the strange ache. This wasn't labor, was it? It couldn't be. If she was in labor, she'd know it! That's what she'd been told by every other woman who had given her advice.

"I'm sure *Mamm* would be happy to show her a few things," Noah replied. "But doesn't having another Englisher around bother you?"

Eve adjusted her position again. "How else do we bring Wollie back? He can't do it without his wife—" She winced.

"You're not okay," Noah said curtly, and when he reached out to take her hand, she let out a slow breath and squeezed his hand.

"Maybe we could pick up the pace a little bit," she admitted, and blew out a slow breath.

Maybe it was just that she'd been in a wagon too long and could use some rest, but she needed to get back to the fabric shop. Lovina would know what to do.

Chapter Ten

When Noah reined the horses to a stop in front of Quilts and Such, a line of cars stopped behind them, and Noah irritably waved them to pass. One by one the cars crept by, keeping him from getting down, and he felt a surge of frustration. Another car slowed, and he gestured for it to go past.

"Go!" he said out loud. "For crying out loud, just go!"

The Englishers in the car looked at him with wide, curious eyes, and he didn't have the patience for them right now. Eve was in labor—or she was in trouble. But he'd been watching her as she rubbed her hand over her belly and leaned forward. She was utterly silent except for the rush of an exhaled breath.

A little group of carolers walked down the sidewalk, singing "Away in a Manger," and a few pirouetting snowflakes drifted from the sky. Had he been a fool to even bring her along to see Wollie's family? She'd been anxious to see her cousin, but a long wagon ride on snowy roads might have been really stupid on his part.

"Let me help you get down," Noah said, as the last car passed and he jumped to the ground on his side. He circled around, past the horses and their clouds of exhaled breath, and he held up his hands to help her. But she grimaced and leaned forward again.

"Is everything okay?" Lovina's voice came from the front door of Quilts and Such, and Noah looked over to see Eve's aunt pulling a shawl around her shoulders. She bustled up and looked at Eve, then exchanged a look with Noah.

"She's pretty uncomfortable," Noah said. "I'm not sure what that means."

"When did this start?" Lovina asked briskly.

"About three miles back," Noah replied, and Lovina rolled her eyes.

"Time, Noah, not distance!" she snapped, and he felt foolish.

"Uh—twenty minutes ago?" he said.

"We have time, then," Lovina said with a nod. "Eve, how are you feeling now?"

"It's getting better," Eve replied. "It's not so bad now. This might be nothing. Maybe just too must jostling, you know?"

"I'm glad you're feeling a little better," Lovina said, and when Eve made a move to try to get down, she shook her head. "No, dear. Noah, I need you to drive Eve back to our place, and I'm going to go fetch the midwife."

Finally—something he could do. Noah nodded. "Of course. I'll get right to it."

"It could be nothing," Eve said, but even as the words came out, she grimaced again.

"Maybe so, but better safe than sorry," Lovina said, and she pulled out a key and passed it over to Noah. "That will get you into the house. I don't think any-one is home right now. Come on. *Schnell!* Let's get moving! I've got the girls to watch the shop for me, so no harm if this is a false alarm, Eve. But I suggest we treat it like it's the real thing, okay?" Eve leaned back against the seat, and Lovina put a hand on Noah's coat sleeve. "Don't leave her alone. You stay with her until I'm back, you hear me?"

"*Yah.* I'll stay," he said.

"Good." Lovina gave a curt nod. "And once you get there, if she's uncomfortable, you could walk with her a little. That tends to help."

"Okay." Noah swallowed, and he headed back around to get up into the wagon again. Once there, he put his arm around Eve and pulled her closer against his side. He wasn't trying to do anything inappropri-ate, but he wanted to make sure that if he had to catch her, he'd be close enough to do it. She leaned against him, and he felt better.

The ride back to the Glick house seemed like an eternity, and Eve leaned against him as he guided the horses down the familiar streets, reining them in at stop signs and waiting on the Englisher traffic. It was a strange relief to be able to be the strong body next to her, to let her press into his shoulder as he flicked the reins and urged the horses on again. He didn't even care who saw them—there were bigger concerns right now.

When they got back to the Glick house, Noah pulled the wagon up close, then hopped down first. He helped Eve down, and she all but fell into his arms as another pain hit her. She leaned forward and moaned.

"Eve, let's get inside," he said. "Your aunt says walking might help."

"Yah..." She straightened. "I don't think I'm ready for this…"

"For what?" he asked feebly.

"For having a baby!" Tears welled in her eyes. "I don't think I can do this!"

Noah had nothing to say to that—this was the women's realm, and he didn't know one thing about childbirth.

"With me here, sure, you feel like it's impossible," he said. "But I'm just a man! When your aunt and the midwife come, they'll take over."

"True…" She smiled faintly, and they walked together toward the door—Noah with his arm around her waist lest she slip, and he caught a handful of her coat, just to be sure. He fiddled with the key, but managed to unlock the door, then he helped her inside.

"Come on," he said. "You sit down, and I'll get a fire started in the stove to warm it up in here."

The natural gas furnace kept the house at a livable temperature, but real comfort came from a woodstove. Noah swung the door shut and helped Eve to step out of her boots, then he peeled off his own coat and boots and headed into the kitchen to get started.

It felt strange to be taking charge in someone else's home like this, but it didn't take him long to locate the wood and kindling, then get a fire started in the cold belly of the black stove. Eve didn't sit, though. She paced back and forth through the kitchen, one hand on the small of her back as she walked.

"Your aunt wants me to stay until she gets here," Noah said, standing up and closing the stove's door as a fire took hold inside. "I hope you don't mind."

"Noah, I *want* you to stay," she said with a faint laugh. "Maybe you can distract me—"

"How?" he asked.

"Tell me about you and Wollie when you were *kinner*," she said. "Natasha said there are stories about the two of you…"

"Oh, *yah*," Noah said with a chuckle. "I'm not sure which of us was the bad influence, but there are stories!"

"So tell me one," she said.

Noah thought back to those childhood years. "Well, there was the time Wollie and I snuck up on Wollie's older sister when she was sitting in a buggy outside his house with her boyfriend. Thomas and I were sleeping over that night because *Mamm* and *Daet* were helping with some community emergency that I can't remember. But us three boys, we snuck outside and made wild animal sounds, hoping to scare his sister and her boyfriend."

"Did it work?" Eve stopped by the stove and put her hand out toward the heat, exhaling slowly. He could tell she was still in pain.

"*Yah*. It worked, but it had also interrupted a proposal." Noah glanced toward the door, wondering how long Lovina would take. "We were forgiven, but only because Wollie's parents were too excited about planning that wedding—that was the longest courtship ever, and everyone was antsy to get things moving forward for those two. So they forgot about punishing us boys in all the excitement."

"Was that Waneta's wedding?" Eve asked, meeting his gaze. "Wollie's sister?"

"*Yah*—Waneta and John. They've got eleven *kinner* now, I believe. They moved away, though."

Eve dropped her gaze, pressing her lips together, and Noah reached out and caught her hand. Her grip was tight and iron-strong, and Noah watched her face as she paled, her nostrils flaring.

"Eve—" He didn't know how to help her, how to make any of this easier.

"I want that…" she whispered.

"Three boys to punish?" he asked, attempting to joke.

"A proposal," she said, her grip on his hand loosening once more, and she let go of him. "I want annoying younger family members, and meddling in-laws, a proposal from a good man and a wedding with as much celery soup as the community can eat." She blew out another slow breath. "If I can manage it."

"You'll manage it," he said. "Trust me on that."

Eve ran her hand over her belly, then she wiped some hair back from her face that had fallen loose from her *kapp*. Tears misted her eyes.

"But more than my own happiness, I want my child to have a happy childhood like we had—getting into trouble, building friendships, learning to sit still on Service Sunday, and all without the burden of a *mamm* who got pregnant outside of marriage."

Noah nodded. "Thomas and Patience will love that baby well—I can guarantee that."

Eve turned away from him. "If you'd known your parents were converts when you were young—if everyone else had known—would it have changed things for you, do you think?"

He wouldn't have felt quite so comfortable in his life. He would have wondered about the Englisher side of the family, and he might not have felt quite so free to make mistakes and learn alongside the other boys. He would have known he was different...

"Yah," he was forced to admit. "It would have."

She nodded. "I thought so..."

Eve leaned forward again and closed her eyes. He grabbed a chair from the table and pulled it over, then helped her to sit down in front of the stove. She let out a shaky breath.

"Noah," she whispered.

"Yah?" He leaned closer.

"I'm having a baby today, and I know for a fact that I'm not ready." Her chin trembled.

"I think you're more ready than you realize," he whispered back. "You're strong, Eve. And *Gott* isn't letting you go—"

Outside he heard the clop of hooves and the crunch of wagon wheels, and he felt a surge of relief. That would be her aunt returning with the midwife.

Whatever he could do for Eve wasn't nearly what

she needed! And the women who could take over and get her safely through this ordeal had arrived.

Gott, take care of her...please.

The door opened and Lovina came inside, another woman behind her. Eve looked up to see a competent-looking older woman, about Lovina's age by appearances, pulling her gloves off and stepping out of her boots in an efficient sort of way. She tossed her gloves onto the table and gave Eve a reassuring smile.

"Eve," she said. "My name is Sarah, and I'm the midwife. How are you doing?"

"I'm—" Eve shook her head. "I have no idea!"

"Are you still feeling contractions?" Sarah asked.

"I think so—it hurts."

Sarah's gaze whisked over to Noah. "Not the father...?"

Apparently, the midwife had been informed about the delicacy of the situation, and Lovina met Eve's gaze and she lifted her shoulders faintly. The fewer people who knew right now, the easier it would be for Eve to go back to her home and not have any telling rumors left to follow her back.

"Not the father," Noah said, his strong voice echoing through the kitchen, and Eve felt a sudden wave of panic. She was about to have a baby, and the man who was standing by her and giving her strength was the brother of the man who'd adopt this child... He wasn't really anything to her—nothing she could claim, at least.

"Then we need you out," Sarah said, her tone having the matter-of-fact timbre of a schoolteacher's. "In fact, if you'd be so kind as to stable the horses so that Lovina and I can get to work here, that would be much appreciated."

"*Yah*. Of course." Noah took a step toward the door, then he looked back at Eve, his eyes filled with sadness, worry and something else she couldn't quite name, but it made her own heart squeeze in response.

"Out!" Sarah said, gesturing toward the door. "I need to check on my little mother, and I can't do that with you here."

Noah nodded quickly and walked briskly toward the door. In a moment, his coat and boots were back on and the door banged shut behind him, leaving the women alone. As soon as he was gone, the feeling of the room immediately changed. It was time to get down to business.

"Now, Eve," Sarah said. "You're scared to death—I can see it. And every first-time mother I've ever helped has felt the exact same way. But don't you worry—this is the hard part, and soon enough it will be over."

"I am scared," Eve said.

"Every single one of us arrived into this world the exact same way," Sarah said. "And then our *mamms* went on to do it again seven or eight more times! This is the way *Gott* has ordained it, and while it's hard, it's a system that works. I can promise you that."

Eve looked toward her aunt, uncertain of what she was even hoping for. Eve was more than frightened of the delivery—she was dreading the moment afterward when she'd see this child and fall in love even more than she already had.

"All right. This is the hard part, but soon enough you'll be able to start the healing. And it will get better. I do promise that, Eve. It will get better…but right now, we're going to be with you, and we'll get you through this, okay?"

How many times had this midwife seen a similar situation when a baby was born and handed off to another family? Was this more common than Eve liked to think? Somehow, this woman's brisk, reassuring way of facing all of it was just what she needed.

"You'll be fine, dear," Lovina said. "Now, I'm going to start some water boiling, and I'll fetch some towels. I'm thinking we need to get you upstairs."

"Yes, we need a bed," Sarah agreed. "But let's get her up and walking first. If she can still talk, this isn't active labor yet."

Eve allowed Sarah to help her to her feet, and as she rose, she was able to see out the side window. Noah was just leading the horses into the stable, and he looked over his shoulder as he passed, his gaze locking on to hers for a split second before Sarah's solid presence blocked her view. He was still here… Why did that comfort her?

If *Gott* blessed her, the next time she gave birth, there would be a husband by her side, and a husband wouldn't be chased out. He'd be proud and happy, and when she delivered that child, it would stay in her arms.

By the time Noah was heading back out with the wagon, it was past closing time at the shop, so instead of going toward town, he turned the horses in the direction of home. He had to tell his brother that Eve was in labor, and everyone would be happy and anxious. They'd all be praying for a safe delivery, but Thomas and Patience would be praying for something more— an addition to their family.

But Noah's prayers went deeper still. He was praying for Eve, for her safety and for her heart, because he knew how horrifically difficult this was going to be for her. Eve loved this baby, and it was only out of the deepest love that she could consider giving it up.

Noah roused himself as they approached the acreage Thomas and Patience shared with *Mamm*. He was the bearer of exciting news, but he couldn't bring himself to feel happy about it.

When he reined the horses in, he saw his mother in the window, looking out at him past the curtain. She smiled and raised a hand. Was it the look on his face that made her seem hesitant, or was it that they'd had so much tension between them the last few years that it was hard to overcome, even at Christmas?

He suddenly felt very tired, and as he got himself down from the wagon, he looked over at the smudge of red that still glowed on the western horizon. For Noah, this was going to be another difficult Christmas, but that was nothing compared to what Eve would endure.

The side door opened and his mother gave him a smile.

"Hello, son!" she called, and Rue appeared behind her skirts.

"Hi, Uncle Noah!" Rue called.

"Are you coming for dinner?" Rachel asked. "Because we have plenty!"

Noah came inside, and Patience smiled at him from the stove where she was stirring a pot of what smelled like chicken stew.

"We do have plenty," Patience confirmed. "It's good to see you, Noah."

"*Mammi* is teaching me to knit, and I'm going to make Toby a sweater!" Rue said, hopping from foot to foot.

"Chickens don't wear sweaters," he said with a chuckle.

"Toby will! And it's going to keep him cozy warm all winter long!"

"I think the hens will keep him warm," he said. "And the chicken house. Sometimes, your *daet* will even put a heater out there."

"But it's a Christmas sweater," Rue replied stubbornly. "I just don't know how to make the arms."

Rue wasn't going to be sidetracked from her mission it seemed, and Noah just laughed, then looked up to meet his sister-in-law's gaze.

"I came by because Eve has gone into labor," he said in Dutch so that his niece wouldn't understand.

"She has!" Patience dropped the spoon onto the stove top with a clatter.

"How long has it been?" Rachel asked.

"A couple of hours?" he replied.

Both women relaxed.

"It'll be a while, then," Rachel replied. "It takes longer than that."

"Do we tell Rue?" Patience said, more to herself than to the rest of them.

"Tell me what?" Rue asked.

"You understood that, did you?" Patience chuckled, switching to English. "Nothing, sugar. I'm just thinking out loud."

"Even if she has the baby in the night, she deserves to hold her child until morning," Rachel said softly in Dutch, and she and Patience exchanged a sad look.

"Yah," Patience said quietly. "She does. Going over there in the morning is soon enough. Tonight, we should pray for *Gott*'s will."

"Rue and I have been getting some toys together to bring to Wollie's *kinner* for Christmas," Rachel said, switching to English again for the girl's benefit. "We've found some very nice toys, haven't we?"

"Yah, and we've got some from the neighbor kids, too!" Rue announced proudly.

"We can bring those to Wollie's family tomorrow morning—just you and me." Rachel bent down with a smile. "Those poor *kinner* have lost all their toys in that fire. And they don't have chickens to play with. But I think they'll be so happy to have the toys we've collected."

"Just us?" Rue whispered delightedly, then she turned to Patience. "Can we, *Mamm*? Can we go bring presents to those Englisher kids with no chickens?"

Patience nodded. "Yes, of course. That's what Christmas is all about."

"Those *kinner* need a chicken, Uncle Noah," Rue said, and he could see her little brain starting to glow with this new idea. "Think how happy they'd be with a Christmas chicken!"

Noah smothered a grin. "Will it make their *mamm* happy, though?"

"How could it not?" Rue asked earnestly.

Noah rubbed a hand over his chin and tried not to smile as he considered the fallout of his niece's grand idea.

"Now, come eat with us," Rachel said, turning to give Noah a hopeful smile. "*Mammi* Mary gets to feed you more often than we do, and I miss my son."

And just like that, everything was arranged. Rue would be off with her grandmother, bringing gifts to the Zook home, which would free up Thomas and Patience to go meet their new baby on the morning of Christmas Eve.

This would be a very happy Christmas for Thomas's home—they'd have a new baby to cuddle and love, and they'd be filled with thankfulness. For this home, at least. Not for Eve.

A buggy rattled up the drive, and Rue hopped back over to the window.

"*Daet*'s home!" she said excitedly. "And I'm going to tell him about Toby's new sweater!"

Thomas, no doubt, would be less than thrilled at the thought of dressing up that scruffy rooster. Someone would have to tell her that it wasn't a possibility, but Noah wasn't going to be the bad guy this evening. A new baby in the home would be enough to distract her later on. Hopefully.

"I suppose I'll stay for supper, then," Noah said,

casting his sister-in-law a smile. "But let me go out and take care of the horses."

Because no matter what excitement was in the air, no matter what change was on the horizon, there was still work to be done. It kept their boots on the ground and their hearts humble.

As he headed back out into the winter chill, he prayed that *Gott* would help him to get his head level again...because Eve wasn't his to worry over. His heart didn't belong in the middle of this baby's birth. This was Thomas and Patience's baby—and they deserved to celebrate.

Chapter Eleven

At one o'clock in the morning on Christmas Eve, while snow swirled outside the window and wind howled around the house, Eve gave birth to a healthy baby boy. He let out a powerful cry after his first breath, and when Sarah wrapped him in a blanket and laid him in Eve's arms, she looked down at that tiny, squished face and her heart cracked in two.

They said that when a baby was born, so was a mother, and Eve had wondered if it would be different for her, because she would never raise this child, but it wasn't. She felt herself change and grow, and turn inside out, if that were even possible, all in a single moment looking down at the baby in her arms.

And yet this transformation would have to remain a secret, and the growth of her heart, swelling to encompass the child, no matter how far away he might go, would be something she could never speak of.

Snow whipped against the windowpane, but the room was warm and cozy as Sarah and Lovina rushed about cleaning things up and carrying towels and basins of water back out of the room again. Eve looked at the baby, and tears trickled down her cheeks.

"I love you," she whispered. "I will always love you. I promise you that…always…"

She didn't want her aunt to hear her—or Sarah. Somehow it felt like showing weakness to let them see this moment between her and her child. Everyone knew that this baby boy would be raised a Wiebe.

Eve had wondered what this baby would look like, this baby that had been forced upon her, that she had not chosen. Would he have an Englisher look about him—whatever that might mean? But he didn't. He looked perfectly innocent, with a shock of black hair that stood straight up, tiny rosebud lips, and a face that looked positively boyish. Whatever trauma had surrounded his conception, he was a beautiful baby.

When he squirmed, she'd talk softly to him, and he'd settle immediately, just like he used to do when he was inside her and she'd rub her hand over her belly. It was like there was something inside him that told him he belonged to her, some physical connection that still lingered…and yet he'd have to learn a different voice and a different touch to trust soon enough.

"You need rest, Eve," Lovina said softly, opening the bedroom door again.

"I'm okay," Eve said.

"A woman needs to recover," Lovina said. "You've gone through a very big ordeal tonight, and you need to let us take care of you."

"I said I'm okay!" Eve's voice strengthened. "I'm not putting him down yet."

"We could put a little cradle next to the bed—" Lovina started.

"No!"

She wouldn't give up a single moment with him— their time together was short enough as it was. There would be time to sleep and grieve and heal… But that time was not now.

Lovina retreated once more, and she could hear the murmur of voices in the hallway. Her cousins, the midwife…and her uncle? Yes, that was who it was, and Eve didn't care. She was taking over a whole room, and she didn't care. For this one night she was going to be selfish and hold her baby.

The baby opened his mouth in a yawn, and she touched his tiny chin with the tip of her finger. Eve knew what she'd name him if she could—Samuel. Because she felt like Hannah having to give up her child, though he would never be out of *Gott*'s care. But it wasn't her place to name this child—his adoptive parents would do that. Her only job was to find a way to let go.

Eve did her best to stay awake that night, although she did doze, but she wouldn't let anyone take the baby from her arms. She'd hand him to one woman—and only when she had to.

Gott, *protect my son*, she prayed, leaning her head back against the cool pillow. *Provide for him, bless him, and as he grows up, show him how very real You are! And please, if You could impress upon his little*

*heart one more thing—let him always know with ab-
solute certainty that his* mamm *loved him…and that
I did my best.*

Tears leaked from the corners of her eyes, and she
let out a shuddering sigh. She didn't want to sleep—she
wanted to stay awake and memorize every detail of her
son's face and fingers and the way he breathed… She
wanted to know that if she saw him again in a crowd,
even after years and years, that she'd recognize him. A
mother should recognize her child anywhere—it was
only right… But she was so very tired, and before she
knew it, she'd drifted into an unsettled sleep.

Eve woke up three more times that night to feed the
baby and to change his diaper. Lovina helped her with
those things—the midwife having left, and her cousins sleeping in another room. Wordlessly, they'd given
the baby his bottle, let him drain it, and then changed
that wee diaper so that he'd be dry and comfortable,
but Eve wouldn't let him be put into the cradle that had
materialized next to the bed.

When Eve awoke the last time, there was daylight
flooding into the bedroom—the snow from last night
had passed, and sunlight sparkled on the snow collected outside the window. She looked down at the baby
in her arms, heard voices downstairs, and her heart
sped up. She knew who was here—it was Patience
and Thomas come to collect their baby. Her mouth
went dry, and she pulled the infant closer against her
as she heard the footsteps coming up the stairs. Her
door opened and Lovina came in first.

"They're here," she said simply.

Eve nodded, and Patience and Thomas came inside, too, the little bedroom suddenly feeling very full. Eve lay on the bed, her arms aching from staying in the same position for so long, but she wouldn't give herself a break. She didn't dare—she'd only regret it later when she tried to remember what he felt like in her arms, and she wouldn't cheat herself of one second with her baby.

"How are you doing?" Patience asked, pulling up a chair next to the bed and sinking into it.

"I'm all right," Eve said.

"Are you in much pain?" Patience asked.

"Some," Eve admitted. "That's to be expected, I suppose."

Patience leaned forward and nudged the blanket away from the baby's face, and a smile tickled her lips.

"He's beautiful, Eve," Patience breathed.

"*Yah*, I know…" Tears welled in her eyes. "He's the most beautiful baby I've ever seen, and I've seen many."

"How much does he weigh?" Patience asked.

"Eight pounds, nine ounces," Lovina said. "And nineteen inches long. He's very healthy, Sarah says."

"*Yah…*" Patience said with a weak smile.

Would Eve forget those details over time? They just felt like numbers right now, swimming in a deeper, more important moment. She might not remember his weight, she realized, but she would remember the way his eyelashes touched his cheeks when he slept, and how his little lips sucked, as if he were dreaming of milk.

"Would you give us a moment?" Patience asked,

turning to look at Lovina and Thomas. "I think that Eve and I could use a little privacy for this…"

They both hesitated, but when Patience met her husband's gaze, he nodded. Thomas and Lovina left the room and shut the door behind them, leaving Patience and Eve alone with the baby.

"They were looming," Patience said with a weak shrug.

"They were," Eve agreed.

"Do you still want to do this?" Patience asked. "Have you changed your mind?"

Eve had asked herself that question a thousand times since she'd first held her son, but while it was going to be an agonizing parting, she knew it was best for him. He needed a proper Amish family, so he could have a happy, carefree life. Keeping him would be selfish, she'd decided. What could she give him but a legacy of shame?

"No, I haven't changed my mind," Eve said, her voice tight.

"I'm glad," Patience said softly. "I've been praying all night for your decision—that you'd make the right one for you, and that *Gott* would give me the strength to accept it, whatever it was."

Eve needed strength, too, for that matter, but it was a bit of a comfort to know that Patience had been praying so earnestly.

"I've been so anxious to meet this little boy," Patience said, her gaze moving down to the baby again.

"What will you name him?" Eve asked.

"We haven't settled on a name yet," Patience replied.

"We'll probably pick a name from someone in our family—he's our first son, after all." Patience reached out and touched the blanket again. "Do you think I could hold him?"

Eve longed to say no—every instinct inside her wanted to push this woman out of the room and lock the door. But she'd promised them this baby because they were better for him than she was.

"Yah." Eve loosened her grip on the infant, and Patience slid him out of her arms.

Eve's arms felt weak and she simply let them drop, her hands loose in her lap as she watched Patience adjust the baby in her arms. Patience rocked him back and forth and let out a happy sigh.

"I love you," Patience whispered. "You're a beautiful little boy, and I love you…"

Eve felt the tears rising inside her, and she pressed her lips together, trying to stop herself from crying. She couldn't give vent to her grief yet.

"Do you think Thomas could come in now?" Patience asked.

"Yah." Eve nodded. Maybe it would help for her to see the baby with both of his adoptive parents— give her a mental image of how he'd look with his new family.

Patience opened the door and Thomas came inside. He looked hesitantly from Eve toward the baby, but when his gaze landed on the infant, his expression melted and his eyes misted.

"Hey, there," he said gruffly, reaching out to touch the baby's cheek. "Oh… Patience… Wow…"

He didn't seem to have words to pull his emotions together, but Eve could see the way Patience and Thomas looked down at her son, and she knew he'd be safe with them—more than safe. He'd be adored. She was making the right choice... Maybe she'd feel more sure about it later.

"I think you should go," Lovina said. "Don't you, Eve? I think it's time for them to head home."

Eve didn't want them to go, but then, this moment wouldn't get easier for waiting. She didn't trust herself to words, so she just nodded. Patience and Thomas left the room, the baby in their arms, and Eve heard the sound of their steps going down the stairs. There was the murmur of voices and Eve's heart seemed to stretch out of her body, following after them.

She could hear the sound of tack jingling on the horses outside, but she was listening for one last sound from her baby...

The door opened, and then she heard it—his plaintive cry. His wail wound upstairs and sank into her chest like a knife. Then the door shut.

Eve pushed back the blankets and let out a grunt of pain as she dragged herself to the edge of the bed and let her legs drop over the side. Her feet hit the cold floor, and she forced herself to stand, even though her body screamed in protest. With one hand under her stomach, she hobbled across the room to the window, and she sank down against the sill, her arms trembling.

"Samuel..." she whispered. Because being allowed to name him or not, that *was* his name—to her, at least.

She could see the bundle of blankets in Patience's

arms, but that was all, and then the horses started forward, the buggy lurching once, then rattling down the snowy drive, taking her baby away.

Eve felt a sob tear through her chest, and she lost her grip on the windowsill, sinking to the cold floor. She wept from such a deep part of her that she thought it might tear her heart right out of her body.

The door opened.

"Eve?" It was Lovina, and then there were hands underneath her, tugging her upward. Eve struggled to rise, and Lovina's strong arms closed around her, and her aunt rocked her back and forth like a baby.

"Oh, Evie..." Lovina crooned. "Oh, Evie..."

There were no words that could explain Eve's grief, and no sympathy that could make it easier to bear. This was a private burden. But all the same, Eve let her aunt help her back into the bed, and when Lovina sat next to her and took her hand, Eve clamped her hand down on her aunt's, refusing to let go.

"You need to eat," Lovina whispered. "Maybe just some tea and sugar? You need your strength, dear. Now it's time to let me take care of you. Please."

Eve didn't answer. Food wasn't going to fix this, because this pain deep in her chest was what it felt like to be a mother without a child in her arms.

Noah worked the shop with Amos that day. It was Christmas Eve, and everyone was picking up last-minute gifts, cheerfully collecting packages as they carried on their way. Outside, the carolers were singing "Jingle Bells," their voices carrying into the showroom where Noah stood, his arms crossed over his chest and his brow furrowed.

They'd finished their orders for the holiday, and they'd all been picked up, except for one. But Noah's mind wasn't on his work. He'd been struggling to keep himself focused all day, but he couldn't seem to do it. Eve was having her baby—or she had it already. How long did these things take? Thomas hadn't come in this morning because they were going to go to the Glick house to wait, and while this wasn't Noah's business, technically, his heart was still lodged in his throat.

A threesome of teenage Amish girls fluttered past the big display window, laughing and carrying boxes from the bakery. He smiled faintly—it wasn't that long ago that he was a teenager, too, and life had been remarkably simple, looking back on it. There was church, and work, and girls that he mooned after…and there had been his mother's visits and his teenage heartbreak over her refusal to stay Amish. His Amish life had given him a structure to grow within. But this Christmas, their Amish life wasn't giving him the comfort he needed.

The bell above the door tinkled, and he looked over to see his mother come inside. She stomped her boots on the mat and looked up with a smile. Her gray hair had some snowflakes clinging to it, and she shook off her coat as she stamped.

"Merry Christmas, Noah," his mother said with a smile.

"Merry Christmas," he said. "Do you have news?"

"It's a boy," Rachel said.

"A boy…" It felt good to know that. "And what about Eve? How is she?"

"Recovering." Rachel's smile slipped. "Giving up her baby is painful for her. But Patience asked her if she was sure, and she was. There was no pressure. But that doesn't necessarily make it easier. So we'll be praying for her as she gets her strength back."

"*Yah*, right." Noah nodded a couple of times. "So the baby…?"

"He's home with Thomas and Patience," Rachel said. "I've come out to buy a few items—more formula, a box of smaller diapers to start off with and one of those little bath seats for newborns you know?"

"Not really," he admitted with a shake of his head.

"Well, anyway, I'm picking that up for them," Rachel said. "And Rue is just overjoyed to have a baby brother."

"*Yah*, I can only imagine," he said. "So…that's that? She's given up the baby, and everything just…continues?"

"There is tragedy and happiness, all twined up together," Rachel said, and she met his gaze. "Son, are *you* all right?"

"I'm fine, it's just—this is very big," he said.

"The arrival of every baby is a very big event," she replied. "When you were born, everything changed. Your *daet* and I became parents for the very first time. It was like the world tipped upside down for us. That was when your father started talking about this Amish life. He wanted something better for you. I daresay he was right." .

"Yah..." Noah shrugged uncomfortably. "I'm just worried about Eve."

"She has her aunt with her," Rachel said. "Lovina even closed up the shop today so that she could be there for Eve."

That was something—and he was glad that Eve had someone by her side.

"Would it be...inappropriate for me to go see her?" Noah asked.

His mother's eyebrows went up. "You two have gotten rather close, haven't you?"

Close didn't describe it. What he was feeling for her was a confusing mess, and he knew that there was no future for them, but their friendship wasn't just about Thomas and Patience adopting her baby, or about their hope to help Wollie. Somewhere, he'd slipped past proprieties with her...

"We're friends, I think," he said, but she was so much more than a friend. Admitting it wasn't going to help, though.

"There are going to be a lot of people visiting Thomas and Patience," Rachel said thoughtfully. "They will be getting a lot of attention and support with their new addition, but there won't be many visiting Eve... I think a visit from her friend would be completely appropriate. And kind."

Noah nodded. *"Yah.* I hoped so. I just wanted to check in on her and see how she is."

"You've grown into a good man, son," Rachel said, putting a hand on his arm. "I'm proud of you."

"Thanks, *Mamm.*" He smiled faintly, but he wasn't

sure that it helped. Thomas and Patience had just gotten their hearts' desire, and Noah couldn't join them in their joy, because his heart was entangled with Eve.

Amos and Noah closed up early that night—all the shops on Main Street did on Christmas Eve. Before they left, he stopped by the candy shop and bought a little box of chocolates before it closed, too. He couldn't think of anything else that might comfort her right now.

Noah and Amos headed toward home together through the crisp, winter evening, passing by the nativity scene—there were no more bags of donations, since Noah had picked up the last of them that afternoon. But still, the crimson sunset reflecting off the snow and the little nativity stable brought a strange lump to his throat.

"I'm going to drop you off at home," Noah said. "I need to see Eve—make sure she's okay."

"*Yah*, of course." Amos cast him a look. "It's Christmas Eve, you know. They'll be celebrating."

"Will *she*?" Noah asked meaningfully. Somehow, he doubted that. He'd gotten to know Eve rather well that last little while, and he didn't think she'd be celebrating anything. "Tell *Mammi* I'm sorry. I'll be home when I can."

"I think *Mammi* will understand," Amos said with a nod. "I know I do."

He felt the weight in Amos's words. How much had the older man guessed about Noah's feelings? Amos had been there for Noah through his adolescence, and of anyone, Amos understood him.

When Noah got to their drive, Amos tapped the

side of the buggy. "Just let me off here. I'll walk down the drive."

Noah reined in the horses and let Amos off, watching for a moment as he strode through the snow toward the house. *Mammi* would be waiting, and there would be good food and fresh baking… But that wasn't what was calling to Noah right now. Home seemed to be farther away than it ever had before.

He flicked the reins and carried on down the road toward the Glick acreage. He just had to know that she was okay, and then he'd rest a little easier.

Chapter Twelve

Eve sat up in bed, a plate of untouched cookies beside her. And next to that plate of cookies was another plate with a sandwich, and next to that, another plate with a cinnamon bun. Every time someone came up to talk to her, they brought her food, hoping to entice her to eat. She'd had a little bit, because everyone wanted her to eat so badly, but she could hardly bring herself to swallow it.

Her cousins had offered to help her downstairs—they'd set up a little nest for her in the sitting room, they said. But this Christmas, Eve didn't want to be downstairs with her family. She'd only bring them down, if she hadn't already.

She could hear the cousins playing some card games at the table—some subdued laughter, the clink of cutlery on plates. They'd likely be talking about this Christmas for years to come. *"Remember that Christmas when Eve had the baby and it was just so sad?"* But her cousins would be able to file this Christmas away as a somber memory. Eve would be carrying it in her heart for the rest of her life.

There was a tap on her door, and she sighed.

"Come in," she said.

The door opened, and this time it wasn't one of her cousins. Noah filled the doorway, his hat in one hand and concern written all over his features, and she felt a rush of relief to see him.

"Eve?" he said quietly. "Can I come in?"

Eve nodded and gestured to the plates.

"Feel free to eat something," she said.

Noah came into the room, a napkin with another sandwich on top in the other hand. He kept the door open, and he tossed his hat next to the plates, then sank into the chair that had replaced the cradle next to her bed.

"I promised I'd try to get you to eat," he said, handing her the sandwich.

Eve felt her eyes mist. "They're taking good care of me."

"But you aren't eating," he said, his gaze moving toward the untouched plates.

"No…" She'd cried out her tears today—and she felt like she was dried from the inside out, but her grief was still there. And she was sure she'd cry some more tomorrow, and the day after.

"Forget the sandwich," he said, putting it down with the other food, and he pulled a little cardboard box from his pocket. "I brought you truffles."

"Chocolate," she said with a faint smile.

Noah licked his lips and looked down for a moment,

and when he looked up, she could see the deep sympathy in his eyes.

"I had to see how you were," Noah said. "I've been so worried."

"Have you seen the baby?" she asked, looking up at him hopefully.

"Not yet," he admitted. "I had to work at the shop, and instead of going to see him... I came to see you."

He'd come... She hadn't even dared hope that he would. She'd told herself that he'd go straight to his brother's house and everyone would celebrate her child. But he'd come here instead.

Eve's chin trembled. "I did the right thing, giving him up."

He didn't answer.

"Didn't I?" she pressed. "Didn't I do the right thing?"

She wasn't sure what she expected him to say, but it wasn't up to him to be certain. And certainty hadn't come in the last few hours separated from her child.

"My mother came by the shop and told me that they're all really happy and doting on him," Noah said. "If that helps."

Did it? Not really. She'd known they would—her son would be loved dearly, but he wouldn't be raised by the one woman who'd love him more dearly than any other.

"What can I do to help you?" he asked, his voice rough with emotion.

Eve shrugged faintly. "Nothing."

"Tell me there's something," he insisted. "Tell me I can buy you something, dig something up for you. Tell me I can tear something apart!"

"Why?" she whispered.

"Because then I could help! I'm just a man, Eve! I want to fix things—"

Eve put the box of chocolates down on the bed beside her. "It will be easier when I go home."

"When is that?" he asked.

"As soon as I can travel," she said. "Sarah—the midwife—will let me know when I'm healed enough, but she thinks in a few days. There is a certain urgency to be rid of me, I think. She'll let me go faster than she would if I were keeping him."

And then she'd be back with her father, and he'd tell people she had been ill and needed to recover, or something—some forgivable lie so that people wouldn't ask too many questions—and she'd heal. She'd be back in the comfort of her childhood home with the father who loved her just as dearly as she loved her own son.

And she'd have a chance at having that beautiful home of her own.

"How can I reach you?" Noah asked. "Once you've left, I mean."

"You won't." She looked away.

"You don't think you could use a friend?" he asked, but she heard the hopeless note in his voice. "Someone who knows about all of this?"

"You're my child's uncle now," she said, her throat tight. "And I have to let go. I can't stay connected to you—because then I'll always want to know about my baby, and I'll never move on. This is better for all of us."

"I don't think so," he countered.

"Don't you understand how this works?" she demanded. "It's better!"

"It's not better for me!" he insisted.

"Can't you see that I'm doing my best?" she pleaded.

"I'm supposed to just not see you again?" he whispered gruffly. "I'm supposed to pretend that whatever happened this Christmas didn't change anything? Eve, I fell in love with you!"

Eve blinked, and she felt like her heart stopped beating in her chest.

"What?"

"This is terrible, and I know it," he breathed. "This wasn't supposed to happen, and trust me when I tell you, I've been very good at protecting my heart in the past. Just ask the single women in this community. But there's something about you—"

"It's just the pregnancy," she said feebly.

"You're no longer pregnant, and I love you still!" he insisted. "This is not so simple. You're like no one I've ever met. When I'm with you, I feel more alive, and when I'm away from you, I'm thinking about you—"

"What would you have me do, stay?" she asked helplessly.

"What if you did?"

"And your brother?" she asked, shaking her head. "Is he supposed to just hand his son over to you, and let you raise him? You don't see any complications there?"

"I don't know..." He shook his head. "Then I go with you back to your people."

"And never see your family..."

He was silent.

"You know that can't work. We're Amish. Family is what we're all about! Are you supposed to be happy with just me?" She felt hot tears on her cheeks. "I'm not enough—"

"You could be."

"You're only saying that because you don't want to say goodbye," she said. "You know it's true. And I came here to find a family for my baby—I found it. I might hate this. I might never fully heal. But what else is there for me to do?"

Noah reached for her hand and covered it with both of his. "Maybe all I have left is to tell you that I love you."

"I love you, too, Noah…" Her lips trembled. "But that isn't enough to make a family, is it?"

They were Amish, and the right way was very often the hard way. They had accepted that, and they lived according to their principles. She wanted her son to have all the benefits of a happy, thriving Amish family, and he would have that with the Wiebes, but only if she walked away and let him go.

If she stayed, if she loved this man in spite of it all, the happy balance she longed for little Samuel to have would be gone. She'd ruin every chance he'd have…

No, loving Noah wasn't enough.

Noah reached for his hat. He was leaving. What did she expect him to do after a confession like that, after she spurned him? But on Christmas Eve, maybe it was time to tell her whole truth, too.

"I can't be the woman you settled for over one strange, emotional Christmas," she said, her voice shaking. "You want a woman to give you security in a proper Amish life after all you went through with your parents, and I'm just the girl who got pregnant at some Englisher party— "

"Don't say that!" he cut in. "That isn't who you are."

"It's exactly who I am, and it's all I'll ever be in the eyes of the community unless I take this second chance at building a life for myself!" she countered. "So I should take my son back? Anyone who gives up her baby to Thomas and Patience is going to go through this misery, you know. In order for them to grow their family, a woman *has* to lose her child..."

"I know," he said, and his chin trembled.

"If all this is, is pity, some hard feelings because you saw the other side of adoption—"

"It isn't pity, and I do love you, Eve," he said, his voice low and agonized. "But you're right that it's possible to love more than is wise..."

If only a romance between them was a possibility— if all of her heartbreak could be fixed with a simple wedding to a good man. But that only worked if her reputation had been whitewashed, and in Redemption, too many people knew the truth. And it only worked if they could be sure that they'd be happy together five years from now, twenty-five years, fifty-five years... that he wouldn't regret the impulse to marry some pregnant girl and thwart his own brother's deepest wish to grow his family. She'd come here to have her baby and leave. Staying still wasn't an option.

If she could let her child go for his own good, then she could let Noah go, too. Her heart had already been shattered, and it couldn't hold any more grief. If she could keep breathing after giving up her son, she could keep putting one foot in front of the other and take herself out of Redemption and go back home.

"So that's it?" he asked hopelessly.

"I have to trust in the plan I pieced together all those months when I was able to think straight," she said. "That's what it was for—so that when my heart was in pieces, I wouldn't have to try to think my way through it. I made a plan…"

Noah lifted her fingers to his lips and pressed a warm kiss against her hand. He shut his eyes for a moment, then lowered her hand and released her.

"I'm going to miss you," he said, his voice thick, then he picked up his hat and put it on his head.

She was going to say "Merry Christmas," or even goodbye, but she couldn't force the words out. Noah went to the door and turned back once to look at her.

"I'll be a good uncle," he said, and his voice caught, then he disappeared and his footsteps echoed down the stairs.

That was the last that Eve could take. Fresh tears leaked from beneath her lashes, and her chest ached within as if her heart had truly broken all over again. She bent her head and cried—for her son she'd never raise, for the man she loved but would never marry, for the life she wished she could have with Noah, but couldn't…

Gott's best would have to change along with her circumstances. She couldn't see any other way around it.

* * *

Noah's throat felt raw as the frigid winter wind blew snow into his face. The horses clopped peacefully along, but his heart refused to be soothed into the rhythm. He hadn't meant to say all of that to Eve tonight—but now that he had, he couldn't deny the truth. He was in love with her. How had he let this happen? Noah had always been the guy who kept things under control, and falling for the mother of his brother's adopted son—he'd prayed so hard for *Gott* to deliver him from his own emotions. But *Gott* hadn't answered. If anything, his feelings for Eve had only grown after his heartfelt prayers.

His chest felt heavy, his throat tight with emotion. He wanted to cry, but he wouldn't. Not yet. He'd rather skip over this part—the heartbreak, the loss. He'd gone through this when his mother left, and he'd been so certain that he could guard himself against feeling this kind of misery again if he only made the right choices...for all that worked. Falling for Eve hadn't been a choice.

He flicked the reins, and the horses picked up their pace. The wind was brisk, hitting his face and numbing his fingers through his gloves. There were the last of the donations in his wagon—some groceries, more clothes. He'd drop these off with Wollie, and then go home to his family to celebrate Christmas...if he could even manage it.

The moon was high, and the snow glittered in the silvery light. Alone out there on the road with only the horses for company, he lifted his heart to *Gott*.

Maybe it was stupid of me to follow my heart, he prayed. *Maybe I should have found a woman a long time ago and simply chosen to love her. But I don't think love is that simple. Am I wrong? Have I just been stubborn all this time? Because the one time I fall head over boots for a woman, and it's someone so completely wrong for me...*

But he loved her. He loved her so much that even knowing he couldn't be her husband, he wanted to make sure she was okay. He still wanted to find a way to make her pain more bearable. Eve was a woman who'd been through more than most endured in a lifetime, and knowing her heartbreak made celebrating with his brother all that more difficult.

Gott...*let her have the desires of her heart, even though I can't be part of it.*

Christmas had never been an easy time for Noah, not since his *mamm* had left, and this Christmas wasn't going to be any easier.

When Noah turned into Wollie's drive, he could see the electric lights on in the house, and through the curtainless windows, he could see the *kinner* bouncing around in the living room.

Maybe this Christmas wasn't going to be about Noah's hopes, but about Wollie's and Thomas's... Not every man got the desires of his heart, but that didn't mean that *Gott* wasn't pouring out blessings on the community around him.

The front door opened and Wollie came outside, pulling a coat on. He waved to Noah as the buggy came to a stop.

"Merry Christmas!" Wollie called out.

"Merry Christmas." Noah tied off the reins and hopped down, hoping that his own sadness didn't show through, but when Wollie came closer, he hesitated.

"Are you all right?" Wollie asked.

"Yah, yah..."

"No, you're not," Wollie countered.

"Eve had the baby," Noah said. "A boy—healthy and strong. He's home with Thomas and Patience now, so..."

"Yah..." Wollie seemed to immediately sense the complication there. "And Eve is without her child."

"Yah." That was part of it, at least.

Wollie was silent for a moment and he nodded a couple of times. "When Caleb came along, he wasn't... planned. I had a choice to make—marry Natasha, or let her live her life. And I couldn't imagine walking away. But Caleb's arrival changed everything—turned my life upside down in the best and the scariest ways."

"I think babies do that," Noah agreed.

"I daresay this baby turned your life upside down, too," Wollie said quietly.

"No—I mean, my brother is adopting this child, and I'm not the father, and—" Noah sighed. "But *yah*. Babies seem to arrive like a bolt of lightning, don't they?"

Wollie smiled faintly. "I have four, and every single of one them changed me in their own ways."

This baby had changed Noah, too...because of his mother. Eve had been the bolt of lightning into his life, and her child was the one who had pulled them all together. And here Noah was, dropping off donations at a friend's house instead of going to see his brother and meet his new nephew. Because he didn't want to be that baby's uncle—

His heartbeat sped up at the realization, and he sucked in a wavery breath. He wanted to be that baby's *daet*. Not that it mattered what he wanted—he and Eve couldn't work. She was right—they were too different, and they both had plans for how to build a satisfying Amish life for themselves. Falling in love with each other didn't fit in!

"I just came by with a few more donations," Noah said, pushing back his private thoughts. "You know, you're more than welcome to come for Christmas Eve at our place. We'd love to have you."

"Natasha has been making Christmas here, and it's really something…" Wollie looked over his shoulder toward the house. His wife looked out the window and waved, and Noah waved back. Then Wollie turned back. "My parents are coming by this evening, too, so we won't be on our own. But thanks all the same. Maybe we can come see you on Christmas Day, or for Second Christmas."

"*Yah*…that would be good." Noah lowered his voice. "Can I ask you something—man to man?"

"Sure." Wollie stilled, and from inside, Noah could hear the kids' laughter filtering out to them in the snowy cold.

"Do you regret it—marrying an Englisher, I mean?" Noah asked cautiously. "Do you ever wish you'd followed the safe path?"

Wollie was silent for a moment, then he sucked in a

breath. "I know this won't make a lot of sense to you, because we were raised to follow the rules and stick to the path. And I know that looking at me right now, you'd think that my life hasn't exactly turned out, but I don't regret it."

"You don't miss the Amish life?" Noah pressed. "You don't wonder if you went against *Gott*'s plan for your life?"

"I do miss it," Wollie said. "And I do want to come back, but marrying Natasha—she wasn't a mistake, Noah. She's…she's everything. She's the one I can turn to, no matter what, and have love and understanding. She's the one I think about when I work long hours, and the one I can't wait to come home to. She's an unexpected gift from *Gott*."

Noah frowned. "I can see how much you love each other, but you can't be Amish with her—"

"Well…" Wollie smiled ruefully. "I can't be Amish with her *yet*, but I'm convinced that *Gott* isn't done with us. Not every path is so direct, but *Gott* is still leading. I know it. I can feel it."

"I admire your faith," Noah said. "Help me unload?"

"Of course."

Noah and Wollie unloaded the last of the donations and carried them into the house. The children were playing in the kitchen with some wooden toys—blocks, carved horses, a little wooden buggy, and some Amish dolls in pink and purple cape dresses. Natasha sat at the kitchen table with a pot of popcorn, and she was stringing it onto some thread.

"Noah's brought over a few more things," Wollie said.

"Thank you so much," Natasha said, standing up. "This means the world to us. I have to admit, we're having a Plain Christmas this year because we don't have any other choice, but I think this is the most grateful we've ever been in our lives."

"We're seeing our grandma and grandpa tonight!" the oldest girl announced. "And we're making popcorn strings to decorate so it will look Christmassy for them."

"That sounds great," Noah said, a smile tugging at his lips. "They'll love that." Then he turned to Wollie. "Come by—anytime. We've got enough to go around, I promise. *Mammi* has outdone herself this year. You know where we're at."

"*Yah*, I know the place," Wollie said. "We'll be driving in the truck—hope that's okay."

"I don't care if you roll over in a snowball," Noah said, winking at the kids who had stopped to look up at him. "Just come."

They said their goodbyes, and Noah headed back out to the buggy. He passed Wollie's parents on his way out, and he waved to them and exchanged a "Merry Christmas."

His heart was heavy, but Wollie's sentiment was rolling over in his mind. *Gott* wasn't finished with them yet… Wollie still had hope that he and his wife could become Amish again together—and that was a phenomenal amount of faith for a man who'd married an Englisher.

And in the sparkling stillness of that Christmas Eve

night, he wondered if *Gott* wasn't finished with Noah yet, either...or Eve.

Still, if a man could marry an Englisher and still have faith that *Gott* was working, it gave Noah something to think about. Had he been making wise choices in following a proper path, or was his faith just not big enough for a leap?

Chapter Thirteen

Christmas morning, Lovina came into Eve's room and swished open the curtains. Watery winter sunlight flooded the room, and Eve pushed herself up onto her elbows.

"Merry Christmas, my dear," Lovina said, sitting down next to her on the bed. "I'm sorry to just come barging in here like this, but your *daet* asked me to be the *mamm* you needed, and I'm trying to do that."

"Oh…" Eve said feebly.

"Now, let me help you with your hair," Lovina said, pulling out a comb. "It will feel better once it's combed."

Eve accepted her aunt's solicitous help, and she submitted to her hair being combed. She had to admit that it did feel nice, and her aunt's gentle touch worked through the tangles.

"I noticed that Noah came over on his own yesterday," Lovina said, the even strokes of the comb continuing. "Did he make things harder for you, or—"

"No, Noah didn't…at least not on purpose." Eve's

chin trembled. "I don't know if it was just that I was vulnerable and lonesome, or that this situation was so complicated, but we…" Eve wiped an errant tear. "He said he loves me."

Lovina straightened, stopped combing and stared at her. "He said that?"

Eve turned to meet her aunt's gaze. *"Yah."*

"And you said…"

"That I love him, too, but Aunty, it isn't going to work."

"I'm sorry, Evie," her aunt said softly.

"What if I didn't leave my son behind?" Eve asked, and she turned to face her aunt.

"What?" Lovina said.

"What if I took him home with me?" she asked, her voice shaking. "If I keep Samuel, it will break those people's hearts—I know that. And it will make me the cruel and stupid woman who put them all through it, but what if I took him home?"

"What would his life be like, you mean?" Lovina asked softly.

"Yah. With a single mother, and a solid grandfather to raise him… What would that be like?"

"It would be complicated," Lovina said quietly. "People would talk."

"Yah…" She knew that. That was why she'd made her choice to begin with, but she'd thought that after Patience left with her son, it would be easier.

"Evie…" Lovina looked toward the window. "I'm going to tell you something, and your father will be angry with me. I might not even be right to tell you…"

"What?" Eve asked.

"People's opinions mean nothing in the eyes of *Gott*." Lovina looked over at Eve with a solemn expression. "Nothing."

"It will affect my son all the same," she said.

"Yah..." Lovina sucked in a slow breath. "But life affects us all in some way or other. Your mother died, and that affected you deeply. There was no avoiding that pain."

"True," Eve said uncertainly.

"And I had a similar experience at a party as you did, Eve, except I remembered every second of it, and I didn't end up pregnant..." Lovina licked her lips and looked at Eve sadly.

"Aunty?" Eve whispered.

"I carry it with me still, all these years later. It's affected me, and it's affected how I raise my girls. I'm careful—too careful, some say. But I won't have them assaulted like I was. It affects you whether you want it to or not. I thought that if you couldn't remember it, you might be able to forget...but how foolish was that? And do you know what makes the pain of life harder to bear?"

Eve shook her head.

"Silence." Lovina's chin quivered. "You need to be able to talk about it, and going home to live in that heavy silence while your heart breaks...it *will* affect you. And your son. And your father..."

"What are you saying?" Eve asked.

"I'm saying that life will be hard no matter what. And I truly did think you'd be better off giving this child up and having your chance at a beautiful life. I know what it's like to have your innocence stolen by a wicked boy, and I wanted you to have the chance at marriage and *kinner* that I did. But I'm not so sure that's the right path anymore...unless it's what you want, Eve. I think you need to follow your heart, no matter what other people think!"

Eve's heart hammered in her chest. Life *would* be hard—and there would be talk. Her son would live with stories and stigma...but life would be hard either way, wouldn't it?

And suddenly it all came together inside her, and she knew what she needed to do.

"I can't be happy without my baby... I know I said I'd give him up, and I know I chose the Wiebes to raise him, but I can't do this! I've been in bed all night missing my baby, missing Noah, and my heart is just aching. So it doesn't matter if I could love Noah or not, because I'm about to do something that is going to break his family's hearts. But I'm going after my baby! And I know his family will never forgive me for doing this, but I can't live without my little boy in my arms."

"You're—" Lovina nodded solemnly. "You're taking him back."

"I'm taking him back!" Eve met her aunt's gaze.

"Are you sure about this?" Lovina asked seriously. "You can't just rush in and cause havoc. Are you sure you don't want to think it through? Talk it through? I haven't mixed you up with my own babble just now?"

"I need my baby," Eve pleaded.

"Let's get you dressed, my dear," Lovina said, rising to her feet. "And you can't overdo it, now. You'll have to take it slow. But I will drive you."

Eve had no idea how this would affect the rest of her life, and it may very well be that her son would have been able to avoid the scandal of her name, but asking her to get in a bus and ride away from her infant was like asking her to leave her beating heart behind. She wouldn't survive it.

Would she be able to get married? Maybe not... but life would carry on. She and her baby would still be in *Gott*'s hands, and that was the safest place they could ever be.

If Patience would give him back...

Christmas morning, Noah, Mary, Amos and Rachel gathered in Thomas and Patience's home. Christmas was always a time for family, and Noah listened absently as Amos read the Christmas story in the book of Matthew, Rue locked in with rapt attention. Bible stories were still a novelty for Rue, and every plot twist left her wide-eyed and filled with awe. She'd heard the story of Jesus's birth before—Noah knew that, because he'd been the one to tell her about the wise men—but watching her serious little face soak in the wonder of the real reason for the season made Noah's heart soften just a little bit more.

Gott was real. Jesus was real. And even if his and Eve's hearts broke, there was hope because of their faith. Strange how watching a little girl listen to the story of a stable, some shepherds and a night with no room in the inn could reawaken his own faith.

After the Bible reading, the women set to work whipping up a big breakfast, and the men sat around the table, their chairs pushed out so they could relax. Thomas held the baby, looking down at him with pride glowing in his eyes, and Noah couldn't help but feel a surge of sadness at the sight.

This wasn't just any baby… This was Eve's son.

"Have you decided on a name yet?" Noah asked.

"Not yet," Thomas said. "It'll either be Jacob for Patience's father, or Elmer, for ours."

"I vote for Elmer," Noah said, reaching for the nutcracker and a walnut from the bowl in the center.

"Your vote doesn't count," Amos replied with a laugh. "Amos is a nice name, too, might I add."

This boy would never just be Noah's nephew. Whatever they named him, to Noah, he'd be the son of the woman he'd fallen in love with, and for years, he knew, he'd be looking into this boy's face searching for his mother.

"Do you want to hold him?" Thomas asked.

Noah felt a wave of misgiving, but Thomas handed the baby over, and Noah took a moment to adjust the little guy in his arms. He was so small—no larger than a loaf of bread. The baby pulled his knees up and squirmed until Noah got him settled against his chest. No, this baby would never be just a nephew to him, but the Amish were practiced in sweeping aside uncomfortable feelings. In a community this size, it was either learn to get over it, or have the community disintegrate.

"It still hardly feels real," Thomas said with a shake of his head. "When Rue arrived, it felt very real right away, and somehow with this baby, I still feel like I'm dreaming."

"*Daet*, I can't reach," Rue called, and Thomas headed over to where his daughter was stretching to get a cup above her head, leaving Noah alone with the baby. The infant opened his mouth in a tiny yawn and Noah touched his cheek with the back of his finger. So small. So soft.

"He's sweet, isn't he?" Rachel asked. His mother came over to where he sat with a dish towel in her hand, and she leaned over his shoulder, looking down at the baby wistfully. Her eyes crinkled when she smiled, and she reached out to touch the baby's toes through the blanket.

"*Yah,*" Noah said. "He's really something."

Rachel tugged a chair up and sank into it, looking at Noah with silent concern.

"I'm fine, *Mamm*," he said.

Rachel pursed her lips. "No, you aren't."

"*Mamm—*" He didn't want to be cruel, but this wasn't something he cared to discuss right now, with anyone.

"You're still angry with me," she said, tears misting her eyes.

"*Mamm*, it's not you."

"And that's why you and I have this chasm between us?" she asked, shaking her head. "It's not me? Of course it's me! I left. Isn't that the problem?"

"We don't have to do this now," he said.

"Then when?" she asked. "Son, I love you! And I left this community, and you've never forgiven me for that. But I've forgiven you!"

"For what?" he demanded.

"For not coming with me," she said, and her lips trembled. "I could have forced you to come. You were my children, and I had every right to bring you with me. But I didn't do that—I didn't want to make it into a power struggle. I wanted you to come with me because you loved your *mamm*."

Noah's heart constricted and he blinked back an unexpected mist of tears. "*Mamm*, I loved you—"

"Not enough to come along," she said, then shook her head. "And you blame me for not staying. But love doesn't demand, Noah. Love is patient. Love believes all things and hopes all things, and... I wouldn't force you."

Noah dropped his gaze. He hadn't considered it in quite that way before. She was right—he'd blamed her for leaving, but he'd never stopped to think what it would be like for her having sons who refused to go with her. They'd stood by their faith—and maybe in some ways she'd been equally abandoned.

"Is it my fault that you didn't marry this girl?" she asked softly.

"What?" He looked up at her.

"Oh, you didn't hide it very well," she said gently. "You fell in love with Eve. And she fell in love with you."

"*Mamm*, she's given her son to my brother. There is no way I can marry her."

"Even loving her like you do?" Rachel asked, then sighed. "Son, you like to keep everything in order, lined up, neat and appropriate. You've been like that since you were little. You measure three times and cut once. But with a woman, you can't do that."

Noah adjusted the baby in his arms and patted the little rump gently. "What?"

"I'm serious," Rachel said. "You have to simply let her...be her! I know you're afraid of everything falling apart on you, so you try to control it and hold it together, but with the most important things in life, we have to let *Gott* hold it together for us. He's the only One who can!"

"I'm not trying to control her," he said with a frown.

"No, you aren't, I agree," she said. "But you're trying to control who you fall in love with, and you're doing your very best to be a good brother. You're trying to control all of the perimeters of your life, and in many ways that's just smart. I raised you to do the right thing, even if it hurts. But sometimes, something hurts because it's *wrong*."

"This is Thomas's son," he said, and his voice caught. "He's not mine..."

"When it comes to your heart, and when it comes to a relationship, even one with your brother, there needs to be some flexibility. If I'd demanded that you come with me to the English world, you would have hated me for different reasons, and we might never have gotten past it."

"You risked losing me completely, though," he countered.

"No, dear," she said with a shake of her head. "I trusted *Gott* to show you your path—and to show me mine. And you know what? *Gott* brought us back together. We were always in His hand. It's not the risk you think when you trust the ones you love to *Gott*."

"Are you suggesting I marry Eve?" he asked. "And be this baby's *daot*?"

"I'm suggesting that you be very certain what *Gott*'s path is for you, and then you walk that path," she said seriously. "And you let *Gott* take care of the rest."

"What if my brother never speaks to me again?" he asked.

"I have two sons with their hearts entangled in this," she said softly. "And your heart matters just as much as your brother's."

Noah looked at his mother, a new realization flooding through him. Was it possible that *Gott* had brought him a son, instead of Thomas? And if that were the case, could his brother ever forgive him?

"Can you take the baby?" he asked.

The baby let out a little sigh in his sleep, and Noah looked down at him tenderly. This child would always be special to him, and he knew it. But right now his mind was spinning with new possibilities. He needed to get alone... He needed to pray.

"Yah." Rachel accepted the infant from his arms.

"I'm just going to take a walk," he said.

"Of course, son."

Noah bent to kiss his mother's cheek. "Thank you for being my *mamm* and loving me steadily, even when I wouldn't come with you."

Rachel's eyes sparkled with unshed tears, and she nodded. Noah grabbed his coat and plunged his feet into his boots, then headed out into the Christmas cold.

Today was the day they celebrated Jesus's birth—a new chance for the world. And as he strode out through the crunchy snow, he wondered if he'd been going about this all wrong. Did he want to spend the next twenty or thirty years watching this child grow up and remembering the woman he loved?

Or was there a way to follow his heart, after all?

But this was a step he would not take without talking it over with *Gott* first.

Chapter Fourteen

The jostle of the buggy made Eve grimace in pain, but she turned away so that her aunt couldn't see it. She didn't want Lovina to slow down—she wanted to get to the Wiebe house as fast as she could. She needed her son back in her arms where he belonged so that her chest could stop aching with grief.

"Will she give him back?" Dread welled up inside her. What if Patience wouldn't return him? What if she said no?

"We'll go and talk it over," Lovina said. "They're good people. Trust in that."

But trusting in anyone but *Gott* alone was hard to do when her child was in their arms and not hers.

Gott, please give me back my baby! she prayed earnestly. *I was wrong to even try to give him up. Please give him back!*

When Lovina turned into the drive, Eve's heart sped up, and when she reined in the horses, Eve didn't wait for help getting down. She slid to the ground, her boots slipping, and she collapsed to her knees in the crunching snow. Then she pushed herself up, staggering toward the house.

"Eve!" Lovina called. "Wait for me! Eve!"

But she couldn't wait—there wasn't another moment to wait. She needed her baby back, and every breath she took without him felt like it would crush her chest. She made it up the steps and pounded on the door with her gloved fist.

"Let me in!" she cried. "I need my baby! Let me in!"

From inside the house she heard her little Samuel's wail start up. He'd heard her, and she knew that he was responding to his mother's voice. Lovina got to the door and stood next to her, just as it opened and Eve stumbled inside.

The kitchen was warm and smelled of cooking. Thomas stared at her in surprise as she moved past him, scanning the room—everyone was standing now, and every eye was pinned to her. But then she saw her baby, cradled safely in Patience's arms. The other woman stared at her, her mouth open and her cheeks pale.

"I changed my mind," Eve breathed. "I need my baby—"

Patience took a step back, holding the infant closer, but he howled louder.

"Please..." Eve said, tears streaming down her cheeks. "Please, Patience. I know I gave him to you, but I can't give him up. I can't!"

Her knees were shaking, and she felt a strong hand under her arm, guiding her to a chair. It was Amos, and she gratefully sank into it.

"You changed your mind?" Patience whispered, tears leaking down her cheeks.

"I'm sorry." Eve met the other woman's gaze and watched as Patience looked down at the baby in her arms. But he was howling now, arching his little back as he wailed his confusion.

Patience looked over at Thomas and he shook his head sadly.

"She can do that, Patience," he said.

"I know, I just—" Patience's chin trembled. "I fell in love with him…"

This little boy was so loved already, hearts breaking all around him. But Eve couldn't leave Redemption without him. Thomas went to his wife's side and ran a hand over the baby's downy head, then bent down and kissed him.

"He's hers…" Thomas murmured softly. "We have to let go."

Patience crossed the kitchen and gently laid the infant in Eve's arms.

Eve closed her arms around him and her tears flowed. The baby nestled against her neck and settled, pushing his tiny, wet face against her. They were together again.

"Oh, my little one…" Eve crooned. "How I missed you…"

Having him in her arms, she felt like her heart came back together again, closing around him and making her whole once more. She'd carried him these nine months, feeling his movements, getting to know him, and she couldn't stop being his *mamm*, even if it meant she'd never have any more *kinner* of her own. He'd be enough.

"Are you sure?" Thomas asked quietly.

"Yah." Eve nodded. "I can't leave him. I'm sorry—I tried! I thought if you left with him, it would get easier, but it didn't! And I can't leave him."

"What will you name him?" Patience asked shakily.

"Samuel. He's my little Samuel," Eve said. "He was Samuel since I first saw him, and he can't be anything else."

"Maybe that's why we couldn't find the right name," Thomas said, and his voice caught. "He already had one."

"It's okay," Rachel said, bending down next to Eve. "We understand...don't we?"

Rachel looked up and Patience had leaned into Thomas's arms, her eyes red and her lips quivering. Thomas looked crumpled—but he nodded.

"Yah, we understand."

Eve wouldn't stay long. She'd crushed this family—it hadn't been intentional, but she knew she'd hurt them more deeply than anyone would be able to express. It would be their turn to grieve, and she couldn't help them in that process.

Lovina gathered up the baby things that Thomas and Patience gracefully gave her, and Eve went outside into the cold, hugging Samuel a little closer. Her legs still felt weak, but they'd hold her—now that she had her baby back, at least. She looked down at his little face and pressed a kiss against his forehead.

Whatever happened now, she had her son. May *Gott* protect him from the cruelty of gossip...

"Eve?"

She knew Noah's voice immediately, and she looked up to see the big man coming toward her from around the stable. He sped up, his steps plunging deep into the snow as he worked his way through.

"Eve!" When he got to her, he looked down at Samuel in her arms, then into her eyes. "What's happened?"

Would he be angry? she wondered. Would he blame her for the catastrophe she'd caused back there?

"I took him back." Eve licked her lips. "I couldn't leave him, Noah. I know I promised, but I couldn't—"

She expected to see anger, confusion, disappointment even, but Noah didn't even let her stop speaking. Noah leaned down and covered her lips with his, the words evaporating on her tongue. He slipped an arm around her, and the other settled protectively over Samuel's back. When he pulled back, she blinked up at him.

"What just happened?" she whispered.

"I kissed you," he said, his voice low. "Eve, I've been thinking, and I've been praying. I know that your baby belongs with you. I'm certain of it. And I know this seems like an impossible solution, but I want you to stay here with me, and I want us to work this out with my family."

"They aren't going to forgive me," she breathed.

"I think they will," he said. "I've been praying, Eve, and my *mamm* pointed out that sometimes something hurts, not because it's the right thing to do, but because it's wrong! I believe *Gott* brought you to me, not your son to my brother…"

Eve stared up at him. "I had a similar thought…but it was my aunt who pointed it out. Life will be hard whatever we choose, but if *Gott* will bless us—"

"Eve, I love you," Noah said. "When I held your son, and I looked down at him, I realized I didn't want to be his uncle. I wanted to be his *daet*."

Eve's heard skipped a beat, and she felt like her breath whooshed out of her body.

"Do you mean that?" she breathed.

"I do. I want to marry you. I want to raise him with you. I want to take care of you both."

But things hadn't gotten any simpler—not when it came to his family! She'd just taken her child out of Patience's arms…

"What about your brother, though?" she asked. "And Patience. I promised them a baby, and I took him back! They aren't going to be able to forgive that!"

"Actually—"

Eve startled and looked behind her to see that Thomas and Patience had come outside. It was Thomas who had spoken.

"Forgive us for overhearing. We love that boy, Eve, that's true, but he's *your* son. And we wanted to raise him as our own, but we can love him as our nephew, too. This family is big enough for both of you."

"*Yah?*" Noah asked in surprise, meeting his brother's gaze. There was a beat of silence between them as the brothers seemed to come to an agreement.

"*Yah,*" Thomas confirmed. "I still believe that *Gott*

has *kinner* for our home. My faith is big enough to keep hoping."

"So is mine," Patience said, and she smiled mistily. "He's yours, Eve."

Was Patience referring to little Samuel or to Noah? But when she looked up into Noah's tender gaze, she knew that both were true.

"Will you marry me?" Noah asked quietly.

She nodded, tears welling in her eyes. "*Yah!* I'll marry you!"

"Can we all just come back inside?" Rachel called from the doorway, trying to hold Rue back from plunging out into the snow. "If there's an engagement to celebrate, let's do it as a family in the warmth!"

Eve looked up at Noah, her heart flooding with love. She'd thought that *Gott*'s plans would have changed for her—lessened perhaps—but they hadn't. Here she was with her son in her arms and the man she would marry at her side, and she'd never felt more blessed in her life.

"Merry Christmas," Noah whispered, and he planted a kiss on her head. "Now, you've been through a lot. Let's get you inside next to the stove. You need rest, and food. And no one is going to ask you to put your son down, I promise you that."

Eve smiled up at him and she brushed a tear from her cheek. "I love you."

"I love you, too."

This was the Christmas that *Gott* gave Eve His very best, and her heart's desire, in the form of a little baby snuggled in her arms—and the man who'd be his *daet*.

Epilogue

In the new year, when the sun shone bright on new fallen snow, Eve stood in the bedroom where she'd delivered her son in her aunt's house. This room was steeped in memory for her, but today she was here getting ready to take her vows.

Eve had always wanted a proper wedding—big and joyous, with celery soup to feed a county. But somehow, after Noah had proposed on Christmas Day, she didn't care so much about the size of the wedding. It seemed more important to be able to settle into a home with Noah as his wife—to start her life as a wife and a mother.

So instead of waiting until the fall, they decided to get married at the end of January in her aunt's living room with extended family only as their guests, and Bishop Glick to perform the ceremony. Eve's *daet* and siblings came out for the wedding, her baby no longer a secret, as they came together as a family to celebrate Eve's new marriage and her precious little boy.

Secrets, after all, had a poison to them, and they'd all agreed that while they could be discreet, they'd always be honest.

Upstairs in the bedroom, Eve adjusted her *kapp* once more in the mirror, then looked over at her father, who sat in a chair with his grandson up on his shoulder, gently rubbing the baby's back.

"You make a beautiful bride, Eve," her *daet* said with a fond smile.

"Yah?" She blushed. "Thank you, *Daet*."

"I'm sorry I tried to make you—" Her father's voice choked. "I'm sorry that I—"

"It's okay, *Daet*," she said. "I suppose we all thought that *Gott*'s best for me would change."

"You're a good woman, Eve," her father said. "And you've got the kind of faith that Samuel will tell his *kinner* about."

Eve went to her father's side and bent down and placed a gentle kiss on Samuel's plump cheek. He was growing fast, a strong, sturdy baby with rolls and dimples in all the proper places. When Eve's mother had told her that she'd done her best, Eve hadn't understood it then. But she felt like she did now, now that she was a mother, too. What else could a wife and mother do but her best? Perhaps those simple words, "I did my best," were a quiet, Amish victory as a woman crossed the threshold into glory.

She'd done her best. She'd given her all. She'd loved with everything she had.

Eve would follow her *mamm*'s example and do the same—she couldn't help it! Noah and Samuel filled up every corner of her heart, and if one day she could tell her *kinner* that she'd done her best, she'd feel like she'd succeeded in walking the path *Gott* had so graciously given her.

She'd be honest. She'd be faithful. She'd love them with everything she had.

Samuel woke up with a squirm and a cry, and Eve eased him out of his grandfather's arms. She snuggled him close, and her son blinked up at her with those dark, round eyes. Perhaps he'd be awake for the ceremony, after all. She'd have to see if he consented to being cuddled by someone other than his mother for the next hour or two.

"Let's go down," her father said with a smile. "Your fiancé is waiting."

And at the thought of Noah downstairs with their mingled families, Eve's heart skipped a beat. She was about to promise this man the rest of her life…and she couldn't wait for it to begin.

* * * * *

Get 3 FREE REWARDS!

We'll send you 2 FREE Books plus a FREE Mystery Gift.

FREE
Value Over
$20

Both the **Harlequin® Special Edition** and **Harlequin® Heartwarming™** series feature compelling novels filled with stories of love and strength where the bonds of friendship, family and community unite.

YES! Please send me 2 FREE novels from the Harlequin Special Edition or Harlequin Heartwarming series and my FREE Gift (gift is worth about $10 retail). After receiving them, if I don't wish to receive any more books, I can return the shipping statement marked "cancel." If I don't cancel, I will receive 6 brand-new Harlequin Special Edition books every month and be billed just $5.49 each in the U.S. or $6.24 each in Canada, a savings of at least 12% off the cover price, or 4 brand-new Harlequin Heartwarming Larger-Print books every month and be billed just $6.24 each in the U.S. or $6.74 each in Canada, a savings of at least 19% off the cover price. It's quite a bargain! Shipping and handling is just 50¢ per book in the U.S. and $1.25 per book in Canada.* I understand that accepting the 2 free books and gift places me under no obligation to buy anything. I can always return a shipment and cancel at any time by calling the number below. The free books and gift are mine to keep no matter what I decide.

Choose one: ☐ **Harlequin**
Special Edition
(235/335 BPA GRMK)

☐ **Harlequin**
Heartwarming
Larger-Print
(161/361 BPA GRMK)

☐ **Or Try Both!**
(235/335 & 161/361
BPA GRPZ)

Name (please print)

Address _____ Apt. #

City _____ State/Province _____ Zip/Postal Code

Email: Please check this box ☐ if you would like to receive newsletters and promotional emails from Harlequin Enterprises ULC and its affiliates. You can unsubscribe anytime.

Mail to the Harlequin Reader Service:
IN U.S.A.: P.O. Box 1341, Buffalo, NY 14240-8531
IN CANADA: P.O. Box 603, Fort Erie, Ontario L2A 5X3

Want to try 2 free books from another series! Call 1-800-873-8635 or visit www.ReaderService.com.

HSEHW23

HARLEQUIN
PLUS

Try the best multimedia subscription service for romance readers like you!

Read, Watch and Play.

Experience the easiest way to get the romance content you crave.

Start your **FREE TRIAL** at
www.harlequinplus.com/freetrial.